Tethered in Time

The Chronicles of Bertha

Volume 1

Michelle Meheux

Tethered in Time

The Chronicles of Bertha

Volume 1

Michelle Meheux

ISBN 9781917109697
A CIP catalogue record for this book
is available from the British Library

Published 2025
Tricorn Books
Treadgolds
1 Bishop Street
Printed in UK

Tethered in Time

The Chronicles of Bertha

Volume 1

For My Mum & Dad …

And For Those Woman Who Inspired

The Very Essence Of Bertha

(GD, Molly & Elly) x

Contents

Tethered in Time

The Chronicles of Bertha

Volume 1

CAMPION
STONEHAVEN
CULLVELLEY
SIRENGUARD

Tethered in Time

A letter from Bertha to the reader,

'I am the voice that calls to you from the ancient echoes of time.

I hear you. I have always heard you, and I come now to share my story with you. To share how we are all connected. All that I write is true. I can only trust that you will soon see the realisation of this for yourself and move forward.

Without my story, all those that have fought, bled, loved and lost, to get me to where I am now, would have done so in vain. And without my story, your story would have been incomplete.

My name is Bertha, and I am here to share the very essence of my soul with you, so that you are able to empower all that you are: A miracle, with a history that goes back to the beginning of time, and a future that spans across worlds. Your life is a tapestry spun over ages by hands no longer visible, so allow me to ignite your dreams, celebrate your life and open up worlds of possibilities through my words that have been waiting in the ether for centuries to find you.

I have been privileged to walk through worlds. I have seen the chambers where tethered Soul Guardians dwell, where stories emerge and start to breathe even before they are born. I have spoken to the Guardians who drift between each heartbeat — the ones who listen when you think no one hears. Call them spirits, guides, holders of the light ... their names may change, but their presence does not.

I live among them now, in a place that touches yours but is not of it. The Realm, the first existence, stitched together from the essence of sound and light, and it is now my home.

It is from here that I write to you, through the narrow seam that still connects us, to help lift the veil of unseen dimensions.

I challenge you to look inwards, because it is there that you rest, and it is there that your own unique story sits and has done so since birth, in eager, yet silent expectation.

You were born to live your story to its fullest and only you will know how to circumnavigate through the challenges that lie ahead of you. Curve with the twists and turns, embrace the dreams, hold onto hope and remember to see life's coincidences for what they are; maps to help direct you.

If you are reading this letter, then I have found you.

Celebrate your birth, and allow those who have walked before you, and are yet to come, to help weave your life's tapestry, because where you sit, a miracle exists. I know it. Why? Because of my own story, which isn't so very different from yours, really, I just lived most of mine in a different time and a slightly different place.

Through the very essence of history, you will now bear witness to my extraordinary life and how I fought to protect those held dear to me from those that inhabited the depths beyond our reflection. You will learn how they found me through the finest of cracks and how I fought the darkened souls that threatened to take over all of our worlds.

We'll live it together now, hand in hand, and bridge the gap between us.

Let's take a walk through time and discover that which has remained, until now in your world, an untold story'.

Yours forever,

Bertha Jay

PROLOGUE
THE REALM

ORIGINS OF BIRTH

The Realm was the world from which all others originated. It would be unfair and inaccurate to impose any physical limits on it. Its atmospheric and spiritual essence captured the beauty and magnetic energies of atoms that have travelled from the dawn of time and space, now standing firmly at the centre of its ethereal universe.

Caught in the eternal orbit of The Realm, vibrant and diverse spheres gracefully danced around its rotational axes. These orbs were destined to be the planets, each cradled under The Realm's attentive gaze, holding unique mirrored particles that reflected their core structure, lovingly referred to as the Source.

One of the planets, Eathia, was the closest to The Realm. It was a tangible manifestation, reflecting The Realm's more ethereal essence. Consequently, it was monitored closely as it began evolving from its original point of creation.

The Realm's formation was one of order and natural division. Within its many layers were segments of life symbolising its celestial origins of sound and light. From this, the essence evolved and became the consciousness of The Realm's own 'Source'.

The Source was embedded in the centre-most point of The Realm. Simply put, it was a bright, evolving mass representing all that was life. Its complex structure could grow and develop continually. It thrived on the vibrations of time, drawn from the sound, energy and light around it. Within its core, the very base of balance was created. It was the truest, purest form of all that was known in existence.

To preserve the delicate equilibrium of the Source, the Celestial Superiors of The Realm ritualistically transmit the status of each planet along its trajectory. Thus, should any discord arise, the Source would restore harmony by invoking a new birth sequence. From its essence, the Source weaves ethereal fragments that evolve into radiant shards. These shards, imbued with strength and wisdom, ultimately transcend their origin, developing into independent entities that wander freely throughout the vast expanse of The Realm.

These shards were to become known as the Soul Guardians.

It was the first planet to exhibit signs of life as it continued to evolve; however, unlike The Realm, Eathia's life forms had a physical presence, while the beings of The Realm were composed of pure energy.

As the Source's consciousness continued to grow, it became apparent that a direct connection to Eathia would be essential if it were to stay aware of its progression.

It achieved this bond by tethering its Soul Guardians to the Eathians from birth. This would provide The Realm with an overview of its evolution and offer its tether a constant spiritual guide deeply embedded in their consciousness. This guide could heal and transfer wisdom and, depending on the order from which the Guardian originated within The Realm, could also transfer some of their skills to them.

Over time, the Soul Guardians realised various groups on Eathia were evolving independently, without The Realm's guidance.

Upon birth, an Eathian's form and tether ignited the essence of life, binding them to what would potentially become an Eathian's lifelong bond. Those Soul Guardians who tethered became deeply involved in the needs of each Eathian, creating a symbiotic relationship that merged their worlds. This subtle connection granted Eathians an intuitive purpose, aiding their life navigation, often without awareness of their constant guidance source.

As time passed, there was something that The Realm had not anticipated. The Soul Guardians' physical tethers on Eathia began to show signs of emotional deviation from their inner connection to The Realm and its Source. It became clear that the Eathian humans were more than capable of redirecting their evolutionary growth; instead, they chose mental, physical and material development to feel rewarded and content with their lives on Eathia.

As a race, the Eathians had started to externalise their emotional needs. They were becoming Eathian-bound, unknowingly relying less on the Soul Guardians for guidance and more on a source of recovery. As many were healers, they had to balance their tethers' physical extremes. It wasn't long before Eathia and its inhabitants began to drain their tethered counterparts. The Realm was starting to suffer, unable to bear the brunt of their emotionally drifting attachments.

It wasn't long before shadows began to appear in the energetic disposition of the Eathians, hidden deep within the spirits of its people. An ever-growing darkness materialised in the voids of inner despair. The darkness began to grow on this new fertile ground, a ground that was slowly becoming too dense for the light of The Realm to penetrate.

It was merely a sliver of this shadow matter, Eathian born, that slowly began to ebb toward The Realm through the tethers created by the now struggling Soul Guardians. Dark energy haemorrhaged through the fine cracks of disillusionment that had started to appear in The Realm among its inhabitants. But that was all it needed to take hold and lie dormant. Despite The Realm's efforts to divert this darkness from the Source and its Soul Guardians, it had become somewhat intriguing to some. Unfortunately for The Realm, it was those Soul Guardians who welcomed the arrival of the dark matter and sought to use it for their selfish agenda.

A divide emerged throughout The Realm. Some were eager to embrace the transformation they were undergoing, along with the darkness it entailed, while others, loyal to the Sources, placed their trust in its ability to guide them, as it had always done.

When a potential uprising appeared on The Realm's horizon, certain safeguards were put into place to protect both The Realm and Eathia, for it was not known how Eathian inhabitants would fare without the support of their tethered Soul Guardians.

The Source saw the future of The Realm deviating from its current path and embedded precautionary measures into the last of the Soul Guardians to be birthed.

No one person or entity could have predicted the outcome or the sequence of events leading up to the final conflict that lay ahead. All had agendas, some for the good of both worlds, others for egotistical gain, all for survival.

Amidst this turmoil, The Source's essence battled to preserve its history and ensure the continuity of the story of The Realm and Eathia, constantly calculating the best outcomes for its survival. Its presence weakened those determined to pursue darker powers, and it recognised the need for human 'transcribers' to safeguard the story's future, existing far from The Realm's reach in case anyone fell prey to its darkened grip. These transcribers would receive specific historical downloads, embedding their insights into journals to create detailed accounts of the history and events leading up to the uprising and its fallout, thereby ensuring the essence's survival within the created journals.

The transcribers were not randomly selected; they held a specific bloodline over time or possessed some of the Source's power.

The first of their kind was a young Eathian girl.

Her name was Bertha.

It wasn't until Kyro a boy from Earth first transcribed her story that we discovered that she was to be the first of her kind to fully understand The Realm's existence and its vital role in Eathia's survival. This is her story, along with that of The Realms, now bestowed upon you with the blessing of The Realm.

Bertha will forever be known as a guiding light who embodies the true meaning of courage, strength and fortitude.

She is a legend that continues to live on, existing across time and space and who has remained, until now, an untold story.

Chapter 1

Eathia - Third Era

Augustus Browne's Emporium

Bertha ran through the morning's dampened cobbled alleyways that would lead her through a winding shortcut to Augustus Browne's Reflector Emporium. Her thin coat was all but useless against the invading chill that relentlessly pushed its way through the loosely woven mesh of her outer garment.

Her heavy breath mistily reached out before her, catching the icy air before trailing off behind her swift pace. Her red curly hair, usually plaited and neat, was unbrushed and wild and, much to her frustration, would kept sweeping over her eyes at every turn, blocking her view as she darted through some of the more windswept lanes. Her attire, thankfully, had been of no concern to her parents that morning. They had other problems to focus on. Bertha had been ushered unceremoniously out of the door by her Nana Nora, with no breakfast, to fetch a reflector 'as quick as possible' she had added, unnecessarily Bertha thought, without any of her usual larking about.

Her empty stomach rebelled, letting out an echoey gripe as she passed the bakery's open door just as they removed their first batch of bread from the oven.

She wondered why her parents had left it so late. A question that hadn't gone down at all well when she'd objected to the whole trip by yelling and stamping her foot in the open doorway of the cottage. It had been her last-ditch attempt at changing her nana's mind as she shouted to be heard over the screams of her mother as she worked relentlessly to overcome her labour pains.

She remembered her pleading conversation and wondered if she could have gone about it differently.

'Why can't Pa go? He's more qualified for things like this. I'm a child.'

‘Only when it suits you, young lady. He isn’t here long, and the little one is arriving two weeks early, so on you go.’

Bertha had shot forward and hugged her. Her small child-length arms hardly reached around her nana’s rounded and homely stature.

It was then that the very foundations of the cottage seemed to start shaking with every scream that reverberated down the small opening of the stairs, piercing its way through the wooden framework of the cottage and out through the open front door. For once, Bertha had been glad they lived on the outskirts of the village. Bertha had heard enough and left without another word.

Bertha skidded and nearly fell as she tried to stop outside her uncle’s shop, a mixture of dew on the slippery stones and a sudden blast of light as it reflected from the other shop window. She reached out for something to hold and grabbed the large brass handle of her Uncle Augustus’s shop door. It thankfully stopped her from falling completely. The latch opened as soon as she gripped it, releasing from the inside, the door suddenly gave way. Still holding on, she was pulled into the entrance of the store as something continued to pull against her from the inside vigorously.

‘For goodness’ sake, child. You can’t come into a shop full of glass with that type of reckless abandonment. More haste, less speed, young lady.’

Mrs Wilhelmina Bullock peered down at her over her rounded metal-framed spectacles before continuing to march past Bertha as she left her uncle’s shop, but not before she had dragged the dirty, musty hem of her ancient dress over Bertha’s face on her way out. Forging ahead, she pounded the cobblestones with every step of her oversized heeled boots.

Picking herself up and dusting down her knees, she looked up towards the counter, squinting to adjust her eyes to the gloom of the store. The rich lavender scent that still lingered in the air from Wilhelmina caught her with her next breath, causing her to sneeze.

Augustus beamed at her from behind a tall wooden counter. His hair was greased back, as usual, and his hands tucked deep into the pockets of his mustard-coloured, immaculately clean tunic.

‘Well, well, little Miss Bertha, quite an entrance. I can guess why you are here.’

Speechless, Bertha stood in the centre of the shop floor. She arched her neck backwards, following the tiers of the randomly shaped reflectors. They reached up to the ceiling. Row upon row of ornate brass, silver, gold and copper reflectors all appeared to be facing the blackened surface of the wall.

For a shop that sells reflectors, it is a mighty dark and gloomy place, she thought. She'd never been into her uncle's shop before now, and she didn't care to step foot into it again after today.

She looked at her uncle with wide, helpless eyes.

'Nana said I'd know which one to choose for our new baby, but I don't.'

Augustus stepped out from behind the counter, but not before pausing and glancing down at the ornate pendant he kept on a shelf below the till. Giving serious consideration for a moment on whether he should put it on before moving closer to Bertha, he decided against it and continued towards her. Crouching down beside her, he whispered into her ear.

'You've already chosen it, Bertha; you just don't know it yet.'

He leaned back to give her space and winked. It was then, still illuminated by the intense reflection of the morning glow in the windows behind her, that she could clearly see her uncle's usual pale complexion. The darkness of his hair against his porcelain skin made him appear even more ominous, that is, if someone didn't know him as well as she did.

His whitish pallor gave her the heebie-jeebies when she was tiny, but she had got used to him now. He was an Ashen, one of two that she knew of. Their skin tone drained easily, depending on the company they kept. It always appeared worse when he was near her, but she had learnt not to take it personally. He sometimes wore a pendant designed to help, but Bertha never understood how it helped.

Augustus tapped his knees for her to climb up. She held onto his cloth-covered hand and jumped up with a bit of a wobble and a giggle.

'Quickly. Close your eyes, Bertha. You will be taken to the right reflector in your mind's eye.'

She squeezed her eyes shut and whispered.

'I spy with my mind's eye.'

She quickly opened one eye, looked straight at her uncle, and laughed.

'That's the game I play with my friends. When we play, I spy, and I get bored of guessing things close to us; I memorise other rooms with my mind's eye, and they must guess what I can see.'

'Sounds complicated. I imagine you are generally the winner of such a game, seeing as your friends don't know what you can see?'

Bertha giggled.

'I am.'

With a wink, he replied 'Concentrate, young lady.'

Bertha eventually did as her uncle suggested, and as quick as a lightning flash, she saw it. A small, ornately crafted, silver oval reflector. Unlike the others, this one had a silver design that extended to the end of the handle, whereas most of the others, hers at home included, were wooden and carved. A blue gemstone was embedded into the base of the handle.

She opened her eyes and found she was looking straight at it. The gem was catching the light, making it stand out even more. Her arm reached to point it out with such gusto that she nearly hit Augustus's nose.

'Wonderful,' he laughed, 'now see, how easy was that?'

Bertha jumped down, and her uncle returned behind the counter, retrieved a ladder from the side of the shop, and gently placed it against the wall, paying close attention so as not to disturb the jigsaw of reflectors that closely surrounded the one she had chosen. He pulled the other white cloth glove out of his tunic pocket and stretched it over his other hand.

'Uncle?'

'Yes?'

'Have we always had reflectors?'

'My father, Gabriel, always used to say that he invented them, but he didn't. He invented the ones that connected us to the … um.'

Augustus paused, wondering how much to divulge. To date, Bertha hadn't been that inquisitive, much to his relief.

Bertha answered for him.

'To the orb in the castle.'

'Yes, exactly. Before that, they just reflected one way if you like; now they open a …'

Augustus went to reach for the reflector and paused again.

'… well, a wealth of knowledge; Past, Present and Future.'

He had momentarily lost concentration, his mind focusing on the orb within the castle and trying to be careful about what he disclosed.

'You see, without the orb, we might never have been reconnected at all. We would have become lost souls, as it were. Just aimlessly floating off into the wilderness of life.'

Augustus returned quickly once he realised he was still speaking but had no recollection of what he said. Looking across at Bertha's blank face gave him the reassurance he needed that his mind had wandered off into safe territory. He reminded himself that he must consider that Bertha had no understanding yet of Eathia's life before the de-tethering of their Soul Guardians. He shuddered when the memory of it all came back to him. He shook it off and focused on what he was doing.

'This little fella has been here the longest. To my recollection, it was one my father made. I was beginning to wonder if anyone would claim it,' Augustus said, his tone reflecting the weight of its history.

'Will I get in trouble for bringing home an old one that no one wants?'

Augustus laughed again, causing a slight quiver on the ladder. He gripped the top of one side, and, calming himself down, he concentrated on the job at hand.

Bertha watched intently as he carefully lifted it from its hook and drew it close towards his body, making sure not to move the felt cloth that had hung behind it ever since it had been placed on that spot.

As Bertha watched, she imagined the cloth was there to stop it from getting scratched; however, it was, in fact, a safeguard so no one inadvertently gazed into it before its keeper. Every newborn would be given a reflector; once they connected to it by looking into it, they would become soulfully tethered to the orb within the castle and all its wisdom.

Augustus turned it carefully and clasped it to his chest before descending.

Bertha glanced past him, bending her body to one side, her hair falling away from her shoulder and hanging in loose auburn ringlets. She counted three wooden columns facing sideways to the shop. All were stacked with an array of differently shaped reflectors. They extended into the rear of the shop. Rows upon rows of shelves stretched as far as she could see. Some were round, some square or rectangular like the one they had on their mantelpiece at home.

Bertha sniffed the air.

'What's burning?'

'Oh, that'll be the Furnace in the back. We make all the reflectors here, you see.'

His arm waved delicately around, his hand gesturing to the walls of the Emporium as if to proudly introduce some old acquaintances to her.

'It smells old. Is it very old?'

'The Furnace?'

'No, the shop.'

Augustus paused, still holding the reflector, then proceeded to put the ladder back where he found it.

'It's the oldest building in Stonehaven, other than the Castle Raphael, where the orb resides. They were built together. If the walls had ears, they could tell you a lot about the secrets of the castles and its connection to this very shop.'

Bertha frowned at her uncle.

'They would surely need a mouth too, not just ears if they were going to tell us anything.'

He stood before her, resisting the urge to giggle at her innocence.

'Now, Bertha!'

Her attention snapped back to her uncle, and she stood upright instantly.

'We are sidestepping slightly, aren't we?'

He held the reflector up carefully.

'You must take this straight home. It's quite a responsibility for a young girl, but I imagine your parents are busy, so here you are. You know I can't offer another. They're all unique,' Augustus reminded her.

'I know, Uncle; I still have mine safe under my bed, but I am due my next one soon.'

'Yes, I know. You'll need a stronger one, won't you, little miss inquisitive. There'll be one here for you, I'm sure.'

Augustus opened the shop door and patted the top of her head as she walked through and out onto a terracotta-tiled floor. They paused momentarily in the doorway. He took a long breath of air, with the strong essence of freshly baked bread still floating amongst its aromas, and then glanced back down at Bertha, who was busily scanning the street ahead. She pushed the reflector under her coat.

Her uncle spoke.

'You know, I think you are my most favourite niece.'

She turned her head awkwardly and looked up at him.

'I'm your only niece. For the time being, anyway. That could all change today but thank you all the same.'

She jumped down from the step with both feet onto the cobbled path.

Augustus watched her walk up the street for a while, then turned back when he heard his wife Anamaya's footsteps coming from the back of the shop. She just caught his distant smile before he turned and adjusted his composure.

'Was that Bertha's voice I heard?'

'Yes, it was. Their new baby is about to be born.'

She set the thought aside, for now.

'I'm just on my way now. No one came to fetch me. I assume Nora has it all under control.'

Anamaya looked down. A wave of sadness unintentionally swept through her. She shook off the sad thought.

'By the sounds of it, she does. I'm sure an extra pair of hands wouldn't go amiss, though. Would you still be able to relieve Pops at the castle afterwards?'

She nodded.

He walked over to Anamaya and embraced her, swinging his shoulders from side to side, rocking her with him as he went.

'I saw that look you gave. Our time will come. You wait and see if it doesn't.'

She looked up at him and tried to smile.

'Always a midwife, never a mother. Isn't that what they say.'

'No, they don't. That's poppycock. The Ashens are built to last; they must. We have a critical job to hand down. The keepers of the castle and, more importantly, the orb. We just need to be patient for a little while longer.'

He smiled down at her, and she found she couldn't fight his jolly mood any longer.

'You're looking slightly pale. You didn't wear the pendant when Bertha was here, did you?'

Augustus shook his head, and Anamaya tutted back at him.

'You must look after yourself. I'll see you later.'

Augustus released her from his embrace and lowered his voice.

'I had to be so careful not to say anything about the reflectors to Bertha that would insight more questions. She is very inquisitive, you know.'

Anamaya turned at the shop door.

'We must always be careful of that little one until she is old enough to understand the full story behind you and your father, the orb's origin, and the castle. In no time, she will become a transcriber. It's such a heavy burden to carry the full weight of the story and all that comes with it in that tiny, innocent mind of hers. I hope she has time to be a child before it happens.'

She smiled and blew Augustus a kiss.

'She has us, she always will,' Augustus reassured her.

Anamaya left and made her way to the cottage before heading back to the castle to take over watch duty from Francis.

~

As Bertha walked back home, she was glad of the fresh air; the shop had an intensity that left you slightly light-headed once you vacated the premises.

She held the reflector tight to her tiny chest. Although she felt overwhelmed initially, the exhilaration far outweighed the worry caused by such a monumental task. It had been a success.

The town clock chimed. *How long had she been?* she wondered. *Had she taken too long?*

As Bertha made her way home, she walked for a little while but then felt the need to speed up with each strike of the bell. She was beginning to feel anxious. What if her little brother or sister would have to live out their life without the reflector's help, and it would be all her fault?

Her marching feet escalated into a jog, quickly turning into a run. She could now see the smoke coming from the chimney of their cottage ahead of her. Surely, she should be able to hear her mother's screaming by now, but there was nothing.

Panic took hold and seemed to grip her ankles, making them feel unnaturally cumbersome. Just as she quickened, her foot caught under a raised cobblestone. At that speed, the sudden jolt caused her to take off from the ground and fly a good half-body length further before she finally crashed down hard onto the path. Her knees took the full weight of the impact. As she instinctively put her arms out to save herself from falling on her face, the reflector fell away from her and hit hard against the stony ground, bouncing on in front of where Bertha had finally come to rest. It landed sideways with a thud against a kerb.

The pain was instantaneous. Bertha was quick to evaluate her situation. She had two options. Curl up and sob at her excruciating pain and misfortune, or get up and run to the cottage and deal with the pain later.

A scream ripped through the street as if to answer her dilemma. It was her mother. She bit her lip and rose, staggered to the reflector, grabbed it, not noticing that there was a fine crack in the glass, wincing with every step at the pain caused in her knees.

As she stumbled up the path, the cottage door flew open, and her Nana Nora was waiting in the doorway, smiling. Somehow, Bertha randomly noticed that she had managed to find the time to set her hair back into a neat and wavy bun. As she approached the gate, Bertha heard the unmistakable wail of a newborn baby.

'Good girl, just in time. On you go and meet your new baby brother.'

Bertha excitedly yelled back as she ascended the stairs, all pain in her knees subsiding for the time being.

'Good. That means I'm still Uncle's favourite niece!'

Chapter 2
Eathia - Third Era

You've Cracked It

It was some time before Bertha could retreat from the excitement of meeting her new brother and head for her bedroom. She desperately wanted to check the damage the falling had done to her knees.

She had given her father the reflector. True to tradition, as soon as her brother opened his eyes, they showed him the face of the reflector. With the ripples starting to flow across the reflector's surface, they could tell that his connection to it was instantaneous. As Bertha leaned against the pillow next to her mother and brother, she was mesmerised by the process.

Something suddenly caught her eye. A darkness seemed to swirl through the glass of the reflector. Not knowing if this was normal, she shrugged it off and beamed at her father when he said that her brother was now officially tethered to the orb and it to him. He ruffled her hair and said she had fetched the perfect reflector for Denis.

However, shortly after, Denis had become unusually disturbed and began to cry relentlessly. He was still screaming as she sat quietly on her bed, deliberating over her knees.

Bertha had no idea what a new baby should sound like, but Denis was reaching decibels almost as high as her mother had done during labour.

Maybe she had chosen the wrong reflector, or worse, what if the crack had affected his tether to the orb?

Unable to shake the feeling, she reached under the bed and grabbed her small handheld reflector. Its copper-moulded frame gleamed as light peeked through the first gap in the clouds that had begun to fill the sky that morning. She stroked its back and gazed at her reflection.

The face looking back at her had wild and unruly hair. As soon as she gazed into her own eyes, the uneasiness from the morning's events magnified.

Deep down, she knew it would. Its unwavering honesty was why she trusted it so much. The orb would always cause the truth to surface. Bertha didn't like the feeling she was experiencing. Her guilt escalated about not saying anything to anyone.

'Well, there's nothing I can do about it now,' she defiantly retorted, throwing the reflector onto a cushion on the bedroom floor.

At the age of six, Bertha was too young to understand the implications of a damaged reflector on her newborn brother. As Denis had connected to the orb, it went unnoticed that there was something far more dangerous lurking within the tether, and that it had been able to make a connection to him.

Deep within the reflector, particles of shadow matter floated untethered for aeons, biding their time to enter Eathia and seek any thread that would lead them to the essence. The darkness they contained had seen him and embedded their seed; a seed ready to grow and consume him at any moment.

The orb became aware instantly. It would need to tread carefully when alerting the young Bertha to what was required to restore the reflector's fractured structure.

If not sealed correctly, it had the potential to change all of their lives forever.

Chapter 3
Eathia - Third Era

Nightmare Waiting to Happen

That night, Bertha's usually uneventful dreams took a dark turn.

She was swinging from a rope swing on an old oak tree she recognised. She remembered having spent many a warm day sitting in its shade and had always delighted in the fact that her name had been etched into its bark. Suddenly, the tree came to life, and its branches began to hit her across the knees. As she was thrown around with such force, she briefly caught sight of her brother, now much older, observing from the doorway of a wooden cabin with an unsettling smile on his face.

She called for him to help her, but he just turned away, walked into the cabin and shut the door behind him.

She looked down just in time to see another branch as it sped towards her. It caught her across both knees and cracked as it hit her legs. The pain finally jolted her awake.

Bertha sat up in bed. Her room seemed dark until her eyes adjusted to the dim light, and she turned and stared at the faint glow under her bedroom door.

She threw herself back down, buried her head into the pillow and sobbed. Her thoughts returned to the intensity of the dream. Eventually, the serenity of her warm room eased her back to sleep.

The light outside her bedroom door was only strong enough to reach a few feet in distance, but its glare was sufficient to highlight Bertha's reflector still laying abandoned on the cushion. Facing up and shining into the room, it caught what little it could from the dim glow, but it held on to what it could and slowly began to build its strength. Above it, each reflective particle began to twin with another and multiply until a swirling iridescent stream of intensifying beams started to rise from the face of her reflector.

Now, stretching out, a shimmering form began to hover over Bertha's peaceful face, its light illuminating parts of it as it expanded until, finally, her entire face as if she were bathed in sunlight. The beams continued to rise, flickering as they went, causing shadows and highlights to dance across the contours of her delicate features. Surprisingly, its radiance did not extend to the other areas of her room. Everything beyond remained in complete darkness; the essence intended to focus solely on Bertha.

It started taking on a life of its own, moving slowly towards her. Its shape bent over her still body, inquisitively watching the small child as she slept.

A faint outline began to take the shape of a young woman with pale golden hair resting over her shoulders. Her body was draped in an opalescent weave of flowing cloth that seemed to ripple with light. An aura surrounded the strange ghostly form, and a slither of light remained anchored to the reflector at its base.

The woman smiled. Her face was alive with colour and intensity that seemed to emanate further as she gazed upon Bertha. She took note of her familiar-shaped nose and chin and how she twitched slightly as she began to re-enter her inner dream world, her nirvana.

There, she intended to meet and introduce herself to Bertha; she wondered if there was any part of her that Bertha would recognise. Possibly not. When Bertha had last seen her, she was an elderly woman. Now, she had chosen to emerge from the orb to show herself to Bertha. Her image was much younger again.

Moving away from Bertha, she settled towards the end of Bertha's bed and waited.

Chapter 4

Eathia - Third Era

The Woman in the Reflector

Unaware of the luminescent form that had entered her room, Bertha had drifted back into a deep sleep, only this time, it was a dream full of mystery and, thankfully, no pain.

In this new dream, she watched as the familiar woman made her way purposefully towards her family's cottage.

Alicia Primrose walked up the cobbled hill that took her to the outskirts of the town. Her leather case was full of her students' homework. The textbooks were sectioned off neatly within their dividers. She was lucky enough to be taking care of the newly enrolled children, and by the time they were ready to move on from her group, she felt satisfied they had a well-rounded start to their school life. Those informative years were so important, and Alicia Primrose put her life and soul into her children and work.

Bertha was due to join at the start of the new term, and she wanted to get to know her first so it wouldn't be such a shock for her on the day she joined.

She flattened down her thin overcoat and adjusted her small brown felt hat. Gently coughing into her brown and black cotton gloves to clear her throat, she paused as she reached the gate. Looking around, she quickly took in the surroundings as she always did at a new child's home. She gazed up at the quaint cottage. Wisteria adorned the frontage and had been carefully clipped to avoid encroaching over the glass of its small windows. It was a pretty cottage; she was satisfied that it was in good order, with a few sloping trellises, but she could overlook that.

Miss Primrose was unable to cope with anything out of place. This was a throwback from growing up with an over-critical aunt.

A scent reached her as she stood, taking in the ambience: jasmine, fresh jasmine. Not the hideous phoney lavender scents her aunt insisted on wearing.

Alicia walked into the front garden, up the path and knocked on the pale green door. The knocker made a louder bang than she expected, making her eyes twitch as she jumped.

She heard laughter and infectious giggles from an open window to the right of the front door. She stepped back and leaned her head further so they could see it was her intruding on their fun. Through the window, Alicia caught a glimpse of Bertha. Her face was alive with happiness and covered in what looked like flour. A new smell reached her now. They were baking. Footsteps left the kitchen as Bertha grabbed some flour from the kitchen surface and launched it at whoever was going to see who had knocked. The door opened and Nora appeared to be looking all together, as covered as Bertha was. She tried to shake it off from her hair as she spoke. Alicia jumped back to avoid the avalanche of white dust from getting into her lungs.

'Mrs Primrose, how lovely to see you. I'm sorry, we're baking and Bertha's slightly excited this morning. As you can see, not much is going into the bowl. Please, come in.'

Alicia smiled and stepped in, still flapping at the airborne flour and carefully avoiding a small crack on the step as she did.

She replied,

'Oh, it's Miss not Mrs, but please call me Alicia. I'm Miss Primrose to my students.'

Nora watched her as she almost tripped over nothing on the step. She went to apologise for whatever had caused her to jump but, on inspection, found there was nothing to apologise for either.

'I'm here to see Bertha if this is a convenient time. To officially introduce myself to her before she joins us next term.'

'Of course, come on through. Bertha! Alicia is here to see you, darling; get that face cleaned up and come to the sitting room, pet.'

Alicia shot a surprised look at Nora.

'Sorry, I'm Miss Primrose to the students. As much as I would love to be on a first-name basis, I am sure our Governors would frown upon it.'

Nora smiled at Alicia, understanding that the poor girl was all tied up in knots of rules and regulations, even out of school.

Bertha appeared at the door and ran towards Alicia just as she started to take a seat in the sitting room. Alicia jumped up in surprise before she even touched the cushion on the chair.

'Miss Primrose? You are here to see me?'

Alicia held out a welcoming hand for Bertha to shake, but she ignored it entirely as she continued to move in for a hug. Alicia froze, unaccustomed to having her body space invaded and quickly glanced at Nora for assistance. Nora just shook her head and laughed as she went back to sort out the mess in the kitchen.

'She's a firecracker, that one.'

'Bertha, hello, um, Bertha?'

Gently detaching Bertha's arms from around her body with her little fingers extended rigidly into the air, Alicia tried to manoeuvre her body back and move Bertha slightly further away, just enough for her to continue sitting down. She preferred to be face-to-face with her students, believing they needed not to feel small and unheard. She also had her aunt to thank for that, having a lifetime of her towering over her.

Once she was sitting, Alicia started to remove her gloves.

'Bertha, I need to speak with you.'

She glanced across at the open door, then tilted her head slightly when she heard a creek from a floorboard in the room above.

'That's my mother. My brother has been asleep. We won't get any peace now, not now he's awake.'

Alicia's eyes became more urgent at the mention of her brother.

'Bertha, I need you to listen to me. I must tell you something very important, but I must be quick before …'

She stopped and listened to sounds being made upstairs once again. More creaks.

'… before your brother comes down.'

Bertha frowned as she tried to understand the urgency and why the thought of her baby brother joining them seemed to bother Miss Primrose.

~

The iridescent form watched patiently as the creases appeared across the sleeping girl's brow. She knew instantly that she was engaged in the meeting.

Alicia reached out to hold onto Bertha's tiny hands as if to intensify the meaning of what she was about to say.

'Bertha, you need to mend the reflector that was given to your brother. The crack must be replaced with a full, undamaged piece of glass. Do you understand? The reflector mustn't remain fragmented in any way.'

Bertha's mouth dropped open.

'How did you know?'

It was Bertha who now turned to see if her grandmother was within earshot.

‘Take it back to your Uncle Augustus. He will fix it for you.’

‘No, he said it was the only one.’

‘Bertha, do you remember when you looked into your reflector and asked about the feeling you had after you …’

Alicia leaned in and whispered,

‘… dropped it?’

Bertha nodded wide-eyed, still amazed that Miss Primrose knew what had happened. She tried to defend herself.

‘I didn’t drop it; it just fell from my arms.’

‘Yes, well, when it “fell from your arms”. Do you remember that feeling you didn’t like? It made you feel bad about what happened. Well, my dear Bertha, it is I who listen to you. Your thoughts, worries, news, I listen to everything when you hold onto the reflector and connect with it.’

Bertha’s mouth fell open again.

‘Bertha, very shortly you will open your eyes and see me as I am, my true form. Don’t be scared. Remember what I said to you. Can you do that for me?’

Far away in Bertha’s unconscious thoughts, things were starting to make sense, but nothing tangible, just a distant sense of acceptance of an extraordinary event. The being from the reflector spoke aloud.

‘Wake up, Bertha. Open your eyes, my child.’

The dream was vivid, but Bertha found herself following a voice that was calling for her.

Bertha’s body was awake, and she sensed she wasn’t alone. She shot open her eyes.

The beautiful golden face of a woman smiled down at her, a look a mother would have when staring into her child’s eyes. Bertha noticed that hers bore an uncanny resemblance to those of the teacher in the dream; at least, she thought they did. Bertha didn’t move an inch but instead allowed the memories of her dream to waft in and continue to comfort and remind her why a strange woman was watching her sleep.

‘You aren’t Miss Primrose at all, are you?’

‘Forgive me for entering your dreams, Bertha, but I needed to talk with you.’

Bertha whispered,

‘Who are you?’

‘I am the essence of who you speak to through your reflector. I come from the orb in the Castle Raphael.’

The woman looked down at the reflector abandoned on the floor. Bertha followed her gaze and gasped. Realising she must already be aware that it had been thrown there. She knew leaving a reflector open was a dangerous occurrence. Who knows who could look inside it?

'Bertha, it is complete and not damaged in any way. If it had not fallen as it did, I would not have been able to come and visit you.'

'Are you in everyone's reflector? Does everyone talk to you?'

'Yes, I am. But you are one of the very few Eathians to have seen me as I am now. This is our secret.'

Bertha's face beamed with importance.

'My nana often talks of you. She says that you come from far away and long ago. She said she knew you when you were, you know, one of us.'

'Yes, I know your nana very well, in fact. She is a very wise lady. You have her exact looks as a child, quite remarkable.'

'Why are you stuck in the orb?' Bertha asked innocently.

The woman laughed and thought for a moment.

'Well. I'm not actually in it. The orb is my soul. I am here to help you all however I can.'

Bertha looked up at her, trying to understand what she was saying as much as a six-year-old could.

The woman's smile faded, and her expression became more serious. She continued,

'You had a nightmare earlier tonight, did you not?'

'Yes, and it had Denis in it. He's my baby brother. He smiled at me, getting hurt.'

The woman continued,

'Bertha, that dream happened because of the crack in your brother's reflector. It's complicated, but we must get that fixed as soon as possible. There is a part of my orb that I don't want anyone connecting to. It's a part I draw away from those who look into their reflectors when they are, shall we say, sad, for want of a better word. It's a part that I keep you all protected from.'

'You have a bad part in you?'

'It's not mine, Bertha; I take it away from the negative thoughts of whoever looks into their reflector.'

Bertha thought for a moment.

'Is that what hurt my brother?'

The woman looked at her confused face. She didn't want to scare her.

You don't have to worry about that Bertha. What I need you to do is fix

Denis's reflector. That would help me tremendously. Can you do that?'

Bertha nodded.

'Now, I need to stop your bad dreams.'

The woman realised Bertha's connection to Denis created a pathway for the darkness to reach her. Ultimately, it was her they desired. She had to stop it by any means necessary. Her options were limited, and only one would prove effective.

It was too early, but this incident with Denis and his reflector had forced her hand and made them all vulnerable.

Bertha moved in the bed and winced as the covers hurt her knees.

'Let me see them before I go.'

Carefully and slightly dramatically, Bertha peeled back the covers to reveal her reddened and bruised knees.

The woman hovered her hand over them until, slowly and steadily, the pain eased and the wounds began to fade. While she silently worked on them, she watched Bertha's face. She remembered the first time she had seen her and thought then, that her features, especially her green eyes, bore such a resemblance to her grandmother's. Someone she had loved so very much.

Bertha watched closely as her knees returned to their unblemished state.

'Wow, you're magical.'

Bertha continued to watch closely.

'I'll get the reflector fixed tomorrow, and everything will be better.'

Although the woman smiled, Bertha could see that it may not be that simple.

Bertha's gaze held onto her every word.

It wasn't just the source of the dark energy that sought Bertha; it extended far beyond the woman's orb, traversing time and space. Until now, she had been successful in protecting her.

The darkness searched and built strength as it reached out to all dark souls whose life purpose was to uncover where the orb's soul had lain. They preyed on anyone, even children, to learn where the essence resided because it was the keeper of the one thing they wished to destroy. The orb's soul held the story of existence. Without her, Eathia would become easy prey for them. Bertha would discover all this for herself; she was destined to. The woman didn't have a choice. She had to prepare Bertha by providing her with the vital knowledge that, until now, she had lacked for her own good.

The crack in her brother's reflector had unfortunately brought her fate closer. It had created an opening within the void behind the reflectors, where all types of matter exist, some of which act as bridges between existences and worlds.

The woman thought for a moment.

'I have an idea, Bertha, to make it easier for you to sleep peacefully.'

In safety, was more to the point, the woman thought.

Bertha nodded before she had even finished, and the woman smiled and slowly nodded in appreciation.

She continued, 'Every night, before you sleep, hold your reflector and place it safely beside you. Through it, I will share stories of distant worlds. Some will be about your ancestors who lived centuries ago. They will fill your mind as you sleep and help keep the nightmares at bay. Your past and my past and future are intertwined, so the stories will help you understand so much, Bertha. I need you to trust me. After each night, I want you to hold a special journal in your hands. You'll feel a tingle in your fingers. That will be the story transferring from your mind to pages within the journal. Your touch will transform the stories into words. I will speak to your Uncle Francis and ask him to bring one to you. That's all you have to do. It will initially feel strange, perhaps tingly on your fingers, but you will become accustomed to it. It is a lot to ask of you, but I believe the time has come for us to act.'

Bertha frowned.

'You know my Uncle Francis? To speak to, I mean?'

'I know him very well. Let's say that he is like a brother to me. We have known each other for a very long time. He will be a good confidant.'

Bertha's frown deepened.

'I mean to say that your uncle will be someone you can speak to about the stories I tell you. He has witnessed so many in his lifetime already.'

They were suddenly interrupted by Bertha's baby brother crying from the room next door. The woman stopped looking at Bertha and followed the sound. Looking back, Bertha saw she had the same look Miss Primrose had shown when she had heard Bertha's brother cry out in her dream. She wondered why they appeared concerned.

'It's only my little brother.'

The woman's expression relaxed.

'Remember to hold onto the reflector, Bertha, as you fall asleep. You will hear my voice and sense a soft glow on your face; it will envelop and protect you as you sleep.' She smiled softly before adding 'No more bad dreams for you.'

She moved closer to Bertha.

'You will learn who I am and discover who you are, my child, my beautiful Bertha. My saviour. Interesting times lie ahead, so be brave and strong, for all our sakes.'

Bertha gazed up at her, unable to take in the seriousness of her words. As the woman began to fade, she spoke once more.

'Bertha, if we ever have to face something scary at any point in the future, I need to be strong and whole. It's crucial to remember this if we're to defeat it together. Do you understand?'

Bertha nodded, not knowing what she was agreeing to. The woman knew that she would once she was a transcriber. It would all make sense to her in time.

'Goodbye, for now, dear Bertha.'

A gentle spectrum of coloured lights danced around the woman's form. She smiled at Bertha just before her image faded, and then she disappeared. The coolness of the air retreated, and the room filled with a natural, warm morning light.

There was nothing unreal about her. There was no question in Bertha's very being that doubted her presence in her dreams and her bedroom that night.

Jumping out of bed, she grabbed the reflector from the floor and investigated it, fully expecting to see the woman disappearing through a tunnel. There was nothing, so she slid it into its felt case and put it back under her bed.

Bertha waited until her mother took her brother downstairs, hurriedly dressed herself, and then crept over to her parents' bedroom.

She had to find her brother's reflector.

Denis's sleeping basket was over towards the back of the cluttered room, next to her mother's side of the bed. The curtains were still closed and the bed was unmade. Their room was packed to the ceiling with boxes. Bags were jammed between them, bulging with old clothes, blankets and materials. None had seen the light of day while Bertha had been alive. Her mother had little time to do anything these days, especially when Denis was awake.

She squeezed between the basket and the wooden frame of the bed. She couldn't see a thing as she scrambled around for the old leather suitcase under the bed. She touched the handle and pulled. It knocked into the potty bowl, and she involuntarily gagged when a tiny drop of liquid hit her hand. Shaking her hand and wiping it on her dress, she grabbed the handle again and dragged the case towards her.

This was the only place it could be. Opening it with a click of the locks, the lid sprung up, and Denis's reflector was on top.

'Yes!' she exclaimed.

She carefully lifted it out. As she did, a musty odour rose as the reflector was freed. Beneath it was something wrapped in an old blanket. She sneaked a quick peek at it and saw it was a book. A name she recognised was on the cover.

'Gabriel Browne – An Inventors Compendium'

Her Great-uncle Francis's father. She was about to look inside when she heard her mother's footsteps. Quickly stashing the item back under the bed, she grabbed the reflector and covered the unmade bed as her mother appeared at the door with Denis.

'Bertha, are you coming down, darling?' She saw that Bertha had made the bed and smiled.

Bertha stared at them momentarily, wanting to tell her mother about everything that had happened.

'I had a bad dream, then the most wonderful dream ever, but it was real. Can I talk about it later? I'm busy now.'

She ducked under Denis's little body as he wriggled in her mother's arms and shot down the stairs with his reflector hidden under her coat. She headed for the door, leaving her mother bemused.

Nora was in the kitchen. When she heard Bertha in the hall, she called out to her.

'Bertha dear, it's baking day today. Are you up for helping me make some cakes?'

Not wanting to get into a detailed conversation about where she was going, Bertha shouted back that she wouldn't be long.

She grabbed the handle of the front door, pulled it open and gasped suddenly in shock, nearly losing her grip on the reflector hidden in her coat.

Standing in the doorway was Miss Primrose, just like in her dream.

Her mouth gaped open.

Chapter 5
Eathia - Third Era

Secrets

As Bertha opened the front door, she was taken aback when she saw Miss Primrose standing there. Her dream the night before came flooding back to her. Was it a coincidence, or did the woman from the reflector know what would happen?

She quickly decided that Miss Primrose was in on the secret about the damaged reflector.

'Hello, Bertha. Just the very girl I wanted to see.'

'I'm doing it now, right now, I promise.'

Alicia Primrose frowned at her and shook her head.

'Sorry? What, what are you doing now? I don't understand.'

Bertha recoiled, realising her confusion.

'I'm here to talk to you about starting school next term. You look like you are off out.'

'I am, but I won't be long. It's baking day, so I need to be back soon.'

'She won't be long, Mrs Primrose; come on in.'

Bertha moved aside and watched as Miss Primrose almost jumped over what could only have been a tiny crack in the floor.

'It's Miss Primrose, Nana, not Mrs, she likes to be known as Miss.'

Bertha looked up at her.

'Don't you.'

With that, she was gone out the door and down the path.

As she made her way to her Uncle Augustus's Emporium, it dawned on Bertha that the woman who had appeared to her that night could, in fact, look into her future. Miss Primrose had indeed knocked on the door the very next morning. She shivered at the thought as she stepped disgruntledly back into her uncle's dreary shop.

He was horrified to hear why she had returned so soon.

'What do you mean it's cracked? But I did explain that it was unique. It's very unlikely that I'll ever be able to fix it again, young lady.'

'Does that mean it's a little bit likely you can?' Bertha said hopefully.

'Bertha, I'm not sure that you understand, and nor should you, the importance of the reflectors and their value …'

Bertha interrupted.

'She said you would be able to. It was her idea, not mine. Have a go at her.'

Augustus was confused.

'Who's she? Sorry, who said that?'

Augustus thought he saw a familiar glint in his niece's eyes but chose not to react.

'Bertha, I need to know.'

'The lady in the reflector. She was all golden and floaty.'

Bertha watched as every remaining colour disappeared from her uncle's face and hands. He wobbled and leaned back onto the counter. She stepped forward to help, but he held out a flattened palm to say he was fine and for her to stop where she was. He became breathless.

'You've seen her?' he said in a high-pitched tone.

'She already knew that I fell and broke the reflector.'

Augustus gasped.

'You fell and broke it, oh my, what to do, what to do?'

He started to pull at his collar, loosening it to get more air into his lungs.

He looked at her, and all he could see was a little six-year-old girl staring back at him, looking completely out of her depth and thankfully unaware of the enormity of the situation.

'You've gone almost completely white, Uncle.'

'Oh, I'm sure I have Bertha. You might need to stand back a little.'

With that, Augustus's eyes rolled back, and he collapsed in a heap onto the shop floor.

Bertha heard a whisper from the reflector. It was a voice she recognised instantly from the previous night.

'Touch his hand, Bertha. You still have some of my energy with you.'

Bertha whispered back to her,

'But I can't get too close. I'll make him worse.'

'It'll be fine, I promise.'

Bertha ran over to where he sat, squatted beside him and grabbed his hand. Slowly, some greyness returned to his cheeks and he opened his eyes.

Bertha stared at him intently. She was so close; he struggled to focus on her.

'Bertha, I feel like I'm still falling.'

Bertha whispered back, 'Not unless you can fall off the floor, you're not.'

Bertha frowned at him and twitched her lips to one side. She got up and ran behind the counter to find the pendant. She then placed it carefully around his neck. He smiled weakly at her. She didn't know why it helped or why he needed it other than it stopped her, her mother, and her nana from making him weak. Her uncle was frail, and that's as much as she understood.

She helped him up, and he dusted himself down. His neat hair had fallen out of shape. His fringe had flopped over one of his eyes.

'I'm sorry I fell and broke it, Uncle. I was trying to get back home quickly.'

'It's alright, Bertha. It's not your fault. Give it to me, and I will see what I can do. A crack, you say; what size of crack are we talking about?'

Bertha held up her little finger and pointed to her nail.

'Oh well, that's tiny. Come back later this morning. I'll shut up shop and get on with it.'

Bertha went to hug him, but he instinctively stepped back out of her reach.

'Oh no, it's alright, my dear, let me keep what energy I have left. You are sweet to worry.'

'Uncle, how can you work on Denis's reflector if you aren't allowed to look into it?'

Augustus quietly sighed to himself. She was indeed becoming inquisitive.

'I wear goggles, just like when I go into the Orbitarium in the castle, that protects …'

He stopped instantly, realising he was waffling and giving away too much information, which would lead to more questions. He smiled and tried to divert her attention again.

'Bertha. I'm so glad you saw her. Is she beautiful?'

Bertha was confused at why he knew of her but had not seen her like his father, Francis. Augustus continued before she had a chance to answer.

'We are merely her keepers and the keyholders of Castle Raphael. Very few have seen her, Bertha, my father being one of them: your Great-uncle Francis. Anyway, now, on you go; let me get on.'

Augustus walked back towards the back of the shop with the small reflector in his hand. Bertha answered, nonetheless.

'She is.'

He turned and looked at her.

'What?' he asked, confused.

'Beautiful.'

She paused and then grinned at him.

'So, she lives in the castle, does she?'

'Yes, she does. Now, Bertha, you need to stop asking questions, now forget I said anything.'

He had said enough, and it was enough to ignite her imagination. She quickly shrugged as if she wasn't bothered by what he said. In truth, she was intrigued.

Augustus suddenly realised. Why had the woman visited her in the first place?

Was it just because of the reflector? he wondered.

'Bertha, is everything OK? Was there anything else she wanted?'

Bertha looked at the floor.

'Uncle Francis is going to give me a book. I have to put words into it from stories she will tell me.'

She shrugged and looked slightly lost.

Augustus knew what this meant and was filled with dread. He needed to talk to his father quickly.

Bertha looked up at him. A worrying thought occurred to her.

'I can't pay you anything to mend the reflector, Uncle.'

Almost disappearing into the darkness at the back of the shop, he called back to her,

'It's baking day, as I remember. A few of your cookies will do just fine.'

Augustus's mind was already on the reflector.

Remembering Miss Primrose was at home waiting for her, she bolted out the door, promising homemade biscuits on her return.

Chapter 6
Eathia - Third Era

Bird Flew

Bertha burst through the school doors and into the fresh air a few months later. She loved her time with her school friends and Miss Primrose, but freedom meant more to her and being cooped up left her with too much energy and too little time to release it.

As she headed home, she heard someone call her name, skidded to a stop and turned.

Most of the children hurtled past her in all directions as they were eager to begin their adventures on what little of the day they had left. As they began to disperse, her aunt, Anamaya, appeared. She called to her.

'Bertha, can you wait a moment, please? I'm so glad I caught you. How are your mother and Nora? I've been meaning to pop over and help a bit, but we've had a bit of a baby boom in the village and what with our duties with the castle …'

Her voice trailed off, seeming to be searching for more reasons to excuse her from not being present or available.

Anamaya worked as a midwife, at the castle and her husband's Emporium. Her true passion was helping bring new children into the world, but her time with the new mothers was limited due to her other duties taking priority.

Bertha answered politely, 'They're doing well, thank you. Mum and Nana are usually busy with Denis, but I try to help as much as possible.'

'Please tell your mother if I can help in any way. We all think she is remarkable how she copes with your father away so much and … well, you know.'

Bertha raised her eyebrows; she had gotten used to living in a disruptive home, but that didn't stop the sympathy given to her and her family because of Denis. He was generally an unhappy baby, unless oddly enough, when she was with him. Bertha felt her aunt's awkwardness and made her excuses to leave.

'I have to go, Aunty. I promised I'd get home quickly today,'

Bertha called back, saying that she would let them know.

Anamaya gave a short and thoughtful smile and walked away, unsure whether she had made herself clear to her niece. Her guilt resurfaced. Since Denis's odd reaction to the reflector and Bertha's connection to the essence in the stories, Francis and Augustus thought it best to keep a closer eye on them, but she had struggled to find the time.

As Bertha approached the cottage, she could see them all in the kitchen. Her nana was baking, and she was missing it. It was just one of the problems with school invading her fun.

When she entered through the front door, Denis's screams were at such a pitch that they felt as though she were eating their way through into her brain. He stopped instantly when she appeared at the door. Her mother looked frazzled, and her nana was flapping a cloth over a burnt cookies she'd just made.

'I shall have to make them again. I'm too hot and flustered to start another batch now.'

'I can help when I get back,' Bertha said calmly. She reached for Denis, taking a wooden spoon out of his mouth and handing it to her nana shortly before it became a weapon.

'Again? You've just come in.'

'I won't be long. I'll take Denis with me.'

Neither her mother nor her nana argued. Instead, both sighed in relief. Bertha headed upstairs to get changed and grab a coat.

When she was a much younger girl, Bertha's father made her a wooden cart with a long handle to help her learn to walk. She had used it to carry her toys in since, but it would be perfect now for Denis. Disappearing back out the front door to the shed, she appeared again in an instant, dragging said object with her. She put a blanket in the base and sat him inside it. Nora appeared at the door.

'Where on Eathia are you going? Is he safe in there?'

'Out for a walk, and no, he isn't, that's why I've tied him to the base of it. He isn't going anywhere.'

Sophia left the sitting room just in time to hear what her daughter had said. She shook her head at Nora, grinning at Bertha's inventiveness.

'Very clever, Bertha. I think your logical mind cartwheeled over my generation; that's for sure.'

Nora laughed.

'Cartwheels, I remember them. If I'd known the last cartwheel I ever did would be the last cartwheel I'd ever do, I'd have made it a spectacular one!'

Sophia laughed at her mother.

Bertha interrupted, still feeling the pinch of the remaining hours before it got dark.

'You're both mad, and I'm leaving now before this gets any weirder. Oh, Anamaya said hi and said she was sorry she hadn't been around to help much. Bye.'

Leaving both her mother and her nana with confused frowns, Bertha took Denis around the back of the cottages. Pulling him behind her, she made her way towards the other side of the town. She knew where she wanted to go, and her brother seemed to enjoy the ride.

Getting him up the hill to the back of the barns was tough, but once she was on the grass, the incline lessened, and she picked up speed.

She stopped to catch her breath momentarily and looked up ahead. The trees were still just about full of leaves, so her view of the castle was hindered, but that didn't matter; she could feel its presence, and so could Denis as he squealed in delight. She picked up a large pine cone and handed it to him to play with.

'You are a little monkey, brother of mine, playing up so all the time for Mum.'

She danced around the cart, making monkey noises to make him laugh, and he chuckled back at her.

A worn track led up to the castle's main stone steps. It was now primarily used by the castle keepers, the Ashens. These were ancient steps. More steps branched to the left side of the castle. They were somewhat overgrown now, but Bertha had used them in the past to hide at the back of the castle. She had always found solace there. Frustratingly for Bertha, none of the windows were low enough to see through. Instead, they were set high in the stonework and featured thick, coloured glass embedded in lead frames. A beautiful glow emanated from them.

She had listened to the few things her uncle had said about the castle, as well as rumours and stories about this place. She had tried for years to capture what it must look like, not realising at the time that all would be revealed through the stories told to her as a transcriber.

She knew the castle contained an invention designed by her great-great-grandfather. It was called the Reflectorscope, and it housed the very orb the woman from the reflector had come from. It shone brightly out of the castle's windows at night, sending beams far into the starlit sky. Because of the orb's constant rotations, its lights danced in the air.

Although loosely connected to its invention, Bertha was denied access to the castle, which only fuelled her curiosity.

The last part of the climb was steep, and she would have to lift Denis out of the cart to make it to the top.

Being near the castle made her feel better, and she hoped it would Denis, too. This place was important to her, and she felt Denis was old enough now to see her secret place. It was somewhere she would relive the stories of the previous night through the journal she kept.

As she climbed, she struggled a little under the extra weight of her brother.

Finally, reaching the top, she flinched when she heard an almighty screech. Moments after, something dark shot towards her from the sky. Bertha ducked in time but hit her head hard against Denis's forehead. He burst into tears, and to her horror, a bump appeared almost immediately below his hairline. Bertha's head pulsed in pain.

Fighting back her tears, she stood fixed to the spot. She tried to calm Denis down. As she pondered whether to return home, it happened again. This time, she lost her footing as she tried to move her body away and protect her little brother. The creature shot past her and almost caught her face with what looked like a claw. As it did, she slipped and fell back down the bank. She held on tightly to Denis as they fell. He had strangely remained silent throughout the fall.

It wasn't until they reached the bottom that she saw he'd been injured again and was holding his breath, ready to erupt with the breath he had been holding on to. The bump that she had unintentionally given him now had a nasty gash across it and was beginning to bleed down the right side of his face.

His scream caused hidden birds to emerge from the trees above, frantically fleeing their sanctuary. They screeched in protest at the disturbance.

Bertha was shaking with shock and fear as she hurriedly put her sobbing brother back into the cart. She dashed back down the path and headed for home, using a cloth handkerchief to try to mop up the blood that still wept from his cut as she went.

Hot and flustered, Bertha burst through their front door with Denis in her arms and ran to the kitchen to her mother.

'I'm sorry, we fell down a hill, and something hit his head. I'm sorry.'

As Sophie took him, Bertha explained that a big black bird had attacked them. She then ran to her room, taking the stairs two at a time. Slamming her door behind her, fury and frustration shot through her body as she scanned the room for something to throw. She ran to her table, grabbed the journal and threw it across the room. For some reason, deciding it was the woman's fault for not making her brother better once the reflector had been fixed. *Why had she made me feel like he would?* her anger raged.

Bertha dramatically threw herself face down on the bed and sobbed. Reaching under her pillow, she pulled out her reflector. Looking into it, she shouted at her reflection, only now she knew 'she' was listening.

'Why do bad things happen when Denis is around? I want him to be normal. You said he would be.'

Even though the reflector had been fixed, her brother continued to cause chaos wherever he went. She blamed herself for all of it. And now, birds, of all things, were attacking them. She calmed herself and thought back to when it happened.

'It wasn't a load of birds; it was just one. She realised it had come down from the window in the castle.'

Everything just kept leading to another question, and nobody would give her any answers, not even her Uncle Francis. She hated everyone! She was starting to feel the pressure of being the only one aware of everything. Other worlds, other people's lives who no longer existed – it was all too much. If she tried to confide in anyone else, she sounded like she was losing her mind.

Her head began to throb as it pleaded with her to close her eyes and relax. Without any response from the reflector, she threw it down next to her. She would talk to her Great Uncle Francis again tomorrow and see if he could help.

Deep inside the reflector, the woman was listening.

She pitied the young girl for all she had endured and all that was to come. It was time to open her up to the full story. In time, it would help her understand her origins and how they shaped their past, present and future. Tonight, when her reflector was next to her, the woman would begin telling her of another altogether different world known as The Realm.

Over the coming months, the woman spent time telling Bertha of The Realm's history until she finally needed her to transcribe the events that, in time, would lead up to the drastic change in Eathia's evolution. Special journals, commissioned years earlier, were made available to Bertha. It would be on these blank pages that her bloodline and soul lineage would be embedded for eternity. The very essence of The Realms' story would live on through her.

She hoped she would be ready. What choice did she have? Time was running out, and the woman feared for the safety of the essence within her.

The darkness felt close, and as long as Denis stayed far away from her, they had no way of discovering them. For now, Stonehaven was safe.

Bertha continued to chronicle all the events that unfolded within The Realm of those who fought to stay tethered to Eathia and those who made it their mission to eliminate those tethers to Eathia forever.

Chapter 7
The Realm

Deeper Still

Deep in the heart of The Realm, Bertha silently watched as the woman began connecting her to the essence, enabling her to see this beautiful, ethereal world. Its translucent tunnel erupted with colour as she was quickly taken through it. Her mind raced as she tried to take in all that surrounded her. It was like nothing she had seen or could imagine.

Eventually, they slowed, and she felt the woman withdraw.

Bertha waited, now familiar with how she, a transcriber, should react to the most extraordinary situations she was taken to.

Keeping calm amid the excitement, she tried not to wake herself up. Eventually, she realised she wasn't alone in this strange world. Although the figure before her was unaware of her presence, she was blissfully aware of theirs.

The essence filled Bertha's consciousness as it began to tell her of The Realm's story.

~

A solitary form waited patiently outside the ethereal chamber surrounding the Source, a mass of pure energy and consciousness from which life originated. Its shape partly resembled that of a female human, a common thread among previously tethered Soul Guardians on Eathia. However, these Guardians had distinctively large eyes, which served as their interface between the Source and their tethers.

Her translucent frame floated effortlessly through The Realm. At the chamber's edge, she paused to ponder her next move. Inside, the Source's power surged, with relentless radiation bleeding from its core. The wall between the Soul Guardian and the Source absorbed this volatile energy, protecting her fragile frame.

From the outside, the surges made the wall look vibrant and alive. Hues of yellows and gold pulsated around its outer surface in a never-ending circuit. This pulse branched off throughout the corridors and tunnels of The Realm, continually feeding and energising it and its inhabitants.

With every ebb and flow, it transmitted a low humming sound. This had intensified as it acknowledged a Superior Soul Guardian was close by and wished for an audience.

Her hesitation stemmed from her realisation of the gravity of what might now be her last time performing this duty. A solemn atmosphere enveloped her as she prepared to initiate the precursor to an extraordinary event within The Realm: the creation of a shard signifying the beginning of a special process, the birth of a new Soul Guardian.

The figure standing gracefully at the entrance to the Source was Verra Mica. She was a newly appointed Superior Soul Guardian who proudly served on the Council and led a Supreme Order within The Realm known as the Seraphytes. This order was one of four divisions that had evolved since the very beginning of The Realm. When all the orders unite, they create a beautiful collective consciousness that resonates with the origins and nuances of the Source's teachings.

The Seraphyte order communicated specifically through the tone and harmonics of sound, which gave it a voice that could be heard through the very essence of the Soul Guardians' central core. The Soul Guardians born to this order would carry with them the melodies and songs of life, enabling them, once tethered, to pass on their gift to their Eathians, allowing them to use their voices in song for expression. The Seraphytes' voices would bring comfort and healing, balancing and enhancing the emotions of their tether. However, this was no more important than other essential ones held within The Realm.

As Verra Mica stood on the threshold of the Source, she drew close to the protective energy field around the chamber. As she did, she felt that an uninvited presence had joined her in the chamber. She waited, trying to clarify if her feelings were justified. Nothing was coming back from her scan of the area. Feeling content that she was alone, she moved slowly towards the entrance. The Source's resonance continued as it acknowledged her arrival, beginning to instigate a process that allowed her safe passage directly into the core of the Source itself via a protective pod-like capsule.

Her tall, ethereal form flowed effortlessly as she moved, her unique aura shimmered around her, reflecting the pureness and clarity that befitted her superiority. Verra Mica had been untethered for only a short while. She had started as a Soul Guardian and then risen in ranks quickly, giving her little time as a Superior to attend many of the births herself. Now, times were changing. The Realm had been pulled into an extraordinary set of circumstances.

Unfortunately, The Realm was now home to this new strain of dark matter; a better understanding of it was needed. A new and evolved Soul Guardian was called for.

There was growing unrest among some of The Realm's inhabitants. Their concerns directly resulted from the dangers existing within their tenuous connections with Eathians and the trouble they were now facing. This unrest began to shatter an otherwise peaceful existence. Signs of a divided allegiance were emerging. Elements of conflict had started to slither through this harmonious homeland, creating a hairline fracture within the attitudes of the Superiors. Some felt that to create balance in the new and changing world, different methods would be required to prioritise and protect the essence of The Realm.

It was true; the balance of The Realm and that of Eathia were definitely and dangerously starting to tilt. An altogether different authority was beginning to appear, intentionally designed to weaken The Realm's foundations as it headed towards a new evolution of its own. If certain actions were not taken, irreversible damage would be inflicted.

Change was coming. But not all would welcome it openly.

Unfortunately, Verra Mica was painfully aware that one would have to fall first to regain any balance at a time such as this.

As she approached the Source, she realised she had never entered the chamber with such apprehension. Never had so much pressure been placed on a Superior and their newborn Soul Guardian. She felt a heavy tug at the thought of what plausible options lay ahead of them if things were to worsen. Was this to be the last of the Soul Guardians born to The Realm? She hoped beyond belief that it was not.

The feeling gripped her. Eathia was falling away from them, and it would take The Realm with it. This was not what she had imagined their future to be. They needed each other.

She felt her attention waning, which was hindering the process. Information needed to be transferred to the Source immediately, revealing the current state of Eathia and The Realm. She needed to be clearer. She wondered what was causing her to lose focus. Backing away slightly, she collected her thoughts and tried again.

Verra Mica was willing and able to tilt along with fate and weather any storm that approached her; her own teacher, Ashtar, had taught her well.

As she focused and released her intention towards the Source, her energetic blueprint would become the key that instigated the process. Now, before her, the portal began to open, allowing her to pass through its wall safely and meet with the Source itself.

Once the opening was complete, a capsule appeared.

It was oval in design with a series of depression-like pores covering its opaque surface. Light energy continually moved around its shell, changing colour and tone, echoing the Source's energetic rhythm. It approached her, as always, on its side with its upper section open, waiting for her to enter. It was in this vessel that Verra Mica would initiate the transference process.

She paused again just before entering, suddenly aware that she was indeed being watched; this time, she could feel the presence of another being close by. She shouted in frustration.

'Who is scanning me?' With her order abrupt and unwelcoming, she continued.

'This is not the time nor the place for interruptions. Reveal yourself at once.'

Alma Tadema, another of The Realm's Superior Soul Guardians, had entered the closed quarters of the Source's Chamber. As with all dignitaries, she wore a headdress, symbolically encapsulating her order within The Realm. She was of an order that connected all of them, for the essence was expressed through her and her Soul Guardians.

A fine ethereal mesh, almost appearing as if it were an Eathian woven fabric, floated away from the base of the headdress and flowed about her as her poised form waited for the right moment to move forward.

She immediately realised that she had been detected and lowered her veil, a shield generally used only for protection or, in this case, to become invisible. She understood that she had silently and stealthily entered Verra Mica's private audience with the Source – two forbidden acts. Only in an emergency could another Superior enter, but to also veil herself, making her hidden and almost undetectable, was unsettling, to say the least, especially since Verra Mica was a dear friend of hers.

'It is I Verra Mica.'

Alma Tadema was from the Nephrolyte order. As a Superior Soul Guardian, she had often worked alongside Verra Mica in Council. The Nephrolytes were the Teachers and Historians, commonly called the

Storytellers. They were an order that passed on wisdom and knowledge to their Soul Guardians. She worked closely with Verra Mica as their factions overlapped in many ways. It was to be the Nephrolytes who had initiated the living story, keeping their history alive to all those that followed.

But now, although old friends, Verra Mica was aggravated and bemused by her presence.

'What would cause you to interfere with this process, and at such a time?'

'I was summoned and advised to intervene. Please accept my apologies, Verra.'

'By whom and for what purpose exactly?'

'The higher order Verra. This is a necessity that I am assured should not be questioned by you or any other Superior.'

In The Realm, the higher order could only be 'The Order of Congress' and was held by only two of the higher-ranked Superiors, Verra Mica herself, recently becoming one and the other a Superior Soul Guardian named Duergar. Together, they had the casting vote that directly reflected that of the Source. Rarely would a condition occur where one of the Higher Council members would be unable to attend such a meeting, causing the need for approval from the remaining Superior Councillors. It was apparent that Alma had agreed that this was one of those rare times.

'You cannot hold a higher-order meeting without my presence. Who gave this order?'

'Duergar had recently received information about a growing turbulent situation on Eathia. Knowing that you were already dedicated here, we all decided that action needed to be taken. He confirmed that the Source mirrored this concern, and permission was given for us to intervene.'

Alma began to move towards her friend but stopped immediately, sensing resistance from her.

'This is inexcusable. He had quite clearly waited until I was unavailable. I cannot begin to imagine a justifiable reason for this. Can you enlighten me on why my opinion on this matter has been disregarded?'

'We are all trying to support the changes required to settle this impending tilt. To do this, Verra, we also must change. Quickly. We can no longer rely on our old ways. They are not enough, not anymore, surely you agree?'

Verra Mica's patience was waning. Her friend continued.

'The time has come now; we need to unite,' Alma implored. 'Duergar does make sense. I am sure you would agree if you only listened to him.'

'We are united. It is not I who needs to be reminded of this. They are his words, not yours. What has happened to you?'

There was something about how Alma said 'unite' that had suddenly stood out from her usual tone, which caused her concern.

Verra Mica began to concentrate more deeply on her friend, and in doing so, became aware that she was still partially veiling. Confused about why, she held fast, untrusting of the reason for the veil's presence. She tried to re-scan Alma.

'What are you suggesting, Alma? Unite in what way, may I ask? Why are you here?'

She glanced down at the heavily veiled area in front of her friend. She was shielding something. Alma continued.

'It has been suggested that we consider merging or uniting the Superiors' Soul Guardians' data. Suppose we collectively input information into the Source this time, rather than relying on only one Superior's contribution. In that case, it would impact the new birth more and lead to a more advanced evolutionary development. It makes sense. You must agree that our current Soul Guardians are struggling to maintain order. We owe it to …'

Verra Mica flared; her aura ignited with a burst of bright fluorescent lights, affirming, with clarity, that she was enraged, to say the least.

'Duergar! That is all I am hearing; I can even feel the dense undercurrent of his tone in everything you say. A merging? Have you gone mad? How far are you going to let this go, Alma?'

As if in response to Verra Mica's outburst, Alma, the more ambivalent of the two, backed down and remained silent. She was starting to feel that she may have quite possibly been swayed by Duergar's powers of persuasion after all.

Verra Mica took her agitation down a notch, realising she was backing her friend into an unenviable corner.

'What exactly have you all agreed to do?'

Alma began to move towards Verra Mica, and as she did, she realised why she could still sense a partial veil. Alma revealed an object she had been holding close to her aura, disguising its presence. As it came into view, Verra Mica could see a small cluster of lights contained in what looked like a miniature dome. Its beautiful colours emanated out from a centre concentration of denser energy. She hadn't seen anything like it before.

Alma released the dome and allowed it to float in front of her. Then, she moved it closer to Verra Mica.

'Please consider taking this in with you?'

As it approached Verra Mica, she could begin to make out a multitude of vibrations that held the characteristics of most of the orders. Alma continued to lift its remaining veil, which now showed its full identity. As it got nearer, she detected something deep within it. It had a certain infinite density, far beyond her ability to scan. She wondered if Alma was aware of this hidden energy. Had she even bothered to check it?

Verra Mica's initial study of the object intrigued her, but she quickly receded her interest as she became more alarmed at her inability to penetrate it completely.

'You're scanning it, aren't you?' Alma said accusingly.

'Of course, I am. And I should, given that "He" has something to do with its origin. Are you aware that part of it is unreadable? Why would this be? What is it for?'

'I am not; I have not felt the need to scan it, and, as I mentioned, you must take it in with you as a collective transference. It contains the ethereal data from ALL of the Superiors Verra, apart from yourself.'

Verra Mica felt horrified at the thought.

'This can't be our only option. We have no idea what the consequences of our actions will be. We are manipulating a process that has safely seen us through our existence.'

'We had the assurance from Duergar; he believes that it is for the greater good of us all, and, as I said before, it comes with the blessing of the Source itself.'

Yet again, Verra Mica flamed at the mention of Duergar. Alma read her reaction ahead of time and again retreated slightly.

'I know of no such acquisition. There is no full blessing without me.'

'Your disregard for my decision makes me feel like a co-conspirator in some appalling plot.'

It was now Alma's turn to show her defiance, a rare outburst considering her calm demeanour.

'Verra, I understand your hesitance, but I implore you to put aside your differences with Duergar and see this for what it is. If we don't change our approach, I am fearful we won't make it through. Otherwise, dear friend, I would not ask you to take this action.'

Verra Mica softened slightly, listening to her friend's tone. Ever the teacher, she thought. Upon seeing that her friend's energy had changed, Alma saw an opportunity to continue and quickly tried to regain her confidence and trust.

'Our new Soul Guardians are being created into an ever-changing environment, and I must be honest, they aren't anywhere near equipped enough for these troubled times. Thankfully, this dark energy is being syphoned off by the Source, but the darkness can piggyback our tethered Soul Guardians without their knowledge. We are running out of choices. We need advanced Soul Guardians, and we need them now.'

Verra Mica responded curtly, '… and the others, do they feel the same?'

'They initially felt the same as you, yet here we are.' Alma moved the orb nearer to Verra Mica.

'… and he sent you? Very astute of him, I must say.'

Ignoring Verra Mica's attempt at being derogatory towards her adversary, she slowly moved towards her.

'Please take it, with our blessings, with my blessing.'

Still trying to read the dome, Verra Mica held fast until the last moment to remain impervious to Alma's pleading, hoping she could think of another way. She felt unable to disagree anymore, incapable of giving reasons to support her concerns. Their current situation was perilous indeed. Reluctantly, Verra Mica opened her aura to accept the obscure dome.

Once inside Verra Mica's aura, she could feel various influences. It was a concentrated synthesis of every order imaginable within The Realm. She felt an obstruction when she tried to penetrate the object to see if she could recognise any of the other Superiors' imprints. Some imprints were very straightforward, while others were trickier, and something about that denseness still alarmed her. She realised that she couldn't sense Duergar's energy at all. When she turned to Alma for an explanation, she found that she had already left.

She recalled her mentor Ashtar's words, 'Embrace change like a long-lost friend.' Tethered to Eathian partners, they formed a courageous union during a pivotal time for the Eathians. Many, on Eathia at the time, claimed to offer spiritual leadership, but most teachings controlled Eathians through fear. Occasionally, there would be someone, as with Ashtar's tether, who was capable of echoing The Realm's guidance. He enabled the Eathians to connect with their own Soul Guardians. Unaware of their inner power, Eathians began to find inner peace, even during their darkest times. With her thoughts returning, she looked down at the orb. Was this one of those moments, she wondered? Should she embrace this thing like a long-lost friend? She flared at the thought.

The capsule remained open, patiently waiting for her to embark.

Her dear friend had left. Misguided or not, Alma Tadema had trusted her to do the right thing. Verra Mica contemplated leaving the small dome behind and continuing without it, as tradition would expect. If these were the last of the births, she had a right to make sure the process would be orchestrated properly. The dome began to vibrate slightly as it neared the energy field surrounding the Source. Verra Mica, once again, hesitated. Finally conceding, she quickly embarked on the waiting vessel, the tiny dome remaining close and protected within her aura as she entered.

For an old soul, she thought, *I am far too pliable ... it will be my downfall.*

The vessel sealed behind her and she started her journey into the centre of the Source.

~

Chapter 8

Eathia - Third Era

The Confident

As she woke from her story-filled sleep, Bertha's excitement bubbled over and she jumped out of bed.

'Another world!' she exclaimed.

She ran to the journal, now abandoned on the floor of her room, and sat at her desk. Scraping her hair back, she absentmindedly ran her hand over the bump from the day before, wincing at the pain. Ignoring it and her previous frustrations, she opened its heavy, leatherbound cover.

The moment she touched it, words started to appear on its pages. Like bubbles rising to the surface of a lake, the words randomly popped up, eventually filling the empty sheets until the story she had witnessed had been transferred. Words and spellings she couldn't possibly know or understand at her age flowed through her hands, her fingers tingling as they did.

Once finished, she sat back. Her head was still full of images of her dream.

Was this all true? she wondered. D*o we all have secret Guardians attached to us?* Her hand reached towards her stomach and she waved it about, expecting to feel something there. She closed her eyes and concentrated.

She almost jumped out of the chair as she heard an abrupt knocking at the door downstairs. Grabbing her dressing gown, she went to put it on until she realised she was still dressed.

'Excellent!' she exclaimed.

She could hear whispering that abruptly stopped as she ran down the stairs. Denis was being handed over to Anamaya, his forehead displaying a rather unnecessarily oversized bandage, she thought. She felt her stomach turn as she relived what had happened to him.

'Where is Denis going?'

Anamaya called over Denis's shoulder,

‘Morning, Bertha. I’m finally free enough to take Denis out for a while. To give you all a bit of a break.’

Anamaya nodded in the direction of her mother, then turned and headed back down the path. Bertha followed her mother into the kitchen, desperate to tell her what had happened.

‘Did you know that there is another world? It’s all around us everywhere.’

Sophia turned and smiled at her daughter. She was well aware of what Bertha was now doing and could only imagine what her young mind was getting filled with. Francis, and now Anamaya, had told Sophia that the orb was helping her because of her nightmares, and she appreciated it, but what she didn’t feel comfortable about was that Bertha thought all of it was true.

As Bertha would soon discover, the stories she observed through the woman in the orb were, to everyone else, just stories, bits of so-called history no one could verify.

Bertha was always destined to become a transcriber. Her soul, her very being, had the right energy anchor for the essence to attach to and become active within her. It allowed her to relive the past as if she were there, hovering just above the scenes as they unfolded. Genuine moments in time. However, she would always be the only one, apart from the Ashens who apparently were sworn to secrecy - who felt the real truth behind them. That’s how the essence survived and kept itself safe.

Stories and legends from long ago guided many throughout their lives. Only when these legends threatened those in power were they suppressed and dismissed, ultimately disregarded as myths and parables. Those who truly believed in them were disgraced or ostracised as witches or soothsayers.

The line between the truth of the past and the myth that The Realm had created had become very fine, and Bertha had to navigate through it. The reality for her was that those closest wouldn’t, no, couldn’t believe her. That wasn’t her fault. It was the way of the essence. To appear untrue was now its veil. One it must hide until those who followed the darkness were no more.

Sophia had decided to tread carefully when Bertha talked to her about the stories. Not wanting her to feel silly.

Nora wasn’t as easily swayed. Her own mother had stories of her own. Although she had left when Nora was still young, she remembered her night terrors, and her mother wholeheartedly believed they were real. Her mother was able to see the future, and that had scared those in charge enough to consider her a witch. Even though life was much less sceptical now, deep down, she was worried for Bertha.

'Another world!' Bertha exclaimed again.

Sophia pushed some jam and toast towards her. Nora listened intently from the sitting room, interested in what Bertha had to say. Sophia continued, choosing not to acknowledge her excited outburst.

'Eat. You missed your dinner last night, young lady.'

Bertha's stomach grumbled at the sight of it but continued speaking regardless.

'A world of Guardians and a … um, what was it called? A place called The Realm.'

Sophia stopped what she was doing and stared at her daughter.

'Were you dreaming again?'

She pushed the plate towards Bertha.

'Please just eat.'

Nora appeared at the door.

'I wasn't dreaming. It came from my reflector, I promise.'

Bertha stopped. If she carried on, she was worried she'd have to admit everything that had happened, including dropping Denis's reflector. She decided to end the conversation.

She felt deflated.

Bertha shrugged, grabbed the plate and sat at the table with her back to her mother. She smiled slightly to comfort the loneliness the story seemed to bring. She wanted to believe the stories were true, but she decided then that it would be safer and less frustrating for all concerned if she kept quiet.

As Sophia left the room, her nana quietly entered. She reached out, pushed her granddaughter's unruly hair behind her ears and saw the bruise.

'Oh, Bertha, look at your head. Did this happen at the same time as your brother's? Why didn't you say something? Let me do your hair and put some cream on that lump.'

She leaned down and whispered in Bertha's car.

'I think your dreams are wonderful. You are a very lucky girl to have such dreams, you know?'

Bertha beamed at her.

There was a tap at the front door, and then it was pushed open.

Suddenly, Bertha heard a familiar voice. She turned to see her great-uncle standing in the kitchen doorway.

'Uncle Francis!'

Bertha threw herself at him, and he just about kept his balance as he held onto her.

Nora stood behind him and intervened.

'Now, young lady, you could do damage with those outbursts. Your poor uncle.'

Bertha looked up apologetically and grinned. Francis smiled and shook his head at her.

The truth was that Francis was Nora's uncle. As an Ashen and a keeper of the castle, the Ashen lifespan exceeded that of an Eathian. They were slower to age. A miraculous occurrence that could only be connected to the energy the orb transmitted.

'I've come to see if you would like to go for a walk with me. My shift has finished at the castle, and I could do with some fresh air. How about it?'

Nora stepped in.

'Your timing couldn't be more perfect.'

She looked wide-eyed at Francis, trying not to bring Bertha's attention to what she was doing.

'Bertha has had an eventful night by all accounts. Dreams and such. Haven't you, Bertha?'

Francis nodded and gestured for Nora to calm down.

'Yes, yes, I know. Now, let me take this wee thing out for a bit. Don't you go worrying about anything, you hear?'

Nora raised an eyebrow. She wasn't one to be silenced easily.

Bertha looked across at her nana and hugged her. Francis winked at Nora over Bertha's head and gave a knowing smile. He then looked down at Bertha. Tweaking her nose, he raised an eyebrow at her.

'Ready to go?'

She giggled as Francis helped her with her coat. She took the slices of toast and they left, chatting to each other as they made their way down the path.

Bertha loved her time with Francis. He was funnier than her Uncle Augustus. Life for him wasn't serious. It was more of an adventure waiting to happen, even at his age.

He leant down towards Bertha and chuckled.

'I think we have some pressing things to discuss, don't we, young lady?'

Francis looked into her eyes. In an instant, the past swept through his mind.

He was the original Ashen and understood what this meant for Bertha.

He was aware of what the future had in store for her and was troubled, to say the least. She was too young to take on the responsibility of carrying the story's life forward from the birth of The Realm to now, her own life as a transcriber. He wondered what could have happened to draw the story to her so quickly. He knew the lady in the orb well from his past and was confused about why she had shown herself to Bertha. That would need to be investigated.

Once Francis had heard from his son, Augustus, explaining that Bertha had seen the woman in the reflector, he prioritised getting across to her as soon as possible. He knew she would need someone to talk to. For now, he'd listen to her and help her understand.

He would become her confidant, just as the woman had promised. Francis understood she would need someone who accepted her belief in the story.

Everything made sense when Bertha admitted to Francis what had happened to the reflector. Now, Francis became worried on a deeper level. Her brother Denis was vulnerable, and because of that, she was too. This event hastened the process of Bertha becoming a transcriber without a doubt. Through this wisdom, she would see how Francis's life was the way it was, an Ashen. The first Ashen to his knowledge.

Francis had spent most of his youth watching and learning from his father, Gabriel. He remembered Gabriel toiling away, diagram after diagram, of the Reflectorscope, trying to create something only he had in his mind. He knew what it meant to break a reflector, let alone look into it once it had been broken, and it worried him that, even though the reflector had now been restored, irreversible damage may have been done.

Only time could tell. For now, he needed to keep a close eye on both Bertha and her brother.

Chapter 9
Eathia - Third Era

The Castle

Once Anamaya had left Bertha and her mother, she made her way towards the castle with Denis still in her arms. It was her shift that morning, and surely, with all that was inside that beautiful building, Denis would find enough distractions to keep him occupied and happy.

As she approached the imposing carved oak doors at the front entrance to the castle, she heard the familiar sound of internal bolts being dragged slowly open for her to enter. A spy hole midway up helping whoever was inside to see who was approaching.

Augustus's pale face peered out at her, shocked at seeing her with an accessory sitting comfortably on her hip. Augustus was still wearing the oculars from just having left the Orbitarium.

He pulled them off quickly when he realised who his wife had with her.

Denis started to cry.

'Oh, we have a visitor, I see, and a noisy one at that.'

He walked out and stood next to Anamaya, one eyebrow raised.

'Is this wise, Ana?'

'It will be fine. He's very heavy. Do you think you could take him for a moment?'

As she handed Denis over, Augustus stood firm.

'Ana, we have never allowed anyone in the castle. This place is sacrosanct.'

'He's just a baby, Augustus,' she implored.

Augustus sighed and stepped inside. Thankfully, Denis had never drained Augustus like Bertha, Sophia and Nora had. The family had only realised this once Denis was born, indicating a maternal bloodline issue.

As soon as they entered the castle, they heard a screech inside another room. Then, without warning, the resident raven flew at them, just missing their heads, making an ear-piercing squawk as it went. Denis's cries reached even higher decibels. He was still very much traumatised from what had happened the day before.

'Quick, get inside. If that's how he's going to be, then I'll keep the raven outside while you have this little one with you. I'll leave the orangery window open so he can get in if need be. I wonder what's got into him?'

Augustus lifted Denis away from him a little and investigated the bandage on his head.

'You look like you have been in the wars, little fella. What happened?'

Ananmaya sighed.

'The raven by the sound of it. It dived at Bertha yesterday when she was over this way.'

Augustus frowned at his wife.

'Why, may I ask, was she over here again? You should have considered that before you brought him back over here again.'

Denis's cries made it impossible for them to speak, so Augustus shook his head and dismissed his question, not having the patience to wait for an answer.

To the left of the main entrance, another oak door lay directly across from where they stood. A large brass sign on the wall indicated that it was the entrance to the 'Orbitarium Room'. The light from the room made the sign shine, catching Denis's attention. He fell silent.

Augustus and Anamaya sighed with relief.

The castle's vast entrance hall was larger than the village's town square. A hexagonal room had wall hangings and tapestries adorning almost every available space, except for one wall to the right of the main doorway opposite the Orbitarium. An ornate, tall reflector was embedded in the wall. On either side were two carved solid oak panels that reached up to the vaulted ceiling. The network of beams and ironwork seemed to give the room even more height. The reflector had required nearly twenty men to lift it into place. Beneath it, an open fireplace roared with a fire whose heat barely penetrated the hall.

Behind the reflector was an opening to the orangery, one of the many secret castle entrances known only to the keepers. The reflector mounted on hinges could be pushed to the wall's left side for an unobstructed view of the orangery. Inside, various herbs and plants flourished, a speciality of Augustus and the castle's former residents. Though well-designed, it thrived only after the Ashens renovated it and finalised the uses for the Orbitarium.

The wooden flooring was partially covered by a large red, gold and green rug with silk tassels. It was perfectly centred in the room. A polished galleried staircase with stone steps was carpeted and led up from the left side of the hall. The gallery curved around half of the hexagonal hall's high walls, providing access to three doors. On the left side of the gallery was a smaller doorway above the main Orbitarium room. Behind it was a simpler room with natural beams, rough stone walls and a vaulted ceiling, mainly used for storage and cleaning products, but it had a small wooden bed for overnight keepers, usually Francis. A wrought iron pulley system was attached to the vaulted ceiling with a curved bare wood observation hatch above it, the purpose of which remained a mystery as it had rusted shut over the years.

The eight joists held the pulley. Large chains threaded through huge hook and eye brackets, each bolted to the floor and extending down into the Orbitarium. Below the chains was a trap door secured with bolts and hinges.

Augustus handed Denis back to Anamaya.

'Will you be alright here on your own?'

'Go and open the shop, I'll be fine. You look tired.'

'I always look tired. As ever, I'll be right as rain in no time.'

Laughing, Augustus tapped his chest where the pendant rested to show that he was wearing armour. He reached for his coat and hat behind where she was standing and took the opportunity to kiss his lovely wife on her rosy cheek.

Anamaya was not Ashen like Augustus. The male side of his family was entirely born into Ashen's lineage, and the family, whether Ashen or not, took on the role of keepers of the castle at Stonehaven. They were usually the only ones permitted to cross the threshold of the castle walls, with few exceptions made in the past.

'Right, little man, let's show you around. You are a very lucky chappie, luckily for me, you won't remember anything on account of you being so tiddly.'

Anamaya laughed and squidged Denis's nose. However, his attention did not veer from the glow that was exuding from the Orbitarium room.

He was silent and had become transfixed.

Chapter 10

Eathia - Third Era

First Steps

Anamaya paused before entering the Orbitarium room. She felt Denis jump in her arms when he caught sight of an ornate metal figure to the right of the door. It was a life-size suit of armour. It was of her height and was affectionately known by the family as Arthur. Ironwork was wrapped around its body, curving around its centre and through its thorax, where a small square opening could be found. It was covered by a hinged door with a tiny hook that kept it shut. An emblem was imprinted on the front of the door. It appeared in odd places about the castle, and as far as Anamaya was aware, it had been created by one of the men who had come to build the Reflectorscope. Friends of her husband's grandfather, as far as she knew, who had said that the symbols came to him in a dream and had admitted that he didn't quite understand their meaning. Four descending circles were held within a vertical eye-shaped design that overlapped.

Inside the door of Arthur's bodywork were hooks that had been welded onto a metal plate within the cavity. This is where they kept the second set of keys for the castle. Much to Augustus's frustration, the head of Arthur was used by his father for his spare hats. Below them, ornate oculars hung on leather straps. The figure's curved metal nose held the front-heavy goggles securely. Two perfect circular darkened lenses were set into brass rims. On either side, soft leather wrapped delicately around them to eradicate any chance of light creeping in from the bright orb.

The oculars were only used by the Ashen keepers. Their safeguard against being drained by the orb was a strange throwback, considering their role as a family was to watch over the safety of the Reflectorscope. They endeavoured to cover their skin as much as possible. Still, their eyes caused them to lose energy, so using the goggles was always imperative when entering the Orbitarium.

Anamaya reached across with her free arm, straightened Francis's hat and the oculars, and nodded to herself in satisfaction.

'That's better, Arthur. Very smart.'

Denis's grip tightened slightly on her shoulders as she proceeded into the room, but thankfully, he showed little sign of fear. His eyes widened, showing more of the swirling lights from the orb in their reflection. With his face aglow, he chuckled happily at the sight of the orb.

Anamaya laughed.

She followed his gaze, never taking for granted the Orb's impact on her and her family, the whole town, and now even further afield. Its iridescent warmth radiated out through the reflectors of so many homes. Guidance was there for everyone at the touch of a reflector, and it all originated from here, from the soul within the orb.

To the right side of the room, an almighty brass construction held in place an illuminated orb. The complex structure seemed to take up a vast proportion of the space.

It grew from the outer edges of the walls and reached out like mechanical octopus arms toward the light. They were made of solid brass and highly polished, increasing the reflectiveness of the light at the centre of their casing. These long arms protruded, each encompassing two sets of hinges, allowing them to bend and manoeuvre into the right position. All were held perfectly in place by chains that hung from the opening above and from spokes that rotated at each base joint, enabling the keepers to alter their intricate alignment.

At the end of each one, two large reflectors sat back to back. Cased in brass, each one was angled towards the central irradiated orb. At least twenty of these enormous, pad-like reflectors were used at any time. They were raised individually in turn through the ceiling into the loft space above and cleaned by one of the Ashen family daily. This ensured that there were no disturbances that might otherwise hinder the reflective surfaces of the glass.

The orb was almost too dazzling to look at with the naked eye. The intense light waves that emanated from it pulsed out towards the room, humming with a self-perpetuating beat. The light bounced from reflector to reflector within its protective field, keeping it central in an eternal reflective state. Above and below, it rested between two vast circular magnets, each bearing a polar opposite charge to the other, thus keeping the orb secured within a strong magnetic pull and preventing it from ever veering off and coming into contact with the ground – a necessary function that would irreversibly damage its balanced state if it failed in any way.

A large circular carpet stretched across most of the floor, covering an ornate mosaic black-and-white tiled surface. Carved wooden furniture edged the left side, its surfaces adorned with various wrought iron tankards, glass jugs, wooden bowls and ornate brass containers featuring insets of reflective glass. Above, a long tapestry hung, its multicoloured embroidered surface depicting the relatively new town's history and those who had become a part of it – those who had travelled far and wide to make Stonehaven their home.

Denis began to wriggle in Anamaya's arms. She grabbed some of the cushions from a bench nearby and placed Denis amongst them on the floor facing away from the orb.

Something started to hit the window high above the orb as she did. Its shadowy figure bashed relentlessly against the glass.

She sighed, frustrated at the raven for causing such a fuss over a small child. She couldn't understand why he was bothered by Denis being there.

The raven had been a castle resident for as long as the orb had. It had a remarkable lifespan, showing no sign of age in the years it had devotedly watched over the soul in the orb. In all her time, Anamaya had never seen him so agitated.

Looking down at Denis, she reassured herself he wasn't going anywhere and ran outside to shoo the raven away. As she unbolted and opened the door, a bird flew in and settled on Arthur's head. Its head twitched as it alternated between looking at her and into the Orbitarium at Denis, who was thankfully unaware of the commotion.

Anamaya took one step forward, and as she did, the bird flew into the room, squawking as it circled Denis. She was now getting cross at its persistence.

Running in, she picked up a cushion and tried to get the raven back into the hall.

'OK, OK, I get it. You don't want him here.'

Not looking where she was going, she flew over one of the cushions on the floor and crash-landed next to Denis, who was now crying, scared and rigid at the sight of the raven swooping over their heads again.

Anamaya was now realising that Augustus's concerns could be valid. She got up and shouted at the raven again.

There was now a banging at the main door. Then, the brass bell was being jangled ferociously.

'For goodness' sake.'

As Anamaya stood to run and open it, now in a complete panic, she slipped on the inner lining of her dress and fell again, her head hitting the tiled floor with a thud. She felt the room spin just before she lost consciousness.

The banging continued and Francis started to call out for her. He was getting concerned at the sound of the raven and Denis's crying.

Upon hearing Francis, the raven flew out of the door, into the hall and beat its wings against the door in a futile attempt to alert Francis.

With the threat of the raven gone, Denis started to calm down. His attention was now drawn towards the orb and its light display.

Denis turned his body around at that moment and balanced on his knees. Gripping Anamaya's motionless back, he rose to his feet for the first time. He never took his eyes off the orb. His attention became solely focused on the centremost part of the orb, its darkened core.

A familiar voice began to call to him from within the darkness. It was as familiar to him as was his mother's voice.

Slowly, Denis's tiny feet began to move forward towards the light. He squealed with delight as he reached out a hand and wiggled his fingers as if trying to sense its energy. He started to gurgle and coo at its rhythmical sound.

Francis had left the main door and shuffled around to the side of the castle to a cellar hatch. It was bolted. Fumbling through his pockets, he found his set of keys.

Meanwhile, Denis had miraculously stayed upright, his desire to reach the orb overriding his hesitation to walk for the first time. He was now starting to move closer to the orb. Once he reached its outer aura, he stretched his tiny hand out until he could feel the static sensation on his fingertips. He beamed at the tingling feeling and pushed his hand in further.

By the time Francis had made it to the cellar, Denis had almost become fully submerged in the orb's light. The raven had flown back into the room and dived onto Anamaya's back. In a panic, it started to peck at her neck, trying to wake her up.

Now fully immersed within the orb, Denis fell into a trance as he started disappearing completely. His arms stretched before him as he tried to reach the innermost, darkened nucleus.

Francis pushed hard against the trap door wedged beneath the rug in the main hall. He pushed with all his frail might to raise the door enough for him to crawl through.

Denis's hand hovered before the dark swirling shadow. He pushed it forward, still glowing in the outer light, until his fingertips disappeared into the dense void. As soon as he did, it was as if a thousand currents of energy swept through his tiny frame. He was thrown backwards away from the core of the orb, then from the outer layer, until he was completely clear of it. His body was thrown sideways across the room as it skidded on the floor's shiny surface. Eventually, it abruptly stopped, hitting hard against the skirting to the left of the main door.

As Francis made enough headway to crawl under the dusty rug, he emerged on all fours. Pulling himself up, he was met by the raven, who tried to lead him to the Orbitarium.

'I know, old friend, I know, I'm coming.'

Panting, Francis entered the room only to find Ananmaya collapsed on the floor and no sign of Denis.

Francis made his way over to Anamaya and crouched down next to her. He heard a murmur as she began to come round.

Then he heard a quiet scuffle. Craning his neck, she tried to hear where it was coming from. There it was again, behind the door he had just entered through. He ran in and saw a tiny boot dancing happily in the air. Francis swung the door away from Denis to find him lying on his back with his legs up against the wall. He looked up at him as Francis awkwardly bent down to grab him.

Sitting up, Anamaya held onto her head.

'Francis, so it was you at the door. Is Denis alright?'

Francis looked at him. 'I think he's OK. What happened to you?'

Anamaya thought back.

'It was the raven; he was getting uptight at Denis being here, and everything went wrong from there on in. I tripped. What made you come here?'

Francis raised his hand to protect his eyes from the orb's glaring light. He reached through the doorway and grabbed the oculars.

'Once Augustus let me know young Denis was here, I thought there may be trouble, and I was right, hey?'

Francis helped Anamaya up, and she sat with Denis on her lap for a while. When she felt better, Francis suggested that she should take him back and he'd finish her shift.

By the time Anamaya had returned Denis, he was asleep in her arms and she had a thumping headache. She stayed for a while until Nora was satisfied she was OK. Bertha ran and got Augustus, who walked her home, and tried very hard on the journey back, not to say he had told her so!

Before putting Denis to bed later that evening, Sophia changed his bandage for a fresh one. When she lifted it, the open wound had gone; in its place was a sealed scar with an unusually darkened bruise beneath it. Sophia winced initially at the sight, then realised the cut had completely healed. It had given his forehead a strange hairline where the dark bruise almost seemed to merge with his hair, causing a widow's peak.

'That's odd,' she thought.

Bertha looked over her shoulder.

'The orb is special, you know it has healing abilities. It does look a bit gruesome, though.'

Sophia smiled as she settled Denis down into his crib.

'Maybe. It will fade, I'm sure. He seems happier, though, don't you think?'

Bertha nodded as her mother left the room. Bertha leant in to kiss her brother goodnight. He watched her draw close to him. As she did, she caught sight of something moving in the iris of both his eyes. She thought she was mistaken in the dim light and pulled back slightly. She lifted his chin gently and looked closer.

There it was again.

A surge of foreboding energy surged through the hazel depths of his eyes, a shadowy whirlwind that twisted like dark tendrils, making Bertha's stomach churn. Then, as quickly as it arrived, it evaporated.

That night, the essence of the story entered her dreams through her reflector, picking up from where it had left off, only this time there was an echo of another voice, and it whispered to her menacingly.

'I saw you, Bertha.'

The essence was strong. It swooped in and dulled the uninvited presence until it retreated. The memory of its voice would fade for Bertha. It would be gone by the morning.

This time, it had got too close for comfort.

Chapter 11

The Realm

The Dome

Verra Mica floated into the mist of the vessel and settled herself into position with the obscure domed object secured close to her. Her alignment commenced as she began to tune in to the Source.

As the vessel advanced deeper into the Source, its movement changed. The inner wall responded to Verra Mica's presence with a distinct pulse. Delicate tendrils began to emerge from the inner lining, gracefully reaching toward her aura. A soft blue current surged from the root of each tendril, travelling through its stem and shimmering at the tips. Fine capillaries illuminated their cushioned ends, glowing through the surrounding opaque matter.

Verra Mica was attuned to this ethereal process. She felt the gentle presence of small data locators weaving through her aura. Once they sensed their alignment, they gently initiated their attachments, preparing to connect with their host and channel the Superiors' recently gathered knowledge.

For Verra Mica, it was a wonderful chance to communicate directly with the Source; throughout the transaction, she could only receive pure and concise information, benefiting her with its healing energy. During the process, she would be given a true and accurate account of Eathia and The Realm's current state.

Some data she was transferring came from her tethered Seraphyte students, who shared information through their tether portals. Her ethereal senses were becoming numb, allowing the tendrils to access her freely.

For a moment, she forgot about the dome completely.

As Verra Mica's senses faded, she was only vaguely aware that something was interfering with the natural progress of transference. The initial instinct that something was amiss came from deep within her being. Her numbness shifted suddenly, reversing back to acute awareness. She could now attentively register every movement of the tendrils as they grew anxious about a strange presence within the capsule.

Now utterly conscious, Verra Mica felt an overwhelming dread enveloping her. A chilling realisation crept in. Something was undeniably wrong, yet she found herself unable to escape. As the tendrils slithered, redirected themselves and edged closer to the small dome, a horrifying thought struck her: without a doubt, she had agreed to invite a dangerous intruder in.

So, she had been right, she thought. *This unorthodox decision was now causing them to alter their sequence.*

Tentatively, the tendrils eased themselves nearer to the outermost part of the dome. Sensing a change in its overall vibration, they slowed their advance. The oscillating sound within the vessel lowered in tone as the tendrils tried to understand what it was. Verra Mica could hear the change and remained as inactive as possible. Vigilantly, the first of the probes reached out to inspect, its flat pads eventually contacting the outer curve of the orb. As it did, it retracted instantaneously, as if shocked by the sensation. Fascinated, more began to hover around it, all trying to evaluate the correct approach.

Verra Mica waited, hoping the dome would be rejected and everything would carry on without it. She had wanted this all along and hoped the Source would sense the intrusion.

She suddenly felt a jolt that caused an energy overload. Then, a flash of an indecipherable image exploded into her vision, if only for a moment, but that was enough.

Without warning, all the remaining tendrils lunged at the dome, attaching themselves in a united strike. As they did, the responding energy coursed through the vessel, sending Verra Mica into an involuntary convulsion. Her being became charged with surge after surge of violent spasms, and with them, the images returned. Memories appeared from her past, The Realm and her time of being tethered to an Eathian human. Then, scenes of fire, floods of water and explosions of cataclysmic proportions within The Realm and Eathia. They dissipated as quickly as they had arrived, until she was finally plunged into total darkness. All she could do was continue to watch and wait, helplessly feeling the devastation that had been shown.

What exactly had she agreed to pass on to the Source, and where was all this information coming from? The past? The future? She had never known of such disasters in either of their worlds. What was she witnessing?

The vessel began to vibrate. Sparks were firing off from the surface of the pads that were now attached to both her and the dome. She continued to watch as Eathia suffered splintering cracks and hot molten liquid pushing up from its depths. Verra Mica watched as The Realm's light began to drain back through the tethers the Soul Guardians had forged to support and nurture. As The Realm's energy depleted, the Soul Guardians' life force faded. Their beautiful forms started to become wispy, shrivelled shadows, unable to lift themselves up, trailing limply next to their tethers and unable to return to The Realm. Such disturbing images would haunt her until she was able to understand their meaning. Was she being warned by the Source or was it showing her the future?

What had she done? What had they all done?

Then, as quickly as it had occurred, all transfers ceased. The deep tone from inside the vessel retreated along with the images. The pale glow returned to the capsule and all was still again.

Verra Mica had been holding onto a sense of dread, which was the last to leave her, replaced instead with relief that it was all over. She started to sense the detachment process. The tendrils released quickly from the dome and then gently from Verra Mica.

Stunned into stillness, she waited, scanning her own being. She checked all her levels, her clarity and her senses. All seemed to be completely unaffected by the incident.

Verra Mica felt the vessel move gently, transporting her back towards the outer edge of the Source.

The dome was now dull in colour, almost grey. It felt heavy against her own being. With no life source, it had become a cold and empty shell, now cleared of all energies within it. Relieved that the ordeal was over and glad to be rid of the dome, Verra released herself from the vessel and discarded it immediately. Behind her, the entrance closed and she was left to ponder what had just happened. She looked down at the orb and studied it with disdain.

Her attention swiftly returned to the Source and the reason she was there. The new birth. All appeared well. The process seemed to continue regardless of her ordeal.

The awful images started to filter back, and she tried her hardest to keep them at bay.

Would she have taken it in now if asked? If she had known the consequences?

Absolutely not!

Chapter 12
The Realm

Conception

Deep within the Source, the transferred data flowed freely, branching into numerous channels. Sparks of intense light dispersed throughout its core, activating sensory receptors along the way. As the Source began to assimilate and filter the new information, the process was hindered by a hidden nucleus energy that Verra Mica had also struggled to interpret. When the sensory receptors encountered this unusual density, they recoiled, much like the tendrils within the vessel had done. Any attempts to access the nucleus were thwarted by what seemed to be a protective force field. An irregular, separate sequence began to emerge, creating an unusual divergence that isolated itself from the rest of the cluster.

This alternative branch continued to move alongside its data counterparts, concealing itself behind them. It enabled entry through similar channels while striving to remain solitary and disconnected from the Source.

The main cluster began to move through the Source's complex labyrinth, where the collaboration of filtered energies started to merge within its primary streaming process. This enabled a two-way transference that, once complete, would allow the stream to either remain whole and singular or be divided, resulting in two identical streams. Unbeknownst to Verra Mica, two distinct clusters began to form. This division would ultimately lead to two separate births – something not uncommon in The Realm but considered quite rare.

The stealthy lone energy stream remained unchanged as things progressed, allowing only a one-way transfer across its protective shield, drawing what it could from the Source.

Once what had now become three streams were ready to vacate the channels, they began to slowly manoeuvre themselves through the outer edges of the Source's walls, their speed increasing to match that of the Source's expulsion rate. On impact, the streams would break through the highly charged perimeter, where the explosion would be felt throughout The Realm.

Having broken free from their polar grip, the perfect streams became individual soul shards, using their energy to break through from the Source.

Once Verra Mica saw the change in the outer wall's energy, her concerns lessened as she became aware of the impending birth. Relieved, she began to channel her consciousness towards them, an aid that would help draw the new soul shard towards her.

Even though Verra Mica had once made this incredible journey, she marvelled at what the young shards would be experiencing. The transformation was astounding, a process known simply as birthing that took a relatively short time, even in its complexity. The knowledge sent to the shards ranged from tens of thousands of years old to the current status of The Realm.

The shards began to embed into the latticed membrane and underwent a 'Shattering' process. During this, simple energy particles transformed into multifaceted energetic particles, creating explosions of light like metal striking metal.

The meshed surface absorbed the shards while bolts of light and colour enveloped them. Particles either attracted and reformed or repelled each other based on their origin. In this process, they rebuilt, forming a near replica of the Source with, however, a modified matrix and consciousness, giving the new young soul its unique individuality.

Verra Mica waited anxiously for the new arrival, completely unaware of the events that had taken place within the Source.

Chapter 13
Eathia - Third Era

Windows to the Soul

The days and nights following Denis's contact with the dark centre of the orb haunted him, leaving scars deeper than anyone could comprehend. Although he hadn't been the happiest of babies, his moods had taken on a much more unsettled note, adding to his anguish, only finding peace when Bertha was with him.

Francis had understood some of what might have happened to him; being near the orb could have profoundly affected him, especially after his initial contact with it through the cracked reflector. A situation that he and Augustus had played down at the time. Neither of them had any idea of what the fallout would be as a result.

One thing that concerned Francis was that he had seen evidence of a noticeable change in its darkened centre within the orb. When did it happen? He could only guess.

It was apparent that Bertha and Denis had a connection that went so much deeper than the usual sibling relationship, and it appeared that it was Bertha who, unfortunately, suffered because of it. There were times when she was vulnerable, and it was through Denis that the darkness within the orb could reach out to her.

It had been Augustus who had come up with the idea of Bertha wearing a version of the oculars designed for the Ashens to use in the castle. He created smaller, plainer versions for Bertha, featuring clear, slightly reflective glass. After being told that she had seen something flash through Denis's eyes, it didn't take long for Francis or Augustus to realise that the eyes were the connection.

'Windows to the Soul,' Francis had muttered thoughtfully.

Chapter 14
The Realm

The Birthing

Verra Mica watched in awe as glorious gold and amber-coloured electrical currents danced and echoed towards the outer shield of the wall.

As they passed her, she was able to attune with the shard. She hesitated, suddenly aware that she was picking up a second energy. She silently whispered to herself,

'So, there are to be two of you; how glorious.'

This made sense to her. Twins had not been born in The Realm for a very long time, not since Makaria and Angelic, and because the Council had intervened, she had expected a slight alteration in the process. She felt content with the outcome.

Now glancing down at the lifeless, small, empty dome as it rested beside her, she directed a sudden blast towards it, sending it flying. She didn't want to look at it anymore.

Her attention was drawn back to the soul shards as they became visible through the outer wall.

'It's time,' she said excitedly, reassuring herself that all was well.

When this process neared completion, Verra Mica would recognise what order they held, usually that of the Superior in attendance, but not always.

Very gradually, the golden and amber lights bulged out from the Source. As Verra Mica moved nearer, the tips of the two energy portals began to move towards her. The velocity and sound coming from the outer wall intensified as they began to connect with each other.

Then, an unexpected turn of events occurred. Completely undetected by her, a third protrusion burst through to the left of the others.

How did she miss it? she thought, feeling agitated at herself for not sensing it.

Verra Mica started to tune in with the unpredicted third birth, but this one appeared to have a life of its own. Any attempt she made to synchronise with it failed. With no attunement, she worried that it would only be able to replicate that of the other births and hoped that it would make it out unaffected.

Side by side, the three soul shards emerged like steady rocks protruding from a fast-flowing stream. They held fast as they edged out in perfect unison.

Finally, the new arrivals were almost free. Verra Mica moved back, sensing the need for distance between her and the platform. As she began to expand her aura, she was able to gain a closer glimpse at The Realm's unique Triplexes.

The third new soul to the far left had started to disconnect first. This one had a stronger pull, but she was not the one drawing it out. It was using Verra Mica's energy to help release itself. Concerned with this encroachment, she felt the sudden need to block its attempts, but it caught her unaware, and before she could, it severed all their connections of its own accord. She paused, monitoring the strange anarchic tendencies of one so new and young. She was starting to sense a darkness about this one, starkly contrasting to the other two, freely moving towards her.

Relief flooded through her; all was well with them.

Content that the others were safe, she quickly moved to the third lone soul again and began to scan it as it hovered before her. As soon as she did, it showed a chameleon-type reaction, possibly sensing danger of some sort, it immediately changed its aura, becoming almost identical to the other two. Aghast at what she had witnessed, concern began to rear its head again.

In truth, all was not well at all.

'This one will be tricky to bond with,' she murmured, contemplating the next phase of her connection to them. She pondered her next move.

Now, she needed to work hard at creating a base for all three that would anchor them into the fabric of The Realm. She was not surprised to sense some disparity as she did.

Verra Mica opened her core portal following the bonding sequence and completed the attachment. As soon as it was open, the third followed suit, finally allowing its energy to connect with Verra Mica, a necessary link for communication and coding. She would now be able to ascertain all their given skills, enabling them to find their place within their orders of The Realm.

She paused momentarily before releasing them; there was something welcomingly familiar about their united energy. At that moment, she felt a sudden tear and the connection with the third soul was severed. Its energy pulled away from her with such unnecessary ferocity that it took her aback. It then proceeded to move away slowly and purposefully from her.

She turned her attention back to her two Souls and watched their final forms appear, revealing exactly who and what they were. They were now officially Soul Guardians and, unusually, had a similarity to the Eathian forms. Considering they hadn't experienced tethering, this was strange, to say the least.

This was the second anomaly she hadn't experienced before; the shards usually only take on a soul's energy field and not a human's.

Still aware that there was a disturbance to the side of her, she waited for the two new Soul Guardians to awaken. In a hushed tone, she announced herself. Her voice was to be an important connection for her Seraphytes. It was now clear that she would be mentoring the two of them.

'I am Verra Mica, and I am your Superior Soul Guardian. You are now ready to come into being. Welcome.'

The two separate forms began to move away from her, their initial connection replaced by a thin, permanent current of translucent pulsing energy.

A young male and a female now hovered before her. Both were incredibly evolved. Verra Mica could see that, but obvious degrees of individuality came with that. Their purity was immense, like no other she had ever seen before. She did not doubt that these beings would bring a wealth of influence to The Realm.

The female of the two was to be known as Christi. She watched Verra Mica intently; her green oval eyes took in every detail of Verra Mica.

Her colours were pale and her fluorescent aura displayed a skin-like quality, as did the other two; hers was by far the softest of tones, with white and gold flowing pulses moving around her being that seemed to fill every part with excitable flashes darting here and there. Above her floated her flaxen hair. Lights seemed to gleam and glisten through their fine tresses as they moved, lifted by the gentle current within the chamber. She smiled and looked across at her twin. He had been given the name Corpus. His form was very different, with pale gold and chestnut tones. He reflected slightly lighter and darker shades within his more refined and stronger figure. His eyes were as intense as Christi's, only blue, made more penetrating by his deeper aura and darker hair that fell in short waves about his face, refining its shape that would resemble, if on Eathia, a strong chiselled jawline.

Verra Mica was intrigued by their appearance.

Behind the Soul Guardians, the surface of the Source's outer wall had resumed its steady stream of rotations and colourful spectrums. The noise dulled to a low hum, and peace finally eclipsed them all.

The third enigma was now going through similar stages to its siblings but, unknown to Verra Mica, had become attached to another Superior Guardian who had silently entered the chamber and resided slightly behind her.

She suddenly realised she was not alone in welcoming them. There was one that was being deliberately concealed. His need to hide made it clear to her that Duergar had become involved in this final stage.

Lowering his veil, the familiar pulsating drone bled out from him and into the chamber. The third Soul Guardian appeared to be completely linked with him, his veil lowering simultaneously with Duergar's.

Verra Mica realised that the third Soul Guardian's own ability to veil throughout the process had been the cause of her not being able to read that there were three of them.

Fury started to bubble up inside her.

She watched and respectfully waited for their process to finish. She could now see how very different the third was in comparison. He was less translucent, with a denser blue tone that seemed to become a lot stronger at his centre point, almost identical to Duergar's core structure.

Why was she not surprised?

Corpus and Christi sensed a change in Verra Mica and watched as their brother fully joined the group. Verra Mica spoke first.

'Christi and Corpus, welcome to The Realm.' She turned to welcome the third, now knowing him to be Elkyne. She gazed at him momentarily before returning to Corpus and Christi. He was as beautiful as the others, but it was clear that he had not been born into her own order. Possibly a rebalance, she thought, but more likely an illegal interference.

So why, she thought, *did something still feel very wrong about Elkyne?*

She let it go and watched all three as they interacted with each other. Verra Mica, for the moment, allowed her anger to pass. Duergar, on the other hand, found her attempts at hiding it amusing.

His resonance changed; it accompanied all musical Soul Guardians, those of the Psybiencian order. He was goading her, acknowledging, if not furtively, that he was aware of what Verra Mica was doing. He smirked at her and made sure she saw it.

She continued to try and ignore him.

'Welcome to you all. You are united and bonded to each other and will remain connected on many levels throughout your existence within The Realm. You are our first-ever Triplex births, and we are proud to have you join us.'

Corpus and Christi lit up, their young personalities showing through. Elkyne, on the other hand, had shown signs that he, too, was beginning to respond to her welcome, and Duergar immediately severed his connection.

'I am glad to see that it is the will of the Source that I have a connection with all three of you.'

She stopped and shot a look at Duergar and then continued.

'Regardless of any attempts to the contrary,' she carried on.

'I sense you are multi-ordered with a higher attunement to either my own Seraphyte order or, as with you, Elkyne, a Psybiencian order. I look forward to working …'

'Can I stop you there if you please?' Duergar interrupted.

With his patience waning, Duergar started to guide Elkyne away from the group.

'If you don't mind, Counsellor, I have other plans for Elkyne for the time being. We will return soon. I won't keep him long unnecessarily.'

He ushered Elkyne away, who was as confused as the others to be leaving.

He bowed slightly to his brother and sister, his gaze lingering on Christi, then turned, veiled once again and retreated.

Even through her agitation, Verra Mica felt a pull as Elkyne left, and as she turned, she realised that both Christi and Corpus felt it too.

Corpus moved forward, taking Verra Mica's attention from Duergar and diffusing momentarily her overwhelming annoyance and partial loss.

'It is our pleasure, Superior Verra Mica; we are proud to be in your favour.'

He looked at Christi for a long while, a knowing look that told of their bond.

Verra Mica bowed at them both and assured them they would all catch up with Elkyne again shortly.

Christi spoke.

'All is as it should be, Superior; we know Elkyne's need to progress as a Psybiencian. We were prepared for this by the Source during our creation.'

'You knew he was to be of another order?'

Verra Mica acknowledged that they were potentially more up to date than she was herself.

'Very well, yes, let's move on. I have much to show you, and many here wish to meet with you; you will all be quite a novelty within The Realm due to your triple birth sequence and timely arrival.'

Corpus and Christi glanced at each other as if to acknowledge their roles and reassure each other that they were indeed united in their purpose. The Source had already communicated this to both of them, or so they thought.

They moved away from the Source without a backwards glance, into the open arms of The Realm, into their new world, one familiar to them before they had even crossed the threshold from the Source's chamber.

As Verra Mica led them away, she turned and looked at the discarded empty dome that still rested nearby. Thankfully, no one had noticed it lying there. With another focused blast of energy from her core, it dissolved into dust, which floated up and fizzled away as if it had never existed.

She then acknowledged her Source and bowed her head, silently asking for forgiveness, knowing full well that she would need to forgive herself for what she had allowed to happen.

'For the greater good,' Alma Tadema had previously stated. She could only hope that it was.

It would become apparent much later that all three had been given slightly different levels of understanding about their roles within The Realm and to what lengths they might have to go to complete them.

After all, they had been born into troubled times.

Chapter 15
Eathia - Third Era

Ashen to Ashen

Francis Eli Browne gradually made his way up towards Castle Raphael. His old legs finally showed signs of giving up on him, but he defiantly ignored the pain in his tired hips and back. At the top, he leaned an arm against the door before opening it to catch his breath so his son didn't witness his wheezing and coughing. His wrinkled, lived-in face looked exhausted by his greyish pallor. He, too, was an Ashen. In the past, a good day would see his cheeks gleaming grey with porcelain white, highlighting his cheekbones. Those days had long since escaped him. A good day now was to make it up those 'damn' steps without choking on his own breath!

He turned and leaned back on the warm wooden door and gazed at the town before him as far as his eyes would let him. He could see the market square, the town's epicentre, with the wrought iron cross reaching high above some buildings. Around it, the grey and golden sun-kissed roofs spread up like the scales on a reptilian back as each one weaved in and out of the naturally sunken valley of Stonehaven.

He had watched this town grow from nothing. When they arrived, all but a small cluster of stone houses with an oversized castle watched over it. Then, the people began to arrive and the town grew.

A sage, or was it a soothsayer they called her, either way, she was his sister. Somehow, word got out that this was her final resting place. A beautiful soul of a woman who had touched so many lives in some way when she walked on Eathian soil, so much so that they journeyed just to be near her.

A lot had happened in that short time since their arrival, and his intuition told him there was more to come long after his time was over.

He'd been alive too long, all thanks to his beloved orb.

As a boy, he was known as a freak in his hometown of Cullvelley. A small village where nothing ever happened until it did.

His father, Gabriel, had called it a miracle and a curse at the same time. He was referring to his invention. A much smaller prototype than the one that now stood in the Orbitarium room.

His father didn't like to speak of what happened that day and could never explain why Francis was born the way he was shortly after, without any colour, but something did happen. His mother, Beatrice, said she had been receiving healing from the machine his father had made. She was pregnant with Francis at the time and had been very ill throughout the pregnancy. The machine malfunctioned, causing an explosion. His parents thought that it was this that was the cause of Francis's unusual pallor.

It wasn't until Francis's own son was born that they realised it was to be a hereditary disorder. They became known as the Ashens, a nickname that stuck and had now become a race. He had heard that there were more elsewhere like him and Augustus but had never seen them or understood how they came to be similar.

The castle door suddenly opened behind him, making him jump and pulling him away from his thoughts.

'Oh, Pops, I wondered if you were here. The bed is all made up for you.'

Augustus looked at his father's tired face.

'Are you sure you still want to do the night shifts?'

'Every day you ask me; every day I say the same bloody thing.'

Augustus smiled and pushed a flask into his hand.

'Made you a brew.'

'Is it that special tea ya make me or just simple tea?'

Augustus was known, on occasion, to add a bit of brandy to the flask.

'Just tea today.'

Francis walked past Augustus and stopped momentarily, looking up at the second staircase he would have to attempt to climb that day. He let out a sigh.

'Thanks for the tea anyhow, son.'

His voice drifted off to a mutter.

Without turning around, he waited for his son to shut the door behind him before he would even consider starting his ascent up the staircase.

Once he finally reached the top, he leant back, exhausted, onto his horsehair mattress and placed the flask, which had lost all interest to him, somewhere near his bed. He thought he probably wouldn't drink it, *no point.*

Memories of his past continued to flood back as if they were yesterday, as they always did when he walked inside the castle walls. The orb had a gift for conjuring up hidden or lost thoughts. His stomach ached as images of his parents appeared in his mind. He missed them terribly, even at his ripe old age, whatever that was, he'd lost count years ago. Then, his sister's face appeared before him. He squeezed his lips together and tried to smile at her with teary eyes.

'Damn it, I'm too old to cry.'

He wiped his cheeks with the back of his sleeve.

He suddenly heard a flapping in the distance. Feeling revived suddenly, he sat up and lifted his arm to protect his face. The raven came sweeping in through the open door to greet his old friend. He landed on Francis's forearm and looked at him inquiringly, tilting his head to one side.

'Here you are. Now, I think I've been banned from having that special tea. Have you been telling on me?'

The raven didn't take his eyes off Francis.

'Ah, well, I guess this place needs a bit of excitement occasionally.'

In truth, Augustus heard the commotion when Francis decided not only to spice up his tea with extra brandy but also thought it would be a good idea to play the piano in the Orbitarium, in the middle of the night. The noise exploded out of the naturally acoustic stone walls and echoed over the roofs of those nearest to the castle. Augustus's home included.

Francis chuckled to himself and tried to get up from the bed. There was work to be done.

After three attempts, Francis eventually exited the bed and shuffled around the loft, looking for his oil and tools.

He was the mechanic behind the machinery and had originally helped to build the Reflectorscope, as it was known by those in the know, with his father's friend, Rent and his grandson Patrick, and it was now his duty of care to keep the old girl going. He had loved those days and thought Patrick was to become his brother-in-law. For a brief time anyhow.

Francis sighed. His stomach ached at the memory that flashed through his mind. He shook his head to try to disperse it.

With the raven still on his arm, he steadily returned down the stairs, gripping the rail as he descended towards the hall and the Orbitarium.

Before he entered, he put his cap on Arthur's head, took the goggles, and placed them over his own. As he walked in, he put his tools down near the long oak cupboard that ran the room length to the left. He noticed something was missing immediately. It was the box his Pa had given him. He scratched his head and looked about the room. All he could see were smudges of dirt here and there, but no box.

'Unlike Augustus, to leave it looking like this.'

The bird flew away from him and landed on the floor beside the sideboard. He bobbed his head, looking under the piece of furniture.

Francis bent back to see if the bird was that clever.

There it was, and yes, he was that clever.

Francis thought for a bit. He couldn't remember when his whole body had been purposefully that close to the floor. He thought he should leave it be and get Augustus to retrieve it. His joints and instincts agreed. But that box was sentimental.

'Ah heck, in for a penny.'

He leant all of his weight against the edge of the sideboard and tried to keep control of the speed as he fell, but that was never going to work, and he grimaced as his knees crashed down hard against the tiled floor.

He hung his head and bit his lip. Lowering his arms down now, he accomplished the first easy part of what looked like a press-up; only it was just the press-down part. As soon as he got his head down level with the floor, he heard the creak of the main door opening.

The raven unexpectedly ignited into action, causing Francis to lift his head too quickly and hit it hard against the lower corner of the wooden beading. But it wasn't that that knocked him out; it was the iron jug that usually rested on top of the cabinet that wobbled precariously, before falling on his head.

He wasn't out for long.

As he came around, his cheek was pressed against the icy cold tiles on the floor, making it ache. His eyes slowly focused on what lay ahead of him. He blinked and frowned when he saw what looked like a bottle of brandy that had been pushed up against one of the legs of the sideboard. His head hurt and so did his knees.

'So that's where he hid it. HAH!'

He became aware of something prodding him in the back, over and over again.

'Damn bird, I'm coming.'

He rolled over, flopped onto his back and groaned.

The poking continued only now on his stomach. He shot his head up to reprimand his feathered friend, but instead, he came face to face with another face. A much younger, dirtier face.

'Denis?'

The boy, now over six, sat cross-legged and quietly stared at him, but irritatingly for Francis, he still insisted on carrying on with the jabs.

'Alright, you can stop now. I'm alive again.'

The boy silently lifted his arm, and the wooden box was in his hand. To Francis's surprise, he also had his father's, Gabriel's, book detailing the building of the Reflectorscope.

Raising himself up, Francis sat back and rested on his straightened arms.

'How did you get in? You can't come in here, son; your mother would have two fits if she knew you were in here, especially after what happened to you.'

Francis pointed at the book.

'You shouldn't have that either. Where did you get that from?'

The boy stood and walked over to Francis, reaching behind him to put the box back.

He leant forward and whispered in his ear.

'The shaft at the back of the fireplace. I found the book under my parents' bed.'

Denis then grabbed the tools and oil from the bag, ran over to the Reflectorscope and began to oil and change the tension on the bolts on the brass arms.

Francis pushed his legs under him and rose awkwardly to get to his feet quickly.

'Hey, no, you don't. You can't do that. Come back over here. NOW.'

Denis disappeared around the back of the orb and continued to adjust the machine quickly. Reappearing on the other side, he stopped and looked across at Francis. His expression was solemn. Francis noticed he wasn't looking for gratitude nor recognition.

Shaken by the events, Francis followed him and checked the joints of the arms one by one, fully expecting to have to re-adjust each one. The boy was making more work for him.

However, each one had perfect tension.

'Well, I'll be blown; you knew exactly what you were doing, you little tyke.'

He looked at him.

'How did you learn to do that?'

Denis held the book out in front of him.

'The book.'

Denis just shook his shoulders.

He quickly walked over to Francis, handed over the tools, put the oil on the floor, threw the book down and ran out of the room without another word. As he exited, the raven, trapped in the hall by Denis, flew in. As soon as the bird reached Francis, Denis slammed the Orbitarium door shut to keep himself separate from the bird. Francis heard the outer door shut. Then there was silence. Francis rubbed his head to see if there was any blood he should worry about.

He glanced across at the sideboard. The box had been returned. He wasn't in the mood to check the contents, so he just lifted the heavy jug from the floor and placed it back, fully expecting to see a dent in the shape of his head on one side. There were just a few tasks he had left to do before he could turn in for the night. Momentarily, he pondered the bottle he'd seen underneath the sideboard but decided, for many reasons, it would be a bad idea to retrieve it.

In the early light of the morning glow, Francis awoke with the sound of familiar footsteps on the stairs.

In the time it took Augustus to reach the door, Francis had decided the events of the previous evening were best kept to himself until he had a chance to understand why Denis had been there.

Ignoring his thumping headache, Francis greeted Augustus and reported that the night had passed without incident.

Chapter 16
Eathia - Third Era

The Birth of a Storyteller

After her lessons that day, Miss Primrose walked with Denis back toward his home. His silence persisted, as it had at school, throughout the journey only responding to her attempts at light conversation with a sideways glance. He was a very clever boy, evident in his work and quick understanding, but not in his voice. He never spoke up in class, a stark contrast to the vocal baby he once was. She realised that he would only talk to Bertha, and that was quite rare, yet it didn't deter her from trying to earn his trust.

Denis walked in just as they reached the cottage door and promptly shut it behind him, startling her as she nearly walked straight into it. She gasped in surprise and immediately lifted her arm to open the handle and continue after him, but stopped, realising she couldn't follow him. It would be rude to enter unannounced.

She waited patiently for someone to come. No one did.

Unbelievable, she thought.

Alicia moved her hand from the handle and knocked loudly.

Sophia opened it almost immediately and beamed at her. On the other hand, Alicia's attention moved on to Denis, who was sitting peering at her from the stairs behind his mother.

'Miss Primrose how lovely to see you. Is everything alright?'

'Yes, yes all fine. I wondered if I could have a word.'

Denis launched himself up the stairs, passing Bertha, who was on the way down as he did. He slammed his door shut. She glanced at Bertha and smiled.

'I hoped to talk with your mother about our little idea.'

They all went into the sitting room and sat down. Bertha's legs danced on the spot as she sat in anticipation. She beamed at Alicia.

‘I was going to ask if you had any objections to Bertha reading to my group on a regular basis. Like a classroom assistant only, to help with quiet time. Her stories are so imaginative that it would be a shame for her not to share them. I would pay her a little something, of course.’

Sophia looked across at Bertha, who grinned back at her.

‘I think that’s a wonderful idea. Some of them might need to be toned down a little, they can be a bit extreme at times.’

Bertha tutted.

‘I will. I know what you’re trying to say, and of course, I’ll tone them down for the young ones.’

Alicia glanced across at Bertha and smiled.

‘She’ll be finishing her studies for this year soon, so I would rather wait until that’s over.’

‘Thank you, that’s very thoughtful.’

Bertha watched her mother’s expression soften to a slight frown only she would have picked up on.

Things were changing for her mother. They had lost Nana Nora last year, and none of them had gotten used to the vacuum left behind in her wake. Her father had also been away longer than usual, fixing and making sails, a job that took him out to sea for extended periods. Additionally, there was Denis, who was fast approaching seven. For him, this transition brought the stress of needing a new reflector. It was a coming-of-age celebration where all children of that age shed their small old reflectors for larger ones.

Bertha felt her mother’s loneliness, and she was bouncing around with glee, knowing full well that it would take her away from the cottage, too.

When she returned from her thoughts, Alicia and her mother were quietly discussing Denis.

She interrupted.

‘Why don’t we have a party for him, to make it more about being with family and friends and not all about that reflector?’

Sophia smiled up at Bertha.

‘I think that’s a lovely idea?’

Alicia picked up on Bertha’s train of thought.

‘Will Tobias be back in time, too, do you think?’

‘Yes, he will, he promised he would.’

Alicia felt they had gotten to a natural end of the conversation and got up to leave. She had a bag full of books to mark. At the door, Sophia paused and stopped Alicia before she disappeared.

'Can I ask how you think Denis is doing?'

Glancing upstairs before she answered, Alicia cleared her throat.

'He is a very bright, clever chap; however, he struggles a little with controlling his outbursts, but we are working on that.'

Both were painfully aware that Alicia was downplaying the situation. Denis's flare-ups were becoming increasingly difficult to manage as he aged. Sophia had noticed that his dark moods were surfacing much more frequently, as was his inability to control them. Since no one understood the consequences or the severity of his cracked reflector on him, nor were they aware of his brush with the darkness of the nucleus within the orb, they might not have viewed him as a difficult child but rather helped him cope. The fact that he felt dread when he looked at his own reflection was completely overlooked, and the gut-wrenching smouldering turmoil he experienced when something triggered his anger only intensified his sense of isolation.

As they said goodbye to Alicia, Sophia turned to Bertha.

'A teacher, a midwife. Is there anything else you would like to do when you leave school? I think you could fit in at least another two vocations, don't you?'

A flash crossed Bertha's face, and Sophia immediately recognised the hereditary fierceness of Nora coming through.

'I'm going to be both. I think they go together well, don't you? Is Denis upstairs? I can't wait to tell him. After all, I will be teaching him at some point.'

Her mother yelled up at her as she climbed the stairs.

'Reading to him, Bertha, not teaching yet!'

Bertha found him lying on the bed facing away from her. She crept up behind him and tickled him until he eventually laughed and turned around.

'I'm going to come and visit you in your class sometimes, Denis, and read to you. Would you like that?'

He smiled and jumped up to hug her. His muffled voice found its way through her cardigan.

'Were they talking about me? Have I done something wrong?'

Bertha shook her head.

'No, silly. Listen to me. You know you're going to be seven soon, don't you?'

He nodded and lifted his head up to meet hers.

'And you know what that means?'

He shook his head.

'I don't want one,' he said with a quivering lower lip.

She hugged him and whispered to him.

'I'll be there. You won't be on your own. Ever, you hear me?'

They both heard a knock at the front door, then their mother's voice. All went quiet. Bertha felt something was wrong and headed for the stairs. She found her mum in the kitchen looking out of the window.

'Are you alright? Who was that?'

Sophia turned and smiled at Bertha, then waggled a piece of paper at her. It was a telegram. She burst out laughing and ran across the kitchen to show Bertha.

It was from Bertha's father, saying he would return soon, in time for Denis's birthday. They both squealed with excitement.

Bertha kept quiet about Denis's refusal to acknowledge his imminent celebration, not wanting to steal her mother's joy, not for anything. She hadn't seen her this happy in so long.

Denis stood in the doorway. He had been listening in. Bertha wasn't sure, but she thought she saw him grin.

Bertha relished the idea of them all being a family again soon.

Chapter 17
The Realm

Conflict of Interest

After their initial introduction, the new Seraphytes, Corpus and Christi, were led from the Source's chamber and through the misty and complex corridors that divided the many segments of The Realm.

This world consisted of many layers and held within its structure unfathomable nuances of vibrations that altered in sound, light and colour pigmentation, depending on their area, each with separate sectors leading off from a complex latticework of ethereal tunnels.

The Soul Guardians could move from one sector to another at astonishing speed. The sectors were layered according to their energetic levels, and some were divided into orders. The higher the sectors, the higher the zone vibration; the Source resided in the highest sector, with only the Council Chamber above. However, a lower level was not considered unevolved. It would be, instead, an area closest to other planets with much lower vibrations, as with Eathia, enabling ease of contact and movement between the two worlds.

Within these areas were the chambers known as the Solescence Chambers. Individual rooms were created to allow Soul Guardians a method of communication and connection to their tethered Eathians.

All Soul Guardians would experience tethering at some stage, and the triplexes would be no exception.

Notice of their arrival had already swept through The Realm. It was apparent to Verra Mica, as they were leaving the final order of the Nephrophytes, that all the Superiors had noticed something different about both Corpus and Christi. Alma Tadema was more obvious about what she felt when they entered her faction, but she hesitated to say anything while being introduced to her class. When all pleasantries had finished, Alma couldn't contain herself and hurried out from her students to follow them as they left and stopped the three of them before they continued to move on.

'Verra Mica, can you wait?'

They all spun around to see her uneasiness as she approached them.

'Is everything alright, Alma? You look concerned?'

Verra Mica was, in her own way, goading her dear friend. She knew that she would be overly interested in them, but did not intend to make it easy for her after the fiasco outside the Source's chamber.

'I … just wanted to welcome you … both. Personally.'

They stared back at Alma, waiting for her to continue. She had already introduced herself earlier and was now making herself look slightly awkward. Corpus and Christi smiled to ease her discomfort. Verra Mica continued to look at her disdainfully, making no effort to make it easy for her.

'Oh, for goodness' sake, Alma, just say it!'

The new arrivals shot a surprised glance at their mentor.

'I thought there were three of you,' Alma blurted out.

'You know very well there were, you saw them born. No doubt you will see their brother at some point when Duergar graces us with his presence; until then, well, you'll have to wait like the rest of us.'

Verra Mica softened, realising her tone was unnecessarily harsh. Still feeling Corpus and Christi's confused attention on her, she backed off slightly.

'His name is Elkyne, Alma. He was born into the order of the Psybiencians, Duergar's order. What a surprise that is, don't you think?'

She really couldn't contain her sarcasm. Alma tried her best to ignore her.

'But they seem to have other orders within them and …'

Alma stopped when she saw a flash of orange sweep through Verra Mica. Her usual pale blues and golds took a back seat as she fought to regain her composure.

Although the young Soul Guardian found the situation amusing, Corpus tried to explain to Alma Tadema why they showed all orders within their energetic make-up.

'Every order we have visited has awakened something in Christi and I, as you have rightly noticed. Not only do we feel akin to all of you, but we also share in some of your abilities, not completely, I might add, for we are and will remain true Seraphytes, and I am imagining that Elkyne will feel the same when he is introduced to you all. Is that what you were referring to?'

'It was Corpus, thank you. I must say, you both have a very familiar energy about you.'

She looked at Verra Mica, wanting her to respond. She was perturbed by this and wondered if her friend had noticed the same.

Verra Mica realised what she was trying to hint at.

'I felt it too, Alma; you are not imagining it. The presence is stronger when they are together, all three of them. I felt it at their birth. We seem to know them already, don't we?'

Verra Mica brought the discussion to a close and moved on.

Christi spoke as they moved from the Nephrocyte division to their next destination.

'As you know, Superior, we are generally aware of how The Realm and Eathia have evolved to date; however, what I find intriguing are the relationships among you all here within The Realm. Our understanding of that is limited, particularly regarding Superior Duergar. We cannot sense Superior Duergar's history or where he fits in among you. I couldn't even detect his current whereabouts and could only discern a small part of him when he was next to us in the Source's chamber. Is there something we should know? Something the Source was unable to convey to us?'

Verra Mica sighed.

'Unfortunately, for as long as I have known him, he has been a law unto himself. He veils as and when it suits him, which appears to be most of the time. All I can say is to be vigilant and always question his motives. As far as his order is concerned, I keep a close watch on them all. There, I've said it.'

Verra Mica's attention returned to their tour as they approached their final chamber.

'Here we are. Let us go in and we can continue here; it will be easier to explain if I can show you.'

Before them was the entrance to a Solescence Chamber. Unlike the walls of The Realm, the doorways were purely electrical currents requiring unique entry codes embedded into the Souls before their birth, staying veiled to any Soul Guardians that did not contain the correct data.

Within each of the many Solescence Chambers stood unique, beautiful and vast vapour lakes. These lakes in The Realm held opaque shimmering clouds of subtle clusters of energy fields. Although waterless, the lakes had a swirling mass of particles capable of magnifying images from Eathia into The Realm. More importantly, they contained portals and individual access tunnels where the tethered Soul Guardians could travel to and from their tethered Eathians.

Verra Mica continued to elaborate on their use to Corpus and Christi, slightly unsure of how much they knew already. Both respectfully remained silent, allowing her time to finish.

'This is as close as you can get to Eathia without being there. It is a mesmerising room; the lake's portal has its own natural magnetic pull. You will be required to build a certain amount of resilience before tethering. Once you tether, however, it will become easier for you.'

She moved ahead of them towards the Solescence Chamber, as they had been doing at every new entry point throughout The Realm; however, as they made their way through the final part of the electric field, they separated from Verra Mica.

The unique imprints of every type of order created multidimensional chambers. This would only occur when a chamber would be utilised by more than one order. Overlapping was common and a necessity. Some bloodlines on Eathia would contain different orders as each family member would show different characteristics and skills, requiring the more universal chambers.

On rare occasions, alternative chambers could be created. Some of those would become illegally veiled, rendering them unseen by other Soul Guardians. Without Verra Mica realising, they had accidentally encountered one of those chambers, their coding allowing them entry: Much to her surprise, when she entered her intended destination, both Corpus and Christi had vanished.

As they reappeared on the other side of another chamber, Corpus and Christi found themselves in an area full of Psybiencians, Duergar's order. They were not only surprised to lose Verra Mica on the way through, but a silence spread throughout the busy chamber as soon as they entered.

One of the Psybiencian Soul Guardians turned to see why her audience had become silent and lost concentration on her speech. Her voice was harsh and was echoed by the sudden sound emanating from her core. A common reaction from an angry Psybiencian.

'Can we help you? How did you manage to enter? This is a private meeting and a private chamber.'

Some of the group had started to whisper amongst themselves as they slowly understood who their leader was addressing. Gallia, one of the higher-ranked Soul Guardian's appeared to be leading a meeting.

As Gallia made a move towards them, Corpus suddenly sensed a different order within the group; a pure Nephrocyte, known as Nemius, was lurking at the back and trying his hardest to go undetected. For the time being, Corpus pretended not to notice and followed Gallia's approach towards them. Her demeanour calmed slightly when she saw who they were.

'Oh, you two, we've heard quite a bit about you already from Elkyne, he'll be here soon. Are you lost, or have you decided to defect?'

Corpus and Christi were thrown; neither could pick up on any of the other Soul Guardians in the chamber, even though they all appeared right before them. They realised quickly that they had all veiled. With no response from either of them, Gallia continued with a semi-sarcastic but mischievous tone.

'Well? Are you looking to come over to our order or not? It was only a matter of time, I guess.'

The group giggled at her remarks.

Christi moved forward, intrigued by her immediate show of passive animosity.

'No, we are still true Seraphytes. Thank you for your ambiguous offer. Unfortunately, I imagine we gained entry because we are also part, and that's a very small part, Psybiencian.'

Corpus reeled at his sister's provocation and silently messaged her, a twin and now triplex advantage over other lone Soul Guardians.

'Christi, easy does it. We've only just got here.'

Now openly.

'We have merely managed to get ourselves lost,' he said with a mild tone of amusement, hoping to calm the mood.

Gallia moved slowly towards him, passing Christi and seductively entering the space within Corpus's aura, an unnatural invasion for a Soul Guardian to instigate. Corpus wanted to move back, but held his ground. The others behind her giggled again at her antics, more so when Christi flared.

'Back off!' she yelled at Gallia.

Verra Mica had now returned to the ingress outside the chambers as soon as she realised that Corpus and Christi had not entered with her. Finding the chamber empty, she realised they must have linked in with another one. She was in the process of scanning them when a slightly bemused Elkyne approached behind her.

'Superior?'

She spun around, shocked at the interruption. She was happy and relieved, however, to see him.

'Elkyne, have you come to join us? I appear to have lost both Corpus and

Christi, which is very strange indeed. I was just in the process of trying to locate them. Somehow I fear they have unfortunately slipped into another chamber.'

Elkyne needed to carry on with his duties without appearing rude or having to answer why he was there. He hadn't counted on this inopportune meeting with Verra Mica quite so early.

'Is everything alright, Elkyne? You left so quickly from the Source's chamber. I didn't really have a chance to …'

'Yes, all is well,' he interrupted. 'I have my duties and must attend; I have Soul Guardians waiting, and I understand their time is short.'

'Very well, of course, you must go and join them. Hopefully, we will meet again soon.'

'That is also my wish, Superior.'

Verra Mica watched him enter his chamber. She hadn't even been aware of his presence behind her. Duergar hadn't wasted any time in teaching him that little trick.

Announcing it was time to go, Corpus quickly moved away from Gallia, who smirked at his retreat.

'Too close for comfort? Brother?' she said sarcastically.

Ignoring Gallia, he pulled at Christi's energy centre and almost dragged her with him before she managed to retaliate.

They passed Elkyne on the way out, and even through the thickness of the partition, Elkyne sensed their presence as they left; he continued to join Gallia and the others. Due to his veil, neither of them noticed his proximity before they exited to the other side. They found Verra Mica waiting for them, still bemused.

'I am finding it impossible to keep up with you all.'

'Apologies, Superior, we found ourselves drawn towards a Psybiencian convention, they were in there waiting for Elkyne to attend apparently.'

'I didn't even consider that, there must have been quite a few Psybiencians in there to pull at that section of your coding. I just saw Elkyne. He entered as you came out. I wonder what is going on in there?'

Christi vented her annoyance.

'I don't know, but they all went silent when we entered, all except Gallia. I don't trust her, and I've only just met her. Why the animosity? We have only just arrived.'

'Oh, embedded history from long ago, I'm afraid. They are the only order you will come up against with such a lack of trust. It has slowly manifested throughout the ages and has managed to filter through. Fuelled by Duergar no doubt. I do apologise. Shall we try again?'

Verra Mica opened her aura to ensure the two entered through her own coded entry so they all arrived at the correct chamber simultaneously.

This chamber stood out distinctly. While Corpus and Christi observed the vast oval void of the lake in the other chamber, it didn't hold the same allure as this one. As they redirected their attention, they started to be drawn toward it. The room was equally tall and wide, with curved grooves carved into the iridescent walls, sloping gently towards the lake's edge. Within these grooves, Soul Guardians watched the misty glimmer on the water's surface. The atmosphere buzzed with laughter, singing and chatter as groups assembled. Some were engaged in profound conversations, while others pondered in quiet contemplation. Those positioned in the grooves were absorbed in their connections and personal stories from Eathia, unaware of what surrounded them.

Corpus and Christi became aware of the different sensation of being in this Solescence Chamber. They started to feel the strange pull on their core that seemed to originate from the lake ahead of them, just as Verra Mica had said it would.

Verra Mica moved away from them and allowed them to experience what was to become their own personal spiritual interface with their future tethers. She watched warmly as they moved on in unison, absorbing new impressions and images gently flowing towards them through the space.

Mesmerised, they moved towards the lake, watching the mist rise and fall, almost overflowing onto the chamber floor. As they approached, a translucent fog appeared in the centre, where gentle light shards illuminated a spectrum of dancing colours. The light rebounded endlessly, creating new hues as it merged. Corpus and Christi spotted two beams emerging from the lake's centre and felt the tug of ghost tethers.

As the sensations reached them, they glanced at each other to see if they were experiencing the same thing. Verra Mica lurched forward, fearing she had left them too long. It was an enticing arena to fall into, but without a real tether it was quite dangerous. She paused, realising they seemed to have it under control.

As they drew nearer, they could feel wave upon wave of almost crude energetic patterns, each with an underlying message and nature. It was a seraphic expression of adoration from those whose world they would soon be a part of. All they could do was stop themselves from falling into the enthralling depths.

Just as Verra Mica was about to move in and break their hypnotic spell, they moved back themselves.

Corpus was the first to see a change in Christi; then, he looked down at his own aura and saw that he was changing, too.

Only a small change at first, but a noticeable one. A swirl of energy was coalescing and igniting within them and moving towards the centre of their beings. The tingling sensation was now becoming an internal, tiny energetic vortex, drawing small amounts of white and blue streams of light inwards.

Verra Mica smiled; she couldn't have ever imagined they would experience this as quickly as they had. The urgency made her feel uneasy. She moved forward.

'You are experiencing your first tether portal. You have both already found your lifelines on Eathia. Those two ghost beams exist in preparation for you and the children soon to be born. This is remarkable, if not possibly a little too soon.'

Christi was the first to hear a multitude of voices. It was overwhelming, and she backed away, shortly followed by Corpus. They both glanced at Verra Mica for an explanation.

'Try to channel the noise away from you. It will be too much for you at first. Eathian dwellers have an irritating ability to express inane babble constantly. It will drive you crazy if you're not used to it. Just shut it out for now; it'll still be there when you come back, and there is no doubt about that.'

She walked forward to join them.

'It may not happen for some time yet. However, what you have both experienced is your link with your future tethers. This is not necessarily their bloodline, where families recreate new life. This is entirely different. These will be the people who circulate around them throughout their existence. Their Soul Lineage if you like.'

Corpus looked at Christi, and they knew they were to be part of the same lineage on Eathia. Verra Mica smiled, acknowledging the same.

'I forget you are both more aware of some things than I am. Well, as you know, we can't say when this will happen. You will know when things move forward. Have things quietened down for you now?'

They both agreed it had.

Verra Mica smiled.

Christi asked, curiosity getting the better of her.

'How was your experience with your tether? May I ask, Superior? Any advice?'

'I have only had one tether, which brought me all I needed to evolve within The Realm to where I am now. The whole experience didn't end quite as I expected. That's all I should say on the matter for now.'

'I am sorry to ask, Superior, it's just that it is the only part of you I cannot read,' Christi said, feeling uncomfortable.

'With good reason, I protect it and those who were a part of it. Now, we should move on. I have work to do, and you must continue acclimatising yourselves. We have achieved a lot, have we not?'

'We are grateful to you. Would it be acceptable for us to continue familiarising ourselves with the divisions and quarters?'

'As you wish. Meet back with me within our own order once you have seen all you need.'

Verra Mica stopped and paused, wanting to ask them both something that concerned her.

'If there is anything that the Source made you aware of, anything you feel I should know about, would you be sure to let me know, please? I had a very unusual experience in there before your birth, and it has left me ill at ease.'

They looked at each other. Corpus spoke up.

'We could not read Elkyne because he appeared to have an established veil from the start of his birth sequence. However, we were, to some extent, able to read some of his programming through our connection with him as Triplexes, which has left us slightly concerned for him.'

Verra Mica looked confused.

'In what way?'

'Well, now we understand the type of leader his Superior is, which explains his stealthy protection of Elkyne. As you are already aware, Elkyne does have a certain amount of Seraphyte factions within him; this should work in our favour in the future, but there is currently an incompatibility of orders. He isn't as settled as we are.'

Verra Mica remained quiet and bid them farewell and left them outside the entrance to their Solescence Chamber. She was well aware of the precarious situation they were in. Elkyne's allegiance, although slight, could either help them or give Duergar the advantage if he ever used Elkyne against them.

Only time will tell.

Chapter 18
Eathia - Third Era

The Reflector

The main garden was to the right of Bertha's cottage, mainly because behind it, a high grassy incline rose into a steep hill that all but towered over the rear of the house, leaving little space for anything other than an outdoor washroom and a storage cupboard for firewood. It wasn't a large garden, but it was enough for their family.

Now home from his travels, Tobias busied himself preparing the garden for their guests. He had set up makeshift tables ready for the ale, pies and punch.

Sophia had been watching her husband through the kitchen window from the side of the house and went out to meet him.

Bertha watched from her window as her parents embraced. Her mother giggled as her father swung her around. She couldn't help but smile at them.

The garden was looking almost ready for her brother's party. Her mother had been out that morning to hang the home-made bunting which was now floating gently up and down on the soft morning breeze. Attached to the branches of the fruit trees, the bunting blended beautifully with the blossom, now starting to burst open like popcorn.

'I love this time of year,' Bertha said aloud to herself.

She realised how secure she felt since her father had returned. Safe was probably a better word. But she could never get to the bottom of why she felt unsafe. The many stories the woman had told her bore no threat to her or her family. But still, there was a feeling of secrecy between them, and that feeling had gotten stronger the older she got.

Francis had spent some time explaining to Sophia that the stories were real, and now Bertha had started to transcribe events that happened to her family and that of Tobias; Sophia could no longer contest their validity. Her daughter was indeed channelling their past. However, she could never quite understand why. To what end? She was aware that they had made her grow up too fast, which made her resentful of them.

Bertha noted how strangely quiet the cottage was. Denis had gone with Francis to the Emporium to choose his own reflector. She tutted out loud, wondering if he would ever use the new one. She wished he would. It would give him a renewed chance to feel connected to all that was good about the orb instead of feeling so alone and acting out most of the time. Denis didn't know why he felt the way he did, or why looking into the reflector filled him with fear and dread.

All Bertha knew was that the whole town and beyond tapped into their reflectors regularly, igniting their own personal relationship with the orb; knowledge, wisdom and intuition were all there as long as they would listen to the answers they sought. Her nana had explained that a person's eyes were the windows to their souls, and the orb created a natural bond with an Eathian soul.

She sat back down on the bed and thought of her brother. The idea of Francis being with him when he chose his reflector made her smile. Not knowing Denis had even stepped into the castle to help Francis, Bertha thought he seemed like an unlikely companion, but her brother appeared to take a shine to him.

As afternoon approached, Bertha heard a few of their guests start to wander up the cobbled street towards their cottage. Pulling herself away from her own random thoughts, she ran downstairs and into the garden to see if she could help and was shocked at how ready everything was.

An uncomfortable noise erupted from a musical threesome wedged into the corner of the garden under a triangular cream awning that her father had acquired from one of the ships he had been working on. The old sail worked perfectly, protecting the older gentlemen musicians from the heat of the day as they played their renditions of folk songs and, what sounded like, other unrehearsed medleys. Bertha was sure they were all playing something different. She winced at the noise they made as she entered the garden to join her father and mother.

Tobias saw scepticism in his daughter's expression.

'They're called The Bonejacquers, apparently, and come highly recommended.'

Bertha raised an eyebrow.

'By whom exactly?'

Sophia responded.

'Not their long-suffering wives, that's for sure.'

She nodded towards three older ladies sitting next to the band, one of whom had just grabbed a handful of crisps, thrown them at her husband and yelled at him not to give up his day job. All three of them cackled like a coven of witches.

Bertha let out a sigh. Suddenly, she heard Wilhelmina Bullock, Miss Primrose's aunt, calling her name sharply from behind.

'Oh, cripes!' she exclaimed.

Wilhelmina ordered her to retrieve a pot of tea and a selection of food from the table. Bertha knew the food wasn't quite ready. However, she had insisted she had to eat at 12 o'clock on the dot as her constitution wouldn't allow her to deviate. She happily continued giving a more in-depth explanation to whoever would listen. Bertha found herself phasing out at the gory details.

The music suddenly got louder. She turned to see why and saw Denis returning with Francis.

Her Uncle Augustus walked over to her and, upon noticing her anxious expression, grinned and nodded at her.

'All went as planned, thankfully. He found it almost as quickly as you found his first one.'

He pulled a large package from the inside pocket of his jacket. It was wrapped in felt cloth like the others had been.

'Why have you got it?' Bertha asked.

'Slight issue with the actual holding of it. Denis won't go anywhere near it just yet. We must overcome that problem before the world and their mother watches him connect to it this afternoon.'

Bertha frowned at the thought.

'Maybe he shouldn't do it in front of everyone?' she said hesitantly.

'I agree. I'll speak with your mother and father, but that would be best. Just keep it to close family. Less explaining to do if he bolts out the door.'

He went to walk away and stopped.

'Oh, Anamaya apologised for not being able to be here. I did offer to swap shifts, but she wouldn't hear of it, I hope you don't mind?'

'I am glad you are here, Uncle. It's right that you are. After all, we are your favourite niece and nephew.'

She winked at her uncle and giggled.

She's a bright one, he mused as he headed into the garden.

Bertha immediately went to her parents' bedroom and went over to the far side of the bed. She carefully dragged the brown leather suitcase out and clicked the locks open. Denis's first reflector was still there, and the dust on the back of the material proved that it hadn't been touched for ages. However, at an angle, it was in a slightly different place, as if something underneath had been taken away. She lifted it, suddenly remembering the knitted shawl that had covered the book that was stored in there, too. She could see the shawl, but the contents had gone by the look of it. She popped the new one on top and closed it, pushing it back under the bed. *Safest place for now*, she thought.

She made a mental note to ask her parents what book was missing.

As she lifted her head above the bed, she saw Denis quietly standing at the door.

'What are you doing?' he asked.

'Putting your reflector away safely. Denis, do you remember there being an old book in this case? It was under your old reflector. It's gone.'

Denis became agitated and yelled at her.

'I don't want to do this. You can't make me.'

Bertha moved out from behind the bed and ran to the other side. Sitting down, she patted the space next to her for him to sit with her. He sat down with a thump and stared straight ahead; his eyes narrowed in anger and his lips squeezed together. She turned to face him.

'Denis, we talk about things. We don't shout at each other. That's our pact, remember?'

'I'm not shouting at you. I'm shouting at everyone else.'

His gaze stayed fixed on the bedroom door.

'Denis?'

He turned and looked at her. Bertha paused, wondering whether she should say what she was about to say. She continued, hoping it would help.

'My reflector helps me to work things out. It's like having an inner friend that has totally got your back, do you understand?'

Bertha watched as Denis's frustration ignited.

'Mine doesn't! It just makes me feel bad. It feels like I'm falling into it, and it will eat me if I stare at it for too long.'

His eyes became tearful and he vigorously wiped them with his sleeve.

'Is that why you don't use it?'

Denis looked down, and Bertha saw him nod tentatively.

'But this one will be different. You chose it, didn't you?'

He nodded again. Then, they both heard a commotion downstairs, followed by footsteps coming up the stairs.

'Bertha, are you up here? Have you seen your brother?'

Sophia reached the landing and saw them sitting down together.

'We've all decided to put the food out and while the family and friends eat, we can secretly initiate the connection with Denis and his new reflector. How does that sound?'

Tobias appeared behind her.

Bertha whispered in Denis's ear, 'Maybe this new one will be better.'

Denis sighed, slowly stood up, walked over to his father, and tightly held his hand. Glancing past him, he saw Augustus and Francis standing at the bottom of the stairs. He half-smiled at Francis, who nodded back.

'Bertha, can you bring it down with you? We'll do it in the sitting room.'

They all turned and headed back down the stairs. Denis let go of Tobias's hand and stayed at the top of the stairs.

He appeared next to her, his hand stretched out.

'I'll do it. I'll take it downstairs.'

A huge victory, Bertha thought and smiled at him proudly.

By the time they reached the sitting room, they were all ready. Her mother beamed at them as they entered the room.

'Shut the door behind you, darling.'

Bertha watched her brother enter the room as the warmth of the afternoon light shone in from behind where he now stood, emphasising thin strands of chestnut in his brown hair. He looked up at his father and, in response, he placed a protective arm around his son. Tobias lowered his head slightly towards Denis.

'Are you ready, little man? I won't be able to call you that anymore after today, hey?'

Denis looked down at his reflector and giggled.

'It tingles.'

His family chuckled at his reaction. Sophia stepped forward and knelt down to be at the same level as him.

'When you are ready, Denis, you know what to do.'

Denis nodded and looked across at Francis.

'Uncle Francis told me what to do.'

The old man winked at him and nodded, giving him the all clear to continue. He couldn't help but have some concern over the boy. His history hadn't been great with the orb. He hoped it was time to put all that behind them.

Denis held on tightly to the handle of the new reflector as he held it out in front of him. He lifted his free arm up, grabbed the top of the material covering it and confidently lifted it off, as though he were showing them a magic trick. All fell silent. Denis, still looking at Francis, then grinned and bravely turned to look at his own reflection.

Meanwhile, outside the cottage, Mrs Bullock sat on an old metal rocking chair to the left of the front door. It was as far as she could get away from the horrific noise currently being made by 'those drunken idiots', as she repeatedly referred to the band. She dug her heels in the grass underneath the chair and denied it the freedom to rock, almost losing one of her boots in the process.

She leaned forward to try and see where her niece, Alicia, was. She wanted to let her know she was ready to go. The infernal drone from the musicians made it hard for her niece to hear her as she continued to serve food to the guests, so she decided to take it up a notch and yell at the top of her voice.

'ALIC-I-A!'

As she screamed, the window of the sitting room suddenly exploded outwards, covering her with shards of glass. If it weren't for her oversized hat, she would have almost definitely been spiked by the dangerous pieces of sharp glass as they shattered over her.

All fell silent as the guests, shocked at the sound, stopped what they were doing and turned in her direction, assuming her voice had caused the explosion.

Further down the hill, two boys, two years ahead of Bertha at school, were late for the party and hurriedly made their way up the cobbled street towards the cottage.

When the explosion hit, they both fell forward. They were sure the blast had come from the south of the village towards the castle. When they turned and looked down the hill, they could see something had happened to the windows at the castle's highest point. They looked at each other, turned, and got to their feet and scampered up towards the cottage to sound the alarm.

Most hadn't realised at that point that the actual source of the explosion had come from the sitting room.

As soon as Denis looked into his reflector and made his connection to it, the glass within its ornate frame began to vibrate. A force from within started to pull Denis towards it, causing him to draw it closer to his face involuntarily. As he did, beams of light began to emanate from its centre.

Confused about what was happening, Bertha glanced over at her mother for an explanation. Sophia turned to Tobias, who shrugged his shoulders, equally perplexed. He tried to recall whether this was what had happened to Bertha when she was Denis's age.

Very slowly at first, thin strands of light caught areas of Denis's face and seemed to draw them back into the reflector. It was almost as though his own image within it was starting to reach out and pull at its counterpart, trying to entice it.

Augustus instinctively felt something was wrong and went to move forward. But his action seemed to antagonise the light strands, intensifying their strength, and they now appeared to be catching more and more of Denis's features.

Denis started to cry.

Augustus lunged forward and tried to pull the reflector out of Denis's hand, but couldn't loosen Denis's grip.

Bertha watched helplessly as her father took the cloth from Denis's other hand and tried to grab hold of the reflector, but again, that only seemed to make it worse. He then tried to put the cloth between Denis's face and the glass, but it burst into flames as soon as it touched the light, burning Tobias's fingers as it did. He pulled back, shaking his hand.

The whole room went into a blind panic. The reflector was now beginning to shake violently. Denis started to scream and so did Sophia and Bertha as they watched his eyes roll back into their sockets. Suddenly, the glass in the reflector exploded, causing an abnormally loud, thunderous crack in the small room. A flash of light spun around the room, creating a secondary explosion. Instantly, the windows were blown outwards from their frames.

Those in the room ducked, expecting to be showered by glass.

Unaffected by the explosion, the glass from the reflector spun dangerously around Denis. The jagged splinters turned in ever-decreasing circles until they eventually started returning to his reflector's empty frame. Although completely cracked, the shards managed somehow to go back into their original places. Slowly, they started to melt back together until the reflector looked as good as new.

Tobias felt his son's body go limp in his arms as it dropped towards the floor. Only then could he retrieve the reflector from his grip. Holding it awkwardly between his thumb and forefinger, he carefully handed it over to Augustus before helping Denis lie more comfortably on the carpet.

Bertha ran towards her brother and knelt down beside his still body. She could see him breathing and looked up at her father, who acknowledged the same with relief.

At the exact moment of the explosion in the cottage, Anamaya had fallen to the floor of the Orbitarium. There had been a thunderous explosion above her. She had covered her head with her arms, fully prepared to have shards of glass from the window cascade down on top of her, but nothing did. The raven screeched, flew from its perch high up and disappeared through one of the now glassless windows.

As she lifted her head towards the orb, she thought she saw a shadow pass through its inner glow, as if someone was floating inside it. She had never seen that before in all her years of maintaining it. She slowly got to her feet and walked towards the orb. Its sound had changed. She wasn't sure why, but she felt like it was in pain.

In the sitting room, Augustus leant down to try and help bring Denis back.

The empty window above them made it easy for them all to hear the frightened shouts from the boys as they approached. Augustus heard clearly that there had been an explosion in the castle. Augustus looked at Tobias, his expression panic-stricken.

'Anamaya.'

'Go, Augustus. Go!' Tobias shouted.

Francis tried to get to his knees.

'I'll be behind ya, son. Go on.'

Augustus ran for the door and out of the cottage towards the castle. He saw the raven flying towards him. He spun around upon seeing Augustus and headed back towards the castle. Augustus realised he coming to warn him.

As he reached the castle and ran all the way to the door, he met Anamaya. He threw his arms around her in relief.

'The windows just exploded, Augustus. A blast seemed to come from the orb and, boom!'

He grabbed her arm, and they raced towards the Orbitarium. Grabbing his oculars, he dragged them over his eyes as they entered. He scanned the orb and looked up at the windows. Then, something caught his eye within the orb.

'Something's in there, Augustus, can you see it? It's been moving around and coming over to the outer shell as if … as if it's trying to get out.'

Augustus quickly started to add all the events up in his head. Deep furrows appeared across his forehead.

'Oh no. Surely not.'

Unaware of the event in the cottage, Anamaya didn't understand her husband's concern.

'What. What is it?'

His bottom lip started to quiver, and although the goggles hid his tears, she knew he was upset.

Shock waves started to pulse through Anamaya's body, and goosebumps bubbled over her skin; she had never seen Augustus like this before.

The raven had now entered the room and circled the orb, screeching.

Anamaya shook Augustus's arm.

'Darling, what is it? You're starting to scare me.'

With that, they both heard a plea for help from the orb.

Behind them, Francis stood gasping for breath. He had finally made it back to the castle. Lifting his arm up to shield himself from the brightness of the orb, he squeezed his eyes closed to see what they were looking at. He steadily and silently walked forward, the bird now coming to rest on his shoulder.

He spoke just loud enough for them to hear.

'It's not what's in there, Ana. It's who.'

They both turned to him.

The pleading cries from the orb echoed around the room. Francis's eyes welled up as he turned away from the brightness of the orb.

'What are you saying?'

'It's Denis. It can only be Denis's soul,' Francis said, shaking his head.

Augustus's mouth dropped and Anamaya shrieked.

'How has this happened? This has never happened before. What can we do?'

Augustus looked down at the floor, vigorously tracing his hand through his hair while he tried to think. He whispered repeatedly, asking how this could have occurred as if waiting for his mind to answer. Instead, he heard his father's voice.

'I think I know what's happened, son. This is my fault.'

They left the room and stood in the main hall while Francis tried to explain how Denis himself might have caused this catastrophe.

'Denis has been helping me occasionally, just working on a few bits here and there. It made him happy, and I just wanted him to feel special; you know, he's such a sad lad sometimes. It seemed to cheer him up a bit.'

Both Augustus and Anamaya fell shockingly silent. Francis continued awkwardly, feeling Augustus's eyes burning into his.

'Anyways, he'd got hold of your grandfather's book from somewhere on how the whole thing was made, you know, the one, and seemed to be a natural at tuning the Reflectorscope and such.'

After he had finished, the raven took flight and headed back towards the cottage, fleeing just in time before Augustus let rip on his father, telling him in no uncertain terms what he thought of him and how dangerous and thoughtless he had been.

Francis stayed silent, letting his son vent at him and wrongly taking the blame for this whole unfortunate episode.

Back at the cottage, they continued to try to bring Denis back from wherever he had gone.

Chapter 19

Eathia - third era

Name and Shame

Tobias carefully lifted Denis up and carried him up the stairs to lay him on his bed. Bertha walked quietly behind them, sat at the side on hers and helplessly watched as her parents hugged each other, one trying to comfort the other.

'The woman in the reflector must be aware of what is happening,' Bertha pondered as she leaned over the back of her bed, fetched her own reflector and quietly walked into her parents' bedroom. Sitting on their bed, she tried to reach the voice. Before she could, something started to tap on their window; looking up, she saw the raven.

Anger washed through her. It must have been the bird that attacked them at the castle, and now he was back. By the look of it, it had come for a second showdown, as if Denis hadn't been through enough. She threw the reflector onto the bed and ran to the window.

Throwing open the side window, she tried to push the bird off the ledge. He flew backwards to avoid her hand, but flew straight over her head and into the bedroom. Furious, she darted around the room, fanning her arms to get him out before her parents heard the commotion. Instead, he shot out the door and down the stairs into the sitting room. Landing on Denis's reflector, he waited for Bertha to enter.

'Get off, that's my brother's.'

She tried to shoo him away, but he flew up and away from her swipe and landed back down on it again.

It was too much for her; sitting down, she put her face in her cupped hands and sobbed.

The raven flew over to the arm of the chair and tilted its head to try and look at her through her fingers. She was aware he was there, but stayed hidden.

'What do you want? Leave us alone!' she shouted.

He gently pecked her smallest finger nearest to him.

Bertha's red and sodden face appeared slowly from the corner of her hand. He flew back over to Denis's reflector.

She dropped her hands down onto her lap and tilted her head slightly. Her tears were calming now as something started to dawn on her. He was showing her something, not attacking like she had originally thought. She stood, moved over to the reflector and picked it up; the raven stayed on it as she lifted it, careful not to show her face to it.

The raven then jumped off and landed on the door frame.

'You want me to follow, are you crazy? I'm not getting this anywhere near my brother, you hear?'

The bird flew up to the top of the stairs and rested on the door frame of her and her brother's room. Tobias came out, realising something had flown into the cottage. Bertha met his gaze halfway up the stairs. When he saw what was in her hands, he marched down to meet her and grabbed the reflector from her.

'What are you doing bringing that back up here?'

She had no answer, nothing believable. She felt mortified by the look on her father's face. Bertha glanced at the raven. He had felt so strongly that he was trying to help.

At that moment, the front door flew open, and Anamaya stood at the bottom of the stairs.

'Quick, Tobias, we don't have long.'

She noticed immediately what he was holding.

'Is that Denis's reflector? We must connect him with it again. Bertha, go and get yours, too. Augustus is on his way.'

Tobias looked at his daughter and his face softened. She ran past him to fetch her reflector from the bed and joined them in her room.

Tobias saw Sophia's reaction to the reflector and held his hand out, gesturing for her to wait before chastising them. The raven began to fidget restlessly on the door. Bertha noticed his disturbed actions and realised there was much more to him.

Anamaya knelt by the bed next to Denis.

'We have to recreate what happened downstairs to reverse it. It's the only chance he has. I'll explain after. Please trust us; we think we know what's happened.'

As Bertha stood in the doorway, she was nearly thrown sideways by her uncle as he entered the room. The raven went flying. He saw she was gripping her own reflector.

'Right, good girl, have it ready, Bertha, for my command?'

He gave a quick look at Sophia and Tobias.

'You must trust me. Tobias, open his eyes and shine the reflector back into them.'

Sophia gasped.

With his left hand, Tobias rested his palm over his son's forehead and lifted his lids with his thumb and index finger. Augustus counted to three and shouted for him to show Denis the face of the reflector.

As soon as they made contact, an immense surge of light shot out from the open surface of the glass. Its brilliance highlighted Denis's face, making it appear contorted. Under its powerful blast, Denis's body convulsed back to life. His eyes stayed wide open of their own accord now, and Tobias pulled his hand away.

'Keep the reflector there until he is fully back. Don't move it away on any account, do you hear?'

Tobias shouted back, but his voice wasn't loud enough over the noise of the reflector. Bertha ran over to her mother and held onto her.

Augustus watched intently as the light continued to crawl towards Denis's face. He was starting to feel the effects it was having, and his complexion was starting to take on an unhealthy translucent grey tone. Anamaya had already noticed and called out to warn him.

Suddenly, the light changed as a fine dark shadow weaved from the reflector towards Denis. Augustus shouted over the noise.

'Pull it away, Tobias, quickly.'

All attempts to free his son from the magnetic pull of the light failed. Augustus jumped in to help, but with little effect.

Sophia freed herself from Bertha's arm and launched herself at the object to help, screaming as she did.

'Get it away from him!'

The raven flew over the bed and landed on Bertha's reflector, this time catching Augustus's attention as it did. Augustus knew now was the right time to intervene.

'Bertha, come over here now. Turn your reflector's face towards your brother's reflector. Put it in between the beam before the dark shadow reaches him.'

She ran over, taking the covering off, she put it into the light, making sure it was facing away from him, just as her uncle had said. The connection was broken immediately, and Denis dropped back. The light ceased and retreated along with the darkened shard, and all the magnetic tension fell away from the reflector.

Augustus fell back onto his knees.

'Clever girl, Bertha. Now cover that back up and Denis's with anything you can find.'

Augustus put his head back and breathed deeply.

Denis stayed still with wild eyes, staring at all the faces looking intently at him. Bertha glanced across at her uncle.

'Did it work?'

He nodded slowly back at her, relief on his face.

'I believe it did.'

He then turned to Sophia and Tobias, who were looking understandably nervous.

'We need to talk about what just happened and why it happened. Just give me a moment to collect myself.'

Bertha waited with Denis and Anamaya before venturing downstairs, ensuring her little brother was completely settled. As she reached the bottom, she realised that the sitting room door was shut, and she could hear hushed voices. She entered the kitchen and found Francis sitting at the table, his head lowered.

'He's much better, Pops. Why don't you go and see him? He'd like that.'

Francis's voice was thin and lifeless.

'Oh, maybe a little later, Bertha. I've helped cause enough damage for one day.'

Bertha frowned, and he tapped the seat next to him so she could sit with him. He then told her about what he felt had happened and what had gone wrong to cause such a reaction from Denis's reflector.

Bertha sat quietly and thought for a moment. She wanted to tell Francis all about the births of new souls in The Realm, but realised now wasn't the right time, so she sat quietly next to Francis and listened to the raised voices across the hall. Francis continued.

'The orb must have understood what was happening, and she sent the raven to guide you through bringing young Denis back. The bird and the orb are sort of connected, you see. He gets a bit frantic occasionally, but he means well. He's protective, that's all.'

They both began to listen to the conversation in the other room.

Augustus was explaining to Tobias and Sophia, in a slightly more graphic way, that Denis had been secretly helping by adjusting the reflectors for Francis over a period of time in the castle. They must have eventually fallen into misalignment. That was the only plausible explanation. He apologised for his father's behaviour but said the responsibility had to fall on himself for letting it happen in the first place.

'We are short of help, and my father was insistent that he wanted to carry on and not let us down.'

Augustus cleared his throat.

'Anamaya and I are trying for our own child, and we have been trying for some time now.'

Tobias and Sophia shot a quick glance at each other. Augustus threw his hands up in the air.

'We vowed to be the keepers of both the orb and the Castle Raphael, and we must continue as best we can until that glorious day arises when we can bring an heir into the world.'

Sophia's attention broke momentarily from Augustus and went to Denis, who was now up and standing in the doorway. She went over to him, picked him up and kissed him. Bringing him back with her, she sat him on her lap.

'How are you feeling, little man? You gave us all a fright. Do you remember what happened at all?'

Denis shook his head and stared blankly back at Augustus.

'I'll take the reflector away with me and put it somewhere safe for the time being.'

'NO!' Denis shouted back at him. 'It's mine now. You can't have it back.'

With that, he pushed himself off Sophia's lap and ran back out of the room and upstairs.

Francis heard it all from the kitchen and sighed. Pushing his chair back, he walked over to the window. The wind had caught hold of the awning and the bunting and thrown them carelessly down the grass and street. All had gone, leaving what was left of the food for the birds.

His stomach found, amazingly, a new lower level to fall to. He hung his head.

'Sorry, I've let you all down.'

Bertha met him at the window, slipped her hand into his and gently squeezed it.

'She'll forgive you. They all will.'

He looked across at her innocent face. She whispered, 'She forgave me, didn't she?'

Francis frowned at her. Not entirely sure what she was referring to.

'The crack in his reflector. How do you know it's not still that causing this?'

Francis sighed. *It could have been something else*, he thought.

By taking the blame, he had stopped everyone from looking further into other reasons why this had happened.

He looked out the window and thought about what Bertha was referring to. The crack in Denis's original reflector. 'Maybe that did have something to do with what just happened?' He nodded thoughtfully to himself.

'What is it, Pops? What are you thinking?'

He smiled affectionately down at Bertha.

'When his old reflector got fixed, I think that was that. But we may need to think about what's going on with this new reflector. Maybe Denis just doesn't need it.'

He shrugged.

'You're never too old to learn a lesson or two, young lady. Let's leave it at that. I'll have a word with the orb and see if she can make sense of this.'

That night, Bertha tried contacting the woman in the reflector, but nothing came back. Part of her wasn't expecting her to. She eventually drifted off to sleep.

The glow of the reflector bathed her face in a warm, golden light, and the woman continued on with her account of The Realm.

It wasn't safe for Bertha to know all of what was happening around her. Her role at that time was to transcribe the past; otherwise, nothing would make sense to anyone in the future.

Chapter 20
The Realm

Veil of Truth

Corpus and Christi returned to the point of entry into the Psybiencian chamber they had found themselves in before. Keeping quiet, they waited to ensure they were on their own before making their next move.

'Shall we try again and see if we can understand why so many Psybiencians have been secretly gathered?'

'If we do, and I agree we should, we'll need to veil, Corpus. Verra Mica will know immediately that we have. It isn't something I want to start doing. Otherwise, we will be as bad as the others.'

Both Christi and Corpus began to receive a message from Verra Mica.

Having scanned their whereabouts, she had pre-empted their intentions. The message was short and clear.

'Continue. Be vigilant.'

They moved forward and through into the chamber. However, this time Gallia did not turn to see them enter, nor did any other Psybiencians. They were now free to edge closer to the group undetected.

Christi saw a lone Soul Guardian, Makaria, at the back of the crowd. She was somehow segregated from the others and stood beside the misty lake. It looked as though she had activated it because a swirling mass was rising to its surface. She gazed down into it, unaware of their presence and paying little attention to Gallia's words to the group. Her thoughts silenced the other voices in the room; instead, they focused on the lake.

Gallia's strong address drew their attention away from Makaria and back to the group.

'It is Duergar's wish that you all start to initiate communications with your tethered Eathians. While you are still tethered, you must return mostly to this Psybiencian chamber to reconnect but also remember to visit the main communal viewing Solescence Chamber so as not to raise an alarm.

You still need to be seen.'

She continued.

'In the unlikely event, you need to contact our floating Soul Guardians on Eathia, use the Psybiencian chamber only. Is that clear?'

Something flickered across Gallia's line of sight, and she turned and looked across at the lake. Noticing Makaria there, she paused and watched her momentarily before continuing. The tell-tale sign of annoyance flared through her aura, agitated at Makaria's rudeness.

'He requires a complete and precise operation with no mistakes. We cannot say when exactly this will happen; however, when he gives the alarm, you must all be prepared and ready.'

Christi looked across at Corpus and silently messaged him. Alarm? What alarm.

He shook his head and looked back at Makaria as she leaned towards the mist. It started to swell up from the lake's depths, making her smile as she touched its vapour adoringly. She hoped for any sign that her sister, Angelica, was alive and safe.

Luckily for Makaria, Gallia herself did not see this act, but Corpus and Christi did and were intrigued as to what she was doing. Sensing danger, Makaria moved away just as Gallia called out her name.

'Is there something that interests you on Eathia, Makaria? More than here, that is?'

With an involuntary flare of light, Makaria showed her shock at being caught out and quickly managed to control it again.

'Not at all, Gallia, I was merely …'

She was unable to complete her explanation before Gallia shot forward and interjected, cutting her short.

'You are already on my watch list. Duergar has asked me to keep a close guard on you, so don't give me any reason to report you. He won't think twice about sending you down to be with your sister. I personally think you have outstayed your usefulness here anyway.'

She threateningly moved closer to her as she had done with Corpus.

'Never trust a twin, especially if they are birthed into different orders.'

Christi and Corpus exchanged a glance once more. They acknowledged their situation with Elkyne and recognised that Makaria was one half of the twins they had heard about from the Source.

Makaria pleaded with Gallia.

'If you know of Angelica's whereabouts, you must tell me. She has gone from my view now. I demand to know where she is.'

Gallia spun round and shouted at the group.

'GO! This meeting is over.'

She turned on Makaria.

'How dare you question our Superior! He will hear of this.'

A booming voice erupted behind where Corpus and Christi now stood.

'Don't bother, I am here.'

Duergar approached Makaria and Gallia, who was moving effortlessly through the mass of Soul Guardians as they hurriedly left the chamber. His controlled tone made him so much more overbearing; they were relieved to escape.

'Don't think for one moment that I am not aware of your outspoken opinion.'

Rather than focusing on Makaria, Duergar was looking straight at Gallia.

'You were asked to communicate my wishes to our fellow Psybiencians. Did you manage to get that across to them before you attempted to voice my authority, may I ask?'

'I was honouring you, Superior.'

'By speaking for me? What gives you that right?'

Being out of favour with him was to be avoided at all costs.

'No, I do not, your Honour, please accept …'

'You are dismissed.'

'Yes, Superior.'

Gallia fled past Corpus and Christi and out of the chamber.

Duergar then focused on Makaria and spoke in a hushed tone.

'What do you have to say for yourself? I noticed what you did, Makaria. I closely monitor my, let's say, more rebellious students.'

Makaria squared up to him, finding a momentary bout of confidence.

'Where is she, Duergar? You said she would be safe, and now I can't find her. She didn't return from her tether as she was supposed to, and all the others with her are now back.'

Her questioning caused Duergar to flash with anger.

'She is safe and on a separate quest. Her veiling is for her own safety and yours, too, Makaria. You must stop trying to contact her; you are one of mine, so you must understand what is at stake here, but still, you push and mistrust me.'

'I thought I knew what we were doing here. I did trust you until you decided to keep us permanently separated. You changed the plan without informing either of us. We have never been out of contact with each other. Something must be wrong.'

'You were separated at birth by the Source, who sought to place you into different orders. That was not my doing; if anything, I have brought your differences closer together; we now fight for the same cause.'

'We had no differences. You gave us no say in this. Release her veil, please, Duergar. I fear for her safety.'

'It is not I that veils her; this is her own doing. She will let me know when she has been successful along with the others, and I, in turn, will let you know. Now, leave here and return with the others to our division. No. On second thoughts, return to your own quarters until I call for you.'

Makaria, furious at Duergar's attempt at control, stormed away. She stopped suddenly and spun around to face Duergar again.

'What of Verra Mica?'

His eyes bore into her.

'What do you mean? I don't understand your question.'

'She has now become the new Superior of the Seraphytes, has she not?'

'I'm still waiting for you to get to the point.'

'She will not bend and shy away. She won't disappear like her predecessor did. She might already be aware that something isn't right. Angelica is one of hers, after all.'

Corpus and Christi moved back slightly from the troublesome pair.

Duergar's vibrations changed without warning from a low hum to a loud, high-pitched, piercing sound, causing Makaria to recoil.

'LEAVE, I will let you know when I hear. Do not think about threatening me with Verra Mica. She is not my concern right now. Remember which order you belong to, Makaria. First and foremost, you are a Psybiencian. Do you understand me?'

Makaria turned and left before he could say any more.

Duergar was still thankfully unaware of the two eavesdropping Seraphytes.

He had been fighting to control his rage over Angelica's disobedience. He hadn't let on to Makaria but had also lost sight of her sister. He moved towards the lake and looked in, hoping to glimpse her whereabouts.

'Where have you gone now, damn you?' he seethed.

Unknown to him, Angelica had diverted her attention, embarking instead on a secretive mercy mission.

While she and Makaria were in the Source, she was shown a young mother and daughter running from their home to save their own lives. They had boarded a ship, but something had gone wrong, and Angelica needed to get to them quickly. They were a vital part of the Source's strategy to protect the essence, and Angelica was aware that no one, not even her sister, should know where she was and why. It was too dangerous.

Duergar had been cleverly placing his Soul Guardians on Eathia, like pawns on a chessboard. However, she still could play part of his game, but in her own way. If only she could intervene in one of his moves. To do so, it would be necessary to veil to enable her to disappear.

Once Duergar had left the chamber, Corpus and Christi relaxed slightly. Christi turned to her brother.

'We need to find Verra Mica quickly, but first I need to speak with Makaria. Something has obviously happened to her sister, and I had no knowledge of this from the Source, did you?'

He stared down into the mist, now calm and still. Then, he looked back at his sister.

'It feels like there are things we aren't supposed to know. Which I find counterproductive. Let's hope this all comes together at some point. I will follow Duergar. We can see Verra Mica together once we have a little more understanding of what's happening here. It feels like we have been born into a Soul Guardian war zone.'

Christi agreed.

'That's why we are here, isn't it? To try and calm the unrest.'

'Apparently so, although they aren't making it easy.'

With that, Christi disappeared to catch up with Makaria.

Corpus glanced back at the lake.

He wondered what was at the root of such divided allegiances within The Realm. The information the Source had given them was by no means enough. This troubled origin hides much deeper, within the shadows of The Realm itself.

He left the chamber to follow the only Superior who seemed to know the most about The Realm's current situation.

Chapter 21
The Realm

Ashtar's Sanctuary

Corpus and Christi eventually found Verra Mica talking with the Nephrocyte Superior, Alma Tadema. They paused before approaching, but heard Alma say that she would be vigilant. They had also stated that there was no cause for concern and that, *he,* would show up soon. When Alma Tadema realised Corpus and Christi had returned, she stopped and excitedly gestured for them to join her and Verra Mica.

'Look at you two. You are truly a wondrous sight. Are you sure I can't tempt you to become a full Nephrocyte?'

The twins moved awkwardly towards them. Alma was gushing, which made for an uncomfortable beginning to any conversation. Verra Mica interjected.

'Yes, yes, Alma, now I think we should continue our conversation a little later. I know these two have many things to discuss with me, so I had better attend to their needs. Is that agreeable with you?'

'Of course, I'll be on my way. It's lovely to see you, and I'm sure Elkyne will show himself soon. It's such a nuisance when siblings are in different orders, don't you think?'

'Yes, thank you, Alma; we are more than aware of who makes that scenario difficult around here.'

They watched as she left to return to her students. Verra Mica lowered her voice.

'Honestly, my patience gets tested with her at times.'

Verra Mica began to move along one of the smaller tunnels. She gestured for them to join her.

'Now, what have you discovered?'

Corpus explained what they had witnessed in the Psybiencian chamber

'It's Duergar, he's up to something, they appear to be planning for something. They are using their own chamber as their meeting point and for their private communications with Eathia.'

'Why would they want to communicate through that lake? Is it merely meant to be an observation platform?'

Verra Mica sighed.

'Anything else?'

'I met with Makaria after the meeting.'

'And?'

'Angelica has disappeared. All Makaria could say was that Angelica didn't return when she was supposed to. A small group of Eathian tethers were all due to return at the same time. Angelica was told to stay and meet up with some free floaters near a cove on Eathia. She told Makaria she would return regardless of what Duergar had insisted on. Something must have happened to make her change her mind and stay; now she has veiled completely and is invisible. We learned that even Duergar cannot locate her, this involves Duergar.'

Verra Mica silently listened on. Christi continued.

'If that's the case, the fact that he cannot locate her gives Makaria hope. It turns out that Makaria and Angelica originally had some plan, albeit a dangerous one, but they abandoned it at the last moment. Angelica mentioned something about a hideout of some sort and was going to investigate it before she returned with the others. That may be where she is now. It could be the cove that was mentioned before.'

Verra Mica showed visible signs of despair.

'Those two twins and their secretive plans. Who's leading whom here? Don't you two be getting any ideas, by the way.'

The Soul Guardians were familiar with the term 'floaters'; they were Soul Guardians trapped on Eathia, either by choice or by accident. Free floaters implied that it was of their own doing. To become untethered while an Eathian human was still alive would not give the Soul Guardian safe passage back to The Realm, as their portal would disappear. Instead, they would be trapped in Eathia. If an Eathian had unfortunately come into visual contact with their Soul Guardians during their point of death and been seen, usually in a reflection in the water, the tethers would be broken before their human's heart stopped. This would also break the link and disconnect the portal from The Realm. It was a rarity for it to be instigated on purpose. However, the recent drop in returning Soul Guardians could only point to foul play of some sort.

The likelihood of Angelica returning now was minimal; re-entering The

Realm without a tethered portal was nearly impossible.

Verra Mica was happy that she had been brought up to date and made ready to leave. Corpus and Christi followed as Verra Mica continued.

'Well, without a time reference, it is very difficult to grasp when and where this might have occurred; we are blind in that way. It's up to us to try and locate her before she is lost for good.'

Verra Mica stopped. Appearing to have reached a destination, Christi was momentarily confused.

'Where are we?'

'We are outside a very unique, private and secret chamber.'

They could feel her enthusiasm.

Another secret, Corpus thought.

Verra Mica continued,

'Duergar isn't the only one with secrets. There is only one code that gains entrance into this chamber. Stay close.'

Corpus and Christi felt themselves being swathed in her energy as they all moved forward through an almost invisible entrance.

They were both taken aback by what they witnessed on the other side.

Verra Mica glowed as she watched their reaction to what lay before them.

It was uniquely beautiful, resembling Eathia's own forest environment with plants, flowers, springs and waterfalls. The Souls of animals mingled amid the vegetation and water. Above them was a sky, bright blue in colour and one that appeared to reach infinity. It was teeming with every variety of bird.

Christi moved forward, completely in awe of the scene before her.

'Verra Mica, this is beautiful, where are we?'

'In my private quarters. They used to be Ashtar's and are completely off The Realm's grid, so hush.'

Corpus interjected.

'But why the secrecy and why the animals?'

'Because this is their home, Corpus. They return here and tell me stories of Eathia. They are my lookouts now. They are one of our strongest natural links to Eathia without a portal. They have, instead, an open link for them to re-join us at any time using a completely different energy, you see. Aren't they beautiful?'

Verra Mica walked forward towards the lake, and Christi noticed movement to one side of the chamber as she did. A large glossy-leaved plant shook, then its stems parted to allow something to come through. Something large.

Slowly, a face appeared under an outstretched arm. Verra Mica turned and welcomed the ape out from the bushes. Its translucent form shimmered excitedly when it saw her.

'Marla, there are some important Soul Guardians I wish for you to meet.'

The powerful creature walked free from the undergrowth and strode to the Superior. She was a female Gorilla; she softened at the sight of her friend. She then looked across at Corpus and Christi, and Verra Mica beckoned them to meet her.

'She has been here for as long as we can remember. This is Marla, and she chooses to be here now, permanently. She has had many visits to Eathia, but as with most of her species, it's getting harder for them to stay there safely.'

As Marla turned towards Christi, she studied her.

'Look at her eyes, they are so knowing. She is beautiful.'

Marla's eyes suddenly shot away from their stare as the sweeping wings of a large black raven circling above them interrupted the moment.

'I realised the animals were feeding us information but had no idea or even considered where they lived within The Realm itself. This is you, all of this, you care for them all?'

Verra Mica smiled, not wanting to take any credit for their welfare.

'I continue to look after them for Ashtar. He and the Source created them to be protectors, unconditional supporters and a source of nourishment for the Eathians, but ultimately to act as living reflectors for Eathians to see how they manage in an increasingly difficult world. Their Eathian forms exist all over the planet, and all have different roles.'

Corpus spoke.

'There is a lot here, Superior. I imagine things aren't going too well for them down there.'

'Some of these animals no longer exist on Eathia. They have lost their Eathian Stars. Without them, they cannot return. With no newborns, the stars fade and die, and with them, the anchors to which they can tether. It is the stars that give them form.'

'Their loss is our gain,' Verra Mica added abruptly.

The black raven that had flown above Marla was now fluttering above Corpus. It attempted to land on him until Marla shot forward and tried to shoo it away.

They all laughed at her antics and watched her as she chased the bird away through the undergrowth.

At that moment, Corpus suddenly felt a tug on his core. Both Verra Mica and Christi noticed something had changed within him. His recently acquired tether portal started pulling him towards his new tether. Verra Mica was shocked.

'It is happening, Corpus, already. You must return to your chamber. Your Eathian tether is about to be born.'

Christi's excitement bubbled over.

'I will follow you as soon as I can, brother.'

'I wish we could have been twins on Eathia, too; then I wouldn't have to wait for you to join me.' He smiled at Christi.

Frustrated at his lack of emergency, Verra Mica flared slightly.

'For goodness' sake, you must go Corpus. I will be in contact with you soon. I didn't have a chance to show you half the things I intended. What is the Source thinking, sending you straight out like this?'

As Corpus went to leave, Verra Mica felt the need to give him a little guidance. She knew where he was heading and why. There was no such thing as a tether by chance. There was a plan, and Corpus and his tether were a fundamental part of that plan.

'Corpus, please wait if you would. I want to say this so you remember that your strength is in your ability to guide. Open your tether's eyes. He might, in Eathian time, become a stubborn old man, but he will learn quickly as a youngster, so get him in tune with you as quickly as possible.'

'I will, your Honour.'

With that, Corpus was gone. Christi moved towards Verra Mica.

'A stubborn old man? So, you must have seen things in the Source, too.'

'Not as much as the two of you, no doubt, but enough, I hope, to see us through these difficult times.'

Christi thought for a moment. There were things about the information the Source passed onto her that didn't quite make sense.

'I have seen so much from Source Verra Mica. However, I am struggling to understand if some of what it has shown me is to come true or if it is just a warning.'

Verra Mica was intrigued.

'Let's return to our division and you can explain.'

Once they had left the chamber and were safely in Seraphyte territory, Christi continued.

'I have seen Eathia in darkness, some of it desolate and burnt to ash, and it felt as though I was in the centre of it. Corpus has made no reference to this vision. This would suggest that some of what the Source embedded into us during our birth sequence differs from the other, Elkyne included. It is important to understand that we all seem to have separate duties and fates. Do you understand why this could be? Considering we are all one-third of a whole.'

'You have answered that yourself, Christi. You are indeed one-third of the whole. Together, although all different, you make up that whole. I can only hope that all three of you will eventually work together to the same end.'

Christi waited as Verra Mica looked like she was scanning something or someone. She continued.

'I will monitor the situation. For the time being, Duergar does not suspect how much we know or that we are suspicious of him to the degree that we are, and it must remain that way; I need him to be his arrogant self, only then will he make a mistake, and when he does, I will be ready for him.'

Christi prepared to leave, but something was bothering her.

'Were you shown my duties in detail, Superior?'

'As far as I am aware, yes.'

Verra Mica watched Christi anxiously.

'Do you need to talk to me about them?'

'No, thank you. As long as we are both aware, your Honour.'

Christi bowed and turned to leave, suddenly conscious of how odd it was not to have Corpus with her.

Verra Mica remained alone for a short while after Christi had left. A little troubled at Christi's mention of what her role would be. She had been shown something about Christi that disturbed her to the very core. She wondered if that was what she was referring to. Surely if it were true, it would be a last resort. How could the Source ask for so much from one Soul Guardian? She hoped it would never come to that. She would do everything in her power to avoid that being Christi's fate.

Verra Mica's attention returned to her reason for scanning earlier. It showed one of the Psybiencian Guardians heading her way, then suddenly disappearing.

Makaria veiled and waited timidly for Verra Mica to draw near to her. As she did, Verra Mica nearly missed Makaria's presence. She paused just in time.

'He'll know you're veiling Makaria; you risk your cover for what?'

'I have finally spoken to Angelica. She has let me know that she is safe, however …'

'You have. Oh, thank goodness. Where is she?'

'… I don't know, but I am still very concerned for her; nonetheless, she is alone. What is disturbing is that she has said there are more like her. Soul Guardians that have never even seen The Realm. I can sense a real fear within her, but that's not all.'

'Go on.'

'She was called to Mary's aid. Your Mary. It was her and her daughter that had to flee their home on board a ship.'

Verra Mica looked visibly shocked. She fell silent, trying to understand why such a situation had arisen. Why would Angelica be needed to attend Verra Mica's past Eathian tether. One that she would have preferred never to have left in the first place.

'Who called her exactly? Do you think it's a trap?'

'Unlikely. It was Ashtar!'

'WHAT? That's not possible.'

'She insisted it was, Superior.'

Verra Mica became suspicious.

'Am I being played here? I won't be lied to, Makaria, by anyone.'

'Why would she lie? For what purpose?'

Verra Mica calmed. She thought about what else Makaria had said.

'Did you say Soul Guardians who have never seen The Realm? That isn't possible either, Makaria; once birthed, they must go through the usual channels of tethering; otherwise, how do they enter Eathia?'

She stepped away from Makaria. Suddenly aware that Makara's being there would cause Duergar to be suspicious. She needed stealth on her side, at the very least.

'Return quickly and be safe, Makaria, no more risks, and remember, as far as Duergar is concerned, I know nothing of this. Christi has updated me about the meeting in the chamber. Very alarming, I must say. Do you feel safe enough with them? I don't want you putting yourself at risk on any account.'

'I do and will continue to be careful, your Honour. I am better placed in the epicentre of this turmoil.'

With that, Makaria left, successfully slipping back while re-veiling to gain imperceptible access to her order.

She was safe for now, she thought, but she would have to be careful not to raise any suspicions. Gallia, Duergar's deputy, was already watching her.

She was finally content that she had been able to contact Angelica. Even though their plan was ever-changing, they both felt happy that they appeared to have the upper hand over Duergar.

Angelica and Makaria were rare for their time, new twin Soul Guardians, very similar in temperament and energies; however, what was rarer still was that their coding and overall fragmented energetic displacements were completely different, showing them to be born into completely different orders, similar, now, to the Triplexes.

Verra Mica realised that both had been born under Duergar's watch but received different orders from the Source, including her own, the Seraphytes. New Soul Guardians, like the twins, revealed signs that something was amiss in an area needing attention. Unaware of this, she recognised Duergar's tendency to disrupt the status quo. His interference repeatedly had consequences, and Verra Mica was fed up with it.

Makaria was a Psybiencian. Born with a connection to the Seraphytes through her sister, she had luckily remained loyal to Verra Mica. She and Angelica recognised that the Psybiencian Superior was less than trustworthy. Makaria decided on her own to remain in the order as a spy.

The Psybiencians were the most secretive order, keeping their work and duties to themselves. Duergar, a great leader, inspired loyalty from his students. While passionate about mentoring and talented musically, concerns arose about his extreme methods. His ability to extract pure sound waves from his students outshone his predecessors. What drove his methods remained a mystery across The Realm. Some rules were clear: these gifts should enhance life, not control it, and veils were for protection, not invisibility. Duergar and his students, however, seemed impervious to these rules.

If Verra Mica had realised that Duergar was becoming slightly nervous at chinks appearing in the armour of his otherwise perfectly orchestrated plans, she would have been in a better position to infiltrate his fortress with more ease.

As for Duergar, he was beginning to sense that he would need to be more careful. He could feel deviations occurring from very specific instructions he had given.

It was clear to him that some reins needed tightening, while others, let's say, breaches, would need eradicating.

Makaria had barely reached her chamber after secretly meeting with Verra Mica when a force of undetectable energy flew past her. She forgot to veil in time, so she froze as it stopped by her. Once it had acknowledged her, it quickly continued on past.

Whoever it was had scanned her; she was sure of it. Her fears began to rise. Veiling quickly now, she waited, not daring to move. Should she follow to investigate or leave it completely alone? Despite herself, she knew she would always investigate. It wasn't long before she realised she was heading towards Duergar's personal quarters.

Duergar was working on his strategy when he felt an imminent encroachment. He frustratingly blocked it, putting yet another shield between them and him. He didn't bother turning around, knowing full well that his lack of theatrical gameplay would only infuriate his adversary. Another game had started. If he hadn't been so busy, he would welcome another opportunity to put this irritation down, once and for all.

He growled as she entered, then spoke first to try and head off any unwanted questions from Verra Mica.

'Apologies for taking young Elkyne away before you could twist his pure Psybiencian soul.'

He turned to look at her.

Verra Mica watched, remaining silent.

He continued, making full use of being centre stage.

'Nice of you to accept the orb by the way, shows good team spirit, well done.'

Verra Mica had heard enough.

'I'm not here about that. Where are they?'

'Sorry, who are, *they*?'

'You know very well who I mean, the ones that are missing. My Seraphytes, and who only knows how many more.'

'Harhh … tut, tut, the high counsellor crown barely warm, and you've gone and lost some of your followers already; how very lackadaisical of you; good to know you're keeping a tight order, Verra Mica.'

'I don't fall for your illusional attempts at creating a smokescreen. Enough, Duergar. It has come to my attention that there are too many new Seraphytes unaccounted for, and believe me, I will go to every extreme measure to find out where they have gone, one by one.'

Duergar remained unfazed by Verra Mica's outburst.

'We all lose Soul Guardians. Verra Mica, it is a sad fact that they get themselves into trouble on Eathia and can't always make it back, but it's not our role to bring the little freedom fighters back home, now is it? I personally have much more vexing things to be getting on with than investigating their whereabouts, and with your new role, I imagine you do too. Is that it? Are you finished?'

'I assume by that you mean, Elkyne. What plans do you have for him? His brother and sister wish to see him, as we all do. Surely, if they were birthed together, they should be able to work together at some point.'

'He is busy for now; they will see him in time. He is in my custody; you have no say on what he does, nor does he.'

'Custody. That's a strong statement. It seems that he hasn't been allowed to tether either and remains a Guardian only. Why? This is not what the Source had in mind for him, surely? When you look at what …'

Duergar cut her off.

'Absolutely NONE of your business. I have been gracious enough and tolerated more than I can stand for the time being, and just for the record, Verra Mica, we don't blast into each other's quarters with petty assumptions. You are a Superior now and a Supreme Council member. Please start acting like one.'

Verra Mica had said her piece. She wanted him to know he was being watched. She left him to stew over her words.

Outside Duergar's quarters, Makaria froze. She had left it too late to retreat. Verra Mica passed her, they glanced quickly at each other, and she quietly spoke to her.

'It appears that we might need some backup, Makaria. Now, please get safely back to your quarters.'

Then she was gone.

Makaria relaxed, knowing it had been Verra Mica scanning her and not one of her own. Relieved, she got as far away from Duergar's quarters as possible.

This was starting to feel increasingly like the onset of a war, she thought.

Sides were being drawn. The necessity for backup signified one thing: tensions were escalating.

Chapter 22
The Realm

Birth of The Story

Once Verra Mica had left Duergar, she headed straight to see Alma Tadema. As she approached, she realised that her friend was in mid-session with her class. Rather than continue, she held herself back from entering the auditorium. She didn't want to interrupt her class unnecessarily, so she waited. It was rare that she could listen to her take her class.

Alma Tadema's Order was the Story's creator, drawn from the essence of the Source. In the beginning, it regularly told stories that went back to the early days of The Realm. When she was new to being a Superior, these stories calmed Verra Mica. They gave her roots that stretched back to when she felt completely at peace. Now, they have helped many as they created a firm foundation for their students. They would hold The Realm's history if it ever went through troubled times. It acted as an anchor for all, and Verra Mica was worried that the time was needed now more than ever.

It wasn't until she focused on what Alma was saying that she realised who it was she was telling the story about.

Verra Mica lit up. *What an opportune moment to choose to eav*esdrop, she thought.

Alma was a respectful and unbiased teacher and a dear friend. Her voice emanated from the front of the auditorium. She was in the process of melodiously reciting an ode about the time that Verra Mica herself and her then mentor, Ashtar, were tethered to two Eathian lovers who had an unenviable task of trying to guide a world away from despair. Two rebellious worlds thwarted their union. Both Eathia and The Realm played a part in their demise. Even then, it seemed The Realm had its own internal wars dividing certain orders.

Ashtar's nemesis, Rammasus, the original Superior to the Psybiencians, leads the revolt against Ashtar and Verra Mica's allocation of tethers. He disagreed with their purpose on Eathia, which sparked a never-ending feud between the Psybiencians and the Seraphytes, which would live on long after Ashtar and Rammasus left The Realm.

What happened as a fallout of the feud shook both Eathia and The Realm to their core, but few saw it first hand as she had.

Was it this that partially fuelled her mistrust of Rammasus and his then young protege at the time, Duergar? she had wondered.

Verra Mica had learnt to grieve. It was an emotion that Soul Guardians cultivated from their Eathian tethers. The story that Alma Tadema now told brought back sadness to her as if it happened only recently, the curse of a timeless existence.

At the time, she wanted to leave with Ashtar and return fully to The Realm and Join her Eathian partner in death. But that wasn't one of the choices available to her. She remembered his agonising expression as he was torn from their entwined tethers. He had tried to return to Eathia and almost made it, which only fuelled Rammasus's anger at him. That was the last time she saw him or felt him.

When she finally returned to The Realm, having to leave her precious, Mary, he was gone, banished by Rammasus and his fellow counsellors for apparently breaking the most important rule in The Realm.

Never try to bring a human body back from death!

Her veil started falling as she evoked the images from her past. She was brought back sharply and recoiled when she heard Alma Tadema's voice.

'I can feel your sadness, Verra.'

Alma was next to her now and was scanning her. She could sense exactly where her friend had gone and felt for her.

'That will teach me to eavesdrop and let my guard down.'

Alma smiled at her dear friend.

'I wonder where he is, Alma; where did that fool go? There is a void that just cannot be filled. All I can do is protect it, hoping he returns.'

Verra Mica decided not to let on yet that Makaria had mentioned his apparent message to Angelica. Not until she was sure.

Alma Tadema responded, 'Ashtar has gone Verra; if you were in my place, you would say the same thing to me.'

'Only he hasn't, has he? We both felt his presence within the Triplexes. It's quite unsettling, don't you think?'

Alma Tadema had felt it so strongly, too. She nodded.

'I am your friend Verra, which I must admit, can be a precarious position to be in at times. I don't always agree with you, which is alright, but I must agree that those three are the essence of Ashtar, not necessarily him. It might explain why you are reacting so much to Elkyne's displacement.'

Verra Mica glared at her friend, then realised she was possibly correct in her evaluation.

'Thank you for that. Alma. I am sure you are right.'

Verra changed the subject as usual when things became too personal.

'Alma, can I ask if you have noticed if any of your tethered and untethered Soul Guardians have gone missing or if your numbers have been reduced in any way at all?'

'What an unusual question. No, not to my knowledge. Having said that, we have not had any replenishments of late. I assumed it was because our order is not as essential now, unlike the more active orders.'

'That should not be the case, Alma.'

'Have you spoken to Baquarrah? Is he concerned at all? Remember, we are to have the Council meeting soon. You should air your concerns then; if something is affecting our Soul Guardians, that will be the place to inform our fellow Superiors, surely, then they can be mindful of it also?'

'Inform the Council about what exactly, losing our Soul Guardians? He'll make a mockery of the mere mention of it.'

'It does sound a strange observation, Verra, but if you sense something isn't right, then yes, you should. Mentioning it will also bring it to the Source's attention.'

Alma flinched when she realised Verra Mica's hesitation and that the 'He' she was referring to was Duergar again.

'How could he take our Soul Guardians without our knowledge? That is slightly far-fetched even for you, Verra, don't you think?'

'Forget I said anything for now. I just wanted you to be more aware of what's happening right before you.'

Alma Tadema sighed.

'Was there anything else you wanted, Verra?'

'No, I was just coming to see you for the sake of it, and when I heard the Story was about me, it threw me off balance for a bit.'

'Maybe you should consider spending some time with Baquarrah. He is a marvellous healer, you know. He likes you very much. He gave a wonderful speech at your ceremony, didn't he?'

'I will see, yes, he was very kind.'

With that, Verra Mica made her leave from Alma Tadema.

She pondered the possibility of approaching Baquarrah, but not necessarily just for the healing. She needed as much support as she could get. Something inside was still causing her to be careful with what she divulged to Alma. *She was so blissfully unaware and trusting*, she thought with a hint of jealousy and frustration.

Baquarrah Korveddio was the head of the Illumacytes. A colourful order developed attunement by utilising their ability to refract and finely rebalance colour and light emanating from both Soul Guardians and Eathians alike. There is little chance of hiding anything from an Illumacyte.

In truth, Alma might have had a point. She would consider visiting Baquarrah.

It wouldn't do any harm, and who knows what she might glean from him prior to their council meeting.

Chapter 23
Eathia - Third era

Last Hope

Denis leant back on the rickety wooden kitchen chair, causing its weak joints to creak under the strain of the solid-framed sixteen-year-old. His muddy boots, still attached to his feet, rested on the side of the kitchen table. He defiantly stared at Tobias as his father continued to prepare their breakfast that morning.

'I want to leave WITH you this time. I don't want to stay here.'

'You're needed here, son. I can't put your mother through that. It isn't fair. This is my last job, and then I'll be back.'

He turned to face Denis.

'For good this time. Now get your boots off the table.'

Denis kicked back, showering mud across the surface of the kitchen table and watched his father's reaction.

'For goodness' sake, Denis, you're nearly seventeen. Behave like a man, not a spoilt brat.'

Denis pushed the chair away as he stood abruptly, sending it crashing against the cupboards behind him. It slid onto the floor with a crash.

Sophia came in wondering what the noise was all about, and Denis just pushed past her on his way out. She was thrown off balance. Tobias moved forward to follow him, but Sophia held his arm and shook her head. The front door slammed, and they quietly turned to watch from the window as he stormed down the garden path.

Tobias turned to Sophia.

'His moods are getting worse. I can cope with his temper, but you won't be able to much longer. I'm wondering if he has a point about coming away with me. I can't leave him here, Sophia, not this time. He's like a ticking bomb. Anyway, although it pains me to say, the town will be glad to see the back of him for a bit, I'd imagine.'

He put the chair right and sat down. He put his elbows on the table and pushed both hands through his weathered blond hair. Sophia sat beside him, and he dropped a hand down into hers, resting them both on the table amid the clusters of mud. He stared at his own hand as it enveloped hers.

'This is your last job, Tobias. Then you'll be home. And, besides, he won't be so angry all the time. I have Bertha, and she can always talk him down.'

Tobias shook his head.

'She's busier now, the town's getting bigger, and she's the only midwife while Anamaya is out of action. She won't be around and you know it. It doesn't feel right this time, Sophia. Leaving you all. I shouldn't have taken on this one; I'm getting too old for this malarkey now.'

'What could we have done differently? He was never the same after the incident with the reflector. We understand that now, and we've tried to support him. He has gone through so much since, and we can't help him in the way he needs. He needs to find himself, find a reason to be happy.'

Tobias leant back and sighed.

'Augustus caught up with me yesterday and said Denis has been hanging around the castle again, asking to be allowed in. It's too much. He isn't going to discover who he is here. Let me take him to the cove and Mary's on the way through. I'll talk to him about our past and try to give him a bit of grounding, a sense of who he is.'

'Grounding? Are you sure that will not just bring up more questions and frustrations?'

'He needs to feel like he belongs, Sophia. He hates it here; he makes that obvious, and now Francis has passed away, and with Augustus and Anamaya's baby due soon, he's losing the people he loves to other things and other places. His differences are becoming increasingly acute; I get it, he feels lonely.'

'But that's not true.'

'It is to him which makes it true in his world.'

Sophia thought for a bit in silence.

'Maybe you're right.'

Tobias smiled at her. A 'knowing he was right' kind of smile.

'OK, OK. You can have this one triumph, but don't get used to it.'

Tobias shuffled towards Sophia.

'Look, I can teach him my trade. The bunch I work with are generally good men. They'll soon pick him up on his attitude. It will do him good to be around the roughest of the species.'

Sophia laughed, knowing Tobias was as soft and clever as they came. It wasn't a bad idea to teach him his skills. Tobias had never been short of work. As fast as the ships were built and their designs were changing, he was adapting his own style of sails. The industry would miss him for sure. Maybe it was time to teach a new dog some old tricks.

~

Denis wasn't sure where he was going when he left the cottage. It wasn't until he lifted himself out of his rage that he realised he had reached the bottom of the stone steps leading up to the castle. He took a deep breath and exhaled the last of his negative energy.

He missed Francis. He was the only one in Stonehaven, other than Bertha, who made any sense.

He turned to walk away, but he thought he heard something as he did. He spun around to look back down the hill as he tried to get an angle on where the sound was coming from.

There it was again. It was a woman's voice.

'Help, please help me. Anyone?'

He turned back towards the castle, realising it was coming from there. He ran up the steps two at a time and pushed the main doors, fully expecting them to be locked inside. Surprisingly, one flew open. He entered the main hall. Anamaya was lying helplessly on the floor at the base of the stairs. She was holding on to her swollen stomach.

'Denis, oh, thank goodness you are here. Please help me. I think I'm having my baby now!'

Denis froze. He looked across at the open doorway leading into the Orbitarium. He hadn't been allowed anywhere near the castle again since Augustus had discovered he was helping Francis.

Anamaya yelled at him again.

'Denis?'

He looked back at Anamaya. The urge was strong to leave her and go into the room where the orb was. Just as he was about to move away from Anamaya, a hidden sense of duty forced him to reconsider. She saw his conflict and all but gave up on him helping.

'Of all the people passing, why did it have to be you?' she agonised.

Another burst of pain shot through her stomach and she cried out. Denis snapped into action, frustrated at having to help but ultimately feeling he had no choice.

'I'll go and get Augustus and Bertha; can I help you up somewhere in the meantime? Off the floor, I mean.'

Anamaya had to admit going back upstairs wasn't an option, so she would have to ask him to take her into the main room, where there was the only couch.

'Will you be alright in there, Denis?'

She nodded towards the Orbitarium.

Not wanting to discuss anything to do with the Orb, he ignored her and lifted her carefully, carrying her towards the open doorway.

'Don't worry about me, I'll be OK. Besides, you're the one who's about to burst.'

'Not quite the bedside manner that your sister has. But I am relieved you're here, Denis.'

He stopped at the doorway when he had a full view of the orb. He took a deep breath and released it slowly, trying to control his racing heart. He then marched across the floor and put her on the soft couch in the room's far left corner.

'I'll go. Will you be alright?'

'Yes, yes, please hurry, I'm worried about my baby, Denis. It's coming too early.'

Denis ran out without looking back. He tried to think where Bertha would be this time of day. Panic rose as he realised that she could be anywhere in the town.

As luck would have it, he saw her with her midwifery bag, and she was walking across to their cottage. After the briefest of conversations, they separated. She ran to the castle, and he went on to get Augustus at the Emporium.

Bertha had never been inside the castle before, and as she approached the open door, she yelled for Anamaya.

'Aunty, are you here?'

Anamaya called back to Bertha and could just be heard above the humming of the orb. As Bertha followed her voice, she was taken aback by how large and bright the orb was. She was mesmerised by all the machinery that surrounded it. It was colossal. She found it hard to pull her attention away from it.

'Bertha?'

She shook her head and headed over to her aunt across the room.

'I fell on the stairs, Bertha, I have been counting my contractions and we are nearly there. Can you run up to the loft and fetch my bag? There are some sheets up there we can use.'

She stopped and grabbed hold of Bertha's hand with the next wave. Bertha waited until the pain began to ease. Then, when she found out she had a small window of time, she quickly ran up to the loft. Shouting back to her, reminding her of her breathing, she immediately felt daft.

What am I saying? she scolded herself, *she knows more than I do.*

Her aunt wasn't due for another four weeks. Bertha wondered if the fall had pushed her into an early labour. She grabbed the last of the things in the loft and ran back just as another of her contractions forced Anamaya to scream out in pain.

Returning, Bertha threw a cushion behind Anamaya's head, making her comfortable. There was no doubt that she was ready for the birth.

Augustus stormed into the hall and yelled for Denis to stay outside.

When Bertha heard him, she called out to let him know where they were.

'It's coming, Uncle. Right now.'

'It's too early, Ana, by my calculations …'

Anamaya's scream cut him off in an instant.

'Hurry, Uncle, I need you to sit behind her and hold on to her hand; she'll need your strength to help her push.'

Bertha turned around and saw that her uncle had suddenly vanished. She shouted at him but still couldn't see him; the light was so bright, it was starting to obscure her vision in the hall. She lowered her glasses, but that made it worse.

Augustus had run back to the door to grab the oculars he needed if he could stay that close to the orb.

'It's coming!'

'Right, start to push when you are ready.'

The room echoed to the sound of Anamaya's labour. The raven, still perched high up on one of the windowsills, became agitated, flew down and started to circle them.

Bertha shouted at Augustus and Anamaya, saying she could see the baby.

'Give one final push.'

Both fear and excitement burst out from Augustus.

'Come on, Ana, let's meet our baby. You can do it, my love.'

Anamaya looked up at him and put all her remaining strength into the final push.

It worked.

'Well done, it's here. Look.'

As she held the baby up for them to see, Bertha's expression changed from glee to concern. She went quiet, immediately sensing something wasn't right. The baby was very pale, even for an Ashen. Augustus moved towards her so he could see his newborn child.

'What is it, Bertha?'

He looked down at the tiny baby boy.

'Is he breathing?'

Anamaya went into a blind panic.

Bertha quickly but calmly wrapped him up and turned him almost upside down and furiously rubbed his back and patted it hard, but nothing was happening.

The raven was now swooping down directly over their heads, only exacerbating an already tense moment. Augustus tried to strike at it and get it away from his distraught wife.

Tears fell down Anamaya's face as she tried to sit up and help Bertha.

All of a sudden, the orb ignited. A thunderous pulse emanated from it, and its swirling light erupted into an almost blinding flash.

Anamaya looked desperately across at Augustus.

'What's happening?'

As soon as Augustus turned to see the cause, a spark appeared to ignite within the orb. An almighty flare floodlit the room, and as fast as it arrived, it was gone.

For some reason, at that moment, the raven circling them now fell suddenly, becoming paralysed in mid-air. It fell to the floor, convulsing on its back until it finally lay still. The flash seemed to have affected it.

No one could ever have realised that a long-standing tether to the bird had been ripped away from it the moment the orb flared. It was harsh enough to cause the bird to pass out.

Augustus was horrified.

'I didn't touch it; I was just trying to scare it off. What on Eathia is going on?'

Bertha was still trying to coax their baby to breathe.

It should have worked by now, she thought. Panic was setting in and the feeling of nausea gripped her throat.

Suddenly, the baby moved in her hands. Augustus was helping Anamaya sit up when he saw the baby's movement for himself. He shouted to Bertha.

'He's alive; look, he moved. Ana, he's going to make it.'

Bertha turned the baby over, continuing to rub his stomach.

His face burst into life; creases appeared on his forehead. Finally, he gave a heart-melting cry.

Her aunt reached out for her to give him to her, with tears now pouring down both her and Augustus's faces, Bertha handed him over to her.

As soon as Anamaya held their baby, she looked across at Augustus.

'We've got a boy, Augustus.'

The two of them hugged the baby and each other. Bertha sat back, exhausted.

She turned to look at the orb. It had now returned to normal.

Her knowledge of the Soul Guardians and The Realm made her suspicious. She now found herself questioning any random event, trying to fathom if anything was due to their interference. Wanted or unwanted. Surely, this could only have been the orb's doing. Something happened to bring that little boy back, she was sure of it.

But that didn't explain the bird's odd reaction. She looked across at it, still motionless on the floor.

'Poor thing,' she whispered.

Something made her glance towards the door. A movement. She turned to see Denis standing there, only his attention wasn't on them. He appeared to be caught in the orb's hypnotic glare.

She called out to him.

'Denis?'

When he finally looked across at her, he couldn't understand why his sister was glaring at him and shaking her head. He looked down at the raven on the floor and raised his eyebrows. He pointed at it, confused. She shrugged her shoulders, then asked him to quickly grab it and take it out.

Denis moved forward cautiously. Lifting it up by its wing and grimacing at the weirdness of being that close to a dead animal, he tiptoed out unnoticed. As he exited the door and onto the front of the castle steps, the bird miraculously exploded back into life. Furious at being held by a wing it started to snap and claw at Denis. His instant reaction was to throw it away from him. Without touching the ground, it curved and started to fly straight for him. He ducked just in time as it flew over him and back into the castle.

'Stupid damn bird. Stupid, stupid.'

He kicked out at the castle's wall, causing little damage to it but sending an excruciating pain up his leg. He hobbled away and down the steps and headed out from the town. He had had enough.

Bertha, unaware of her brother's misfortune and perplexed at the re-entrance of the raven, sat still and watched her aunt and uncle study their new baby. He was, indeed, a true Ashen, just like his father and grandfather.

Augustus became slightly agitated.

'We must get out of this room, my love. I'm not feeling at all well, and I don't know if this little fella can take this extreme light for much longer either.'

Bertha looked across at Anamaya and tutted. Considering what she had just been through, it was her uncle who was feeling a little under the weather! She tried to help him by offering an arm, forgetting that her contact might just tip him over the edge. He waved his hand gently, rejecting her offer, and stood with his new son cupped safely in his bent arm.

'Have you had a chance to think of a name yet?' Bertha asked excitedly.

They looked at each other and smiled. Anamaya spoke first.

'Maddox, his name will be Maddox Francis Browne.'

Bertha giggled with approval.

'Wow, that's a big name. He's going to have to grow into that one.'

She moved forward and looked at the tiny grey boy and gasped.

'We need a reflector.'

Augustus smiled.

'Oh, we Ashens don't need them. I am surprised this is the first time it has come up. He has a natural connection with the orb, you see.'

Bertha nodded in acceptance. That made perfect sense.

'I'll go and get Mum, and we'll be back to help you home if you'd like.'

Augustus waved her towards the door.

'We'll be fine. Baby or no baby, we must secure the castle again, then we'll get home when Ana is feeling well enough.'

'Well, I'll bring some food up and leave it outside.'

'Now that I will agree to.'

Augustus walked towards the door, leaned to the left, grabbed hold of his oculars and threw them back on top of Arthur's metal head. He reached down and pulled the blanket over the baby's closed eyes for extra protection. He smiled to himself and then glanced up and stared at the raven who was now calmly back on the windowsill.

He shook his head at Bertha as she reached the main door.

'Wasn't that the strangest thing? I swear I never even touched it, and down it went, and the light that flared up from the orb, all very strange.'

Bertha shook her head, then nodded in agreement. 'He's never shown any sign of bad health in all these years.'

She hesitated before addressing a point that may explain the odd light from the orb.

'I think she saved Maddox, Uncle. I truly do. I know you are going to say that it isn't possible after all this time, but he wasn't breathing, and then he was.'

Augustus nodded at her.

'Maybe we'll never know. Maybe we aren't supposed to. We'll see. I'm so grateful Maddox is here, if not a little early.'

Bertha looked up at the ceiling, then continued her gaze, taking in the rest of the room and the orb.

'What a beautiful place. I am thankful to have been allowed in.'

'Under the circumstances, I think we are the ones who are grateful. I can't thank you enough for helping to bring our little Maddox into the world, Bertha.'

Augustus quietly commented on her having a good teacher, but Bertha didn't hear him as she continued to look at the ornate design of the room's tall ceiling.

She looked back down thoughtfully.

'We were lucky, Uncle. Very lucky.'

Bertha smiled at him and walked out the door, back towards the cottage, leaving them in peace to focus on their new baby.

Light years away in time and space, a Soul Guardian had felt a pull at his core. Aeons had gone by since the last tether had drawn one of them back to Eathia, now a world cut off from The Realm. The Soul Guardian had no time to wait; the pull was frantic, a baby was dying and he needed to revive it; otherwise, all would be lost on Eathia forever.

A plan was still in play and Maddox was to be the final move against the Dark Soul Guardians.

Chapter 24
Eathia - Third Era

The Final Journey

By the time Denis made it back to the cottage, his father was waiting for him in the sitting room, now doubling up as Denis's bedroom. Bertha and Sophia were quietly watching and waiting for him to walk in. Bertha had updated them both on that morning's events.

As Denis walked in, he felt all eyes looking at him.

'I didn't do anything. I was walking past and she was screaming. What would you have done?'

'We know, son, and the little chap wouldn't have made it without you, from what I hear.'

Denis frowned at his father.

'It's been born. It's a boy!'

Denis couldn't stop the smile that was determined to break out from his usually serious demeanour.

'Wow.'

He then caught sight of something leaning against his father's feet. A large sack was lying on the floor and it was bursting at the seams.

Anger flashed through Denis.

'So, you're going then?'

He turned to leave the room.

'See ya.'

He went to go upstairs and paused when he heard his father's voice.

'Tomorrow morning, first thing. Be ready at first light, or I'll leave without you.'

As Denis re-entered the room, Tobias kicked the sack towards him.

'It's yours, you numpty.'

Tobias grinned at him.

'Seriously, you mean it? I'm coming with you?'

Chapter 25
The Realm

Smokescreen

Verra Mica was on her way to greet a small group of returning Seraphyte Soul Guardians when she received Duergar's call to Council earlier than initially planned. Knowing this wasn't a meeting she wanted to miss, she turned and headed speedily towards the Council Chambers instead.

She responded and summoned Alma Tadema, who replied immediately. Baquarrah had remained silent and non-responsive, which she found unusual.

She had visited him and did receive healing, but was unable to gain any insight as to whether he was missing any Soul Guardians. He was as horrified as Alma Tadema had been at the thought of them disappearing without them having made their presence known within The Realm.

Surely Duergar would know not to rearrange a meeting when one or more Superiors could be busy elsewhere? she mused.

She continued her inner dialogue.

Of course, he would. He had done that very same thing when she had been attending the births of the Triplexes, had he not? She felt herself getting agitated already.

Verra Mica asked to meet with Alma briefly before entering the Council Chamber. Alma had explained that Duergar would assume that Verra Mica would naturally take a back seat to learn the ropes before diving in and getting involved with matters already in hand. This was not the case, as she explained to Alma as they made their way to the meeting.

'He is a bigger fool than I originally realised. If he thinks, I will sit back and let him run the meeting. There are two of us now, for a good reason; I didn't ask to be appointed, did I?'

'I know, Verra, it was decided by all of us. I might add, Duergar included, at our last Council meeting, which I have to say feels like an awful long time ago now. We all agreed with the Source inasmuch as The Realm required a more balanced collection of representatives to act on its behalf, however …'

Alma stopped and looked straight at her dear friend and sighed.

'… it is advisable to go slowly at first and listen to some of the issues and be led slightly by those who have been doing this for a while now.'

Alma watched Verra Mica's pained expression, knowing full well that she would ignore her advice. She sighed again and continued.

'Well, it was worth a shot.'

'Well, we all know what happened at the Council's last meeting, don't we? That was supposed to be my first one. I will try Alma, for your sake. I haven't heard back from Baquarrah. I hope he knows we have a meeting?'

'Apparently, yes, he does.'

'How do you know?'

Alma felt uncomfortable again with the directness of Verra Mica's accusatory tone.

'Baquarrah was otherwise momentarily engaged, and Duergar has let me know that they would be along in due course.'

'And so it begins, just like the last meeting. Duergar kept me out of the loop. On purpose, I might add.'

'What meeting?'

'The meeting before the births, that's the meeting I'm talking about. I was not informed as a Superior that it was taking place, and I was not involved in the decision to input all your data into the Source. So Baquarrah is with Duergar now, as we speak, is that correct?'

Alma Tadema started to feel flustered.

'Now I'm confused; which would you like me to respond to first? You get me in a dither, as well you know.'

Ignoring her friend's bewilderment, Verra Mica continued.

'What exactly happened at that meeting, Alma? How did the orb come into being? Who suggested it? I need to know before we enter.'

'You know very well it was Duergar. He brought it in with him and asked us to imprint on it so it would contain all our data. I have told you this already.'

'Did he imprint with you all?'

Alma Tadema thought back to Duergar's actions.

'No, he had already uploaded his information when he created the orb.'

'And you all just went along with it? Am I the only one who thinks this is suspicious?'

'Yes, Verra, you are.'

'Did you not realise it was partially blocked at the time?'

'What are you talking about? Of course it wasn't.'

Verra Mica remained silent and contemplated her friend's reaction. She hadn't imagined it. The orb was partially veiled. She decided to drop it before she upset Alma anymore, as they had arrived at the entrance to the chamber.

'Don't worry about it now, Alma, let's go in.'

'I wasn't worried until you mentioned it. Now I'm worried AND confused. I do like our little get-togethers, Verra, don't you?'

Verra Mica snorted in disdain.

Alma Tadema paused and looked up at the ornate entrance to the Council Chambers. No code would gain them entry into this chamber; instead, just above the entrance shone an oval-shaped globe, a direct link with Source, and it was the Source that would allow them to continue. While they waited, Alma continued to comment.

'Thank goodness we're here. What happened to the old, relaxed Verra Mica I knew? That was a statement, not a question, before you start again.'

Verra Mica chuckled at her dear friend's manner, and once they had been scanned, they proceeded through the wall of the chamber and into its vast open sanctum.

The Council Chamber differed noticeably from all the other chambers within The Realm. Its chamber was the closest you could get to the Source itself, other than entering it directly via its own capsule, as Verra Mica had done when the Triplexes had arrived.

A beam of its divine energy shone through a domed light which rested on one side of the chambers. A strong magnetic field functioned as a shield and an intermediary communication device, giving the Superiors a safe connection directly to the Source. Its presence here acted as a silent member of the Council.

At this dome, all members would register their arrival and departure. Any items raised that the Superiors could not agree on would then require the Source's attention before any final decisions could be made. Duergar rarely let them escalate to that degree, and he would be less inclined, even more so now that Verra Mica had risen to the higher ranks to stand at the same level as him.

For a while now, Duergar had been the sole High Councillor. Having a seconder was not going to be an easy adjustment, but, as the other Superiors were present at the decision to honour her with that status, Duergar had to take it as an uncomfortable short-term defeat.

In the centre of the chamber stood a circular columned forum. This allowed Superiors the opportunity to face each other on an equal stage, not giving anyone the hierarchy of looking down on others. The golden dome rose from the centre, pulsating a gentle thrum as its lights swirled beneath the glass like a protective shield. Beneath each of the Superiors rested a magnetic base designed for them to tether to, thus giving the Source full involvement in the proceedings.

As Verra Mica and Alma Tadema entered, they realised they were the first to attend. They both went to the dome to register to the Source. Their attunement was straightforward.

As they were ready to make their way to their podiums, Duergar appeared behind them and, with him, Baquarrah.

'Very good, you are all here finally. Now, possibly, we can proceed.'

Verra Mica immediately turned on Duergar.

'We were here on time, Duergar; what are you suggesting?'

'I was here on time but had to leave to inform Baquarrah and to ask for a favour. Please do me the honour of addressing me as Councillor while we attend this meeting. We are required to be respectful throughout our general assembly with no exceptions.'

Alma silently messaged Verra Mica.

'This will be a long session if you don't behave. There are a lot of things I could be getting on with.'

Duergar reacted with a twisted grin, registering that he had heard Alma's quip; her allegiance amused him. Verra Mica saw the flash of smugness and fought hard to contain her own annoyance.

Baquarrah went straight to the dome to register. However, Duergar continued past it and took his place at his rostrum.

'Aren't you going to attune to Source, or do you not need to, seeing as you already consider yourself beyond reproach?'

'I have already attuned Verra Mica. As I said, I was here on time.'

'Shouldn't you also be addressing me as Councillor?'

As Baquarrah moved away from the dome and towards his own podium, he glanced across at Alma Tadema and relayed a frustrated gesture.

Duergar bowed.

A trifle overacted, Verra Mica thought. *For the other's benefit, no doubt, not hers.*

'Yes, of course. You are, as you say, a Councillor. Please accept my apologies.'

Verra Mica backed down, for the time being, wary of his need for point-scoring and recognising it would be a long meeting if she picked him up on every detail she disagreed with.

'Now, if we are ready, I would like to begin this meeting. For the Councillors' benefit, I will run through the procedures.'

'I have attended other similar meetings before this one. Please do not waste unnecessary time on my account.'

'As you wish, we will proceed. If you have any concerns, please raise them at an appropriate time.'

Verra Mica bowed her head in acknowledgement.

The meeting ran smoothly, with everyone updating one another on their progress and highlighting their general concerns. All tried to avoid inflammatory subjects that would provoke either Duergar or Verra Mica. That was until Baquarrah brought up the uncomfortable subject of an apparent issue with his own Illumacyte-tethered Soul Guardians, a point Duergar had urged him to mention when he met with him before joining the others.

'It has come to my attention that my tethered Soul Guardians, within the Illumacyte order, need to spend longer periods of time when attuned to their Eathians. They are unable to de-tether often enough to either continue duties within The Realm as their Eathians appear to be needing their presence more and more.'

Verra Mica knew why this was but wanted to hear what Duergar had to say about it. However, Baquarrah continued.

'It's been a slow increase, Councillor, sorry, Councillors. Many more Eathians are becoming unsettled, and they are, whether they realise it or not, relying on their Soul Guardians to rebalance these issues.'

Duergar remained disingenuous in his response, which made Verra Mica suspicious.

'Yes, I have noticed this. Thank you for bringing it to the Council's attention. Can we continue supporting the tethered Soul Guardians as we have been? Possibly, yes, by enlisting our untethered Soul Guardians, those in The Ream and those currently free-floating on Eathia. I hear from Verra Mica that we may have a few there now?'

Duergar nodded towards Verra Mica in an attempt to openly involve her in the subject of the free floaters. She mentioned it in his chamber in their private, slightly heated discussion. Only now, he was using it to his advantage.

Verra Mica felt the bubbles rise, agitated by Duergar's obviously scripted response.

Baquarrah lit up with enthusiasm, and Alma Tadema glanced across at her friend, elated that she had finally decided to see Duergar as a trusted ally.

Baquarrah, now feeling that all were on board with the issue, continued.

'Yes, yes, that is exactly what I was hoping for. Duergar, sorry, Councillor, was saying something along these lines earlier when we spoke before the meeting. He thought it prudent to let you all know.'

Duergar glanced at Baquarrah, not wanting him to divulge too much of their pre-meeting conversation. It was wasted as Baquarrah was busily watching out for his fellow Councillor's approval. However, Verra Mica was not intending to let it pass.

'I would like to interject at this point if I may.'

Duergar tried to regain Baquarrahs attention, wanting control of the meeting.

'Had you finished Superior Baquarrah?' Duergar said abruptly, hoping he hadn't.

Duergar glanced over to Verra Mica.

'I thought we were to wait for "an appropriate time" before we interrupted a fellow Councillor?'

Baquarrah gratefully acknowledged Duergar's gesture.

'Oh, yes, thank you, yes.'

Baquarrah looked awkwardly at Duergar as his voice raised slightly.

'As I was saying. It is becoming obvious that we need to intervene somehow to reduce the energy fallout felt by The Realm from Eathia through our tethered Soul Guardians. I feel it is imperative that we urgently consider ways to lessen these effects, and I would ask the Council to consider my suggestions.'

Verra Mica watched the dome closely, awaiting any fluctuations in its energetic display in response to Duergar's statement. So far, it had remained balanced and calm. Alma Tadema addressed him.

'Please continue, Councillor Duergar.'

'Thank you. You remarked, Superior Baquarrah, quite astutely, that our Soul Guardians require support, and I concur. Recently, Verra Mica brought to my attention the possibility that some of our Soul Guardians may struggle to return safely. This could stem from insufficient training to prepare for all eventualities, and we understand the potential fallout if they are unprepared. Do you not agree, Superior Verra Mica?'

'Oh, I am allowed to speak now, am I? Well, that is not what I said, Duergar. You know very well what I meant, and this is one of the points I would like to raise.'

Duergar ignored Verra Mica's outburst and continued to look straight at Alma Tadema. He caught her quite by surprise. Flustered, she responded by agreeing with him. Verra Mica frustratingly wanted to gain her attention before she could answer him, but she felt her friend was being evasive on purpose, as she avoided Verra Mica's gaze.

Duergar continued.

'It is my opinion, and one I hope we can all agree on, that we should begin allowing those Soul Guardians who are becoming untethered to remain in The Realm, where they can be supported and re-trained by our more evolved Soul Guardians such as Elkyne. I have spent a considerable amount of time with him, ensuring he is at the top of his field before he is allowed to venture out as a tether. Those who are still tethered and permitted to remain so without any advancement in their training are being stretched beyond their natural energetic abilities.'

Duergar turned and directed his next statement directly towards Verra Mica, his voice becoming smug and condescending.

'Councillor, had you perhaps prepared Corpus and Christi slightly more before sending them out on their own, would they not fare a little better? What do you think?'

The niceties were over. If Duergar wanted to cause a reaction in Verra Mica, that was the one subject he could guarantee would set her aflame.

'What are you suggesting? The Source has made every allowance for the new Soul Guardians. You made damn sure of that. Are you saying that from now on, we ignore the pull from a newborn Eathian to focus on our Soul Guardians training here in The Realm? That's tantamount to abandonment, a complete disregard for our obligation and vows to that planet. Is that what you want? We would be going against the essence of the Source's wish.'

Verra Mica glanced across at the dome again, still confused by the absence of any reaction.

Duergar's voice was now rising, and a low pounding vibration emanated from his core.

'You implied that they needed support; how would you provide that service, pray tell?'

'I did no such thing. I stated that we are losing some of our Soul Guardians. Yes, more training would help, of course, but we ourselves are supposed to be looking after them, monitoring them and mentoring them.'

Duergar looked at Baquarrah.

'Do you feel you have the necessary capabilities to support your order and the whole Realm through this very challenging time? Have you tried helping your own Soul Guardians thus far?'

Baquarrah suddenly felt caught in Duergar's trap but was paralysed by his domineering directness.

'I have, Councillor. I have closely watched the Source and taught my students to recognise their limitations. I am not sure we could cope with all of the tethered Soul Guardians.'

He looked at Verra Mica pleadingly, trying to bring peace to the meeting.

'It is our order that suffers the most; we have to try and heal both the Eathians and the Soul Guardians. Even you, yourself, have considered coming to me, have you not?'

Verra Mica was shocked that he would state such private knowledge to the others. Before she could respond, Duergar pushed the conversation along.

'Please stick to the point at hand. Councillor Baquarrah? Please continue with what you have discovered so far.'

'The Eathians initially responded adequately and were doing well. However, there has been a wave of, shall we say, disbelief in our fundamental supportive roles, and instead they are relying on more external needs and expectations. I would suggest more immediate material pleasures than inner guidance. We are still meeting some of their needs, but at this point, Eathia itself is becoming their source of expansion. As we know, that will not be infinitely available, physically and spiritually speaking. This drains my Soul Guardians, not that their tethers are ill; they are becoming …'

Baquarrah tried to search for the right word but was cut short by Duergar.

'Lazy. That's the word you are looking for. Lazy and Lost.'

The pause allowed a response from Verra Mica.

'And your answer to them losing touch with us is to withdraw your support completely? Is this where you are going with this line of discussion?'

She addressed her next question to Baquarrah directly before Duergar could defend his stance.

'Disbelief in what exactly? Us?'

'I'd say more in "themselves", Councillor, as they are primarily unaware of our tethers.'

'What? What do you mean, themselves?'

'Their evolution is slowing down. Their thirst for personal spiritual growth is waning; with it, they are losing a need for us. We are all caught up in a very strange and unexpected transition.'

Verra Mica moved away from where she stood and approached the dome. She connected immediately, not waiting for the others.

Sure enough, the Source supported what Baquarrah was saying, but that was surely why the latest Triplexes were born. To balance any tilt. She pulled away and looked at the three Superiors.

'How has this happened? I don't understand how the Eathians have reached this point so quickly. We were told of this, and it was a future issue with gentle alterations to be instigated as a long-term process. The Triplexes were to be part of that process; otherwise, why take such extreme measures to bring them here in the first place?'

'And yet here we are. We could not have known that this would happen at such a quickened rate, Councillor.'

She turned to look straight at Duergar.

'There must be a reason for this. It hasn't just happened; something must have intervened and increased the rate of this whole devolution. This is what we are looking at. Devolution? And it's happened on our watch. We should be ashamed of ourselves.'

'You appear to be looking around here for someone to blame.'

'I don't need to look very far for that Councillor Duergar, do I?'

Alma Tadema intervened.

'That is uncalled for, Verra, and this meeting is losing direction fast; we must stick to the point.'

Alma moved towards her to divert her attention, but Duergar was now fully engaged and on a roll. This was exactly what he wanted.

'If you want to blame someone, look no further than your predecessor, Ashtar.'

Alma Tadema moved back immediately, knowing her friend too well and knowing which subjects to bring up and those that should be completely left alone. Unfortunately, Duergar was well aware of them, too, and his first response was to fight fire with fire and incite a reaction in front of the others.

'How dare you mention Ashtar! How dare you even use his name in relation to any of this.'

Alma was now imploring both Councillors.

'This meeting is digressing; we should reconvene again once things have settled. Don't you think?'

Duergar was first to reply.

'I think you should both bid your farewells. We have achieved some of what we intended, and the rest is for Councillor Verra Mica and I to discuss. I would not like to detain you both any longer than necessary. As you say, you are both extremely busy. Thank you for your attendance.'

Baquarrah and Alma nodded and began to leave. Before deregistering from the dome and exiting, Alma gave a helpless look back at Verra Mica, but she was not looking; her sights were on Duergar only, and they both appeared to be locked in and ready for battle.

'Why must you constantly use his name in vain? He took you under his wing when Rammasus abandoned you. He gave himself to bring about change and balance, thanklessly to protect and support us and Eathia.'

'Balance? Just what does "balance" mean to you, Verra? Let's ensure we are actually talking about the same thing before flippantly brandishing it.'

'Oh, so who's lost all "respect" now? No more "Councillor"?'

'No, on the contrary. This is now a discussion between you and I, and it is long overdue.'

'Damn right, it is. To answer your question, the Source, that is The Realm's and Eathia's balance.'

'How predictable. You are overlooking one very large addition. The Accumulator. A creation of the Source itself, and you chose to see it as a forbidden curse. The Source may have decided to mirror Eathia's current status or, to put it another way, it is a deliberate attempt to help us evolve alongside Eathia; after all, this was supposed to be a two-way existence, was it not?' Duergar spoke with an indignant air.

'The Accumulator is the dark energy vortex, syphoned away from Eathia. It was designed to protect them and us.'

'You are wrong, Verra. You have an outdated viewpoint, one which will bring about the downfall of us all, Eathia included.'

Strangely, Duergar remained calm, and Verra Mica was still in defence mode. This made her feel as if she were having to justify her stance. She decided to calm down; this was a debate, after all, and not an inquisition.

Duergar continued.

'It is high time we let the Eathians embrace all within them, light and dark, good and bad, etc. We must give them the freedom to discover their path and live out their fates on their terms, possibly even let them go.'

Verra Mica flared at what he was suggesting; she was right. This is where he was heading. Withdraw from Eathia completely, was he mad? He continued before she could interject.

'Your old ways are fuelling their hatred and anger and provoking extreme emotions by suppressing their true nature, natures we helped to create in the first place.'

'So, what are you suggesting, Duergar? We withdraw our tethers from Eathia, then what? You will be destroying our history within it. The essence is embedded into the core of Eathia. You have no idea of the repercussions that detethering will cause.'

Duergar remained quiet and watched Verra Mica's energy as it swirled about her form, wondering if now was the right time to reveal his intentions. He decided to dilute them slightly.

'You and your mentor may have been on to something when you both felt the need to guide Eathians in a more, shall we say, hands-on approach.'

He waited for Verra Mica to grasp his point.

She glared at him.

'You are fully aware that Ashtar was exiled for that very misinterpretation. There was never a need for a hands-on approach. What are you getting at, Duergar?'

'My suggestion is to embrace the Accumulator as an equal to the Source and use it to our advantage when communicating with the Eathians.'

Verra Mica flew at Duergar, but he quickly countered her attack. Having breached his aura before he could block her, she felt the full force of his response. A thunderous symphony of sound blasted through her, and she flew backwards. She quickly reestablished her ground and manoeuvred herself to a hair's breadth away from him.

Duergar felt slightly underwhelmed at her reaction. He should have given her the undiluted version after all. He found this all very amusing.

'You are making them feel unworthy if they dare to fall from your grace, his grace.'

Verra Mica shot a look at the dome, at the Source's reaction to what he was saying, but there was still nothing. What had he done to it?

'So, this is your intention? Are the others aware of this?'

Duergar moved away from her.

'They will in due course. I thought I would run it by you first. Judging by your reaction ...'

He smiled.

'... I think it will go down quite well.'

'You are living proof that any connection to the Accumulator could be fatal. For goodness' sake, Duergar, you nearly got obliterated at the hands of your mentor. Now you are suggesting we embrace the same ridiculous idea as Rammasus.'

Duergar briefly pondered the memory; he was well aware of his history and didn't need Verra to drag it up to make a point. It was, after all, a shame Rammasus couldn't have stayed around longer. Instead, he had left him to carry on his legacy.

Verra Mica implored Duergar.

'If Ashtar were still here, he would be enraged at the thought of the Accumulator being given credence alongside the Source and for the thought of de-tethering from Eathia. Why can you not understand that it has always been this way for good reason?'

'That does not mean it continues to be the right way.'

Verra Mica paused, still confused at his actions with the recent births.

'So why manipulate the birth of the Triplexes? To what end?'

Duergar smiled.

'Balance, Verra.'

Verra Mica remained silent and thoughtful. Duergar continued.

'We now, finally, have balance.'

A chill swept through Verra Mica's aura. She thought, *and all this from a soul that had never been tethered himself. What a hypocrite.* A realisation deepened in Verra Mica's mind.

'You don't intend to let Elkyne tether, do you? You are doing the same to him that Rammasus did to you.'

Duergar was slightly taken aback by the change in Verra Mica's tactics, but relished a new enlightened perspective.

'Both I and Elkyne are meant for a much higher purpose, not that it has anything to do with you. And this is coming from someone who not only abandoned her own tether midway through her life; Mary, was it? But she also left her young daughter, Sara, if I'm not mistaken. Tut, tut Verra Mica.'

'Because I had no choice but to come back and babysit you! Do you think I wanted to leave Mary without my guidance and protection? I had no choice because Ashtar didn't trust you or Rammasus, and for good reason.'

Duergar didn't rise to the bait. He spoke calmly.

'Speaking of which, I understand from Alma that you feel Ashtar's presence within the Triplexes. How very closed-minded of you. What you are actually saying is that Ashtar had a smidgen of darkness in him too.'

Verra Mica was surprised by his perplexing observation.

He turned to leave and hesitated.

'One more thing, Verra. It will be better for you in the long run if you get on board with the concept of The Realm's evolution. It would be a shame to leave you behind when the time comes.'

Verra Mica hid her despair and disappointment.

With that, Duergar disconnected from the Source and left.

Verra Mica had monitored the Source throughout their conversation. Nothing, no reaction at all. She was confused.

'So, he had attuned after all.' She was baffled.

The images that she was shown within the Source were of destruction, Eathia in turmoil. 'Was this because of Duergar's push for change or, and far more worryingly, if they failed to heed his warning. Or, which was a worse scenario, were they damned either way?' She wondered.

Upon leaving, Duergar sent a message to Baquarrah to release him from his healing. It worked perfectly, and Baquarrah could never have imagined why Duergar needed his help. By creating an impermeable healing field around his aura, not only had it blocked his attendance within the Council altogether, rendering the meeting ineffective, which was the whole point of it, but it had kept him as non-responsive to Verra Mica as possible. No healing could take place without the healer's aura engulfing the receiver. The Source had stayed blissfully unaware of his attendance and his conversation.

Verra Mica gathered her thoughts outside the Council Chamber before returning to her order. She muttered to herself, 'He thinks I'm a gullible idiot. We'll see about that. I'm not falling for his attempts at putting up all these smokescreens. I'll make sure I pull them down, one by one.'

Feeling pleased with himself, Duergar returned to his quarters to organise the next phase. The Accumulator's bravado was indeed a smokescreen and had bought him some time. It had given Verra Mica something to focus on while he got on with the pivotal part of his plan.

Chapter 26
Eathia - Third Era

The Cove of Secrets

After many days and nights, Tobias and Denis finally reached Sirenguard with just enough time to spare before their meeting at the bay and joining his ship. Where they now stood was the highest accessible viewpoint in the south. Laid before them stretched the valley that led to the sea. Rough gravel roads branched off to the left and right, with only the narrow footpath behind from where they had come.

Tobias left it as a surprise for Denis, and his face made it worthwhile.

'So that's the sea? And we're going on that?'

'Yes, that's it. Down there is the forest where my grandparents are laid to rest.'

Tobias pointed towards a large cluster of oak trees. He continued.

'Over there, just to the side of where the mountain range starts.'

Denis studied the vista in awe of its vastness and beauty.

'Why is it called Sirenguard?'

Tobias smiled warmly.

'It's a local folktale, told by many with similar experiences of this area. It became a legend over time. The source of the name is a tale for tonight, by a campfire. Come on, let's keep going.'

He ruffled his son's head, catching a glimpse of his scar, still noticeable on his forehead. Denis darted his head sideways and frowned at him. Then, he gave in and grinned.

'Why are we staying here? I thought we were heading out today?'

'The ship arrives tomorrow. Why?'

Denis scuffed the heel of one of his shoes along the dusty path.

'I just didn't want to stay here. Feels weird sleeping near your dead grandparents.'

Tobias couldn't help but laugh at his son's discomfort. Denis reluctantly followed him down the steep, winding path to the cabin his grandfather, Thomas, had built for his grandmother, Mary.

As the ground became flatter, the path disappeared. Grass lay underfoot, slightly covered by fallen leaves. As they moved on, the landscape began to open, and Denis could finally see the start of what looked like a farm dwelling with a wooden cabin nestled in at the far side. He was surprised to see movement on the porch and smoke rising up from the cabin.

'The chimney's alight, there's smoke.'

'That'll be Guss. He stays here to look after the old place. He'll be with us on the ship, too. He's an old friend and, more importantly, a great cook.'

'You never said there'd be someone here,' Denis exclaimed, feeling awkward.

'What does it matter, son? You've got to get used to strangers now until they become friends, that is.'

Tobias winked at him, stopped, dropped his sack and called out to the old guy with a bird-like crow. Denis winced, feeling embarrassed.

'Is that necessary?'

'It is if you don't want to get shot. This is a smuggler's cove now. It can get a bit dangerous if the wrong sort comes in unannounced. That and Guss's eyesight isn't what it used to be.'

Denis visibly retreated a little.

'I don't like it here.'

As they drew nearer, Denis could see a shortish, elderly man with grey hair. He had a large green knitted hat covering most of it. The hair that wasn't trying to escape from the sides of the hat merged with the same unruly mass of grey beard. Denis inquisitively scanned the rest of the old gent. His belly was protruding out from the bottom of his jumper.

Denis watched as the man leaned forward, resting his hands on his knees. He squinted at them as he tried to focus. His trousers were rolled up to his knees, and he didn't appear to wear shoes or socks. Denis tutted and looked away. Once the old guy recognised Tobias, he slapped his leg and danced off the porch, yipping with delight at the sight of his friend.

'I was wondering if you were coming at all, you rascal. Who's this handsome chap? Can't be one of yours. You're too ugly.'

He laughed aloud, and now Denis was nearer he could see the gaps in his mouth where teeth should have been.

'Dad?'

Tobias was too caught up in the joys of seeing Guss again. Guss looked at Denis and continued.

'You here to follow in ya Da's footsteps, hey son?'

They met at the gate, and Guss slapped Denis hard on his back.

Denis rubbed at the sting left behind.

'Ouch, that was unnecessarily hard.'

'Nice to meet ya, boy.'

'Denis, my name is Denis.'

Guss hugged Tobias and turned back towards the house, not registering an ounce of Denis's discomfort.

'Denis, ya say. Yeah, well, there's nothing we can do about that now, son. We all have our crosses to bear.'

Denis frowned at Tobias, waiting for him to stand up for him. Instead, his dad just laughed.

'You'll get used to their sense of humour.'

'What? How many are in there?'

'Oh, just Guss. You'll meet the rest of them tomorrow.'

'Can't wait,' Denis said sarcastically.

Denis's attention was drawn to Guss's bare feet again.

Why, he thought, *would he let himself look at the things that freaked him out the most about people? These were the worst he'd ever seen.*

He started to feel slightly nauseous at the sight of the stained, dirty toes. He shook his head to try loosening the image from his mind.

A little later that afternoon, after they cleaned up and ate, Tobias took Denis out to show him around and to take him to his grandparents' graves before it got too dark. His father didn't just want to introduce him to his home. He had a few surprises he could only tell Denis about when they were at his homestead.

They walked towards a large oak that towered over all the trees around it, making them look more like saplings. Its shadow spread low and long across the ground in the late afternoon light. The dappled rays twinkled in the breeze and danced across three large stones erected evenly next to each other. Tobias hung his head for a moment, a respectful silence, before walking to where they rested.

Denis followed cautiously, not knowing the right etiquette for this situation.

'Why are there three?'

'That's one of the things I wanted to tell you while we were here.'

Tobias knelt by the smaller of the three and cleared some of the fallen twigs and leaves from the small mound.

'It's my aunt. Her name was Sara.'

He looked up at his son but could only see his silhouette. Which, at that moment, might have been a blessing. He hadn't finished by a long shot. He didn't want the look on Denis's face to cause him to put this off any longer. He looked back at Sara's headstone.

'I never met her, but she was a courageous little thing by all accounts. They were shipwrecked here, of all things. Decided to stay.'

Denis looked at all three graves and the faded names engraved on them. They showed enough for him to see for himself the inconsistencies.

Sara's and Mary's surname was Speranza, and his grandfather was Thomas (Gully) Grinder.

'Why does he have a different surname?'

'My grandfather wasn't her father …'

Tobias stopped. His body tensed as it had done so many times before when he wanted to sit Denis down and explain, not just the truth about his family's history, but their current family situation too. He dug deep to try and find the courage to continue. Denis was immediately aware that Tobias had cut the sentence short and was curious why.

'What is it?'

Tobias stood up. Now, he did need to see his son's face. He walked away from the graves, leading Denis away from them, as if the bodies below them might judge what he had to say.

'That's one of the things I needed to talk to you about. I figured you should know, and here seemed the best place to tell you.'

Denis raised a mistrusting eyebrow.

'It's about your sister, Bertha.'

Tobias continued quickly.

'She wasn't born into our family like you were. I'm trying to say that she isn't mine like you. She is mum's but from a previous … situation.'

Tobias frowned at himself for not being able to find the words he needed to make this all sound better. He had had long enough, after all.

Denis's mouth dropped open.

'She had a different father.'

He turned to look back at Sara's grave.

'Just like my aunt. Thomas wasn't her father either. Not in the biological sense of the word, anyhow. I mean, he brought her up like she was his own, but …'

He felt Denis pull himself together enough to start the myriads of questions he obviously had every right to ask; Tobias knew that but continued anyway.

'Bertha was born in a place where your mother lived before. A village called Cullvelley. Shortly after that, we fled here to Sirenguard for safety.'

'So, what you're saying is that she isn't my sister?'

His words were calmer than Tobias expected, maybe a little too cold for his liking.'Of course, she is Denis; she is every part your sister as she is my daughter.'

'What? But that's not true, is it? Why hasn't she said anything to me?'

Tobias looked down. His silence spoke volumes.

'You're kidding me. She doesn't even know, does she? Have neither of you told her?'

'Your mother and I decided it was safer that she …'

'SAFER?'

Denis went to walk away, and Tobias urged him to wait.

'The stories she transcribes. They come from the orb, the reflector. For years, she has been told about the past, our past. Other worlds.'

Denis glared at Tobias.

'I know, she's read them to me enough. So?'

'Over time, we have realised the stories are real. They are real moments captured by the orb and passed on to Bertha for safekeeping. Anyway, the one story she hasn't been told is her own.'

Denis frowned at his father, confused about what point he was trying to make. Tobias continued.

'Her story reaches further than she can see. Her story is happening now, with us, but she can't see it for good reason. So, your mother and I decided it should stay that way and not divulge everything to her. And yes, for her safety.'

'Safe from what or who. What are you trying to protect her from?'

Tobias shook his head. Even to him, this all sounded so far-fetched, and he had known about it for years. How could he have expected Denis, of all people, to just take it as valid?

'Does everyone know about this? Uncle Augustus? Did Francis know?'

Tobias sighed and nodded, feeling defeated.

'Well, I'm going to talk to Uncle Augustus when I get back. Maybe he'll finally tell me the truth, too.'

Denis stormed back towards the graves, his anger starting to rise. He stared down at them, trying to work out the flood of emotions beating against his head and his heart. He looked up at the sky, at the slow-moving clouds and had to stop himself from swaying with them. He felt giddy. He looked at the top of the tree to get some sense of stillness, down at the branches, continuing down to the sturdy, heavily barked trunk. He stopped looking further when he couldn't believe what he saw.

There, etched into the trunk, was her name.

B E R T H A

Denis spun around and faced his father.

'What else haven't you told me? You know what, don't bother. I can't take all this in.'

With that, Denis turned and stormed back towards the cabin.

Tobias shouted after him.

He went to follow him, then stopped and sighed in frustration. He turned, walked back and stood in front of the graves; kneeling, he looked at his grandmother Mary's gravestone.

'That went slightly worse than I expected.'

His eyes naturally lifted to read the engraved name on the tree. He smiled and remembered the day they had all picnicked next to it.

Mary had carved Bertha's name and had said that one day, her name would be etched on everyone's hearts. He looked back at her gravestone.

Mary was a sage; her knowledge and wisdom outweighed her slight, unassuming appearance. Tobias remembered how she always saw something other worldly in Bertha that no one else was aware of. She was special, and Mary was always worried about her safety. Knowing what he did now, she had good reason, but how would he pass any of this knowledge down to Denis? It was one of the reasons Sophia had agreed to his coming, so he could finally know, in the future, that he had as much of a role to play in Bertha's safety as they all did.

Goose pimples ran across Tobias's body. He hadn't even started telling Denis the history of Bertha's past.

Tobias looked about, taking in the hillside's contours and the change in the trees, which had been much taller since his last visit. The breeze rolled up from the sea and swathed his face in warm sea air. His gaze followed the roughly made path as it led away from him. Ghostly images of his parents, bags in hand, materialised in front of him. He was just a young boy. He had watched as they turned and waved, his mother blew a kiss, and his father placed his arm around her to ensure she wasn't having any last-minute doubts. He never knew if she had or not. He never saw either of them again.

Tobias was only four when his parents left Sirenguard to return to their homeland, but his grandmother and Thomas forbade them from taking Tobias. After the loss of Sara, from what they thought was because of the treacherous journey they had undertaken, there was no way Tobias could be put through the same trauma. So, he had been raised by his grandparents. Occasionally, they received letters from his parents, but they stopped suddenly and never heard from them again.

Tobias stood up and stretched his legs. The days of wondering had long left him, and he turned to look in the direction where Denis had stormed off.

Denis was nowhere to be seen.

The door flew open in the cabin as an angry Denis entered.

Guss, who'd been sitting peacefully by the stove, suddenly jumped at the shock of the intrusion. He involuntarily spat his pipe out, emptying all its burning contents over his trousers and the floor.

'Bloody hell fire, what the … Oh Denis, it's you.'

Guss coughed and started to swipe away the hot ashes from his trousers as they began to singe the material.

'He's told you then?'

'What, you knew too. Who else? So, you know my sister? No, stop, scratch that. You know Bertha, the girl who's posing as my sister?'

'Well …'

'You know what, forget it. I've got to get out of here.'

His eyes were drawn down to Guss's feet again.

'Why don't you ever wear shoes or socks?'

Denis grabbed his coat from the back of the chair and left, slamming the door behind him.

Still patting down the glowing scorched holes in his trousers, Guss started to clear the tobacco up from the rug before that caught fire, too. He glanced down at his feet. He muttered to an empty room.

'Never felt the need, till now, that is.'

He tutted before setting off in search of Tobias.

He chuckled when he remembered little Bertha's name for the graves. Father Oakleigh's Teeth. She called them. She never liked the thought of them as graves with dead bodies underneath them.

Denis headed for the cove. He'd roughly worked out where it was from the cabin, following the direction of his father's nod of the head when he was explaining where they would meet the other men on the ship the next day.

As he neared the edge of the grass, he could see a sheer drop in the rock's face as it fell away ahead of him. As he looked over the edge, a 'v' shape gap emerged, eventually leading down to the pebbled shoreline.

Denis considered returning as dusk approached but continued down the rocky slope. The cove was still beautiful even in the fading light, with hills curving around it and rocks scattered near the shore. The pale sand and the sound of the tide made it even more breathtaking. Denis understood why his father found it hard to leave this place.

Burning wood smoke, trapped in the gap of the small cove, was starting to push up towards him, caught on the breeze. It caught the back of his throat. He coughed, then muffled it, realising he wasn't alone. *Maybe the men are here early?* he thought, *camping out, ready for an early start tomorrow.* But there was no ship as far as he could see.

He carefully moved over to the right side of the ridge, clinging to its rock face as he continued down the hill.

The campfire crackled and sputtered as one of the men tossed a damp piece of wood onto the smouldering embers. A thick, pungent smoke billowed upwards, then vanished into the irregular wind tunnels formed by the shape of the cove. Two long wooden torches were lit on the right side of the waterfront, one on each side of what appeared to be a cavern. Denis could hear water sloshing toward a darkened tunnel in the rock face. The man walked away from the fire, passed through the torches and entered the opening, then disappeared.

Still trying to hug the rock surface, he quietly scaled its sharp edges as he lowered himself to get a closer look without risking being seen.

A banging sound repeatedly hit the side of the rocks near the cavern. In the dim light, Denis could make out a small boat floating in and out with the motion of the waves. It had been secured to a rock on the shore, and it was this that kept hitting the side of the rock.

Denis muttered to himself, 'I'm no sailor, but even I know that's a stupid thing to do.'

He slowly made his way over to the tunnel. Other than the rhythmical thudding, all seemed quiet both on the shore and in the cave.

Denis grinned to himself.

This is better than Stonehaven any day, he thought. Grabbing one of the torches, he decided to venture into the abyss. 'Nothing ventured, nothing gained.' Confidently quoting one of his father's sayings to himself.

As he moved slowly onward, the sounds of the shore retreated gradually.

His new surroundings became echoey as the regular lapping of the water rolled in and up the slippery sides of the tunnel with each wave. The arched walls curved up and around him. Their covering of mineral deposits and algae shimmered silver, green and grey in mottled fusions in the half-light of the flame from the torch. As his eyes became more accustomed to the cave's darkness, he could see an orange glow ahead of him. The tunnel's entrance curved to the right. The aperture naturally dimmed any light from it.

He paused and listened.

I can't turn back now, he thought.

Then he noticed that the water around his feet started gushing and swirling. There was regular swooshing from behind him that felt almost as though …

The voice boomed in his ears.

'Who the bloody hell are you?'

Denis was grabbed violently from behind and thrown against the wall, its slippery surface causing him to slide down into the water. The man grabbed him again and dragged him upwards until he was level with his face.

'Oi, lads, we've got ourselves a snooper. Get in there.'

He pushed Denis forward, keeping a tight grip on his shirt.

'I didn't know anything was in here. Let me go.'

As they turned the corner, the cave opened into a multi-layered cavern. It reminded Denis of a beehive. The water level was higher as the sea crashed in from at least three large openings to the side. Rows upon rows of barrels and boxes had been stacked up on the higher levels of the ledges. The lower ones showing signs of white salt-like deposits around them.

Three men waded towards them. His untimely entrance had stopped two of the men from arguing.

Denis was now being dragged into an open space in the centre of the cave, which was brighter; more torches were wedged between the rock's natural crevices.

'Just let me go. I just came down to see the cove.'

'Can't let you go, laddie; you've seen too much.'

'Well, I wouldn't have done if you hadn't dragged me in here, would I?'

A fist came from the man before him and caught him completely unaware. His head jolted backwards, paralysing his neck muscles so his head fell forward, completely immersing him in the seawater. He felt like he was going to pass out. The coldness of the water brought him back quickly before he inhaled too much into his lungs. When he was pulled out again, he was coughing and choking up salty water.

'I don't think he realises the trouble he's in, Toff.'

'We didn't need this; we're supposed to be leaving tomorra.'

Denis suddenly realised that they could be his father's shipmates after all, and the knot in his stomach relaxed slightly.

'Are you going on the ship tomorrow? You must know my father.'

'Ship, what ship?'

The man behind him, still holding him, pulled him back and looked at the others to see if they heard him, too.

'WHAT SHIP?'

'I'm going out tomorrow with my father. We're working, making new sails.'

He brought Denis's face up close to his again. He stank of alcohol. Denis kicked back to try and get away.

'Get in there now where we can keep an eye on ya.'

The smaller of the men, who had remained silent until now, grunted.

'We weren't told of no ship; he's lying. If it's true, it'll ruin everything.'

With his eyes still stinging from the seawater, Denis could now make out all three men in front of him. He blinked and shook the water out of his ear. They had gone quiet, and if he wasn't mistaken, they were staring past him and at something behind him. Denis groaned and waited for the blow to come from the man who still had hold of his collar.

Instead, he heard a familiar voice.

'Let go of my son and turn around slowly. NOW!'

Tobias and Guss stood firm, both with rifles in their hands and resting on their hips, aiming them straight at the smugglers.

Tobias urged Denis to join them.

'Come on, son, we're leaving.'

Denis's legs felt heavy and weak as he pushed through the water and made his way over to his father.

'You got this, Guss?'

'Yep. Go on, take the lad back up, I'll just be a minute.'

Denis looked sideways at his father as they left; he then turned to watch Guss to see what he would do. Tobias talked calmly to his son.

'Just keep walking.'

As they cleared the mouth of the cave, the shots started to ring out, their sounds reverberating from the walls. Denis put his arms over his head and ducked, slipping forward and falling onto his knees. They continued to echo as the sound ricocheted through his waterlogged ears, which only reignited his fear. His body became weak and he felt himself collapse forward.

Tobias showed no such fear; he kept hold of his son's arm and pulled him back up onto his legs. Half dragged, half supported him back towards the cabin, almost pulling him along as he went. Still in shock, Denis remained silent throughout the journey, the gravity of what had just happened slowly seeping through his emotional numbness.

At the cabin, Tobias led Denis over to Guss's chair, and he then disappeared into one of the rooms. He shouted back at Denis.

'Sit down and warm up by the fire, and I'll get you a coffee.'

'I don't drink coffee.'

It was out of his mouth before he thought to be slightly more gracious, considering the predicament his dad and Guss had just saved him from.

Tobias threw a dry shirt at his son.

'On second thoughts, get that wet stuff off first.'

As Denis stood up from the chair, Guss came in through the door, followed by a gust of cold air caught on the breeze, Denis could smell the unmistakable aroma of gun smoke. Leaning the rifle against the wall, he clapped his hands together and walked past Denis and over to the fire. Taking his pipe out of his pocket, he looked at him and winked. Denis backed away slightly. Pulling the wet shirt off in one tug, he quickly dragged the dry one over his head. Not taking his eyes from Guss as he tried to read his expression.

'Why did you only shoot three of them? There were four and you only shot three times?'

Guss glanced over to Tobias and his lips quivered until he burst into laughter.

'Shoot them? What son? You think I shot, um?'

Tobias joined in initially but quickly calmed himself when he realised his son wasn't joking.

'I didn't kill anyone, lad. I hit them where it hurt.'

He turned back to Tobias.

'Right through their stinking thieving barrels of rum. You should have seen them. All running to find something to plug the holes with. That'll teach'em.'

He lit his pipe and puffed a few times to get it going. Denis watched the smoke as it got dragged towards the open hearth, disappearing up into the chimney.

Guss went to kick his boots off but looked up at Denis and thought better of it. He tutted and shook his head.

'We have an agreement, lad. We turn a blind eye to them if they leave us alone. We can't stop um, as long as there's a bit of mutual respect. They stepped over the line this time. Mind you, so did you, boy, vanishing like that.'

'Go on, have a coffee, there's one on the stove, and just relax. You've had a hell of a day.'

'I don't drink … oh, what's the use!'

'Hellfire boy, calm down. What then? Ale?'

'Tea. I drink tea.'

'You, soppy sod. That's an old lady's drink, tea.'

He looked across at Tobias.

'What sort of stuff have you been teaching this lad?'

Guss turned to Denis.

'Just as well you've come to the cove now, son, and in the nick of time by the looks of it. Uncle Guss'll teach you a few things. You'll be downing kegs of ale for breakfast by the time I finish with you.'

He chuckled, finding himself amusing.

Tobias watched his son in the warm light of the fire. He looked seven again and completely out of his depth with this whole trip, but it would make him stronger. He was sure of that.

'Come on, son, turn in. Guss is right; you've had more than enough for one day.'

Leading his son towards his bed for the night, Tobias glanced back at Guss, who nodded reassuringly. A silent gesture between the two men signified that it would all turn out fine in the end.

But it couldn't.

They would never allow it.

He would make sure of it.

Chapter 27
The Realm

Hidden History

Once Christi left Makaria, she caught up with Verra Mica while exiting the Council meeting. Being in The Realm without Elkyne or Corpus felt strange to her. Both were out of sight; Elkyne's whereabouts remained unknown, and Corpus was now tethered to a young boy named Gabriel on Eathia. Christi hoped to be tethered soon as well. As she approached Verra Mica, she sensed that something was wrong.

'Something has happened. Was it the meeting?'

'Yes indeed. Would you come with me? I need to update you fully before I return to my students. Do you have any news for me?'

Verra Mica stopped to listen to Christi at the tunnel that led to her quarters.

'I have met with Makaria; she insists that Angelica initially went missing because of Duergar, but she has matters in her own hands for now. She also feels that there is tension in the ranks of the Psybiencians. She senses that things aren't quite going Duergar's way at present. But you are correct in being cautious of him. They do have something going on. Were you able to glean anything from him during the meeting?'

'Oh yes. Do you know, I hadn't realised how many followers Duergar had cajoled into his twisted mindset?'

When she was sure they could not be heard, she continued.

'Christi, I must start by letting you know that what I say is only between us now. Is that understood?'

'Even from Corpus?'

'You can let Corpus know the details as you see fit.'

She continued in a hushed tone.

'What hasn't been passed onto us from the Source became clear during the meeting of the Council. You are right, it appears that Duergar is planning some sort of mass exodus from Eathia. I can't see how he thinks he will get away with this. I assume it will be a gradual event where we fail to replenish those Soul Guardians who leave their tethers once they have passed away. That will take time and allow us to think of a plan ourselves. I have never known of a Soul Guardian ignoring a pull from a new birth on Eathia; it just doesn't make sense, but then I don't have Duergar's convictions.'

'He said this in the meeting. What of the rest of the Council, what did they say to his suggestions?'

'He twists words; he thought he was being clever, and it appeared they bought into it all, agreeing with him and accepting his reasoning. I don't trust him. By the time the other council members wise up to him and his devious secrets, it will be too late.'

'I was shown nothing of Duergar. He is a mystery to both Corpus and me. Is it possible that the Source is unaware of his actions? Is he able to disconnect from it somehow?'

'I believe Duergar is shrouding the Source in some way. Keeping his movements secret from it. I don't know how yet. If that's the case, he managed to keep all of our conversations separate from it.'

Interfering with the Source was unthinkable. Christi wondered if all three of the Triplexes had been manipulated.

'Have we been created by the Source, or Duergar Superior?'

Verra Mica was shocked at her frankness.

'All three of you were born to create a wonderful change. From my time in the Source, I see that your purpose is to support The Realm, not to oppose it. Yet, Duergar seems quite determined to keep you all separated. It's becoming clearer that the knowledge you've received may lead you down very different paths. His plans are external and not inspired by the Source.'

'You say you know little of Duergar based on what the Source has told you. I will, therefore, update you as soon as possible. Our time is short, Christi, your tether could activate your core at any moment so rather than waste your valuable time discussing it. I will transfer the information directly to you.'

'I need more details, Superior. If I am to conduct myself from the wishes of the Source, I need to know more about Duergar and his past.'

Verra Mica thought and quickly decided to transfer what she knew of him to her. It was safer than openly expressing it and quicker.

Duergar and Verra Mica were born to restore balance due to Eathia and The Realm's misguidance. He was the firstborn and a pure Psybiencian, like his mentor, Rammasus. While merely a student, Duergar's mentor suddenly disappeared, believed to have ventured into the Accumulator, which was his obsession. In his absence, Ashtar, leader of the Seraphytes, watched over Duergar and was set to mentor Verra Mica.

Then, unexpectedly, Rammasus returned. Ashtar, whom Duergar admired, had to relinquish care of him due to Rammasus's return and Ashtar's impending tethering, which at the time was vital to Eathia.

Duergar shone in Ashtar's favour until Rammasus returned. Duergar never was the same again, nor was Rammasus after his absence. Something changed him; his perspective shifted and Duergar bore the consequences.

Christi's attention wandered from the message Verra Mica had sent her.

'What happened to Rammasus? Do we know anything?'

Verra Mica spoke aloud.

'The fool had entered the Accumulator but had somehow made it back to The Realm, which, by all accounts, is an impossibility.'

Verra Mica continued.

'After that, Duergar began to withdraw. His admiration for Ashtar faded into contempt, especially after what happened.'

'What do you mean?'

Verra Mica realised that Christi knew nothing of her own and Ashtar's withdrawal from Eathia.

'Once tethered, Ashtar broke the divine rule of The Realm and was forced to leave due to his actions. He felt he had good reason to do so, but the consequences for the Source, me included, and for him were felt to outweigh his decision to … well … bring his tether back to life.'

Christi was astonished; it wasn't what she expected.

'His tether? He brought an Eathian back to life?'

'Ashtar had no choice. There was something he had to tell his Eathian wife, Mary. He had seen something during his journey back to The Realm. She was my tether, you see. His re-tethering did indeed bring his Eathian back to life, but his energy was drained significantly. Ashtar struggled to return to The Realm, where he needed the Illumacytes' healing.'

Christi tried to comprehend everything that her Superior was saying. Verra Mica continued.

'When he did return, he was brought to order by the High Council and accused of manipulating an Eathian's life while trying to fulfil his own agenda. They couldn't have got it any more wrong, but Ashtar realised he could not stay and left The Realm, wounded and without a word about where he was going. Certain planets were in alignment at that time, and it was thought he had managed to salvage his little energy and use it to portal himself away.'

'So why did he say you had to leave your tether, Mary, so quickly?'

'I was needed here. Considering what Ashtar witnessed at the time of his initial return when his Eathian tether had died, he became aware of some revolt fuelled by Rammasus. When he realised he would need to leave The Realm for good, I was the only Soul Guardian to take his place. I had to choose between staying with Mary or returning to protect The Realm from their anarchism. I've been fighting it ever since.'

Christi was horrified.

'Some choice! I'm unsure what I would have done in your position, but I am grateful you protected The Realm. For all our sakes.'

'Which brings us to the Duergar we know and love today. He now feels that the experiences he had back then were the making of him. He has become a true force to be reckoned with since. His students adore him and he achieves tremendous results with them. I can't deny that.'

Christi admired Verra Mica's attempt at being gracious.

'The Psybiencians have always been a private order, Christi; they regularly veil, which results in them being separated from the Source, so endless amounts of actions never get recorded. Duergar relies on this. I genuinely feel my rise to Superiority and then on to High Councillor was to balance Duergar's extremism.'

'Do you have any idea where Ashtar might be now?'

'My honest answer is that I felt he had possibly gone to another world. One aligned at the time was a planet known as Quitara. That could be a logical answer.'

'Do you still believe that now?'

'I think it is very likely that he has chosen to resurrect himself in you three. I felt him when you were born, and so did Alma Tadema, and at the time, she was closer to him than I.'

Verra Mica then explained what had happened with the dome before their birth sequence.

Christi thought for a moment. She was about to reply, but then stopped. Both she and Verra Mica suddenly noticed a change in her energetic core.

'It is happening, Christi. Your tether is ready and it is a timely interruption. Let's move to your Solescence Chamber, at least you will be nearer should she be born imminently.'

Christi's aura began to glow.

Corpus was waiting for Christi once they reached the chamber. He knew that her tether had become active and wanted to wish her luck. Christi burst into excitement when she saw him. They flew to each other with lights ablaze and Verra Mica watched, admiring their natural connection.

'How is it? Is it what you thought it would be, Corpus?'

Corpus laughed.

'Yes, it is and more. I've missed you and can't wait for you to join me.'

He looked across at their Superior. They composed themselves and joined her.

'Superior, I trust all is well?'

'All is a little unsure at present, Corpus; however, I feel we are getting somewhere thanks to my loyal Soul Guardians.'

Verra Mica backed away from them.

'Now, I have taken much of your time. Please go with my blessing. Know that I am very proud of you both.'

They bowed, and Corpus led Christi to the edge of the well. The mist rose to meet her as if to offer her safe passage. The baby girl, Beatrice, would be born on Eathia. They both jumped and disappeared, leaving Verra Mica alone with her thoughts. Just as they disappeared from her sight, a new presence was felt and it was close by.

He unveiled himself fully.

'Elkyne!'

Chapter 28
The Realm

Allegiance

Elkyne moved towards Verra Mica from the chamber entrance where he had been silently watching.

'My apologies for not lowering my veil sooner, Superior.'

'You keep popping up everywhere, but I never get to speak with you properly. You have just missed Corpus and Christi.'

Elkyne's energy fluctuated and dropped, a sign of despair. He seemed distant to Verra Mica.

'Was it them you had come to see?'

'I did not come to eavesdrop if that's what you think.'

'I didn't think that for one moment. I imagine it was simply that you were aware that Christi was to be tethered.'

'I wished to speak with her before she left, but it was not to be.'

Elkyne's sadness again emanated from his aura, and Verra Mica felt deeply for him.

'Elkyne, Christi is very fond of you, they both are. They and I want what's best for you. You do understand that, don't you?'

Elkyne's manner stiffened. Either he didn't want to hear her words, or couldn't allow himself to listen to them.

'I am divided, your Honour. My allegiance is with The Realm; however, my ties are with your adversary. Made even more complicated by what I have just understood to be a download between yourself and Christi.'

Verra Mica was horrified at the thought that Elkyne could have overheard what she had spoken to Christi about earlier. They were Triplexes; why hadn't she realised that downloading information had the potential of going to all three of them? She must be careful in the future. Elkyne realised her shock and continued, wanting to reassure her.

'I have no intention of mentioning it to Duergar. It appears I am forced to live out my time torn between those I love and admire and those I am in allegiance with. History appears to be repeating itself.'

'I understand Elkyne, and I am grateful to you. You have been born into a challenging time for The Realm. Please know that I am always here for you, too. May I ask if there has been any mention of a tether for you?'

'No, not for me, another thing I have in common with Duergar and Rammasus. It's an easily avoidable subject for Duergar, one I have given up enquiring about.'

Elkyne fell silent and watched the lake. It had settled, and all signs of Christi and Corpus had gone. Verra Mica spoke quietly and with affection.

'I will leave you in peace with your thoughts. Know that I am proud of you also, and Elkyne, there is never a need to veil when you are with me or your brother and sister. I am always happy to share my thoughts with you, just as much as Corpus and Christi; our only concern is that we compromise your situation even more.'

Verra Mica did not wait; a response was not what she intended for Elkyne to feel he had to offer her. Once she had left, he walked over to the lake and peered in. Mist obscured his view of his siblings falling to their Eathian tethers, and he could only imagine how it must have felt. A cold shard ran through his being and his mournfulness severed instantly. Without looking back, he left the chamber quickly, eager to go anywhere but here or the Psybiencian order. He was not ready to return there, not yet.

Waiting outside the Accumulator, Duergar stared at its walls, deep in thought. The energy emitted from it was colossal, and the noise that now bled from the Axion Chiral field that webbed around its outer remit continued its thunderous warning to all, not to come any closer.

It was a forbidden zone within The Realm and for good reason. Duergar, however, absorbed all the vibrations it had to offer with an unnatural hunger, drawing them into the centre of his being for his assimilation. Through these immense vibrations, he could read exactly where the alignment of the Accumulator's portal was in relation to Eathia and its ever-moving orbit about The Realm. It was close. Everything was falling together, well, *nearly everything*, he thought.

Duergar shouted into the space around him as his aura flared.

'Where is he?'

Frustrated, he scanned Elkyne and thankfully found him quickly. What was he doing in a Solescence Chamber? As the many chambers overlapped, luckily for Elkyne, Duergar could not see which one he was in, so he could not draw any conclusion from his direct disobedience. He could see that Elkyne was now moving on.

'Good. Finally.'

Duergar watched his movements, slightly confused at his lack of urgency. Then Elkyne took a detour.

'NO! Now, where are you going? Not this way, that's for sure. Damn you, boy.'

He angrily sent a message to him again and waited for a response. Nothing, not one acknowledgement. He couldn't contain his fury anymore and unintentionally sent out a blast wave that impacted against the sides of the Axion field's wall. As it hit its extremely dense surface, the blast reverberated back at him, causing him to be pushed away.

Regaining his composure, he laughed at himself, amused at his quick temper. Spinning round, he turned to leave and return to his quarters.

'You're wasting my precious time, Elkyne.'

Once Elkyne had left Verra Mica, he decided to go and find a reliable and sympathetic friend instead of returning to his order.

Olpheira was an Illumacyte Soul Guardian who, because of her skills and position as a healer, had a naturally unbiased and impartial opinion, which, considering Elkyne's complex situation, was the only Soul Guardian in The Realm who made any sense to him.

Her confidential role was to support the Soul Guardians only within The Realm, and like Elkyne, she seemed destined never to tether, so she knew what frustrations that brought.

As he approached Olpheira, he felt the call come in from Duergar. The pressure erupted within his core and he found it hard to disguise his anger.

When she saw him, she glowed. A natural response from an Illumacyte when healing was needed, but it was also heightened by her feelings for him.

'You are troubled again, Elkyne. No need to ask why you are here. What's he been up to this time?'

'I just want peace, and I cannot seem to achieve it in whatever I do or wherever I go. I am lost, Olpheira, you and only you can give me the space to think. I appreciate your friendship and your gift, believe me.'

Elkyne entered the Illumacytes chamber and rested.

'Elkyne, as a gifted Soul Guardian, you possess the ability to understand all our ways through the Source. However, you lack direction and commitment because of your Triplex status. Speaking with Makaria may help. She has experience in this area, and, be it short-lived, she may be able to help.'

'She's the last Soul Guardian who would want to see me. Makaria is angry with me. She thinks I know Angelica's whereabouts and that I am in some way in league with Duergar regarding her sister's disappearance. I don't think she'd want to talk openly to me now, least about sibling relationships.'

'I heard about the situation with Angelica. I know you could not be involved, Elkyne.'

'I have nothing to do with it. I need to have boundaries that I cannot keep crossing over from one order to another without weaving a web of lies and deceit everywhere I go, and I am losing myself trying to support and be loyal to both sides. What would you have me do?'

'It is not I who needs to make peace with my destiny, Elkyne. I understand you love Christi and Corpus, but I sense that you are mixing up your allegiances because you have deep and natural feelings for …'

Elkyne interrupted abruptly.

'Corpus is a joke; I feel nothing for him.'

'I was going to say feelings for all the orders; however, you have made your predicament slightly clearer. It is, in fact, Christi that is compromising you.'

Elkyne realised he had let slip his fondness and loyalty for Christi.

'Speak with Christi, Elkyne. She will understand, and maybe out of that connection, a bridge can be made between you and the Seraphytes that will enable you not to feel so out on the edge of everything; you two could be the answer to ending this constant conflict that's gone on since Ashtar and Rammasus supervised The Realm. Goodness knows we could all do with peace as far as that is concerned. And as for Corpus, well, he has a strong, confident nature, which, to be honest, he will need if he is truly going to be able to turn our fates around. We all have a part to play, Elkyne. You need to settle on yours.'

Elkyne grimaced and a wave of anger washed through him again. Olpheira saw something change in him.

'What is happening?'

'Duergar is trying to reach me, but I don't want to meet him. He can be overpowering and I rarely agree with him. It's frustrating to be stunted by his wishes and whims. You are right; Corpus is an active and forthright Soul Guardian making a difference, and I, his twin, am beholden. For what, I am at a loss.'

'Come here, close to me.'

Olpheira drew Elkyne in towards her aura and tuned in to him. Elkyne felt a beautiful numbing sensation and all the turmoil seemed to float away, blocked momentarily from entering his aura. He looked at Olpheira and realised that she was healing him. He let go and allowed her to take control. As she did, he became invisible to all in The Realm, a by-product of having healing. She was shocked at his anguish, and it was getting worse. If he could only see just how special he was. She gazed down at him, full of love and admiration, a look that would fall unseen and unnoticed by him.

Once her healing was complete, his anger became a distant whisper. He looked up at her in awe of her abilities to care so much.

'What would I do without you?'

'Make a difference.'

Elkyne recoiled slightly, not expecting Olpheira to bring him back from his trance-like state with such bluntness.

'What do you mean?'

'Elkyne, I enjoy helping you, but you must start acting on your instincts. Masking your pain only delays the inevitable. You must decide who you are and trust the Source's choice. Make peace with your siblings and focus on your work.'

This was the honesty and the beauty of Olpheira, love with a truthful sting.

'I never know what I will feel when I leave you. Thank you, as ever, for your kindness.'

'My dear Elkyne …'

Before Olpheira could finish, Elkyne was preparing to leave, and she sensed his veil returning.

'I will consider your observations of me as ever, I promise. Being with you offers me clarity. I think you are right; it is time to move forward. I appear to be the only one questioning my role, so again, thank you for your morality and wisdom.'

She had him there for a moment, and all she could do, all she was allowed to do, was watch him close himself down and leave. Maybe it was for the best.

As Elkyne left the Illumacytes, he felt Duergar's increasingly agitated call for attendance. Thanks to Olpheira, he felt resolute. He would set aside his feelings for Christi and what he overheard from Verra Mica and would not think or discuss it again. There was only one path for him; he no longer had the luxury of choice, as that had already been decided.

He finally left to meet up with Duergar, ready to show his allegiance.

Chapter 29
Eathia - Third Era

Shalako's Grace

At first light, Tobias, Denis and Guss made their way down to the cove to meet the ship. Not another word was mentioned about the previous day's events.

Denis stepped over dry land and onto land that seemed to be able to live half underwater and half outside of it. He could smell where both merged, aromas he had never encountered before. He wasn't sure if he wanted to inhale it. Bright green slippery seaweed mingled in with perfectly formed oval pebbles that spread out around where he stood and stretched out into the water. After the previous night's darkness, the view he now saw had been completely hidden and lost to him. He stopped and took in its beauty.

Tobias quietly came over and stood next to him.

'There's nothing like it, hey?'

Denis smiled as his hair was blown back from his face. He decided that it smelled of freedom if freedom had a smell.

Tobias noticed the scar again on his son's hairline. One Denis was careful to keep covered, not liking the memory it brought back to him when he was attacked by the black bird from the castle as a small boy. He hadn't wanted to be near ravens, or any other birds since. He quickly ruffled his brown wavy fringe forward when he realised what his father had seen.

He looked at the cave entrance, remembering the previous night's events. Two men were there lifting barrels onto a makeshift raft. One doffed his hat at Tobias and then nodded at Denis. A flash of anger moved through him.

'Why do you let them stay there? They're thieves.'

'They have a living to make. Don't judge them. These people have helped us more than you can imagine when no one else would. You can be sure they don't judge you and that my son is a rare commodity.'

'I felt pretty judged last night.'

'That was different. That was territorial.'

Out of nowhere, a small boat appeared from behind the rocks to the left of the cove. Two men guided it in, their bodies bouncing up and down as the waves broke against the rocks.

'Here we go.'

Denis felt a pang of nervousness and excitement.

Guss moved first and started to clamber over the rougher side of the shore, slipping occasionally and cursing until finally making it over to the finer, steadier shingle. He shouted out to one of the men.

'Alright there, Bill?'

'Hey, still as nimble-footed as ever, I see, you old codger.'

'Shut ya face and get further in, so I don't have to bleedin drown before I get to ya.'

Bill looked over to Tobias and laughed, then saw the others on the other side of the shore.

He shouted out to the men.

'That looks like rum to me. HEY! Fancy bringing some of that over here?'

All he got was a rude hand gesture back.

Bill chuckled and lowered his voice to Guss.

'Charming. Who's the lad?'

Guss waded into the water, threw his sack and rope into the boat, and held on to the side.

'Oh, that's Tobias's young boy. We're babysitting.'

'Oh really, teaching him the ropes, hey?'

The ship came into view as Bill manoeuvred them back through the rocks. Guss looked across at Denis and his chest puffed out with pride at seeing the vessel.

'What a beaut, hey, Denis? Her name is Shalako. She's named after a mythical lady who brings a homely feeling, shall we say, to sailors who spend too long at sea. When she comes, she generally brings the breeze and rain.'

'It's big.'

'Well, yes, she is that.'

'How are we going to get on it?'

'Oh, we'll get you on board safely.'

As the boat approached the ship's bow, the waves threw them up and down, making it almost impossible to grab hold of the ladder ropes that hung over its side. The lower section was embedded with crustaceans and slippery algae, making it even harder to get a hold, but they all made it up safely as Guss promised. Behind them, the small boat was hauled up and secured alongside another identical one.

On board, Guss and Tobias were greeted with manly hugs and slaps on the back. Denis watched on, seeing a side of his father he'd never witnessed before. *So, this is my father's second family*, he thought.

'Good to have you on board again, Toby; I hear this is your last trip with us. Who's this skinny so-and-so, your replacement?'

Tobias turned to look at his son and signalled for him to step forward to meet his oldest friend, Loaf.

'I'm Denis, his son, actually.'

'Oh, well, good to meet ya, Denis. You along for the ride, or are we dropping ya off somewhere?'

'Haven't got a clue, suppose I'm learning a bit of what my father does.'

'I see your plan, Toby. Teaching the young'un your skills, hey? Well, I'll let you all settle and then I'll go through the issues we've been having with these sails. They're knackered if you ask me.'

Loaf moved on and shouted back that they'd set sail any minute. Denis heard him muttering about never liking this cove, and the quicker it was behind them, the better. Its legend felt too believable to the sailors who stayed too long.

Denis turned to his father and whispered,

'You never did explain how Sirengard got its name.'

One of the crew overheard him.

'Hey, don't mention this place out loud. It's a sure sign they'll get ya.'

Tobias smiled at his son, put a fatherly arm around him and led him to where they would both be working.

The first few days saw blustery weather giving Denis a perfect chance to find his sea legs, which he spent most of the time swinging in one of the hammocks below deck or supporting himself when the rest of his body was bent over the rails while he was being sick into the swaying grey tide below.

When the weather eased and the calmer waters came, Tobias could begin repairs on the mast and make necessary alterations on the sails. Denis took to climbing the shrouds and shimmying across the smaller mizzen mast. The ship had a double crow's nest, the smaller acting as more of a fighting top with less support. From there, Denis looked across to the mainmast.

A complex network of ropes stretched from where he was to the foremast. *How did any of them understand which ones to pull and which to secure?* he wondered.

Tobias stood atop the mainmast's crow's nest and called for Denis to unbuckle a hook just below him. Denis checked his rope was secure around his waist before leaning out to grapple with the heavy clasp. It was locked in place with a sliding spring which had to be disengaged before he could lift it off.

Tobias assumed it would take him a while to free it and got ready to throw him the rope to tie it to so he could winch it across. Unfortunately, Denis was keen to impress and released and dropped it in one move. Tobias leaned and yelled at two of the crew below them.

'Watch out below.'

Luckily, both ducked and moved away from where they were working, not without giving Denis a hard stare as they went. He shouted down at them.

'Sorry.'

Tobias laughed.

'Just go slower; we have a while on board and need the crew.'

Tobias looked down and shouted at the men.

'Well, some of them anyway.'

Denis called across to his dad.

'What's wrong with the sails? They look fine to me.'

'They aren't the right ones for this type of ship. They're being overstretched and they're tearing. And, whoever put them on needs shooting, far too many hoists and ropes. It's putting too much strain on the smaller masts if the weather were to get a bit rough.'

Tobias dropped the rope down, and Guss tied the loose swing hook to it for him to lift back up again.

Denis looked about him. He didn't mind the height so much. It was just the trip down that looked a lot harder than the one coming up. The sea merged on the horizon with the sky and only a fine white line seemed to separate them. The breeze was warm, and he closed his eyes. Now he was out of Sirengard, free from the hassles that seemed to follow him; he should have started to feel lighter, like a weight was lifting from him. He looked out at sea again. Nothing was in his way, and there were no memories or people to blame. So why did he still feel a heaviness in the pit of his stomach? If not here, then where was he going to feel happiness like everyone else seemed to have?

'Do you want me to come back later?'

Denis jumped out of his skin at the sight of his father right next to him and instinctively grabbed at the side of the mast, wrapping both arms around it as he did.

Tobias laughed from his belly.

'I thought you'd need a bit of help coming down. It's a bit daunting the first time.'

'How did you get over here so fast?'

Tobias took his son's arm and, step by step, he helped him back down to the deck.

They ate lunch while Denis watched his father start to make sketches for a new design for the sails.

'Right, down we go. What's the weather looking like, Guss?'

'I think you've got a good couple of days; you want help down there?'

'I think we've got it covered; I'll call if I need anything. Come on, son, we'll be working on this below. We'll come back up and take the mainsail down when we've set up.'

Denis spent his nights sleeping in the hold at the ship's stern. His father took him down another set of stairs, which led into a much larger area at the front of the ship. This was where their fruit and vegetables, livestock and barrels of dried rice and barley were kept. The floor had been cleared for them, and two low milking stools had been left next to Tobias's large leather bag of tools, now sitting in the centre of the room.

'It's dark. How can you see anything down here?'

'Your eyes get used to it. I don't like working with oil lamps. It is too dangerous with all this cloth and wood. Right, grab the bag and the stools and we'll sit over here under the hatch and give you a chance to get used to the light. In that bag, you'll find a wire brush. I'll need you to clean the tools first, son, before we start anything else. I haven't used them in a while.'

Denis snorted.

'What did your last slave die of?'

'He didn't. He's alive and happy up on deck, laughing because you've stupidly offered to take his place down here.'

'Ha, ha, very funny. Why am I the butt of everyone's jokes; my name, my appearance, everything?'

Tobias, choosing to ignore him, pointed back at the bag.

Denis all but dragged the heavy bag over to his father. Two long wooden handles ran through the leather loops at the top and a metal clasp was pushed over one of them to keep it together. When he opened it, a mixture of musty and fishy-smelling aromas rose from the wooden and rusty metal tools. The brush, thankfully, was lying on top of them.

'Right, I'm going back up top to get the sail with Guss, so son, if you would be so kind as to go through all the metalwork and brush the rust off. It'll take a bit of force, but it'll come off. Over there's a bucket and water. Just use that water to rinse them off. It's not seawater and it's in short supply, so go easy. I'll be back in a bit.'

He disappeared through the hatch, and Denis wandered around the hold. Finding little interest, he resigned himself to doing what was asked of him. He started to pull out the tools and lay them on a rug. As he grabbed the first one and ran the brush over it, his mind wandered back to what his father had said about Bertha. He adored her and never thought that anything would or could ever change that. He thought for a bit and realised he still felt the same about her. It made no difference; his father was right, and he wasn't planning on telling her either. Besides, she was the light of his dreary life. Why would he want to knowingly extinguish that?

With bits of rusty dust still in his eyes, he clambered up the steps, hearing shouts and noises from above. The midday light was bright and he used his hand to shield his eyes as he stuck his head out of the hatch. He was just in time to see the sail fall. Three of the crew ran to lift it off the deck, folding it and calling on a fourth because of the weight; they manoeuvred it over to where Denis was.

'In or out, lad, quick.'

He shot up and out so they could awkwardly attempt to carry the canvas sheeting down through the tight gap where he had just exited.

Tobias jumped down from the last few rungs of the rope ladder and rubbed his hands together. He walked over to Denis, picking at a splinter in his palm.

'All done down there?'

'Yep. Never seen tools like those before.'

'Well, they're yours if you want them. I won't be needing them after this trip.'

He glanced up at the mainmast and shook his head.

'That took far too long, damn ropes were all over the place, we'll have to get it back quicker than that.'

Tobias sighed and headed back down to make a start on the sail.

'Right, ready, I'll go through what needs doing.'

He shouted across to Loaf, ensuring they had enough spare canvas onboard.

'A bit late if we haven't. Hey, have ya seen this?'

Loaf gestured over the quarterdeck and out at sea. Tobias jumped up the steps and stood beside him. Denis quietly followed.

'They've been following us since we left.'

Denis squinted to try and focus through the bright daylight.

'What are they?'

'Shoal of some kind or other. Probably dolphins, not like I've ever seen before, though. They're keeping away from us, which is odd. They're just watching us.'

Loaf explained to Denis.

'If they were dolphins, they'd usually swim alongside us, having fun with us, ya see.'

Denis felt a nervousness bubble up. He looked for reassurance from the crew standing around him as they looked out at the creatures.

'What does that mean? Is it bad?'

It was then he heard someone whisper his name.

'Denis. Come and join us.'

Denis spun around to see who had spoken to him.

Tobias pulled his son away before Loaf could answer.

'Oh, it's just fishermen's omens and superstitions. If I listened to all that stuff, I'd be dead ten times over.'

Denis waited to see if he could hear anything. Nothing. His father tugged at him again and led him towards the hatch.

Tobias was happy at sea but surprisingly spent little time looking out at it. Over the years, the crew had noticed his aversion and tried not to draw his attention to it. Guss tutted at Loaf for doing it, knowing full well the stories still swirled around in Tobias's head. Those stories told to him long ago by his grandparents, of half-Eathian, half-fish-like creatures in the sea. He pretended not to believe them, but Guss knew him better than that.

Sliding down the stairs that led back to the hold, Tobias clapped his hands together to motivate himself and get on with the job at hand.

By all accounts, you are familiar with tools, from what I hear.'

Denis frowned, confused at what point his father was making.

'Francis told us how you knew of the Reflectorscope before you had even set foot in the castle. He said you were a natural. So, this should be easy for you.'

Denis lowered his head, unsure of what to say.

Tobias was intrigued.

'I've never asked, but how did you become so familiar with it?'

Denis sighed.

'There's this book. I found it under your bed. It has loads of pictures, mainly drawings and calculations. I read it over and over and understood it. Don't know how, just did.'

Tobias smiled.

'Oh, that's Gabriel's old journal. Fair enough. I'm proud of you, son. That's pretty darn clever. '

He nodded at his son and held his hand out.

Denis raised one eyebrow, beginning to feel uncomfortable.

'Are we having a moment here?'

'Nope. Not unless you want one. Meanwhile, pass us the cutters and the measure. Then start to pull that cord out from the old sail on both sides. It's gonna get in the way and one of us will end up cutting straight through it.'

'By one of us, you mean me?'

Denis didn't bother looking up at his father. He grabbed the rope at one end of the sail and started to weave it back through the metal holes.

Some way off, the creatures in the sea mused at how they would all be in Duergars good books. One of them split from the others, returning to let their Superior know that by happenstance, Denis and his father were in the right place at the right time.

The other creatures continued to watch and observe the ship. Keeping a safe distance as they did.

Chapter 30
The Realm

Tethered Love

Corpus and Christi fell side by side within the tether stream, down towards their Eathians. Corpus watched her as she took in the surroundings and the exhilarating feeling of falling. Again, she made him smile. She made him happy.

'Christi, we will separate soon. Enjoy your time with her, and very soon we'll be together again, understand? See you back at the Solescence Chamber when you can. Remember, life on Eathia is as quick as a blink of an eye to us, so relish in its beauty dear sister. Don't forget to come and find me down there.'

The excitement ran through every part of Christi's being. The elation as she fell, knowing that soon she would unite with her first tether. As she drew nearer, the first pulling sensation she had felt in The Realm started to become stronger and so did her sense of who she was to be bonding with.

She watched as Corpus swerved away from her, his gaze still very much on her. The sudden sense of loneliness and the fear it brought only heightened her awareness of what was coming.

A fast-moving stream of energy designed to withstand different atmospheric conditions acted as a unique portal from The Realm to Eathia. It had a specialised data cord running through its centre, which connected with Christi, providing her with the knowledge of her destination and the person she was seeking.

Echoes in the portal changed as she moved. A twang turned to a drone when she hit the shield while learning to navigate safely. Christi watched the colours as they flew past her, their density blocking any view of what was beyond her tether and portal completely.

As the sounds faded, a new rhythmic beat emerged, drawing her in with swishes and whooshes. She felt a calling to unite.

Christi saw vibrant colours flash past her as she let go and felt another's energy join her. She tried to stabilise as she drew closer and heard only one fast heartbeat. Then she saw her.

She felt a perfect fit with the union, tethered and bonded with a child of Eathia. It brought an overwhelming sense of wholeness and a complete change in her awareness. She tried to understand the contrast in her feelings to those she had just moments before.

At that moment, she realised she couldn't connect with Corpus but felt dedicated to someone else instead. New emotions, sensations and sounds began to overwhelm her.

The bond between a Soul Guardian and their tether is indescribable. An Eathian becomes a physical representation of the Soul Guardian's essence. This unique and natural bond cannot be replicated between any other Eathian or Soul Guardian. Christi felt love in that instant. That's what it was, love for the tiny new life form on the other side of a translucent energy cord, her companion until the end of her time on Eathia.

As Christi was filling with adoration, the light suddenly flooded her senses and a heavy coldness felt harsh against her sensitive aura.

The little girl started to communicate with her at once. Tentatively, at first, as her awareness poured through the tethered cord towards Christi.

She remembered to let them pass through her.

Subtle feelings rose through Christi as she sampled each emotion and nuance separately as they worked their way through her towards The Realm. The little one's ability to experience and let go was so pure and perfect.

Christi tuned into the colours, light and sound around her. As she bonded with the Eathian child, she grounded herself through the baby and into the Eathian Star below. This created an anchor for communication and expansion back to The Realm. She remembered what Verra Mica had said about the Eathian Star and its importance to both Soul Guardian and their tether at that moment. It lay beneath Eathia's surface, formed simultaneously with the planet itself, creating a perfect base for a newborn child to fasten onto throughout life.

Her aura assimilated new communications and sensations from the Eathian Star. She unknowingly scanned the baby, and as alien energy returned from the star, she braced herself for impact. However, she was pleasantly surprised as an invisible shield created distance between them. Now, she could sense the baby and its environment.

Warmth, touch, smell, fleeting moments of vision and so much more.

She watched her tether's mind fire up. Colours and messages shot between nerves, and Christi could decipher every one of them. There appeared to be a language bridge, a common energy that she could read, already embedded in the Eathian brain.

Was this the closest I could get to living, fully? she wondered.

Another voice harshly echoed around them.

'You are beautiful, my darling; we have a girl. Finally, we have our little girl.'

She watched as the child warmly reacted to the voice of her mother and made noises back to her. These she couldn't decipher, but she could feel the contentment.

Another flood of energy came at Christi, but this time it had not come directly from the baby; it had passed through her from her mother. It was weaker, a less significant vibration to Christi, one that continued to pass through her tether, through her being and back to The Realm and the Source. She realised quickly that others around the baby would also have an impact on what Christi felt and sensed.

Christi tried to speak to the newborn through thoughts. Judging by her reaction, they were heard loud and clear.

Another voice came through, and she heard the name Beatrice.

'Beatrice, you are the most beautiful vision I have ever seen.'

As Christi's words passed through the tether, the baby became quiet, her attention turning inwards towards Christi.

Had she heard her? She must have.

Christi watched in awe as their combined aura burst into life, fired up by a torrent of energies reacting from her voice. The colours swirled around the baby just like those around the Soul Guardians in The Realm.

'Hello, little one.'

Then Beatrice started to convey her message to Christi with no sound or words, just pure communication through their tether. Christi realised instantly that the baby knew she was there.

'This is love in your world. Now I know why we are here with you. I hope you can feel my love in return.'

Something ignited within Christi and she started to feel an energy moving towards her from The Realm. It joined with her own and continued towards the little girl.

They were fully tethered.

She spent a while attuning to the small child, and once she fell asleep, the pull from The Realm became stronger, confirming she was free and able to go back, and although still tethered, she could now fully experience both worlds.

She returned, excited to tell Corpus.

She found him in their Solescence Chamber waiting for her return. He didn't need to wait long before she exploded through the gentle mist in the well. He beamed when he caught sight of her.

'Corpus, that was truly amazing. I saw how she connected to the Source. I tried to sense you there, and I did, but I couldn't see you?'

Laughing, Corpus beckoned to her to slow down.

'I am there, but remember, we haven't met yet; we have that to look forward to. So, now you see what an incredible journey we have ahead of us, be it all, a slightly intense one.'

They had entered a unique Seraphyte Solescence Chamber. It was theirs and all the Soul Guardians that were part of the same lifeline on Eathia. The same Soul Guardians would be tethered again and again to clusters of family members and friends. Each life would be different and have different relationships; however, the Soul Guardians would still have a similar bond, drawn with each life towards each other repeatedly. Once those tethers were back in The Realm, they would enter and leave through the same portals within the chambers, their imprint making it impossible for any other Soul Guardian to enter other than the Superiors.

Corpus left to return to his tether a little before Christi. She was not ready to return yet and instead moved to the main collective chamber to overview her whole family, which, of course, included Corpus's family; now that she was to be a part of his lifeline, she could watch his Eathian child wake before she needed to go.

It was here that Elkyne found her, sensing her return. He was unveiled.

'Elkyne, I can't believe it's you. I have missed you, brother. You have just missed Corpus.'

Elkyne looked down at her noticeable tether and his energy dropped.

'Any news on tethering yet? Please say you are going to join us soon, is that why you are here?'

She instantly felt his aura's controlled adjustment, which should have been glowing about him.

'No, not yet although I still hold out hope I will be given the opportunity very soon.'

He paused and suddenly appeared vexed. Christi's concern for him grew.

'What is it?'

'I have just been summoned again. I was going to see Duergar but took this detour when I felt you had returned.'

Christi giggled.

'You found me.'

'I cannot stay long though, Christi, although it would be my wish to do so; I missed you before you left; I am sorry.'

'Is everything good with you? I am concerned for you and your wellbeing, brother.'

'With all this attention and concern you'd think I'd be the most popular Soul Guardian in The Realm, which is odd, considering I have felt so very alone. I imagine that's just the feeling of having a twin and not being able to be with her.'

He was suddenly distracted by another communication from Duergar.

'If you are needed elsewhere, I shouldn't keep you too long, Elkyne; the last thing I wish to do is cause you problems.'

He bowed and went to leave.

'Elkyne?'

Elkyne remained still and waited for Christi to speak. He always felt weakened in her presence, but a weakness he would gladly feel if only to linger in the added warmth she brought.

'You are our brother and …'

'I have to go.'

Elkyne began to move away towards the exit, but before leaving he turned back towards her.

'I have you, Christi, and I have my order. It appears that we have been born into opposing forces where discord and devotion appear to be enveloping our true purpose. My apparent "lack" of loyalty is making things worse, and it will continue to do so until I let go of …'

Christi finished his sentence for him.

'Us?'

Something was burning inside Elkyne's being. *Why was this so difficult?* He looked at her and tried to say 'YOU'.

Instead, he responded the only way he could.

'Yes. Forgive my bluntness. I really must bid my leave now.'

'I love you Elkyne. Please keep hold of your belief in us. We will always support you and so will Verra Mica. Always.'

The scales were tipping, Elkyne could feel it with every word Christi uttered. He fled from the chamber unable to shield himself successfully any longer. The further he moved away from her the easier it became to numb out the sensation of his arduous divided loyalty. The truth was that he only felt like he belonged when he was with her and that was dangerous. For both their sakes, he couldn't allow Duergar to be aware of his vulnerability.

He had made his decision and he had to uphold that even though, in truth, that was the lie.

He had no choice. Olpheira was right. He had to decide and get on with it.

Chapter 31
Eathia – Third Era

Fall from Grace

While they sat in the semi-darkness of the hull, Denis watched his father as he laid out the enormous expanse of cloth on the ground and placed a couple of tools at each end to keep it stretched out. His measurements were clearly written across it; he used it as a constant reference between darting around the sail, measuring angles, diameters and lengths. Once he had taken all the rope from the sail, Denis continued to do so as Tobias had asked and measured it, making marks at every ten-metre point. After he had finished, he quietly watched for Tobias to show signs of completing the calculations in his head. While he waited, his mind returned to when they had stood by the graves at Sirenguard.

'I'm sorry about overreacting. You know, when you told me about Bertha? No wonder you waited to tell me. I acted exactly as you expected, didn't I?'

Behind Denis, Guss had started to climb down through the hatch to see how they were getting on, but as soon as he heard Denis, he stopped and clambered back up again, not wanting to intrude on their discussion.

Tobias looked up at Denis and half-grinned at Guss as he awkwardly left the hull.

'You had every right to kick off. It wasn't an easy thing to bring up. There never seemed to be a right moment.'

Denis shifted on his stool; part of his bum was going numb. He flared.

'How do you sit on these things for so long?'

Tobias knew it was a rhetorical question and carried on.

'Is there anything you want to ask?'

Denis rubbed the back of his neck; sweat seeped through as he tried to contain his emotions long enough to hold a proper conversation with his father.

'Can you tell me a bit about her real dad, Bertha's, I mean?'

Tobias inhaled and looked into space for a while, wondering how much to tell and what to leave out.

He sighed.

'His name was Daniel.'

'Was?'

'I don't know if he's still alive. He came from a town known as Campion to your mother's home town of Cullvelley, apparently to hunt down a man.'

'What, he was a sheriff?'

Tobias smiled at Denis's speedy assumption.

'No. His town had been taken over, and his people had been forced to live like slaves; some of them were Ashen, too, by all accounts. Daniel's father was an inventor, like Gabriel, Francis's father. Daniel's father built a system underground to eradicate the intruders; apparently, the key to its success was somewhere in Cullvelley. I believe it might have had a connection with what Gabriel had been able to build with the Reflectorscope's prototype.'

Tobias shrugged.

'At the time, a man and his son had taken a keen interest in your mother, and they were bad news. It was the same guy Daniel had been looking for. My grandmother, Mary, remembered him – Marcus, I think his name was – from the ship she was on. Anyway, he met your mother there, and because she wasn't in the best of situations at the time, they just fell towards each other. For a while, he was her knight in shining armour.'

'Then he left her? Pregnant? Some knight he was,' Denis snarled.

'No, he got himself captured. It all turned a bit nasty, and in all fairness, he didn't know she was pregnant.'

Tobias paused for a moment as if in turmoil about whether to continue or not. Denis spoke.

'So, when did you get involved? When did you meet Mum?'

'Mary knew your great-grandmother. They had been close, and Mary helped her get back on her feet. They were similar, you see. Unlike Bertha, who can see the past, they could see things and future events. Your great-grandmother's ability had nearly driven her into madness. If it hadn't been for Mary, I don't know what would have happened to her. She always kept that connection to her, and one day she had an image connected to your mother and Bertha that made her scared enough to send me to Cullvelley to fetch them. Eventually, we all made our way to Stonehaven.'

Denis tried to process this new information.

'Hang on. You're saying Bertha's ridiculous stories are true?'

He laughed sarcastically, stood up and began to pace around.

Tobias nodded.

'I don't understand. Why us? Why was this happening to our family?'

Tobias was getting slightly anxious. He understood Denis's interest in hearing all this for the first time, but they had work to do.

'Let's work while we talk, son. Otherwise, we'll get nothing done.'

Tobia showed Denis what to do, and they cracked on with changing the sail. Tobias was impressed with how quickly Denis worked with accuracy and, unusually, perseverance.

After a while, Tobias continued.

Denis listened quietly, immersed in his work on the sail, finding it a distraction to curb his anger towards his father.

'Your great-grandmother became a bit of a mystic traveller. Until she, too, made her way to Stonehaven, where she died. Following another of Mary's insights, we left Sirenguard to be by her side during her failing health. We only just made it before she died. Thankfully, your grandmother, Nora, and your mother were close to her when it happened. You see, there's a direct bloodline with the female side of the family. Something special has been passed through to each one, Bertha being the last.'

Denis stopped and looked across at his father. A flash of anger broke through, gripping his gut as it did. Tobias saw and tried to calm him down.

'It was decided a long time ago, Denis, that this was something we'd keep under wraps for our safety.'

Denis finally flipped.

'Safety. You repeated safety. Why? It's like you're protecting Bertha from something dangerous. Has this got something to do with me?' Are you worried about me causing problems? Is that why I'm here?'

'What, no, not at all. Why would you think that?'

'I'm the one that nearly lost my life when I looked into that damn reflector. You haven't mentioned my safety once. Francis was the only one who understood me and what I went through back then, and now he's gone.'

Denis started to feel like he was an outsider in the family. The ache under his ribs began to make him feel suffocated. A feeling he was all too familiar with.

'I have your back, son. I always will. There is something bigger going on, Denis, bigger than all of us, or at least there was. We fled Sirenguard to be close to to be close to a special woman. Your Great-Grandmother. She had disappeared and then, after years, we heard that she had turned up in Stonehaven.

She was important, you see, all of them are, especially Bertha.'

'Of course, she is. She's a descendant of blah, blah, blah.'

Guss's head appeared in the opening of the hatch. Both men looked up at his timely interruption.

'I'm sorry to butt in, Tobe. Are you nearly done with the sail? Captain now thinks we have a bit of bad weather coming this way. Idiot. I couldn't leave it any longer to tell you.'

Tobias looked past Guss and, craning his neck, he tried to see the sky through the hatch.

'What? But we're losing the light.'

He looked across at Denis to check he had finished his work. Denis nodded.

'Yes, it's done.'

'Can we do it, do ya think? Only you know, Tobes. I'm not doing nought without your say so.'

Tobias looked apologetically at Denis.

'Can we carry on with this a little later, son? I want to tell you everything.'

Denis reluctantly nodded. He'd waited this long. Then he realised what was about to happen.

'What, we're putting the sail back up now?'

'Looks like it. You stay on deck; I can feel the change in the weather already; I should have known this was coming.'

Tobias grabbed the sketches, jumped up two rungs of the steps and handed them to Guss, telling him to show the crew. They were all going to help, like it or not.

Two of the crew slid down into the hold and lifted the rolled-up sail.

'Come on, lad, grab hold of the middle and follow old Taylor up.'

Tobias lunged for his tools and jumped in front of them so that Guss could take it and drop it ready at the base of the mast.

Once the sail was through the gap, Denis helped move it, but kept his sights on his father. Watching him strap on a large leather belt of tools, looking for any tell-tale signs in his expression to gauge just how much of a stupid and dangerous idea this was. The look he saw suggested that it was indeed 'stupid'. They shouldn't even be attempting to secure the sail with a potential storm coming.

Denis fell silent with a growing fear that had started to bubble up deep inside his stomach.

Loaf and Taylor climbed up the two outer masts, and Guss followed his father up the main one, stopping midway and securing himself to one of the rungs above him via a rope he had tied around his waist.

The other men had reached the top and were calling across to his father, who was busy securing himself at the crow's nest.

Denis realised he was still supporting the sail, the others now elsewhere, so he dropped it and stepped back to get a better look at what his father was doing. Even in the dulling sky, he still lifted his hand to his eyes to shield them from the brighter light, his eyes having gotten used to the gloom of the hold.

The brace beam started to sway as the wind began to pick up. It was the first thing Tobias needed to secure before lowering it down for the sail to be attached. He threw heavy hooks to the men who fed the rope through large loops and sent them back to him. He climbed higher to the uppermost of the mast and rerouted some of the thicker ropes. He held four in all and began to lower them towards Guss, who climbed down and started to open the sail that had been left on deck. Denis ran forward to help.

The ship was starting to bob around quite vigorously now and, to make things worse, the light was disappearing fast. Guss looked up to see Tobias's progress. He muttered to himself, but loud enough for Denis to hear.

'That staysail's gonna catch if he's not quick.'

He yelled at Loaf at the mizzen mast.

'Try and release that jib, mate.'

He looked at Denis, who was taking his cap off and scratching his head.

'They've been too keen to get the other up and secure.'

It was another language to Denis, but he could sense that Guss, usually the clown of the group, was concerned.

There was a sudden gust of wind just as Loaf released the upper jib. Now loose, the sail between him and the mainmast blew upwards and swung one of its heavy hooks up in the air, arching over where Tobias had climbed. From the point of the crew's location on deck, their view of its whereabouts was obscured, getting lost against the darkening sky; however, knowing it was dangerous to have it hanging loose, Guss shouted for Tobias to watch for it. It was a long way up and now no one below had sight of Tobias. Suddenly, the bracket and the rope attached to it went taut.

'Shit.'

Guss launched into action and began to climb the mainmast. Denis was confused.

'What's happening?'

'Just stay there, Denis.'

Denis ran backwards to the ship's edge and saw the sail flapping freely. Then the wind changed, the sail blew to one side, and he saw his father hanging in the air with only the rope around his waist holding him secure. Everything looked loose, knocking and swaying around his swinging body.

Blind panic hit Denis. A surge of energy propelled him onto the rigging. He saw in seconds a way to get to his father. Up onto the foremast, grab the brace, secure it, swing across it into the crow's nest, pull his father in, or lower him whatever was best, but he had to get there first.

He heard Guss yelling for him to stop. Taylor, already at the top, was calling for him to go back.

'You've got no rope on ya, Denis, get down.'

Before he could shout again, Denis was on top of him and climbed onto the other side of the mast. He reached out to grab the long brace as it swung by. Taylor was now stuck on the wrong side of the mast and unable to help other than hold on to Denis's free hand as it gripped one of the pegs protruding from the mast.

He finally managed to reach and take hold of the end of the brace and pulled it towards him. He saw Guss now almost at the top, but he couldn't reach across from where he was to pull Tobias to safety.

The ship arched up, and even Guss had to hold on and stop himself from falling. He instinctively glanced out at sea, confused at why the ship was swaying so much. He'd seen much worse storms, and it had managed those easily.

Something dulled his senses. Guss shook his head to focus.

The sound of the waves slowly became music and voices echoed amongst the melody. He slapped at his face to bring himself back just in time to see Tobias swing towards Loaf. The sail suddenly flipped up between them, hindering his attempts to catch his legs.

Denis called for Taylor to hold the brace and try to tie it down. He was going to monkey crawl along it. Once at the end, he told him to push it the rest of the way and he'd jump.

Denis's long, thin frame precariously moved along the wooden beam, one hand following the other as he went, his legs kicking up against the ship's movement. It was too late for any of the crew to reason with him now; all they could do was pray that he didn't fall.

From those left on the deck, all sight of them had gone now. The night sky had put a veil between them.

As Denis reached the end of the brace, he called for Taylor to push it forward hard.

Denis started to swing his legs to give himself more momentum. As Taylor released the beam and pushed it, he threw himself towards the crow's nest. His feet encountered the edge and he clasped them together to hold on. The brace started to swing back, giving Denis seconds to decide which end he would let go of.

He heard his father groan. At this distance, he could see the head wound and the blood seeping down the left side of his father's face. He shouted down to Guss that he'd been hit.

Then he started to hear someone calling him. He felt his fear recede.

He watched on as a man precariously hung before him. Distant shouts floated through his mind, making little impact, drowned out by a beautiful voice singing to him.

He relaxed his limbs. As he did, he let go of the brace. He swung mid-air before hitting his legs hard against the wooden cage of the nest. His senses came back with a start. He started to slip and his feet lost their hold. While still hanging upside down, he desperately tried to grab the pegs sticking out from the mast. The crew's voices reverberated around his mind, now free of the strange voice and music.

Guss had gone back down to try to release Tobias's rope from the bracket and attempt to lower him down with the other men, but he couldn't guarantee that they could hold him firm enough. The deck was constantly moving and swaying and, by doing so, they could make it more dangerous for Tobias, leaving him freer to crash into both masts with the swaying of the ship. Instead, Guss stood at the base of the mainmast and started back up again towards his helpless friend.

He called out to let Denis know he was coming.

Denis had lost all sense of direction as his feet finally gave way and slipped off the cage. His lower body fell and crashed against one of the metal pegs. Pain ripped through his leg as it cut through his trousers and into his skin. Wrapping his other leg around the mast, he pulled his damaged leg away and stabilised himself, his forehead resting on the wood of the mast while he waited for the pain to lessen. He felt himself losing focus on any plan he might have had. He glanced across at his father and their eyes met.

'Denis, what are you doing, son?'

His father's voice helped him to refocus. He reached out for him to grab hold of his hand. But his father was going in and out of consciousness.

He was muttering about a lullaby.

Denis climbed up to the nest and pulled at the brace as it rocked towards him, pushing it towards Loaf. He shouted at him to catch hold of it.

Guss came up from beneath him and climbed in with him.

'Catch your breath, son. That was a crazy stunt. I see what ya doing, but it's too dangerous to go out there again now.'

From a strap attached to his back, he pulled out a long stick with a dangerous-looking fishhook at one end.

'I'll try and pull him in and you catch him; you'll have to get lower, though.'

As he climbed back onto the mast below, he saw Guss hook the top of the rope at the knot on his father's back. He pulled him in, and his father's body went into a spin, nearly kicking Denis as it went around. Denis reached out with all his might and caught hold of one of his father's trouser legs. There was still some distance between them, so he wrapped his legs tighter around the mast and released his other hand to try to pull him in towards him. It worked, and he could take hold of the rope and arch his arm over his back. With a much tighter hold, he pulled back against the mast. He smiled with relief as he took a stronger hold of his father.

Then the ship lurched back and Denis felt his father start falling away from his grip.

Guss quickly ducked under the railings and climbed down towards Denis and Tobias.

'I'm coming, son, hold on.'

The angle of the ship became too much. Denis realised he had to either let go or hold on. He made the instinctive decision not to let his father go. He released his grip on the only thing that was keeping him safe. The mast seemed to fall away from his hand, and as tight as he was holding on with his legs, they weren't strong enough to steady them both. He started to slip again, finally falling away from the mast altogether as he continued to hold onto his father's motionless body.

The two men swung for what seemed like an eternity before the rope gave way under their combined weight. Now, without restraint, Denis and his father plummeted downwards.

Denis clutched desperately at his father's body as they fell. Hitting the side of the ship, he felt the punch from the impact pass through his father's body and into his own. The force split them apart, and they fell beyond the safety of the ship, carrying on down until the cold water enveloped them both, and they were lost to the depths of the darkened sea.

Guss yelled as he watched their bodies disappear. He knew too well that the sea had claimed them and that there would be no chance of finding them now.

He buried his face in his cap, collapsed in a heap and screamed for it not to be true. Not Tobias and his son. It couldn't be true.

Beneath the waves, the shoal of creatures silently rejoiced in their good fortune and retreated.

They had succeeded in their endeavour to secure the death of two more from the ill fated bloodline.

A bloodline, Duergar wanted to eliminate at any cost.

Chapter 32
Eathia – Third Era

Divine Intervention?

Back at home in Stonehaven, Bertha wrapped her scarf around her neck to fend off the chill of the night air. She was heading toward her uncle's Emporium. Her nightly visits gave him a breather while Anamaya was at the castle. It was an unfortunate routine that neither she nor Augustus could change for the time being. The castle and the orb required constant vigilance day and night, as did little Maddox.

The warmth of his kitchen made her face tingle and itch as it came back to life from the cold. She tugged at her scarf, its tightness now excessive in the sudden heat.

Augustus heard her come and called out.

'We're in here, Bertha. It's bath time and I've had to warm the house.'

Bertha appeared red-faced at the door of the sitting room. Augustus could see her colour, breathed heavily and fanned the air around him, acknowledging the heat.

'I may have gone a little over the top with the heat. The trouble is that it takes a while to cool down once you stoke that stove up.'

Bertha laughed and reached for Maddox, who was snuggled up in a towel. He grinned up at her.

'He recognises you, look.'

Bertha still half expected to see rosy cheeks on Maddox, which was a regular occurrence on all the other babies she delivered. It still surprised her that he was a healthy shade of grey even in all this heat.

'I'll just make us some tea. Are you alright there for a bit? Silly me, of course you are. You could do it standing on your head. Oh ...'

Augustus opened the sideboard drawer, lifted out his pendant, and handed it to Bertha.

'... before I forget, here we are. We still need to be careful. I do wish my grandfather had the foresight to make more of these things. I haven't a clue how to reproduce it.'

Taking a seat with Maddox stretched out on her lap, she giggled up at him and placed the pendant over her head. Maddox's eyes widened and he laughed when he saw his reflection in the pendant's reflector. She called to Augustus, now in the kitchen.

'How is Aunty? Is she still feeling well?'

Augustus responded, saying that she was in good health. He then joined her with two steaming cups of tea.

'Well, that's one good thing about having a furnace next door, it heats water quicker than the blink of an eye. How's your father and Denis? Have you heard anything from them at all?

Bertha shook her head.

'I half expected Denis to be home before my father; it was a leap in the dark for him, and I wasn't sure how he'd get on. Things have been much quieter around here, though.'

She went quiet for a moment. Augustus noticed her mind was elsewhere.

'What is it?'

Bertha had been troubled by something. After all this time, she still dipped in and out of the stories she had spent so much time transcribing. Now, she only had to hold the journals that contained the words of the stories she had been told, and the images flooded back to her as if she were reliving them.

The Realm had always intrigued her. Knowing as much as she did about its struggles, she couldn't help but go back to when Maddox was born. She was sure he had been tethered, too, but had never been shown that part of the story, even after all this time.

Surely, if the woman in the reflector wanted to pass that information on, Bertha would know by now.

'Uncle? Why do you think so much of my story has been held from me? Unlike my great-grandmother, I can see so much but very little about my life. She could see her own destiny, whereas I don't have a clue about mine.'

Augustus waited before he jumped in to answer. Bertha hadn't quite finished.

'The day Maddox was born. I am so sure the orb intervened to save him. From what I understand, the only way it could have helped was to tether a Soul Guardian to him, but she hasn't allowed me to see that for myself. Why do you think that is?'

'Your wonderful great-grandmother could, unfortunately, see everything, which, eventually, became her downfall. Her insight came from within her, through night dreams or terrors, as some of them were. That ability to see things in the future drove her away from those she loved, including my father. I'm not sure it would benefit you in any way to see your life laid out before you. I think the orb is very wise to restrict this. Some things are just too close to home. You need to be able to live your life to some degree. I know it hasn't been easy for you by a long shot, but it would be a lot more difficult if you saw everything before it was about to happen.'

Augustus thought for a moment.

'As far as Maddox is concerned. It's not possible, not anymore. The orb may have triggered an energy surge, helping little Maddox come around and breathe again, or it was you, Bertha. You never gave up on him. I imagine we will discover what happened one day, and that day will come when someone else transcribes your story.

Bertha was shocked at the thought of someone else seeing her life.

'Oh, good heavens. Really?'

'Yes, really.'

Maddox began to wriggle.

'Look, Bertha, I am not entirely sure where you are in the story, but I can't divulge anything you haven't seen for yourself. I am not permitted to. You know this, so maybe it would be best if we changed the subject.'

He stopped and took a mouthful of tea. When he finished, Bertha expected him to continue.

But he didn't.

'Shall I get this one ready for bed?'

Relieved at the change in conversation, Augustus agreed and set about clearing the sitting room of the bath and all his toys.

As Bertha went home after a light supper with her uncle, she relished the cool night air. The thought of tethering still niggled her. As definite as her uncle was, she, on the other hand, wasn't quite as quick to disregard the idea, although he did say, 'Not anymore'. She thought that it had been a strange response. She wondered how aware of The Realm's current state he was.

She knew she still had so much to learn and to understand.

She wondered what it must feel like to have someone tethered to you.

Then she remembered what her uncle had said. If someone was transcribing her, then they would be watching her now, but in the future.

She looked up and instinctively waved at the night sky. Her other hand shot up to stop herself as if it were an involuntary movement, acted out by someone else.

'You idiot, Bertha!'

Scolding herself, she sank her head down into her scarf and hurried home.

Chapter 33
Eathia – Third Era

Unwanted Visitor

Bertha wandered through the quiet, cobbled streets of Stonehaven. Images and stories from The Realm and her past ancestors flashed through her mind as clearly as if she had been there in that moment. She still felt the gut-wrenching turmoil some of them provoked. She had become so accustomed to the feelings that came with them that she sometimes forgot they were about her family. Some as recent as her great uncle. She often wondered where all their lives were leading and to what end. They were important enough to keep a record of, but would the need for them ever end? *When would they all be allowed to become just history?* she pondered.

Her Uncle Francis had always said that the stories were collectively about the keepers and the seekers. Those who would live out their lives protecting the essence of the stories and keeping them safe and alive, and those who sought to find and destroy it and all those connected to it.

Initially, it sounded far-fetched, but as Bertha delved deeper into each transcription, she realised that Francis wasn't downplaying it in any way.

She, herself, had never felt in any danger. All she had was a distant memory of the woman from the reflector telling her that one day, she would need her help.

Maybe the danger had passed? she deliberated.

She began to walk up the steep street towards the cottage. She appreciated its location but always wondered why this cottage was so remote compared to the others.

It was only when her footsteps were the sole sound echoing back to her from the stone and cobbled ground that she heard a scream – a gut-wrenching, heartfelt scream emanating from the cottage.

Panic washed through her. Memories flooded back to when she was young; her mother was in labour and Denis was born. That had been the time when she had dropped the reflector.

The fear within her, which had initially caused her to freeze, was now the driving force that propelled her up the remaining path to her cottage.

As she neared it, she saw a horse and cart tethered to the fence in front of it.

The sound could have only come from her mother. Whoever was in there was hurting her. Her first thought was Denis, but feeling guilty for even thinking it, she banished it from her mind.

Bertha ran, pushed her way through the gate and stormed in through the front door.

A rough-looking man was standing in the kitchen with his back to Bertha. As she entered the room, she could see her mother in a heap on the floor. She was sobbing.

The man turned around and looked at Bertha. There was something in his weather worn face that she recognised.

'Guss? Is that you?'

She ran to her mother's side and put her arm around her.

'What's happened?'

Guss was twisting his woollen hat in his hands over and over again. His cheeks were soaked with tears.

Bertha started to put the few pieces of the puzzle together. Sophia turned to her, fell into her arms and cried uncontrollably. She tried to speak, but Bertha couldn't understand what she was saying. She looked up at Guss.

'There was an accident, Bertha. Both ya Da and Denis fell.'

Bertha felt her limbs go numb. She couldn't carry the weight of her mother for much longer.

'Fell. What do you mean? Fell where. Are they all right?'

Guss slowly started to shake his head.

'No, Bertha. They're not. They fell into the sea in a storm and …'

Upon hearing it again, Sophia groaned loudly, causing Guss to stop.

He silently shook his head instead. Not wanting to cause any more pain.

What little strength Bertha had now left her, and she fell into her mother, somehow propping each other up.

Guss didn't know what to do. He had the whole journey there to dread telling them. When he pulled up, he'd seen Sophia singing in the kitchen. He knew her life would never be the same again when he entered their front door..

He reached for a chair and sat down. His legs were starting to give way.

Bertha and Sophia joined Guss at the table once they could focus and listen to what he had to say.

They understood that it had been an accident and that Denis had tried to save his father.

Sophia reached out her hand and held onto Guss's across the table. She knew it must have been so hard for him to have to come all this way with such awful news.

'Thank you for coming, Guss. I'm sorry you've had to go through this, too.'

She stood and went to put the kettle on the stove.

Guss looked across at Bertha.

'You've grown so much since I last saw you, but I'd recognise you anywhere.'

His eyes began to fill again, and Bertha reached out and held on to his arm.

When she spoke, her voice was weak and quiet.

'Is there any way they could have survived?'

This was the question he had been dreading. He had seen them fall. He had heard Tobias's back break as it hit the ship's side before they had both fallen into the sea. He had also heard Denis yell in pain at the impact.

He lowered his head. Aware that Sophia, now standing by the stove, was watching him and was also waiting for an answer.

'There's no chance, no. I was there and saw it happen.'

Sophia closed her eyes and gripped the handle on the stove for support. She tried not to imagine what Guss had seen.

Bertha's eyes filled again. She squeezed them shut and wished with all her heart that she could have been warned that this was coming; if she had seen it, she might have been able to stop them from going in the first place.

Her mind drifted back to her conversation that evening with Augustus.

For the second time in her life, she found herself resenting the woman in the reflector.

It was all she could do to stop herself from running upstairs and throwing it out of the window for good.

She lowered her head onto Guss's arm and cried into his sleeve. Guilt flooded through her at thinking it was Denis causing heartache.

It was, but in a different, more final way.

Chapter 34
The Realm

Forbidden Gem

Duergar continued to pace frustratingly around his quarters, waiting for his protégé to arrive. He had to confess that there were times, more regular than he wished to admit, that he was beginning to struggle with holding everything in place. He monitored both worlds, managed his own and his Soul Guardians, and maintained his post while trying not to attract unwanted attention. This juggling act was getting difficult, and he was being monitored regularly. He needed an undetectable ally devoted to his cause.

'You called for me, Superior?'

Duergar, caught by surprise, greeted Elkyne with an agitated and overly friendly façade.

'Ah, Elkyne, thank you for finding time to see me. I know how busy you are.'

'With respect, Superior. You control my duties, and I am amazed that you have found time amongst them to receive me.'

Duergar paused, a little uncertain if that was a dig or, indeed, an act of respect. He decided the latter and continued to get to the reason he had requested this meeting in the first place.

'I'll get straight to the point, Elkyne. I want to show you something within The Realm. It is time you understood the truth about its function and potential if used correctly. I don't believe in boundaries being put up as deterrents; I believe instead in being fully prepared and informed so that one can make their judgement regarding certain, shall we say, limitations placed on our kind. Do you understand what I am saying?'

Elkyne was aware of how Duergar twisted his words to support his own opinions; not all of them, as far as he was concerned, were morally right, but he was a powerful persuader and rarely lost a discussion or argument. On this occasion, he had to agree that forewarned was to be forearmed. Now, he had decided to be a true Psybiencian and he wanted to stand by it and support his

Superior.

'I understand, Superior, as ever, you wish for me to have a wider knowledge and a more in-depth view; however, just to clarify, what boundaries do you speak of? Surely not ones within The Realm?'

'You are my top Soul Guardian, are you not?'

Without waiting for a reply, Duergar continued.

'We must understand our race's full capabilities to continue supporting and working with Eathians. We can't limit ourselves to our own dated expectations. You may be tethered in the future if necessary. That is an ancient way of thinking and, as you know, a rationale that Verra Mica holds dear. She prioritises the Eathians, while her world is falling apart beneath her. I will not stagnate, unable to evolve, Elkyne, it is unhealthy for our race, and, in the end, it dishonours our Eathian counterparts and our promise to do the very best for them.'

'Surely it is the Source that controls our evolution and not an individual such as Verra Mica, your Honour?'

'The Source alone will take us to extinction if we are not careful. The Eathians, I'm sure, will eventually understand the measure I wish to take, and no doubt will, in time, come back to us on their terms, but until then, we are being forced to watch on helplessly as both worlds are being drained beyond recognition. Our world ultimately gets engulfed in Eathia's lack of, for want of a better word, boundaries! Who protects us, our world? Without us, nothing would exist.'

'Where is this leading, your Honour? What is your point?'

'They don't retain knowledge or use it to their advantage. Instead, they're driven by greed and lust for material possessions that pollute their environment. They lack the wisdom and capability to save themselves. Most aren't even aware of our existence, and those who are enlightened are eliminated. To them, we're an insane voice in their heads. I won't wait to be drained into an endless void. We've come too close to this before.'

Duergar saw the doubt in Elkyne. He was getting fed up with trying to cajole him. Anger flooded his being.

'Your diplomacy has kept you at a constant disadvantage. You can't feel part of either order; I see that now. Even though I am your Superior, you still struggle with your loyalties. Would I be correct, Elkyne?'

Elkyn was stunned by Duergar's frankness. He knew he had to choose his beliefs in The Realm, but was torn between following Duergar and staying true to himself. Christi's words echoed in his mind, urging him to stay strong. Why was it easier to feel strong doing the wrong thing? He had thought his decision was absolute, but standing before Duergar, he realised he was still undecided.

Duergar calmed himself, feeling he was losing Elkyne and that couldn't happen, not on his watch.

'Let me show you what my Superior showed me, and then you can freely make your choice, Elkyne; it's all about choices. Sometimes, it is necessary to lose oneself before the truth rises to save you, and it is from this place that you will fully understand your capabilities and those of The Realm. You have been lied to, all of you have been lied to, and I plan to change that.'

Elkyne felt defeated. He was relentless.

'Where do you wish to take me that I haven't already seen or heard of myself?'

'Why don't you just come with me now? It's best that way, trust me please, Elkyne, if only just this once.'

Elkyne remained motionless, trying to work out what Duergar was up to. Secrecy was rarely a good thing in his experience, and the need for it made him uneasy. He was getting agitated again.

'Does Verra Mica know of this place, and Corpus and Christi do they know about it also? Is it part of their teaching too?'

An uncontrolled flash passed through Duergar, and he banished it quickly. Unveiled and open, he was not expecting to be questioned at such a level by his own Soul Guardian. Elkyne saw it before Duergar masked it.

'It is not my intention to be disrespectful, your Honour; I am merely being inquisitive as to the source of my knowledge; I have not been made aware of the existence of any such place.'

'Oh, I think you have. Never mind. Diplomacy is an admirable quality, Elkyne. I would expect no less. Now then, shall we go? I want to give you some insight into the truth behind this forbidden gem.'

Duergar moved to exit his quarters, and Elkyne reluctantly followed, trying to shield himself; he decided he needed, on this one occasion, to give Duergar the benefit of the doubt. He pushed back all thoughts of betrayal from those he cared for and those who cared for him.

Then he realised what Duergar had said.

Forbidden gem? It couldn't be. He now had an inkling of where his Superior intended to take him. He thought back to what he had overheard Verra Mica saying to Christi.

Dread began to seep into the void left by his banished doubt.

~

Chapter 35
The Realm

Necessary Evil

Verra Mica entered the Council Chamber alone and walked towards the dome to connect with the Source for guidance on locating Angelica on Eathia. Unusually, she didn't call for a Council meeting, unsure who she could trust. Even Alma Tadema showed signs of wavering at times.

She connected with the dome. It was a dangerous act for a Superior Soul Guardian, leaving them quite vulnerable to others in The Realm; necessary, however, if the circumstances justify the outcome.

It also opened her up to the current layout of The Realm. A momentary overview of others' whereabouts. However, this was a two-way observation; once open, other Superiors could also know what she was doing. In The Realm, this never proved an issue before with a naturally trusting environment, that is, until recently.

Verra Mica noticed someone else was out of place for one swift moment, and the speed with which they veiled proved they did not want to be seen. He had ventured into the forbidden sector of The Realm. A place where he should know better than to enter again.

As far as she could recall, Duergar, a young, spirited Soul Guardian, had been egged on by his Superior, Rammasus, to venture too near to the sector containing the Accumulator.

It was a negative quantum vortex held deep within The Realm's core, surrounded by a protective field. A dark negative nucleus of lifeless matter, and if any Soul Guardian dared to venture in, they would quickly lose their senses and direction and become disorientated. They would lose all connection and contact with The Realm if their stay were prolonged.

The Accumulator was a necessary evil, the dark counterpart to the ever-increasing light of the Source, drawing shadow energy from Eathia as it bypassed the Source's protective energy filters. The Accumulator had been growing due to the ongoing struggle on Eathia; the more it grew, the faster the tilt and the bigger the impact it had on The Realm.

This had happened to Duergar, and his Superior thankfully saved him before becoming immersed in the endless darkness, although he had unfortunately suffered for his mistake. Darkness began to grow within him, but he managed somehow to turn the experience around to his advantage. He worked tirelessly up through the ranks to become a Superior Soul Guardian. It was a risky move by Rammasus; he could have lost him in the abyss. Verra Mica never understood why he wasn't held accountable for his defiance in the same way Ashtar had been.

Being of the Psybiencian order, Duergar used music, whereas other orders worked with colours, songs, light or other energies. He was able to use harmonics in the same way, bending and forming musical notes to deliver various forms of messages, healing and wellbeing.

On a darker note, the music extricated from the Psybiencian was at best mesmerising, at worst hypnotic, rendering the receiver powerless, which depended entirely on the nature and motive of the source it came from. This was more in line with Duergar's beliefs.

Duergar's exceptional musical talent earned him great respect after returning from the brink of oblivion. However, some Soul Guardians believed he could manipulate other Soul Guardians' energies, causing them to act against their will. Verra Mica was among the few who remained wary of him due to his past.

She had picked up Duergar's vibrations right next to the Accumulator. No matter how fast he veiled, she had learnt to trust her initial observations and instincts, especially where he was concerned.

She continued to study the Source. Waiting to retrieve confirmation for the reason Angelica was there in the first place, details that had come to light from Makaria.

Nothing came back. That in itself was proof.

She knew of every birth within The Realm, and she would, eventually, catch Duergar out if he was manipulating the records. Unknown by any Superiors, Duergar helped create an immense number of births, some of which, she was now beginning to realise, had never been shared with The Realm. Instead, he veiled them at birth and sent them straight down through hidden portals. For all she knew, they were left to fend for themselves as free floaters on Eathia.

Verra Mica had to act on the information that had now come to light, but she had a class waiting for her.

After that, she would need to be quick. She needed backup and fast; she sent a message to Alma Tadema requesting an immediate audience.

The time had come to trust and hope she had made the right move.

Chapter 36

The Realm

Wonder Boy

While Verra Mica continued with her duties and waited for Alma Tadema, Makaria had started to grow curious as to the whereabouts of their Superior Duergar. A scheduled training session was delayed by his absence, which, even for Duergar, was an unusual occurrence.

Gallia, now positioned next to Makaria, noticed her frustration. Makaria felt she needed to make some sort of peace gesture after the confrontation in the Solescence Chamber.

'Strange, both Duergar and Wonder Boy are missing at the same time, don't you think?'

Gallia had to agree, but was not concerned.

'He will be here soon, I imagine, and as for his star pupil, he'll be off on some vital mission, no doubt. It appears that he's far too advanced to need these ridiculous training classes.'

Makaria now wished she hadn't drawn Gallia's attention to her thoughts and tried to change her approach instead.

'Oh yes, he's a wonder boy all right. Gallia, do I have your permission to leave? I have a quick errand I need to do. I'll make sure I am back before Duergar returns.'

Gallia appreciated that Makaria was finally elevating her above her own level, particularly since she had previously highlighted this very fact. It demonstrated her respect, and she valued that.

'What? Why? Oh, go on, but be quick, I won't cover for you.'

With that, Makaria exited the zone. She veiled herself and rushed towards Verra Mica's quarters. Finding them empty, she continued to remain shielded until she could return. She changed direction and cautiously headed toward the Seraphytes' training zone. Waiting just outside the entrance, she hesitated, and upon hearing Verra Mica, she slowly entered at the back of the group.

Verra Mica was now on the forum addressing her students. Makaria dropped her veil for just a moment and Verra Mica briefly stopped what she was saying when she realised she was there. Makaria's tactless announcement had caused others to sense her attendance.

One of the younger Seraphyte Soul Guardians moved closely to her nearest pupil.

'That's Angelica's twin sister Makaria, you know the one who went missing.'

A few around her overheard and tried to see who she was talking about. Verra Mica picked up on the disturbance.

'Hush, Corra, I can hear you, and so can most of the group. One moment please.'

Verra Mica left the rostrum and approached Makaria, quickly ushering her out of the zone.

'What are you thinking, drawing attention to yourself like that?'

She looked back, ensuring that none of the class had followed her.

'They're both missing this time. You said to let you know if anything strange happened. Well, it's happened.'

'Who exactly?'

'Duergar and Elkyne.'

'Are you saying that they are still there?'

'You know of this? What do you mean, there? Where?'

'I caught a glimpse earlier, very quickly, mind you, of two forms near the … '

Verra Mica trailed off, realising what she was about to divulge.

Makaria understood at once. Not mentioning it made it obvious.

'The Accumulator?'

'Right! Enough of this, leave it with me for the time being. You return to your group, Makaria, and let me finish mine. Unfortunately, I cannot leave just yet. I will keep you posted as much as I can. Go back quickly and keep that veil up; I don't want you going on the missing list, too.'

Makaria surmised that the situation was indeed bad. Leaving Verra Mica, she could but wonder if it might be too late. She couldn't help being intrigued to see what they were up to in the forbidden zone.

If they were still there, she had enough time to spy and get back before anyone realised. Quickly, she made her way through the zones, ensuring she went unnoticed.

She missed her sister, *She would have loved this*, she thought.

Chapter 37
The Realm

Very Big Butt

Unaware of any issues involving Verra Mica and Duergar, Alma Tadema remained semi-veiled to avoid any more interruptions as she manoeuvred her class through an in-depth and significant historical topic. Unfortunately, she started to receive messages from Verra Mica again. She tried to block them, but her friend irritatingly knew what she was up to and skillfully deviated away from her protective coding.

'Damn that woman!' she suddenly exclaimed which unfortunately brought the class's meditative state abruptly back to the present.

'I am sorry, I am being beckoned. Adamus, could you carry on for me? We were nearly at the end. Confounded disruptions.'

As Alma left her students and the auditorium, she was surprised to see that Verra Mica was waiting for her outside.

'For goodness' sake, you made me jump. What is so important that it couldn't wait?'

'My apologies, Alma, but you have known me long enough that I wouldn't contact you unless I needed to speak with you. Something has come to my attention and I need to discuss it with you.'

'That's very well, Verra, but I was just getting to an exciting and monumental part with our historical founders' group, and then you kept ... anyway, let's move on. Where would you like to speak? Do we need somewhere private?'

'Yes, if possible. Can we go back to my quarters?'

Verra Mica led the way. She started to fill Alma in en route.

'I really must implore you to keep this to yourself, Alma, it's vital we keep these concerns as quiet as possible, otherwise they're likely to blow up before we are ready to act.'

'I haven't the foggiest idea what you are talking about, Verra. Can you be more specific?'

Once they were in the confines of her quarters, she made sure she couldn't detect anyone scanning nearby before continuing.

'We have a situation. Right now, as we speak.'

Alma interrupted.

'We always have a situation nowadays, which one, in particular, is it this time?'

'Will you listen to me?'

Alma stopped and allowed her friend to speak.

'Duergar is game-playing. He appears to be manoeuvring certain Soul Guardians into a position where he can be most useful to him. If I am right, he is recruiting some of them even before they have reached their respective orders and using them to enter Eathia as floaters who will ultimately become his followers, regardless of what order they have been birthed into.

'This is pure supposition, Verra. Where are you getting this information from?'

'The fact that Duergar is currently at the Accumulator with Elkyne is a bad sign, and that there have been far too many other occurrences that are unexplainable, one of which includes your student, Nemius.'

'What do you mean, has something happened to him?'

'Corpus saw him at a Psybiencian meeting and suspects he is secretly following Duergar's orders, not yours.'

'Why would Duergar have anything to do with Nemius?'

'Why indeed. This is what I plan to find out, but I need further proof.'

'But even if he is taking our new births, how would he be getting them to Eathia without our knowledge? It seems too far-fetched to me.'

Verra Mica moved back from Alma and pondered whether to involve her in her plans. She was a good friend, which was not in question, but she was gullible and pliable, and Duergar somehow had an overbearing advantage with her.

'Listen, Alma, I have done what you have said. I took the orb into the Source against my better judgement.'

Alma Tadema tried to be positive.

'And that turned out well, don't you think?'

'Not yet, it hasn't. Anyway, as I was saying, I listened to you in Council. I took on board that things must change if we are all to survive, and I believe I am sympathetic to the idea that we may need to de-tether some of our Soul Guardians if they are to remain healthy, BUT, it's a big but ...'

Alma laughed, stopping Verra in her tracks.

'Sorry, you said, big butt. It just made me...' She trailed off as Verra Mica's expression became unimpressed 'You're making me doubt if I should even be talking to you.'

'You make me like this, Verra You're so intense, I can't help but lighten things up.'

'It is serious, Alma.'

'Very well. Yes, you have listened, and you have tried to understand, and I agree that it is very odd for Duergar to be seen anywhere near the Accumulator. How are you planning on going forward from here?'

Verra Mica moved closer to her friend.

'Can I trust you?'

'Of course,.'

Once Verra Mica felt assured, she informed Alma of all her doubts and what steps she was taking to counter Duergar's attempts to control Eathia's fate. Alma was horrified at some of what Verra Mica said and had to admit she had been a little naïve where he was concerned.

'So, will you speak to Nemius, try to gauge where his allegiance lies, without alerting him, of course.'

'I will, Verra. Things are turning very nasty indeed. You are sure this is our only option? I mean, do all the Triplexes know of this outcome if things escalate? It seems such a harsh choice.'

'No, just Christi, and it must stay that way; we have had guidance on this matter. At least we know that Eathia will have a chance if Duergar gets his way, and we are forced to pull away from our beloved tethers. If ever there was a time I needed the wisdom of Ashtar, it would be now. I should go; thank you, dear friend, for listening and trusting in me. Now, open yourself up to what's really going on here, I implore you.'

Relieved, Verra Mica eventually returned to her students and Alma Tadema to her auditorium. Now, she didn't feel like she was fighting this cause alone. It was a risk to involve Alma, but one she needed to take now that her own Soul Guardian, Nemius, had become so involved, too.

In the far corner of The Realm, Duergar fought to keep Elkyne focused.

'Do I have your undivided attention, Elkyne? And by undivided, I mean undivided. What I am about to tell you was told to me by my mentor, Rammasus.'

'Yes, you do, Superior. From what I understand, he was quite a shady character. And by shady, I mean Dark.'

'Spare me your sarcastic, sanctimonious comments, please, Elkyne. You are still just a naïve student who, instead of listening to his preordained order, chooses to heed the gossip of an ill-advised relic. Perhaps I was wrong about you. It appears you remain a nonessential embellishment to the Psybiencian order after all. Why do you choose to test me so, when it is I that can raise you to The Realm's higher order?'

'With respect, Superior, I am aware of many things, Naïve I am not. I "test" you, your word, not mine, because I continue to seek the truth. If I am to be your prodigy, I would rather not have my foundations built on a narcissistic and inflated point of view.'

Duergar bellowed with laughter at Elkyne's effrontery. He decided encouragement would be a better tactic. They were getting nowhere fast, and he was running out of time.

'You are indeed my "prodigy". Hah! I'll make you a force to be reckoned with, Elkyne. Naïve was a little crude. I apologise, I have enough proof of naïvety in The Realm, and it appears you show no evidence of such a weakness.'

Elkyne felt he was beginning to see how Duergar functioned. If he was finally settling as a Psybiencian, he had to be sure he believed in what the order stood for. His newfound camaraderie with his Superior relieved his concerns for the time being, but, as with every meeting with Duergar, something gnawed away at him; something wasn't right.

'Shall we continue?'

Duergar allowed Elkyne his moment of glory. His tone was sharp, and he trusted that he believed in his words. It didn't matter what he believed in; he assured himself he'd come around to my his of thinking, one way or another.

'Follow me, please; I want to take you to the Accumulator.'

Elkyne stopped in his tracks.

'My concerns appear to be founded after all. The Accumulator, Superior. Why there of all places?'

'There we have it; this is exactly my point. Your immediate reaction is that of nearly every damn Soul Guardian, bar one that has ever existed here, and that is, unfortunately, to be expected. However, you are an advanced being, Elkyne. Start acting like one. Put aside your scepticism. I am confident that you will be able to embrace this concept alongside those you have naturally taken to be true with no questions asked. Let us leave now.'

Elkyne felt he had a point. He only questioned what he had yet to understand in his search for truth. Duergar trusted him as his mentor and for his advancement. He would continue. Duergar already sensed he had him intrigued, and that was all he needed. They moved on.

The Accumulator, embedded into the deepest part of The Realm, sat in a dangerous and forbidden zone. The force field that surrounded it was heavy with an intense, magnetic undulating interface, which worked at transferring the darker matter away from the Source itself. Its primary function was to balance the opposing energy forces created, historically, on Eathia. However, of late, it had also been necessary to draw on these forces from The Realm.

Within the confines of its outer casing, its baryonic matter created a self-perpetuating, anti-gravitational abyss in a constant state of self-consumption through its limitless energetic vortex, folding and turning in on itself, making its centre an eternal one-way tunnel to oblivion.

Each dark matter particle naturally shielded itself with a formation like a veiled protective field created by a Soul Guardian. Particles merged and then radiated out, surrounding the Accumulator's outermost layer. The thin layer within it gave the impression it was safe to be near, as it held the magnetic pull away from the atmosphere just enough to give whoever came close a false sense of security. But this was not the description that Duergar gave Elkyne.

They approached the outer perimeter of the forbidden sector.

Elkyne wanted to know Duergar's explanation of its reason for being there to see if it differed from his understanding from Source.

'How has this energy come to be, from what origins?'

'Eathia's natural organic matter contains particles that form what is known to them as "Original" matter. It is the basis of all that is Eathia. Each of these original matter particles has a reflective, or let's say, mirror image of themselves. The image is a perfect reflection, except that it is the opposite image – a particle that acts differently from its original counterpart. It is what's known as mirror matter. These symmetrical reflections can exist as an exact symmetry of nature, provided that a mirror particle exists for every ordinary particle, and that is very important. Now, this is where it gets interesting. Are you with me so far?'

Elkyne gestured that he was. He was intrigued.

'Good, well, the mirror matter throws off a shadow that goes unnoticed on Eathia because it is invisible to the Eathian eye, even though it contains similar properties to the reflective mirror matter. It is this uncontained shadow energy that has a much weaker unfaithful link to its particle; given this, it becomes a free-floating shadow which, because of its need to have a complete charge, gets drawn towards the stronger polar pull of our dark energetic vortex through our very own Source; the Source then rejects it, transferring it out towards the Accumulator. Each particle contains its very own protective veil, the Axion Chiral field, which surrounds and protects it.'

They had begun to approach the outer edges of the Accumulator.

'You talk about it as if it is living.'

'In a way, it is. Do you see now that we, in The Realm, are holding the Dark Shadow matter away from Eathia? A dangerous position, do you not think?'

'We hold Eathia's dark energy here? How big is it, the Accumulator that is?'

'It is eternal, Elkyne. There is no end to it. It only gains energy in momentum. The field around it acts as a one-way interstitial membrane, disabling the continuation of the reflective matter beyond into an eternal ether.'

Duergar paused, waiting to see Elkyne's reaction, but he did not comment.

'It's the dark side of the Source; it's a shadowed, altered image if you like.'

Elkyne remained silent, taking it in, giving himself a chance to assimilate all this new information.

'There is also another fundamental difference. The Accumulator has no consciousness. The Source can take on consciousness, an important part of understanding and learning from Eathians. This energy can't pass through into the Accumulator. This, together with the dark matter, creates a very dark energy where no consciousness dwells; light cannot penetrate, causing eternal darkness and eternal lifelessness.'

'And it is this Accumulator you wanted to show me? I would hate to see where you would take your enemies, your Honour. With respect.'

Duergar roared again at Elkyne's response, and then he suddenly stopped.

'Veil Elkyne, quickly, we are being scanned. Do it now, I say!'

Waiting just outside of the Accumulator, they both veiled. Elkyne waited for the coast to be clear.

'Who is scanning us?'

'Verra Mica. We must continue quickly.'

Elkyne was confused.

'Continue, where to now?'

Duergar looked at the pulsating wall of the Accumulator, then back at Elkyne.

'Inside, of course.'

Chapter 38
The Realm

Unauthorised Entry

Elkyne thought that he must have misheard Duergar.

'So, let me clarify – forbidden, dangerous, no entry on any account are phrases that mean nothing to you?'

'It means something is being hidden, and everyone goes along with it without questioning the reason behind it.'

The pause riled Duergar. This was taking too long.

'I have a class waiting, Elkyne. I really cannot be missing much longer.'

'Fine! What is it you would like to show me?'

As if on stage in front of his master class, Duergar proceeded to explain in more detail the workings of the Accumulator; this he did with flamboyant enthusiasm, a necessary shield he used from time to time when struggling with something that tapped into his unhealed wounds at the hands of Rammasus.

'The Accumulator is a portal, Elkyne. A portal to Eathia. A back door, if you like, but not for the faint-spirited. Its polar attraction to the shadow matter draws energy from Eathia via the Source. This, in turn, creates an interface with it. It is not one way as they would have you believe. There is a risk, but not to Soul Guardians in my order. I have ensured you are all prepared for such an eventuality, you see?'

Elkyne felt uneasy again as he noticed a strange sound emanating from Duergar's direction.'

'You're humming; I can hear your drone. Why?'

'It is not my drone that you hear but that of the vortex. It recognises you as one of its own.'

Elkyne lost interest in what he was saying, aware now of a different sensation. He had started to feel a sensory numbness and found it increasingly difficult to interpret what Duergar was saying.

'What's happening, Duergar? I don't feel right.'

'I need you to go into the Accumulator, Elkyne, and see why it is so important to us that we continue to watch Eathia in our own way. Tethering or using animals is becoming too tiresome. We are evolving separately; however, we must still understand what is happening there. Learning through a controlled, monitored and biased approach, by which I mean the Source, is not enough. Once you realise your true capability, you will see that we have evolved far beyond the Eathian requirements. We need to stop tethering if we are to survive. You will only trust me and your capabilities once you experience this for yourself.'

Elkyne heard his words but could not absorb them. Duergar's hypnotic drone held him in a vice-like grip. The rhythmical sensation around him was intensifying, and he was now involuntarily moving towards the exterior glow that had started to emanate from the surface of the chamber. As he was moved closer to the wall of the Accumulator, he could see someone approaching, another being. Then he realised it was an image of him, beckoning him to follow. The image's substance was of an altogether different form, with energies much denser than his own. As he felt himself move forward, he blended with his image, merging spirits and advancing into a different formation. It was glorious to experience such harmony. He let go and allowed the merger.

Duergar tried hard to pull himself back. The draw was so strong when he was near it. It was a wonderful experience, but maintaining a safe distance from it became increasingly difficult for him without being drawn into its powerful magnetic pull.

He knew there was little time left and it had already taken too long. The real reason for Duergar's concern was not his class that were waiting on his arrival but that they would soon be out of alignment with Eathia. The window was closing. If that happened during his descent, the consequences would be disastrous for Elkyne.

As Makaria approached the Accumulator, she raised her shield. Nearing the tunnel, she slowed down and entered the final corridor, sensing movement ahead. Gradually, she edged closer, keeping near the inner wall. Curious, she studied the forbidden area, her senses attuned to an unusual sound. Monitoring it, she noticed a heavy drone, denser than typical Psybiencian noises, indicating nearby beings; she realised that anything close would be engulfed by its hypnotic pulse.

She lowered her own vibration and energy and slowly moved out from the side of the wall's surface, stopping suddenly when she saw Duergar in front of her. That noise was coming from him. There was movement to the side of him, and leaning out just a little more, she thought she saw another Soul Guardian.

What were they doing? she wondered.

Torn between alerting Verra Mica or staying to see what Duergar was up to, she waited and continued to watch in horror as the other being disappeared into some kind of pulsating force field.

As Elkyne descended further into the Accumulator's heart, the other form's oppressive density consumed him, invading his own lightened core with suffocating force. He felt he was being pulled away from The Realm, dragged into an inescapable darkness. The heavy drone of Duergar faded into its shadows, and with its retreat, Elkyne's senses ebbed away amidst the encroaching void. In the fleeting moments left to him, caught between Duergar's suffocating grip and the new, malevolent force emanating from the Accumulator, he realised escape was impossible. Now spiralling entirely out of control, he plunged deeper into the vortex, self-recognition slipping away into the abyss. He struggled to recall anything of himself.

Suddenly, he heard a voice screaming at him to 'SHIELD'. Was it his own words? 'Shield, SHIELD NOW.' Just as the last of his form and energy dispersed, he drew in what little remained, increasing his vibration and forcing his shield up and around him. Sparks of energy firing and fading into shadows continued to forge some form of energetic ignition – this was the same detonation used to bring an Eathian back from death. He felt as though he was experiencing a rebirth. 'Come on!' he screamed, falling faster and faster. Darkness was seeping into Elkyne's very soul as he struggled to hold it at bay. Now, his own drone was beginning to rise, stronger and louder than he had ever known possible.

He screamed as searing, burning energy exploded like lava from volcanic mountains. At that moment, his being ignited back into life. His complete, energetic form returned in an immense atomic reversal. He felt nearly every part of himself get torn away, and in one almighty burst, it returned fully; the force field around him started to become visible.

With this new awareness came a new terror. He was plunging out of control, his speed increasing.

He realised it was too late to avoid the inevitable impact.

The numbness returned, only this time it was of his own making. His drone took him away from the horror of what was about to be inflicted on him. He entered the darkened force without sound or feeling, shielded from his self-imposed doom.

It was then that distant voices began to echo about him.

Within The Realm, Duergar, now satisfied that Elkyne had made it into Eathia in the nick of time, moved away from the Accumulator, weak and needing healing. It had taken longer for him to lure Elkyne into the vortex; this, he realised, had been his one opportunity to get him anywhere near the damn Accumulator.

It's finally done, he thought.

Still weak and uncertain, Duergar felt it prudent to check in on Verra Mica before attending his own session with his Psybiencians. This would relinquish any concerns of his own that it might have been she who had been watching him and Elkyne at the Accumulator.

He was aware that he was now significantly behind schedule.

He realised what she was teaching as he approached Verra Mica's students' training group.

Fantastic timing, he thought.

On Eathia, Christi felt the tear as her connection to Elkyne severed. Her Eathian baby cried out as anguish ripped through Christi. Unable to console her and realising she was the cause of her pain, she headed back to The Realm.

Corpus reeled at the sensation now building within his core. His first thought was of Christi. *Had something happened to her or to her tether?*

Then, like a bolt of lightning, he felt the full force of the separation. Gabriel, now two, happily played on the kitchen floor until he felt it through Corpus. It burst out of him in a flurry of emotions, and he screamed for his mother for comfort.

Corpus tried to contact Christi, already knowing it would be fruitless. He would have to return to The Realm, and quickly.

Makaria realised that the person standing next to Duergar had now fully entered the Accumulator. The shock jolted her, causing her to drop her veil momentarily. She retreated quickly, backing up against the wall, collecting herself and re-veiling; she carefully worked her way towards the exit. Then, when she knew she was clear, she launched herself free of the area and away from Duergar, not knowing if he had sensed her watching him. As she fled, she tried not to relive the vision of seeing that poor Soul Guardian being sucked into the dark Axion field.

The awful realisation that it could only have been Elkyne caused her to stop and take stock. '*What was happening? Why would a Superior endanger one of his own? She wondered.*

Something Duergar had once said to her regarding her sister's disappearance came back to her.

'*The means justify the cause'.*

She thought about its meaning and wondered why hadn't she questioned him at the time.

He was saying that even a morally wrong action is justified if the outcome was for the greater good.

He didn't care about any of them. The Realm, his own order, his followers – none of them.

Chapter 39
The Realm

Hello Old Friend

Unaware of the seriousness unfolding within the Accumulator, Verra Mica had scheduled a training session that would require her utmost attention and concentration, which was not the best time for such an exercise with all that was happening around her. This would not be easy on this occasion as her thoughts were naturally elsewhere.

The session itself was her final session with her current group of students. Her group was now nearing the end of their attainment before entering a new level. She would show them how to control and deliver the right correlation of energetic harmonics for healing. As Seraphytes, once they were tethered, they would be able to heal through the sound of their voices, an act they would demonstrate initially within the confines and safety of their group. For an Eathian to receive healing, especially this type of healing, it was generally administered while they slept or at times of complete turmoil.

As Verra Mica readied herself for her group, she took a little longer to settle, initially torn between choosing whether to cancel the session altogether or continue to avoid further disruption. Besides, Duergar could have simply been showing Elkyne what had happened to him as a student, just as a father would a son on Eathia, creating a stronger bond between them. He was his mentor, after all. It was hard to give him the benefit of the doubt, but she would have to try not to overreact.

Her students were starting to become a little unsettled. Their noise brought her back to the group.

'Right, this is it: your final lesson at this level. To begin, I want to hear your voices harmonising the Setheria. Listen carefully to one another and adapt to any natural changes in vibration and sound. I don't want any leaders. Do you understand? If you take the lead, you lose control and disrupt the process of natural feedback. We want unity at all times. We will go through this once and only once, and when I am ready, I will start to lower my vibration, causing you to see the colours fade from me. I will become more transparent and vulnerable, so please be careful with me. My energy centre will remain intact, of course, but my vital signs will begin to diminish. You MUST listen out for my choral tone. That is the key to knowing when to flow alongside it and initially raise it. What you aim to see is my vital signs starting to return. Be gentle; I am in your care. I do not want any of you breaking free. Keep your focus and make this count. There will not be another opportunity to retake this exercise. That said, I have the utmost confidence in all of you; you are capable and extremely knowledgeable in this process, and we have discussed it enough. When you are ready, I will initiate, and then it will be up to you. Good luck, for my sake.'

The class laughed nervously until they were ready to start.

Verra Mica needed to lower her guard, shield and veil to create the right level for her student to gain a connection to her. Her energetic vibrations would be reduced to a minimal level, almost to the point of senselessness. This was a dangerous state as it left her vulnerable to mistakes, but she had raised many groups to very high levels with her training methods and felt just as confident in this group's abilities.

When she was ready, the group naturally settled and focused on her, primed to begin simulating her tone; then, it was up to them.

The auditorium fell silent.

No number, letter or word can describe the essence of sound emanating from a Seraphyte. They can mimic all sound and imagery, enabling them to communicate in every living language and culture of all worlds, including the animal world on Eathia.

Verra Mica set the tone for the expectant audience. Each Soul Guardian connected with their energy, following her steady voice. This vibration could travel thousands of miles on Eathia to one target or a nearby individual. They absorbed the sound, perfectly reflecting it back, their response flawless as their tenor rose with growing confidence and energy.

Verra Mica relaxed her harmony back and lowered her energetic levels. She sensed proudly that the group was with her. Now free, she could plunge into unconsciousness, a defenceless state that gave her students a unique opportunity to grow into pure Seraphytes. Her translucent frame began to float weightlessly before her group, her consciousness drifting far away from The Realm and into an oblivious state of numbness.

Moving in on the healing vibration, Duergar felt it was safe enough to open his own depleted aura up to the students, a parasite using the Seraphytes' healing to help himself regain his energetic levels. He dared not go to Baquarrah in case he tapped into why his energy was low. He decided this would do just fine for the time being.

He watched Verra Mica's radiant form, defenceless to any Soul Guardian wishing to annihilate her life force. The risks she took in the name of training were ludicrous.

He scoffed at his own hypocrisy.

Good to know, though, he thought.

As good as it was to stay within the beautiful healing, he had to leave. His energy was now strong enough to do so, and to stay longer would risk unsettling the group. He returned to his students, who he was sure would have sent out a search party by now. He would need to come up with reasons not just for his absence but also to explain Elkyne's disappearance if he failed to return.

At the time, Verra Mica had been unaware of Duergar's presence, an uninvited parasite feeding off the healing at the back of the room.

Her students' voices became a distant calling, their tones mingling and recreating her own vibrational harmonics that sent out sound waves towards her that hooked into her core and kept her steady. They were doing well.

As she opened up to them, she fought hard to keep their information influx flooding her senses. This was a common occurrence once her protective wall was lowered. It was like having thousands of voices speaking simultaneously. She steadied the current and centred herself again, but within the chaos was a voice she wasn't expecting. It was a call for help. Without her response, the Soul Guardian had chosen to send a complete message instead. Verra Mica had a sudden image appear before her.

It was of Mary, her only Eathian tether. Verra Mica bolted at the sight of Mary almost drowning in dark murky water. The shock at seeing her passed on an anxious current straight onto the group of students she was training. They thankfully held fast and continued as if this was part of the exercise. When the message had dispersed, Verra Mica tried hard to work through the remaining process for the group's sake, stage by stage, allowing her students to complete their tests.

When she felt she had regained her composure, another voice entered her awareness, a familiar one from long ago.

'Surely it couldn't be, not after all this time?' she questioned.

Verra Mica seemed to freeze in time.

‘It is I, Verra Mica. Please do not alarm yourself.’

His communication with her seemed to push her group’s vibrations back to a distant base level as if their connection with her was being paused. His communication, now freely attuned to Vera Mica’s, allowed his words to filter through her as if he were again by her side.

‘Ashtar? Is that you?’

‘Yes, it is I. I have waited a long time to be able to speak with you, Verra. Only now that we are in alignment and you are open to receiving can I be heard.’

Verra Mica felt overwhelmed. After all this time, her dear mentor and friend was here with her.

‘Where have you been? It has been so long, and so much has happened.’

‘I am needed to work on the outer planes, an overseer, if you like, of all our planets.’

Upon hearing his voice, the time spent apart vanished, and she found herself back with him again.

‘I intended to speak of all that has happened since we last were together. However, the current events are now quite overwhelming, and my original intended conversation falls into insignificance.’

His voice was reassuring, yet Verra Mica could detect an element of intensity in his tone.

‘I understand, Ashtar. We are in an unusual predicament, to say the least. Any input you have would be of great value to me.’

‘I have seen disturbing events on Eathia, and now I fear there is evidence that all is not well within The Realm either, and I see Rammasus’s ideologies have bled into Duergar now too. And you, Verra, you have had to lose your tether; I am truly sorry for asking you to leave Eathia with me. I had hoped you would have a long life with Mary and our Eathian child. I am truly sorry this was not as we hoped.’

Verra Mica suddenly felt despair. She was concerned for her students, not knowing whether she was safe, but the overwhelming loss of both Ashtar and Mary returned and was no less painful than the moment it happened.

‘I feel I have lost her all over again, Ashtar. I have seen her fall into the dark, cold waters of Eathia, and she is with our child.’

‘She lives, Verra. Angelica had fled to be with her now. I understand your grief, but it is our Eathian daughter who is in danger now. She will soon be suffering at the hands of dark forces. I am unable to act or help her. I have comforted and been healing them, but the darkness will consume her soon;

they are closing in. Verra, he must not be allowed to use her to get back. Can you hear my words, Verra? I need you to understand. On no account must you let him return.'

Verra Mica felt herself begin to divide; this was not good. Ashtar's voice was retreating, and she was fighting against her natural return to the group, which was making it impossible for the group to draw her back safely. She had to go. She had to let him go for now. She called to him.

'Who must not return, Ashtar?'

She was being pulled away, and now the soft vibrations of her students were washing over her senses. She thought she heard Ashtar's voice as it retreated into the ether, but she could not make sense of his answer. He was gone. Their worlds, wherever he was, had fallen out of alignment; with it, he had gone too.

She returned to a very anxious group, whom she could see by their reaction, felt they had failed her in some way.

She tried to reassure them.

'That was perfect, yes, very good. I … I was taken aback by something that wasn't your fault, but you coped well. Thank you. I must go if you'll all excuse me.'

Verra Mica realised that she was making no sense to her class in her daze of what had just happened. One of the Seraphyte Soul Guardians at the front moved forward.

'Are you sure you are well, Superior?'

The Soul Guardian looked back at the group as if to show that she was speaking for all of them.

'You were gone for quite some time, and we thought we had lost you at one point. Did we make mistakes?'

'No, it was I; I unintentionally made it difficult for you, and you succeeded well and in a very unexpected situation. On the contrary, you have all excelled. Besides, if it had gone wrong, I would have become a part of history and one of Superior Alma Tadema's odes, no doubt, but I am still here, thankfully.'

The group, relieved at her humour, laughed and prepared to leave.

Verra Mica sent an urgent message to Corpus and Christi for immediate counsel.

Chapter 40
The Realm

Lost

On her route to meet Christi and Corpus, she ran into Makaria. She was disturbed, to say the least, and Verra Mica appealed for her to stop and calm herself.

At that moment, Verra Mica received a message from Christi. She needed to see her in the Solescence Chamber immediately.

She addressed Makaria.

'What has happened? Do you know something?'

'It's Duergar. He was in the forbidden zone with a Soul Guardian. I couldn't see clearly who it was, but I can guess … he entered the Accumulator.'

Shock swept through Verra Mica.

'Who did? Duergar?'

'No, the Soul Guardian that was with him.'

Another message came through to her; this time, it was Corpus, pleading for her to meet them.

'I have to go. Go safely back to your group and say nothing of this until I understand what is going on.'

As Makaria disappeared, Verra Mica rushed to join Corpus and Christi.

Then she received an unexpected message from Olpheria. She advised her that she would meet her on the way to the Solescence Chamber.

As Corpus had risen from the portal in the lake, he saw Christi waiting at its edge. She looked as shaken as he was.

'What has happened? Are you alright?'

Christi looked at him with an almost vacant expression.

'Can't you feel it, now you're here? He's gone. Elkyne has gone.'

Corpus tuned in to his core and felt the void immediately. He messaged Verra Mica again.

'I don't understand.'

Within moments, Verra Mica and Olpheria were storming into the chamber.

Christi shot forward towards them.

'We have lost all contact with Elkyne. He has severed his connection,' Christi declared.

Verra Mica looked visibly shaken. Her aura paled and she became sullen. Then, the anger hit.

'Damn that fool.'

Verra Mica glanced across at Olpheria.

'Tell them what you sensed.'

They could see that she was struggling too.

'I am closely connected to Elkyne because of our healing sessions. So, when he is in trouble, I can get a secondary sense that all is not well. I tuned into him when it happened earlier and it was just awful.'

Olpheria froze. Unable to continue, Verra Mica carried on.

'He's sent Elkyne into the Accumulator. We've lost him.'

Chapter 41
The Realm

What Darkness Awaits

As Elkyne fell, shadowy figures eagerly awaited him beneath a shimmering portal that appeared to them like a mercury lake on the roof of a cave hidden deep within a cove. These forms were the Dark Soul Guardians, originating from The Realm. They consisted of both Psybiencians and Seraphytes. All had been sent down to Eathia one way or another, either by choice or by deceit.

These Dark Soul Guardians were free to move across Eathia, having been recruited by Duergar to observe and bide their time until he initiated his plan. They inhabited the elements of water (sirens), air (Airians) and land (Terraneans) and were completely detached from The Realm. Their state of being untethered or free-floating on Eathia would jeopardise their chances of ever returning home.

Their forms remained invisible to Eathians unless they tethered with one or to an animal, as in the case of the sirens.

Eathia was becoming a breeding ground for all dark forces, culminating in many forms, living freely amongst the unsuspecting Eathians.

They were gradually increasing their presence in Eathia. Duergar had started recruiting long ago, and they remained loyal followers, patiently awaiting his commands. Other Dark Soul Guardians were taken from The Realm at the instant of their own birth, entering Eathia through the secret portal, which, at the time, was known only to Duergar.

It was through this portal that Elkyne now travelled.

Once Elkyne entered the Accumulator, Duergar maintained his field as long as possible. Sensing Elkyne's presence within the vortex, he stayed with him until it faded, draining most of Duergar's energy. The dark matter rapidly depleted a Soul Guardian, making it nearly impossible to sustain protective fields, which were vital for their existence. Duergar was unique; he was the only one to return from the Accumulator without being annihilated or passing through its portal entirely. His predecessor, Rammasus, had adequately prepared him for safety.

His intention for Elkyne, as far as Elkyne was concerned, was for him to see Eathia for himself. He was to be untethered and meet with Duergar's army of Dark Soul Guardians and, with their help, return him in one piece.

However, Duergar's reasoning for this absurd act was for Elkyne to experience the Accumulator and it's energ. Duergar hadn't told Elkyne that entering the dark matter would change him forever. He believed this would help dull the upstart's conflicted mind and turn even the strongest objectors. It also provided a blinding clarity about the possibilities within one's being; it led to the vortex's darkest centre, leaving an eternal imprint on their soul, a darkened corner that could gradually grow from within. In Duergar's view, this darkness was essential for a complete Soul Guardian, providing the balance needed to be a true Soul Guardian, as he was and his mentor before him.

Duergar was sure he had felt another's presence towards the end of his contact with Elkyne and just before he disappeared. The energy given off hindered any scanning attempts; in any case, Duergar no longer felt it important as, by now, he was sure Elkyne would be on Eathia. He would leave it to Nephelia to welcome him, a meeting that would alter his perspective permanently.

She was a siren. The first of many Dark Soul Guardians of the water, and one of the original followers of Duergar. She was first class at luring sailors in towards the rocks using her talent for echoing sound and music out towards them, enchanting and spellbinding them to be drawn towards her. Now, part of a much larger shoal, she could bring down whole ships while sending out mesmerising sounds from her siren choir.

Their existence lived on in sailors' superstitions, too scared to admit they were real. Their stories were pushed to the back of their minds, where they found solace in ignorance.

But they were real, and Sirenguard was the first of many coves they inhabited.

~

Chapter 42
The Realm

King of Secrecy

Verra Mica called for an urgent meeting with the Superiors. Still, it wasn't until then that she realised her unexpected communication with Ashtar had been overridden by the shocking news of Elkyne.

Once the meeting had happened and once they had all spoken to Duergar themselves, she would talk to Corpus and Christi again to see if they could shed any light on Ashtar's message to her. The strange mention of their Eathian daughter, Sara, baffled her and any connection with her and a request to not allow someone access back into The Realm made no sense to her.

Things were starting to escalate. But why and to what end, she wondered. She hadn't had time to revel in the glory of hearing from Ashtar before she was launched into the despair of losing Elkyne.

Baquarrah responded quickly, aware of what had happened from his Soul Guardian, Olpheria. Once Alma Tadema had replied, they decided to meet at Verra Mica's quarters. Seeing as none of them had heard from Duergar since his last session with his class, they felt that was the best place to convene.

Verra Mica started immediately once her chamber had been secured,

'What was he thinking? Can any of you think of why he would do such a thing?'

Alma Tadema spoke hesitantly.

'Are we sure that is what has happened? Before we go blazing after Duergar without having all of the facts.'

Baquarrah reassured her.

'Olpheria felt him fall, Alma, she knew exactly where he was and called for him to shield. He was fracturing from the denseness of the abyss. She doesn't know if he made it or if he is lost for good. It is alarming. There is no doubt about what Duergar has done. None at all.'

They all felt a sudden high-pitched tone coming from just beyond the entrance to Verra Mica's chambers. They all turned to see Duergar emerging from the supposedly locked doorway.

'How dare you enter my chamber uninvited!'

Verra Mica realised immediately that she had invited him initially. The fact that he had disappeared was irrelevant.

Duergar just quietly looked at each of them in turn. There was an uncomfortable silence. Then he spoke.

'I assume you are all gathered here to discuss my unorthodox approach to teaching my latest protégée. I imagine you all have something to say about it. I would have rather you come to me directly rather than gather here secretly.'

Verra Mica seethed with fury at the hypocrisy. *He is the king of secrecy!* she thought, as her aura flared.

'You left us no choice. What you have done is despicable. To risk losing a pure Soul Guardian is beyond our beliefs.'

'Do I tell any of you how to teach your students? I only ever look out for them. I have made it clear that you are not preparing them. I, on the other hand, am making sure Elkyne is completely aware and ready for all measures of eventualities that lie ahead of him.'

He addressed Verra Mica.

'How dare you question my methods!'

He went to walk away, but turned to the group, all staring at him in disbelief.

'Elkyne is safe and will rejoin us in due course.'

With that, he left.

Alma Tadema remained silent. Baquarrah had heard enough.

'I owe you an apology, Verra Mica. I have completely misjudged Duergar's motives. Elkyne is far from safe. Should you require further support in this and any matter – concerning Duergar, you shall have it, unequivocally. I see we have quite a lot of catching up to do. I am happy to hear what you have discovered thus far.'

Baquarrah bowed at both the Superiors, left quietly and returned to his chamber.

Alma Tadema looked across at her friend.

'I'm sorry, Verra. I have been a fool. He's gone too far. Let's talk again and …

Verra Mica interrupted her.

'I've heard from Ashtar.'

Chapter 43
The Realm

Artius

Despite their son's half-hearted attempts at derailing their lives, for the most part, Corpus's tether, Gabriel, now middle aged was starting to make some progress, and together, they were having fun through his development of skills and studies. There was now an unexpected surprise for both of them: a new unplanned baby was on the way.

While Gabriel and Beatrice's cottage was peaceful, an unexpected message came to Corpus and Christi. They both felt the urgency in Verra Mica's tone, but it was the middle of their day on Eathia. They sent out a rare blast of healing to lower their tethers' vibrations enough to induce tiredness. Sleep was inevitable, especially as Christi's tether was getting increasingly tired as her pregnancy term went on.

Content that they could de-tether, they returned to the Solescence Chamber to find their extremely volatile Superior waiting for them.

Corpus entered just ahead of Christi.

'What is it, your Honour? Have you heard anything about Elkyne?'

Verra Mica, who was about to launch into what had happened during her study group, suddenly became sidetracked and jumped when she read from Christi's aura that there was to be another child born into their Eathian family.

'A baby? That was not accounted for. See what I mean when I say Eathians cannot be relied upon? Things can change in an instant. Leave that one with me. I might have the perfect solution.'

She adjusted her energy and continued with the reason she called them to her ward.

'Right, I hardly know where to start. We need to speed things up. We have no time. Where is your tether in his advancements? Is he getting somewhere, Corpus?'

'Yes, we are getting there, slowly. He has the first drafts of the machine.'

Christi stepped forward, sensing her edginess.

'What has happened, your Honour? Have you heard anything of Elkyne?'

'Unfortunately, no The little I have is a pathetic assurance from Duergar that he is safe.'

She paused and became aware of the possibility they could be overheard.

'No, this isn't safe. Come with me.'

She exited the chamber, waited for them to join her, and then embedded a code into them both. They re-entered another chamber altogether. It was the private animal sanctuary where Verra Mica had taken them before.

Verra Mica paused, waiting for the atmosphere in the room to calm down at their arrival.

'I have heard from Ashtar.'

Both Corpus and Christi were stunned into silence. Verra Mica continued.

'It was during my training class. He entered, or rather, I entered his ether. He informed me of Angelica's whereabouts and explained why. I was shocked to hear that she has now managed to tether to my original Eathian, Mary. She is alive, my Mary is alive. Now, I understand Angelica's need to stay veiled from Duergar's view. She has been able to continue in my place. I am so grateful for her loyalty and courage in adversity.'

Verra Mica's form was filled with abundant colour, a rare occurrence.

'Ashtar has seen her, but he is concerned about her Eathian child, our Eathian child I should say. She is being used in some way by dark forces. He had some knowledge of our current situation here. That was all I could glean from him, but it was enough. Oh, and he mentioned that we mustn't, on any account, allow him to return.'

They glanced at each other.

'Who?' Corpus questioned.

'Who was he talking about?'

'I don't know. I lost contact with him.'

She looked at Corpus.

'We need to speed things up with Gabriel before it becomes too late for us to act. I apologise for pulling you both away at such short notice. Let us leave now, and you can re-enter your chamber and return to your tethers.'

Once Verra Mica had gone, they remained in her private chamber for a while. Before they could discuss Ashtar's return, the large black bird flew towards them, eventually resting with Corpus.

'Hello, my friend. Thank you for not blowing my cover.'

Christi scowled at him.

'How do you know this one? Secrets, brother?'

Corpus laughed.

'We are old friends. I have flown with him often, but please keep it between us.'

'But why the secret from me?'

'Because I wanted to surprise you and take you with me, but we just haven't had the chance. Isn't he beautiful? Christi? His name is Artius. When I am tethered to him, it's like free flying. Only on Eathia can you feel it in that way. When I am joined with him, the stimulation of air pushing at you brings so many other senses to life like nothing else can here.'

'You do surprise me, brother.'

The bird flew away and re-joined the others, barely missing a swot from Marla, the gorilla, who had been watching them from a distance.

Corpus watched and laughed at the ape's antics.

'Christi, for Ashtar to come forward now, after so long, must mean things are worsening. I think he knows Duergar's intentions and is trying to help us, albeit from a distance.'

He continued.

'I think my tether needs a little push in the right direction to help speed things up, as Verra Mica suggested. With this in mind, I have an idea, but I need you to trust me. After all, this is why we are here, is it not?'

'What are you up to, Corpus? Shouldn't you run it by Verra Mica first?'

'I will, at the right time, but now, please let me try to, how did she put it, "open his eyes" in the best way I can. I am sure now is the right time, so I must go.'

As they left and re-entered their own Solescence Chamber, Corpus hurried over to the lake's edge. He looked back at Christi.

'Wish us luck.'

And then he jumped.

Christi hesitated before joining him. Should she return and let Verra Mica know he was being Corpus again? *Great, well, we know how this will end*, she thought.

Instead, she chose to give him the benefit of her doubt. She followed him to rejoin her tether.

When she re-entered, Beatrice slept soundly, so Christi stayed outside her vibration for a while. Using her melody, she let it stream over her while she slept. She should focus on them for now, her tether and the new baby growing inside her. She was still concerned for Corpus, a worry that remained close by like an indistinguishable niggle deep inside her soul.

Corpus now knew what he should do. *Was it unethical?* he wondered. *Possibly!* he thought. *Slightly precarious?* Not if he was careful. Besides, being back with the animals reminded him that he had done it countless times on his own and oh, what an experience! How could his tether not want to experience that joy and awareness? There was nothing like it. To be both Eathian and Soul Guardian, with a foot in The Realm and Eathia. That should be enough to turn the smallest tides and help him understand what was at stake and why he had to finish the machine quickly.

Chapter 44
The Realm

Duty of Care

To draw an Eathian consciousness away from their body was something Corpus assumed to be rudimentary. If said Eathian was to be asleep at the time, then surely he wouldn't miss it.

Once Gabriel had fallen asleep that evening, Corpus began to draw the essence of his soul away from him. It clung to its life form initially, but eventually, trusting in the familiar energy of Corpus, it gently followed him through the tether up into The Realm.

Corpus watched as Gabriel began to settle into his alternative state, intrigued by his awareness and clarity of perception.

He had spoken to Gabriel once he was asleep. Sending out a low, harmonious tone at the same time had worked in pulling Gabriel's consciousness to him. It slipped away easily once Gabriel had connected to the familiar tones and nuances of Corpus's voice.

Corpus introduced himself, being cautious not to alarm his Eathian visitor as they hovered on the outskirts of The Realm.

Once some of the expected teething problems were ironed out, Corpus could show Gabriel The Realm and explain why he had brought him there in the first place.

Initially, Corpus knew that while Gabriel felt he was dreaming, he would be able to maintain his sense of equilibrium while he was there. If, for any reason, fear took over, then he would need to work harder at keeping Gabriel stable in that reality, that being The Realm.

Corpus showed him vistas from Gabriel's past lives, and for that moment in time, Gabriel remembered every one of them. As Gabriel watched, the scenery transformed, moving from one image to another.

He was mesmerised by their beauty.

It took a while for Gabriel to realise he wasn't physically there. When he spoke, he had no lips to form the word, and when he looked for his hand, it didn't exist, just a translucent form that floated in front of him.

The first problem came when Gabriel instinctively looked down, assuming Eathia was below him. As he did so, the shock of floating caused him to panic, and his subconscious awareness faltered before he had the chance to regain control.

Realising that there was no ground beneath him only compounded his loss of composure, and he continued to fall. Initially, it was more of a visual falling, without the physical attributes, until finally, they joined in, too. Together, they became the embodiment of falling, a feeling he recognised. He tried to scream but felt instead an illusion of a hefty thud as his body felt as though it had hit hard against the mattress of his bed. The air in his lungs was exhaled, along with an involuntary groan.

Once Gabriel's heart steadied itself from the shock of the impact of falling, he began to drift off towards Corpus's voice again. With ease, he slowly lifted and returned to him once more.

Eventually, Corpus was able to fully explain the concept of The Realm. The Source and now the Accumulator, and how Eathia had begun to affect them. He told him of the urgency of building the machine Gabriel had been working on and how he hoped it would help Eathia in the future.

Once Gabriel eventually realised he wasn't experiencing a dream, his time in The Realm helped confirm that he was indeed on the right track with his inventions. He understood that with Corpus aiding him, things would possibly start to run a little smoother now that he knew of his existence. The difficulty would be for him to learn how to listen to Corpus while on Eathia. That would take some practice. However, their link would be stronger now that they had officially met.

When Corpus felt that Gabriel had understood and realised his role in the larger scheme of things, he wanted to give him a treat. Something that would lift him, like flying, as he had done so many times with the raven, Artius, when Gabriel had been sleeping. He felt that taking him over his homestead would expand his knowledge simultaneously.

Veiling them both, Corpus entered the tunnels of The Realm and took him at speed to the outer door of the animal chambers. He quickly took

Gabriel through, similar to Verra Mica, and guided him towards the lake.

The raven instinctively flew to Corpus's side and called for another to join them. Each of them tethered by merging their soul to the birds and entered the lake.

Corpus kept a close eye on his friend as they fell together, in tandem through the clouds of the lake and then into the sky of Eathia. Gabriel felt no gush of wind, no sinking feeling in his stomach as he imagined he would, just the exhilaration of travelling at such a speed.

Gabriel looked in awe at the view, a perspective he would never have the pleasure of witnessing again.

Looking down through the early penetrating light of dawn, he could see the ocean beneath them. Never had he seen the sea for himself; it was spread as far as his vision could stretch. Mountains rose up from its depths and curved around in arches as if to hold a part of the ocean still within its protection. He looked up and saw the sky still holding onto some of the night stars even as light slowly emanated far over the horizon. Part of Eathia's sky was still in darkness.

Suddenly, they plummeted down towards the sea. Gabriel shrieked with delight as the waves quickly rose and fell before them. He looked at the mountains and saw their contours turning into smaller hills and valleys. Trees began to appear and disappear beneath them. He looked across at Corpus; he was looking back at the ocean, and Gabriel followed his gaze. In an instant, the sea was upon them. He felt sure he was about to dive in through its surface, but Corpus pulled them up again before he could react, curving their small bodies towards the sky. Gabriel let out a cry of excitement.

Then, at that moment, they stopped in mid-air. Corpus was looking down at something; Gabriel saw something in the water. Then, in a moment, the sea became full of moving objects, swimming, diving and swirling, rising to its surface and back down into its depths.

Corpus's attention became lost on these sea creatures. Then, he saw some Eathians from the water crawl onto the land.

A woman with a child in her arms was being dragged to shore by a man. They both fell into a heap and remained still.

Corpus drew nearer and watched as they unwrapped clothing to reveal the child. It was a young girl. Corpus couldn't see if she was alive.

He glanced across at Gabriel and immediately instigated a change in their course as they began to dive back down towards the sea. There was something he needed to investigate.

The nearer to the water, the more they became aware of another sound other than the crashing waves. Corpus thought he could hear beautiful singing, but it had a sinister undertone. As it seeped into his consciousness, he felt like an invisible energy was pulling him away.

Down they went, nearer and nearer to the water. Corpus became unable to keep them both airborne.

They both entered the water; Corpus was now intensely focusing on something else and, for that moment, appeared to be oblivious to Gabriel's presence.

Above Gabriel, surrounded in floating colours, Corpus drifted upwards away from him. Corpus fought to stay present. He turned to try to find Gabriel and saw instead something behind him, propelling his Eathian ward upwards. He wasn't sure if it was one of the creatures, but he was sure he was going too fast.

Corpus yelled at them to stop.

It was too late. Corpus watched helplessly as Gabriel seemed to fly into the air and fall uncontrollably back into the water.

At that moment, Gabriel detached from the experience and lost all vision. All about him plunged into darkness.

Christi was in her Solescence Chamber when she felt the tug from Beatrice.

She was awake, and she could feel she was anxious. It was still the middle of the night on Eathia. She wondered briefly if it was the baby.

Corpus hadn't returned to The Realm as far as she was aware.

She swiftly bid her goodbyes to the others in the chamber and entered the lake to rejoin her tether.

Beatrice was alert when Christi re-entered her aura. Initially, she still wasn't clear what had woken her; it hadn't been the baby kicking. The echoes of Beatrice's thoughts lifted into Christi's awareness. She listened in. Beatrice remembered it had been a strange sound that had awoken her. She lay still and listened, expecting to hear if it was a nocturnal animal calling from outside the window. Nothing. Then, Gabriel began making a screeching noise in his sleep. Christi watched as Beatrice sat up and fumbled for the bedside lamp. It had been he who had woken her. What an awful noise! She realised he was having a nightmare and it was distressing him.

She continued to observe as Gabriel remained still and in a deep sleep.

His face twitched, his arms began to jolt, and his legs kicked at the covers. Then he was gasping for air as if something was blocking his throat; just as her tether was about to try and shake him awake, he suddenly stopped thrashing and became still once again.

Christi heard her speak to Gabriel.

'Come back, love.'

She wondered why Corpus wasn't aware and coming to help calm him. There was also something odd about Gabriel. He seemed to be more dense, less present, even in sleep; she could feel a difference in him.

Suddenly, he jumped and his eyes shot open; he turned and looked straight at Beatrice.

That's when Christi realised what was different about him.

His soul was missing.

'Corpus, what have you done?'

Her anxieties flashed, unintentionally passing them on to her tether, who became more concerned for Gabriel.

Beatrice spoke again.

'It's all right, Gabe, you're just dreaming, my love.'

Christi floated above Gabriel as he started to gurgle as if trying to gasp for air again. Her tether spun back around, nearly knocking the lamp off the side table as she frantically tried to relight it.

Christi tried to lower her vibrations to help keep her calm.

Beatrice took hold of his shoulders and started to try to shake him awake.

'Gabe, Gabe, wake up, love, please.'

His eyes were now open, staring at her pleadingly. Then the reality hit Christi: he was awake, he wasn't dreaming anymore and something was wrong.

To Christi, it looked like he was suffocating, unable to breathe and get any air into his lungs properly.

Christi was torn. There was definitely something wrong. She desperately wanted to head back to The Realm to see if she could find Corpus, but knew she needed to be with Beatrice.

She messaged Verra Mica.

Christi watched on in horror, his eyes rolled back into their sockets and the colour drained from his face, his pallor turning pale blue.

He became deathly still.

She had to return to The Realm. She sent another message to Nemius, their son's, Soul Guardian. She needed him to rejoin his tether and help.

That was if his tether was even in the vicinity.

Their wayward son, Avery, just like Nemius, had allegiances elsewhere nowadays. She hoped they would both do the right thing, for once.

Corpus went down after Gabriel, but stopped mid-air when he saw Elkyne.

He involuntarily called out to him. Then veiled quickly, realising his mistake.

He was with a siren and they were heading towards the shore. They seemed to be focused on the Eathian mother and daughter that Corpus had noticed earlier.

The siren looked up, aware of something above them.

Corpus could see her flare, but was happy he had veiled in time before she had seen him.

The singing started again. It was her, he could see her smirking as she swam behind Elkyne.

Unable to hold his position, Corpus felt his soul separate from that of the ravens, falling instead now, towards the Eathians on the shore

The two ravens that had carried them there swooped under him, catching him in mid-flight. The jolt brought him back again.

When he was able to regain his focus he realised he was face to face with Angelica.

Chapter 45
The Realm

Close Shave

Verra Mica first became aware of Corpus's plan when Christi messaged her and had to flee from her tether. She was concerned when Gabriel started struggling in his sleep, showing little or no sign of breathing. Knowing, as she did, that Corpus had warned her he was going to try something that evening, she realised that the plan wasn't going the way he intended.

Verra Mica was ready for her when she arrived. She found Christi waiting in her chambers.

Christi explained in as much detail as possible, but not knowing what was happening with Corpus made it difficult.

'So, something had shocked him so much that he struggled to stay coherent? If you hadn't sent out an alarm, Christi, we would be discussing a different outcome now.'

Corpus, now also en route to Verra Mica, sensed that Christi was there too, a welcome ally at this juncture. He hoped she was on his side. However, as soon as he saw them, he realised she wasn't, and he would be explaining his reasons for such an action on his own. He paused at the entrance, hearing the final part of Verra Mica's statement. So, it was Verra Mica who had saved Gabriel and guided his soul back to him.

When Christi realised Corpus had arrived, she silently messaged him to be cautious.

Corpus moved forward to make his presence noticed and explained almost immediately.

'It's far more complicated than you may think if you'd allow me to run through what happened?'

'What was it you thought you were doing exactly?'

Verra Mica appeared twice the size, a state he had only seen once before when she had been agitated, and Duergar had been involved then. Looking at her now, he could see she was slightly more than agitated. She was about to blow.

'I am sorry, your Honour. I planned to inform him of our plight to help him come to a mutually beneficial conclusion regarding his invention and the direction he should take from that moment onwards. I felt it was important for him to gain a better overall picture of what is happening to us all and, more importantly, to let him know he wasn't on his own with this quest.'

Verra Mica had heard enough.

'What! You are an advanced Soul Guardian and one of our best; do you even realise the consequences of what you just said, Corpus?'

'I was trying to help and …'

Another coded message came through from Christi.

'Just stop, Corpus, and listen to her.'

Corpus held back; any explanation was futile.

Verra Mica continued.

'By ending the life of our last chance, our ONLY chance at present.'

'I had it under control, but then …'

'Oh, did you indeed? What part exactly did you have under control, pray tell?'

'At present, I admit I still don't understand what happened. I lost sight of him when he fell back into the water.'

'Because of your intervention, Gabriel thought that he was drowning, so much so that his Eathian form reacted as if it were real. He momentarily stopped breathing, Corpus. He would have died if it hadn't been for Christi's quick actions. I had to re-tether, something I am forbidden to do. Do you realise the predicament you have put me in?'

Corpus looked at her and bowed his head.

'I am sorry, I …'

Christi's look implored him to stay quiet.

'I'm sorry, your Honour.'

'Now, having said this, Corpus, without this near disaster, we would not have been made aware of those creatures; well, let's call them what they are, sirens.'

'You know of them?'

'I do now. Ironic, isn't it? But don't you think you are off the hook for one moment! I could have done without your little jaunt.'

Her mood lifted, and Corpus relaxed slightly as another supportive comment came in from Christi; just for a moment, Corpus spoke only to her.

'It's not all bad, brother.'

'So, it did work. It was worth the risk?'

'Possibly, but Verra Mica won't admit that, understandably.'

Verra Mica interrupted.

'Once you two have finished with your internal babble, I would like to continue if I may?'

Both remained silent.

'These sirens used to be Soul Guardians before they were darkened in some way. I fear that if what I saw through you, Corpus, is correct, the fact that they were using their voices to lure those fallen Eathians and to block your powers, most of them can only be my poor, lost Seraphytes, lured down to Eathia before I even knew they existed. And now, of course, we know exactly where Angelica is. Near the shoreline and very much unhurt and undetected, regardless of Duergar's attempts at finding her.'

Corpus spoke cautiously.

'Angelica was guarding something or someone. She is on her own down there. I also caught a brief glimpse of other dark beings, but this time on land, too. They seemed to be moving in on Angelica's tether. I am assuming that Duergar might be aware of her after all.'

'I don't think it was her they were after. After what Ashtar indicated, it was more likely to be the young girl, her daughter. How were you able to see them?'

'They must have been veiled initially, but then I saw Angelica because she had sent a blast of energy to push the dark Guardians away from them; it briefly dropped their veils. I imagine she had remained veiled and secure there this whole time.'

'Was she seen?'

'No, I don't think so, but I was. Momentarily.'

It took Verra Mica a while to take in the implications of what Corpus had said. Then, she seemed to have decided and come to terms with Corpus's irrational actions.

'Corpus, I will overlook this, with no more to be said on this matter. You should have known better, however, I understand what you were trying to achieve.'

She hesitated and looked at Christi.

'It is now clear to me that we actually have no choice.'

She then bowed her head to dismiss them, turned and retired to her quarters.

Corpus was confused.

'What does she mean, no choice?'

Christi started to leave and gestured for Corpus to go with her.

'No more can be done at present. Let Verra Mica absorb your information further. Be assured, whatever it is, it will now be done out of necessity and not choice. Now we know a little more about what Duergar is up to. Choice is a luxury we don't have anymore.'

'They drew me in Christi; I haven't experienced that before. I fought back, but they tried to draw me into the water too. My guard was down. I had no idea of their strength. I will be ready for the next time.'

'Yes, you will. So, sirens from the Seraphyte order. Duergar has been planning this for some time.'

Christi kept her gaze on Corpus.

'What?'

He could see she wanted to say something.

'It wasn't entirely your fault, Corpus; you couldn't have known they were down there.'

For a moment, he appeared as a younger soul, one she wanted to protect, sometimes even from himself. She felt there was something else, something he was holding on to.

Then he opened up.

'I didn't mention it to Verra Mica, but Elkyne was on Eathia. I think he might have seen me, too. Angelica definitely saw him.'

'That explains why we can't feel him here. Leave him to me, Corpus. If it is him, he won't say anything; he has enough to handle. I sense he carries enough of our order within him to navigate this situation. I believe in him, and you should as well, Corpus. It takes immense strength to stay impartial and steadfast in the face of Duergar's harsh teaching methods.'

'Yes, however, my sister, possessing that knowledge, can be perilous. He was unhappy and angry, I believe that is why I felt his presence so strongly. He harbours a misguided loyalty to Duergar; how can we trust him completely? He likely isn't aware of what's occurring on both sides. Eventually, he will be compelled to choose and potentially ruin everything.'

'He's your brother, Corpus.'

Corpus found himself at a loss for words at Christi's statement. He couldn't decide if it was because he disagreed with her final remark or if she was right, and they should trust one another unconditionally because of their bond.

He remained silent.

Christi turned to Corpus before vanishing.

'If you can't trust Elkyne, at least trust the Source's reasoning for making us who we are. I shall inform you as soon as I have spoken with him to ease your mind. Do you think you can keep out of trouble until then?'

She smiled and disappeared, leaving Corpus with the unenviable task of tethering back to Gabriel.

He needed first to make himself known to him, then apologise for almost killing him!

Chapter 46
Eathia - Third Era

Sooner or Later

The following day, Bertha, her mother and Guss made their way down to Augustus and Anamaya. None of them had slept, spending most of the night reminiscing over past meetings with Guss at Sirenguard as a family when Bertha was just a young child.

Something was troubling Bertha. She needed to talk to Augustus about an uncomfortable feeling she was having regarding the circumstances of her father's and brother's accident.

Her transcribing of The Realm and those awful experiences she witnessed when Corpus had encountered the sirens made her fearful that they were dealing with something far more disturbing.

The sudden news of Tobias and Denis put Augustus into shock. Anamaya was at the castle. He grabbed at the pendant to keep what little energy he had from being passed on to Bertha and Sophia.

'How bad was this storm? For goodness' sake, what were they doing up there in the first place?'

Augustus posed the question to them as they stood awkwardly in the kitchen.

Guss was worn out and had no energy to explain it all again.

Bertha stepped forward and sat down next to Augustus.

'It was a random sequence of events that caused it, Uncle. The storm just came out of nowhere, and the ship went into a dangerous tilt. It couldn't regain its balance, catching them off guard.'

Bertha thought she had cried all she could for one day, but seeing Augustus break down seemed to renew her vat of tears. It was unbearable to feel the way she did and to see the ones she loved in such pain.

Sophia had gone numb. When they heard Maddox cry from his room, she silently lifted the pendant from Augustus's neck, put it on her own and went to see him.

Bertha tried to smile at her uncle.

'She hasn't spoken very much. She is in shock. We all are.'

Augustus waved a hand at Guss, gesturing for him to sit down.

'I'll make some tea.'

While her mother was out of the room, Bertha posed a difficult question to Augustus and Guss.

'Was this an accident, do you think?'

Guss was taken aback.

'Of course it was, Missy. What makes you say that?'

'Where were you all when it happened?'

Guss scratched at his beard.

'Well, we hadn't got far. Sirenguard was still in sight, if that's what you're asking. Why?'

Augustus looked intently at Bertha, trying to see where she was going with this line of questions.

'What is it, Bertha?'

She looked at Guss.

'Have you ever known your ship to struggle like that at sea? Ever?'

'Well, no. But it was a bad storm. It was all over so quickly. We couldn't control the ship because our main sail was down. We were at the mercy of the sea, Missy.'

'What are you getting at, Bertha?'

Augustus put a teapot and cups on the table and sat down.

She stupidly started a conversation in front of Guss about things she couldn't openly discuss. She hoped her uncle would catch on.

There were no signs of it happening any time soon, so she continued carefully.

'I just thought that cove had a weird history attached to it. Father talked about it occasionally and said odd things had happened there to his grandparents, or rather, to people they had known.'

Both Guss and Augustus clicked on to what she was suggesting. Both understood it in different ways, of course. To Guss, it was a superstition. To Augustus, it was a reality.

Guss sat back in his chair.

'Oh, no, Missy. Get that out of your head. There was none of that.'

He went quiet and appeared to be thinking about something. He shook his head and seemed to be having a conversation with himself. He looked at Augustus, appearing suddenly uncomfortable.

Augustus acknowledged his discomfort and addressed Bertha.

'Could you go and make sure your mother is alright, Bertha? She has been away for a while.'

Bertha looked shocked. Then conceded and left the kitchen.

'Guss? What is it?'

'It's odd for Bertha to ask such a thing, but it has jogged my memory.'

He stared past Augustus into the distance as if reliving something.

'Go on.'

Well, going on what Bertha was talking about. We did see a shoal of creatures off the shore for a bit. Tobes looked visibly shaken by it and went to work on the sail. We all thought nothing of it. Well, some of us did, but now I think of it, they were there when the ship was tipping all over the place. They were right up close. I was so focused on Tobes and Denis that I forgot about them. Then that was when I heard the singing.'

He looked back at Augustus.

Augustus cast a horrified glance back at him. Guss continued.

'Do you think they had something to do with what happened?'

Now, Augustus had to be careful how he approached this subject. After all, no one outside the family knew the truth about Sirenguard and its history with Stonehaven and their family.

He had to bluff his way out of the situation.

'You think a shoal of fish attacked you?'

'Well, no, not really. It sounds ridiculous when you put it like that.'

'Bertha is clutching at straws. I understand why, Guss; really, I do. We all want to find a reason for this, but, in truth, it's been an awful accident.'

Guss nodded and sighed.

'Look, there are a few things I need to do in town before I head back to the cove. Would you tell them I'll catch up with them a little later?'

Augustus showed Guss out and turned to see Sophia and Bertha descending the stairs. Maddox was in Sophia's arms. Bertha didn't take her eyes off her uncle.

He nodded and mouthed, 'Later,' to her.

Bertha felt a chilling dread coursing through her veins; deep down, she knew her suspicions were not just fears. They were haunting truths ready to consume her.

She didn't want to wait. The doubt would eat away at her until she could speak to her uncle again.

Chapter 47
The Realm

Elkynes Fall to Eathia

Once Elkyne had regained all of his faculties, thanks to whoever had shouted at him to shield, the first thing he felt was the overwhelming force that struck him as he exited the portal. The bright, flashing lights gave way to a murky glow.

He wasn't sure if he was through the portal or had exited elsewhere.

Unable to get his bearings, he waited and allowed his senses to register the new atmosphere surrounding him. It was not what he expected. He wasn't even sure if he was expected to have reached this far.

Muffled sounds echoed around him. He struggled to decipher strange languages with background sounds. As he tried to focus on it, it began to retreat and fade back, ebbing away towards a fluctuating light. The darkness was slowly lifting, and the light started to filter through from above him more strongly.

He was submerged in liquid of some kind.

Glistening ripples carried light particles, illuminating colours as they seeped into the misty space around him. Images, three-dimensional forms and evidence that had made it through started to appear. It was then that something grabbed him and pulled him up.

The flash of light was as bright as the one that had announced his departure from the portal. The sounds around him had completely changed and become harsher in tone as they reverberated off the surrounding stone walls above the water's surface.

'Finally, he graces us with his presence. Welcome, brother, your arrival has caused quite a stir.'

Slowly, a face filtered into his view. He naturally attempted to scan her but could gain nothing. *Could he even scan from where he was?* he wondered.

'Are you from The Realm?'

'Of sorts, yes, but this is our home for now.'

There was something enthralling about the Eathian Soul Guardian. She felt familiar but gave nothing of her true nature away.

There was laughter behind her, and similar forms moved into view. All were facially unique but with similar forms that seemed to aid them in floating in the water.

'Am I in the right place? Do you know who I am?'

'Yes, brother. You are Elkyne. Duergar has told us all about you, and you're late.'

More faces slowly joined the already growing group around him. *It makes quite a change to be popular*, he thought.

'Did you all arrive from this portal?'

'No, not all. Let me introduce myself, as I will be escorting you around this forsaken land. I am Nephelia, the leader of this band of slithering troublemakers. We are all at your service, Elkyne, and are happy to meet with you finally.'

Nephelia floated back from him and joined the front of the group. Only then was he able to see her full form. She did hold a partial Eathian appearance, but she had taken on another, altogether, stranger form too. Her lower section tapered out into a fan-like tail. Nephelia watched as he tried to identify what he was looking at. She laughed, and the giggles spread through the group.

'You will find it difficult to move in water, Elkyne, as you must have already realised. The portal brings you out into the water, within this cave. The particles make it difficult for us to move through that, and there is a heavy gravitational pull down here. It will take you time to adjust. We'll probably have to drag you everywhere as time, apparently, is not on our side.'

Elkyne was confused about how much they seemed to be aware of.

'Have you spoken to Duergar?'

'Yes, often. We were expecting you some time ago. There was only a small opportunity for you to make it through the portal safely. Did Duergar not tell you this? Eathia needs to be perfectly aligned so the portal can reach us here. If you missed it, that would have been your lot. Poof.'

She clicked her fingers together.

'No, he didn't. That explains his temperament when I left. I knew nothing of this, nothing. Where would I have exited if not here?'

'You wouldn't have done. You would have been lost in the Accumulator.

I sensed you going off-stream and helped you through the last part of your journey.'

'So, it was you I heard telling me to shield.'

Nephelia changed; her appearance immediately became darker and less reflective. Her form moved towards him, taking on more of the cold blues and purples of the water.

'It was not I who called you. Who was it? Who knew you would be coming here?'

'No one apart from Duergar. Look, I must have been mistaken; I heard a voice. Whoever it was helped me get here safely. I was struggling to hold on.'

'And you didn't recognise their voice?'

'No, like I said, I thought it was you.'

Slowly, the darkness lifted from her, returning her translucent form. Elkyne watched, confused. She appeared content for the time being.

'Well, no harm done. I see that you are intact and have managed to enhance your capabilities. Duergar was correct; you are an advanced being, are you not?'

Slightly unsure how to respond, Elkyne remained silent. He realised that there was more to these Soul Guardians than met the eye.

'Come, let us show you around.'

Two of the sirens moved forward and offered him their aura, opening themselves up so he could blend and hook onto them. Nephelia had moved on towards the opening of the stone cave, where the light was streaming in. Just the four left, and Elkyne felt a little easier at not being watched by so many.

As they moved through the opening, Nephelia took them down into the depths of the water. He felt the same drag on him, but the impact was lessened with the help of his two stronger, more agile aids.

The cave opened to one of Eathia's oceans, where more water than land covered its globe. As Elkyne travelled through its depths, he bore witness to the extreme beauty it held. Unusual forms, some semi-translucent, floated past him; some were enormous mammals whose bodies effortlessly swayed as they moved. Others, much smaller, darted here and there, completely oblivious to his and the sirens' presence.

'This is their world beneath the sea. Very different to above the water, it's far more harmonious and in tune with its environment. It's up there that things tend to get slightly out of hand.'

'In what way? I'm not sure I understand.'

'Well, let me put it this way: thank goodness they can't breathe underwater. We have watched them and what they can do to the animals they can reach.'

'Careful, it sounds like you care for them.'

'I care for the animals, yes. I can take or leave the Eathians.'

'What are you exactly? All of you. Do you all have a name, a type?'

'We are sirens. Here, we are allowed to use our harmonics and our voices. All to our advantage.'

'So, have you ever been tethered before, Nephelia?'

'No. Perish the thought. Why do you ask?'

'If I am to accept what it is that Duergar is trying to show me via your good selves for reasons in his words "to expand my awareness about the truth of his plight", then I would like to make sure the information I am given comes from the best and most accurate standpoint.'

Nephelia suddenly instructed all to stop, and they all came to a standstill. The darkness within her reappeared, branching out like veins of black blood from a merciless heart.

'Now you come to mention it, Duergar warned me about your cynicism. He said you'd be left unsure whether you have just had a compliment or been criticised. Which one would you have me believe? Actually, don't worry. You know it's not about anything I show you down here anyway. It's all about the journey, Elkyne, and not the destination.'

The sirens smiled a knowing smile at each other.

'You're ready to go back anytime now if you wish. I'm just being a good host and showing you around.'

'What do you mean, the journey?'

'You have already been embedded. That was why Duergar sent you through the Accumulator, to be embedded. He really didn't tell you anything, did he?'

'Embedded with what?'

Nephelia looked down at Elkyne's core, and the other two followed her gaze; they seemed amused at something. Nephelia retreated back.

Elkyne looked down at his energy centre. Until now, it had always been primarily connected to the source; however, now it was sharing its position with another denser energy. Startled, he looked up at the three of them, then down at their centres. They had only a dark shadow at their core.

'Ahh, he gets it now.'

'What is it? What has happened to me?'

‘It’s what you wanted, Elkyne. To be given a more informed and balanced viewpoint. It wasn’t we who were supposed to enlighten you. It was the Accumulator whose purpose was to, shall we say, *endarken* you.’

Again, more laughter.

‘Why is it there?’

Nephelia ushered the other two away. She was now becoming irritated with this naïve idiot.

‘So much for being advanced. What exactly did Duergar say to you, Elkyne? You seem oblivious to his methods and reasons for sending you through the Accumulator, and you suggest that I may not be fit for purpose. I assumed you were in favour of entering it. Honestly, you appear completely unaware of what happened to you.’

Suddenly, Nephelia shot away from Elkyne and seemed to be listening to something; the others heard it, too.

‘We have to get back to the cave. The tour and the niceties are over.’

The two sirens quickly attached to Elkyne again, leading him back towards the cave’s opening. Before he could protest, Elkyne heard a chorus of voices emanating from the cave.

‘Oh, can you shield? Now! otherwise, you’ll lose what little sense you have.’

Elkyne had had enough of being kept in the dark.

‘Can you stop? Stop dragging me and talking to me like an idiot!’

He pulled hard against the sirens supporting him, causing them to stop abruptly. He heaved himself free of them and rose to the surface to try and get out of the viscous water, only to find it altogether too difficult to manoeuvre through with ease.

‘Come back down. You are an idiot. You don’t know what you are doing.’

At that moment, an imposing darkness fell over them all. A shadow that slowly ate away at the light above them, casting them all into semi-darkness.

Nephelia had had enough, too.

‘Leave him, we have to get back.’

The three sirens took off before Elkyne had a chance to regroup. Leaving the safety of the deeper water, he began to resurface.

The cause of the shadow, which was now completely towering over him, became obvious as it began to rise with the motion of the waves, only to crash down a short distance away from where he was.

Elkyne could hear screams coming from inside it. Then a much nearer cry could be heard as an Eathian dweller fell from the ship’s mast and crashed into the water beside him. The voices from the cave started to sing a hypnotising tune, and it began to bleed into his consciousness; he felt his attention dissipate.

'Veil, you idiot.'

He heard Nephelia's voice again.

Elkyne lifted his veil, and the lure of the siren's voices retreated.

He dived back down just before the ship came crashing down again, almost on top of him this time. As he did, more men on board the wooden beast fell into the water around him.

Feeling overwhelmed and helpless, Elkyne turned to return to the cave, but was confronted by a shoal of sirens coming straight towards him.

As the vessel crashed down again, it pushed the water around him, downwards, forcing him deeper into the sea; he was beginning to lose direction. He kept looking up at the small fragments of light that shone through as the vessel moved. Suddenly, an immense crack sent shards of the beast's frame flying past him, followed by bits of debris. He watched in horror as the sirens continued to swim past him towards the falling Eathians. He remembered what Nephelia had said: they couldn't breathe underwater. Were they then saving them? He began to feel some relief.

Unfortunately, it wasn't long before Elkyne realised that the victims would soon become the hosts of the Darker Soul Guardians.

He was disgusted by them.

He watched in horror, witnessing the departure and de-tethering of those fallen Eathians as their Soul Guardians were forced to leave them and return to The Realm. Then, without reprieve and as fast as their tails could take them, the Dark Guardians re-tethered to the dying Eathians. This act was causing the men to spring back to life and frantically swim to the surface.

Why would you lure them in only to save them again? he wondered.

Nephelia swam past him, then stopped and begrudgingly turned back towards him.

'You need to re-tether if you want to get back, Elkyne; find a body; it's the only way to return to The Realm. Hitch a lift with one of the do-gooders. I didn't have time to clarify; The Realm is completely out of alignment now. Go back. You aren't needed or wanted here.'

Frenzied movements of sirens and the bodies of the men still chaotically moved about him. Lifeless bodies were brought back to life, some opening their eyes, looking straight at him, and grinning before reaching up to the water's surface again.

Elkyne shouted at Nephelia.

'I don't know how to tether. How can that help me get back anyway?'

'We can no longer use the cave's portal, now, all the tethers are closed.'

She gestured to all of the Eathians, who were now making it to the surface.

'There's only one other way. It was how we initially intended for you to get back if this were to happen; more exciting but a little more complicated. Follow me.'

Instead of swimming towards the cave, Nephelia guided him towards the shoreline to the right of them. Thankfully, he found that he could direct himself through the water more easily now.

As they surfaced, she briefly caught sight of what she thought was an Airian Soul Guardian above her. It was looking down towards her from the sky. It all happened quickly, so she couldn't be sure. In an instant, it was gone.

It was enough time for Elkyne to gain a brief glimpse of him. It was Corpus. He recognised him immediately before he was plunged back under the water; Nephelia had forced Elkyne to submerge, much to his dismay. He tried to push against her, getting angrier as he did, but she remained firm and overpowered him easily, having the advantage of being in her natural surroundings. When she thought it was safe, she released him. Elkyne yelled at her.

'JUST WHAT DO YOU THINK YOU ARE DOING?'

His explosion of anger even surprised him. Elkyne turned and faced Nephelia. He appeared to grow twice his size, and his voice resonated as if amplified by an unseen force.

Nephelia noted the change immediately and was impressed.

'I was protecting your cover, you imbecile. I thought I saw what looked like a Soul Guardian watching us.'

'Look, I have no idea what just happened back there, or why, for that matter, you were claiming the lives of all those Eathians. Can you please tell me what you are all doing down here? What are your orders?'

Nephelia watched as the darkness within Elkyne receded. She remained silent while the last of the Eathians swam past them and began to stagger out from the water onto dry land. They glanced at the two of them with little interest as they passed. She eventually turned back to address Elkyne.

'Now you have had a taster of what your new energy is capable of. It is powerful, so be careful. As to what we were doing …'

Elkyne stopped her from continuing.

'What power?'

She looked down at the dark surge of energy within him.

He followed her gaze.

'This? This is where the anger came from. I thought …'

'Best not do that, Elkyne. Doesn't seem to be one of your strong points.'

She watched him carefully as she continued to provoke another reaction. Elkyne was starting to feel the difference in his being, an apparent lack of control. It wasn't a pleasant feeling.

She continued.

'As to what we were doing here. We are recruiting Eathians but using our own Dark Soul Guardians to re-tether. It seems that we are more in tune with Eathia's current state. We are all over Eathia, Elkyne. We've been working on this for ages now. This is part of Duergar's plan, which I am sure he will elaborate on when, or should I say, if, you can return.'

Elkyne countered.

'From what I have seen so far, it appears you and your renegades are forcing the people here to meet such a fate and bringing an unnatural end to their lives. You are making that decision for them. I have seen enough. I want to return now; this place holds no interest for me. Not like this.'

'You are in no state to cast judgement, Elkyne. Remember, you can't get back without my help.'

Elkyne stared at her, knowing she was right, and he backed down.

'That's better. Very well, I will tell you how to re-tether, but it isn't as straightforward as you'd hoped. You might need to dig deep under that self-righteous moral high ground you have created for yourself.'

She looked back at the shore. He followed her gaze.

'You will need to travel on land to start with.'

He looked confused.

'Just for a bit. There is an Eathian out there, almost ready to leave; you can use her as a launch base; it will take you to her original tether's Solescence Chamber. Her own tether has long since left; however, her portal is still there, with no energy field around it, so it's unprotected and open to the dark matter. Before you ask, that makes it easy for us to enter. It should be an easy ride, especially after the Accumulator.'

'What do you mean, ready to leave?'

'She is still alive, just. So, stay out of the way until the right time. Our Dark Soul Guardians are currently watching her, but they won't all be able to track her into the mountains. That's where she is heading.'

'Wait, you said, her. You know of her?'

'Oh yes, we know of her. It's perfect, actually.'

She continued to watch the shore, looking pleased with herself.

'I will talk you through it and guide you through as much as I can from here because when it's time for you to go, you'll need all the help you can get to reach her.'

She watched the anger build in Elkyne. A coldness spread through her, and her usual appearance changed to a grey, menacing stare.

'Before you go, Elkyne, allow me to show you a little of the power we have "Accumulated" by being here.'

Her glare turned to a sinister grin.

'What do you mean?'

Ignoring him, Nephelia retreated slightly and bowed her head. The vortex within her began to churn, and the shadows that had started to stir throughout her being began to get drawn inwards again. She slowly looked up and, to Elkyne's surprise, her eyes, now deep violet, burned into him. Then she almost seemed to implode in towards her centre. The energy turned and expanded without warning, projecting its explosion straight at him.

As the water burst forward at a tremendous rate, neither of them noticed an uninvited soul had been caught in the crossfire. Gabriel was smothered by the wave and disappeared within its embrace. It was on him before he could brace himself. At the same time, Elkyne was thrown out of the water high into the air. She held him there laughing as he rode helplessly on top of the wave. Then she released him, pulling the water out from under him in a whipping motion and happily watched him free-fall back down again.

Corpus, now veiled, watched in horror as Elkyne's body was thrown backwards from the creature and Gabriel disappeared beneath them.

Nephelia swam quickly to where Elkyne was flailing, as he tried to regain his control.

'That is for your arrogance. You didn't think I'd ignore your rudeness, did you?'

Once Elkyne had collected himself, he retaliated.

'I thought we were supposed to be on the same side?'

'And yet here you are questioning all that we are. Elkyne, you are a weak link in our armour, and we cannot afford your need for constant explanations and reassurance. I will report to Duergar and let him know you are on your way. Now go before it's too late. The last thing I want is for you to get stuck here where I'll have to babysit you.'

She looked back at the shore.

'You sound just like him.'

She ignored him.

'You will find it considerably easier to travel through the air than through water. I shall inform the Airians to meet you on your arrival.'

'Airians?'

'The flying version of us.'

Elkyne paused.

'What became of her? My only way back.'

Nephelia tutted at him. Her patience now wearing thin.

'So, she drowned too? When?'

'You do not need to know. All you should know is that she is your only way back, so take it and be grateful. The rest of us cannot return as easily, even if we could. There is no place for us in The Realm now, so your ungracious attitude is beginning to try my patience.'

With that, Nephelia dived back under the water's surface and disappeared.

Good riddance, he thought.

He glanced up to see if Corpus was anywhere to be seen. He had gone. Elkyne turned to face the shore. A female Eathian was waiting to die somewhere on land, unknowingly providing him with his portal home.

The thought sickened him to his darkened core.

Chapter 48
Eathia - Third Era

Fish Tales

Guss had packed up his provisions and had climbed back onto his cart. He looked vacantly down the cobbled street, then turned to face Sophia and Bertha.

'I don't want to leave you.'

He felt himself welling up again. A spasm caught his throat as he tried to contain the tears.

Sophia held onto his hand.

'I'll come and see you, Guss. We'll wait for the gravestones to be ready, then I'll come and we can put them under the tree. It may take a while, but I will be there.'

Guss nodded and gave a half smile.

'Will you be all right, the pair of you?'

Sophia nodded.

'We'll be fine. Now on you go before you lose the light at the other end.'

Guss clicked for the horse to move on, and his cart creaked and jolted as the wheels bumped over the cobbles.

Bertha watched as he made his way down the street, then turned and followed her mother into the house.

'Actually, do you mind if I have a quick word with Uncle? I shouldn't be too long.'

Sophia gave a half-hearted smile. *That will be all she can manage for a while*, Bertha thought. She felt the same. Seeing Guss leave seemed to open up a void for both of them. One, they were going to have to live with from now on.

Bertha sighed quietly and carried on towards Augustus's Emporium.

It was shut when she arrived, and she wandered around the back. When she saw him, she realised he had his own void to come to terms with.

He was sitting at the kitchen table. His hair was unusually hanging down in front of his face. His shirt was half out of his trousers and his collar was loose and open. He was staring into a cup of tea.

When he heard the door shut and saw Bertha, he jumped up, embarrassed to be seen in such a state.

'Oh, Bertha. It's you. Thank goodness. I'm sorry, I haven't quite got myself together this morning.'

Bertha touched his teacup. It was ice cold. *He's been sitting there for ages*, she realised.

As he tucked himself in and put a comb through his hair, he began to look a little more like himself.

'I'll put the kettle on, Uncle. You relax. It's hit us all hard, and no one expects you to carry on as usual. Where's Maddox?'

'Oh, he's with Ana. He wanted to go and play on that old piano in the Orbitarium. He's taken to it amazingly well for a boy his age.'

Augustus glanced in the direction of the shop.

'Uncle, leave it closed for today at least. I have a first-hand guarantee that no babies are due for a while. The four that are pregnant are some way off yet.'

'Oh. Yes. Ana told me about those couples. How strange. They all have the same due date. You'll both be busy then.'

He attempted a weak laugh.

'I imagine you would like to continue where we left off. About the cove?'

Bertha was quiet for a while. Then spoke quietly.

'I was actually thinking about what you said. When you said about "me not knowing about my life" before it happened.'

'Oh, Bertha. Don't do that to yourself.'

'No, it's all right. I was angry initially. But now, I can't imagine, through the transcribing, experiencing what happened to Father and Denis. I mean, actually, seeing it. I understand why now. She must have known and …'

'It's probably best not to think about that.'

He took a slurp of tea.

'You make the best tea.'

'Anamaya won't like you saying that.'

'I have to be honest; I can't drink it when she has made it. I've run out of places to pour it.'

He looked across at a sad-looking plant in the corner of the kitchen.

The tension was broken and they both laughed.

'Right, dear girl. Talk to me. What are your thoughts on what we discussed? I had to redirect Guss on the matter. He shouldn't be made aware of them. It's best left as a sailor's superstition.'

'He said the creatures had fishtails and were butting against the ship. In hindsight, he felt the vessel had become perilously unsteady, despite its lack of sail. Then there is the odd case of the singing he heard.'

Bertha sat back in the chair.

'Singing. What, like sirens?'

She frowned at her uncle.

'I know about Mary and what happened at the cove. But that was a long time ago. Any threat from The Realm's renegades is over now, surely? If it was so-called sirens, then why now? What provoked them? Guss has never mentioned them before now.'

Augustus thought for a while.

Bertha suddenly made a connection.

'The place is where they are supposed to be on land. The town, what was it called? Campion. Their hideout years ago. Has anyone ever spoken of it again? Has anyone ever seen them?'

The skin on Augustus's neck and arms bristled with goosebumps.

'Err. No. As far as I'm aware, they have long gone, Bertha. We are getting away from the point.'

She noted his discomfort.

Bertha's real father, Daniel, was the only person who had ever told him and his father of such a place. That was a long time ago; for all he knew, it had been destroyed. He remembered Daniel's father had built a system to eradicate the creatures. He tried to keep his face from looking awkward, which for an Ashen was mighty tricky.

Bertha watched him intently.

'What aren't you telling me, Uncle?'

He looked up at her.

'Nothing, dear. It just brought back memories.'

Suddenly, the back door flew open, and Anamaya came rushing in with Maddox. On seeing Bertha, she ran and hugged her.

'Bertha, I'm sorry to hear about your father and brother. I can't imagine what you and your mother are going through.'

Maddox had headed over to the couch, nose-dived into the cushion, and stayed there with his head buried. His mini set of oculars was still dangling from his neck.

Augustus looked round at him, knowing he did that when he was scared.

'What's happened now?'

Anamaya was torn between consoling Bertha and telling Augustus what had happened at the castle.

Bertha could see something was up.

'It's OK, Aunty. Tell us.'

'Something strange has happened to the orb. It suddenly fluctuated and sent out sparks towards the reflectors. It was all over very quickly.'

Augustus frowned.

'What's going on, I wonder? I'll pop over and have a look. Why don't you stay here with Bertha?'

He looked across at Maddox, who was still lying on the sofa.

'Did he see it too?'

Anamaya nodded.

'It completely freaked him out.'

As Augustus grabbed his coat. Maddox made for the door as if he wanted to go with him.

'Oh no. You stay here, little man. I won't be long.

Maddox grabbed hold of his leg and squeezed tightly. His muffled voice yelled at him from deep within Augustus's trouser leg.

'I want to see her again.'

'Oh, for goodness' sake. It can't have freaked him out that much. Come on then.'

Then it dawned on Augustus what his son just said.

'See her? Who?'

Someone knocked at the door. Augustus had to drag his leg towards the door with the weight of Maddox still gripping on tightly.

As Augustus opened the door, a man was standing there, his arm still stretched up, about to knock again. Augustus jumped.

'Mr … err … Emporium?'

'What? Who? No, that's not my surname. It's Mr Browne if you wish to be on second-name terms. How can I help you?'

'Well, it's Mrs … Browne I was after. Is she here?'

Augustus called for Anamaya.

She appeared at the door behind Augustus.

'Hello, Alais, how can I help?'

'Well, it's Lilly. She's …'

Augustus interrupted.

'Look, I'm sorry. I need to get to the castle. Excuse me. Sorry.'

He manoeuvred past the man and reached for Maddox to join him, who edged his way around him.

'Come in. Come in. Bertha is here too.'

Bertha stood as Alais walked into the kitchen. He seemed uncomfortable.

'Sorry to intrude. I wonder if one of you could come and look at Lilly. She had a nasty spasm earlier and seems a little under the weather now. She is so early on in her pregnancy, it worried us that something may have happened.'

Bertha grabbed her coat and went to leave with him. Anamaya intervened.

'Absolutely not, Bertha, I'll go. I'll leave a note for Augustus. You go home to your mother and give her my love. I'll pop over later.'

With that, they both left, leaving Bertha on her own. One thing she didn't want to be at that moment. She left shortly after and went to be with her mother.

She had witnessed the orb acting up when Maddox was born. Her mind, unable to not question everything now, fired up.

It was only a small flame, but it had been ignited.

Why had the orb flared again?

Chapter 49
The Realm - Eathia

Illiandra

Elkyne scanned the shore for any survivors. Now, with Nephelia gone, he could focus on trying to get back to The Realm, even if he wasn't sure how that would happen at that moment.

Most of the men from the wrecked ship who had left the water had dispersed. Some ran towards the hills just ahead of him, through a small opening in the rocks, and others headed for the mountains to the right.

There was movement at the far end of the cove that drew his attention.

Now able to veil himself, Elkyne moved freely through the water undetected. Upon reaching the shore, he saw that the movement had come from three Eathians. A strange blur drifted between him and them, making them appear slightly out of focus. He soon realised they were translucent figures, swaying and shifting on the land, circling the small group he had observed.

They weren't sirens but had very similar darkened energies about them. They hovered just above the ground. One turned to look at Elkyne, he felt her gaze penetrate his core, then he heard her speak to him.

'We have them now, come with us. Although she isn't quite ready yet.'

Elkyne was surprised.

'You can see me?'

'I can hear you. Your internal conversation is deafening to us. So, you are an advanced pure Psybiencian.'

She turned away from him.

'Again, with the insults.'

'Shh.'

As he silently drew nearer, he could see a woman, a man and a small child, a girl, to be exact. He could see that the child had indeed lost her tether and looked unwell.

'What happened? Where is her tether?'

'The Dark Soul Guardian that had been speaking to him separated from the group and made her way over to him.'

'Gone, left her for dead, but we revived her for you. We had our orders.'

'What? For me?'

'We will stay with you until she is ready. You need us, Elkyne. To get home, I thought Nephelia had told you of this?'

'She did, but is there no other way?'

He heard the Dark Soul Guardians behind her begin to laugh and hiss at him.

Elkyne felt a profound internal conflict raging within him. The darkness that had infiltrated him in the Accumulator incited a deep-seated rage, or perhaps it was the Source itself responding to the profound injustice of his predicament. He couldn't tell anymore.

What appeared to be the leader of the group watched and waited for him to work through his inner battle, interested in which side he would fall.

Elkyne managed to silence the turmoil within him. Unbeknownst to him, this had given him a second chance with this particular Dark Soul Guardian.

The small cluster of Eathians left and slowly made their way towards the mountains. The young girl looked almost too weak to walk but tried her best to keep up. It was obvious that the woman needed to be carried by the man; she herself was looking close to death. Elkyne crushed the anguish he felt, burying it as deep as he could, so as not to be detectable. Inside his core, the darkness began to grow ever so slightly, as if his grief was somehow feeding it.

'Am I correct in calling your group, Airians?'

The leader glanced at him. Although she contemplated dismissing him, she chose to temper the hostility. This animosity was a collective burden, and it felt refreshing to be less inclined towards harshness.

'We are Terraneans. We stay close to the ground.'

With that, she turned and continued.

They followed them up to a small clearing, and it appeared they were heading towards the more substantial part of the three mountain range.

Elkyne watched in awe not only at the Eathians but also at Eathia. Its natural vegetation, colours and shapes all had such beauty.

So, this is what it is to be tethered, he thought.

He then realised the Eathians had stopped, seeking shelter from the biting cold wind and relentless rain among the small trees and bushes. He watched as the man built a fire, conjuring flames from nothing but wood and stone. When he laid the young girl beside it, Elkyne realised it was for her warmth, their concern for the child etched deeply across their faces. He wondered how it would affect her now that her tether had vanished. He tried to block his thoughts, they would not serve him well in the end.

These were the first Eathians he had encountered and they appeared to be good people; he could sense that about them.

The Source inside him stirred and started to ache; this caught the attention of the Terranean who had welcomed him. She looked over at him while hovering near the small child before turning back to Elkyne.

'Stop making this difficult for yourself, Elkyne.'

'How can you not? Wasn't she born with a purpose, just like us? We are taking that away from her.'

She rested next to him and looked back, watching as the group closed in around the girl as she slept. She started to groan and whimper, her head moved from side to side. They watched as the Eathian woman, her mother, ran to her side and embraced her. The other Terraneans moved back, hissing at her as they did. They turned and looked at Elkyne and their leader for direction.

She addressed the cluster as they hung on her command.

'Leave it for now, let them rest. She won't always be there to protect her.'

Elkyne was confused.

'The woman? Is it she that protects her?'

'No. This woman has help. We caught sight of her Soul Guardian, just for a moment, then she was gone. A traitor to our cause.'

'Why do I feel as though we are the traitors to these people? Taking over their lives for what exactly?'

She turned to Elkyne.

'She had already died, Elkyne, we are just keeping her alive for you. She will die for a great purpose; can't you see that?'

Elkyne felt at a loss.

'Maybe I should try to contact Duergar and see if there is another way.'

'NO! You are in our care, and he wants you back. Now! He expects us to return you. You cannot make it any harder for us.'

Elkyne sensed a slither of resentment in her words, but not against him this time.

'It is your wish to be here, to follow him, surely?'

She softened.

'We are dedicated to him and his ideologies. We believe in what he is trying to do, most of the time. We are here because we were placed here, and yes, I heard your thoughts, Elkyne; yes, there is some resentment. This was never our home. We were told that we were escaping from a world in conflict and had been chosen to be mercenaries, born or enrolled into a desperate and necessary need for change, unlike any before. We are honoured to support such a cause, but …'

Her voice pierced his energy like a cold blade. What had he done, believing in this awful plan when even some of Duergar's private army weren't completely happy with what they were doing?

'But …?'

She looked down at his core, an area she seemed unable to stop focusing on.

'You are here, having both the Source and the darkness inside you and questioning him. You are opening up wounds by being here, Elkyne. Whatever our doubt, you are giving it life; we can't have that here. You must go.'

She knew exactly what she was doing. It was the one thing that would push him into taking this route home. It was not a calculated manipulation; she was honest with him, and she could see the doubt he was carrying and how it reflected her own. She momentarily took pity on him. Elkyne tried to appeal to the better side of her nature, if she even had one.

'Is it possible that fate has brought me here, so you can see that there might be an alternative way?'

The darkness within Elkyne began to roar, as if it were angry at his attempt to dampen the Terranean's spirit.

'You underestimate our strength, Elkyne. We only regard you this much because you are in Duergar's favour. For now, at least. You appear determined to undermine that with every word you speak. I was mistaken in confiding in such a confused and lost Soul Guardian. I believe he has erred in placing his faith in you.'

Now her fire was igniting, and Elkyne moved away from her as he observed it grow. He did not want to be caught off guard in the same manner he had been with Nephelia.

'Maybe fate has brought us together so I can assist you in another way.'

As she spoke, swirls of dark energy extended out from her towards him.

They stroked his aura, feeling and sensing as they worked through the subtle layers. Then a single dark tendril shot forward into him and entered his own dark vortex. He felt himself spasm and contract. This excited the group, and they moved nearer to watch. It felt like he was back in the Accumulator again when his whole being felt like it had started to shatter.

He screamed at her to stop.

His voice boomed out, only this time, it was carried on a thunderous vibration of a single deafening tone, surprising even Elkyne at the strength and force behind it.

She pulled away and with her the tendrils retracted rapidly back into her darkened core. The group hissed at him as they retreated, as if his actions had caused them to experience pain somehow.

She laughed, happy at his reaction.

She moved uncomfortably close to him, all spiral feelers back within her aura.

'You have no idea of your strength, do you? You have Duergar to thank for that. It's sickening to watch you waste it.'

She looked back at the Eathians.

'You and I will follow them from here. No need for the entourage any more, they have accomplished what they set out to. Partially anyway.'

'That being?'

She looked back at him. Trying to read his thoughts.

'To stop them re-tethering and to protect our interests from intruders.'

Elkyne laughed.

'Intruders, do you not think we are the intruders?'

He looked across at them for a moment.

'What of the man?'

'He is insignificant to us.'

Elkyne looked back at the woman, still cradling the girl as she slept. She was talking under her breath, but not to her; her face was lifted to the sky, her eyes closed. Elkyne tried to listen but didn't want to draw attention to them anymore. They deserved peace now. He backed away while their leader dismissed her group. She then returned to his side.

'You are different to Nephelia.'

'Yes, I am. I am a free floater of the land, but not the sea or air. I can enter the oceans, but they are not my natural habitat.'

'Can I ask how you got here?'

She was happy to indulge in light conversation while they waited for the

Eathians to move on again.

'We are forbidden to look into our tether's eyes, are we not? Sometimes, here on Eathia, it can happen quite by chance, no matter how hard you try to avoid it.'

'I don't understand.'

She was silent for a short moment while she remembered her own Eathian tether.'

'My tether drowned.' She looked away from him.

'Like the others here?' he questioned.

'No, she was murdered by two other Eathian men. They attacked her as she washed her clothes by a lake far from here. She had a small child with her who, fortunately, survived.'

She continued to look out in the direction of the sea, falling silent again.

'Please go on.'

Elkyne was intrigued to hear about her experience.

'They pushed her face into the water. Just before she was submerged, she saw my reflection, and I briefly looked into her eyes. It took us both by surprise. We both felt the rip of being separated, and then she drowned. They were not armed, but she had a knife hidden in her washing basket. Her husband had insisted she carry it with her. She was beautiful and she unintentionally drew others' unwanted attention.'

'Why did she not defend herself, if she had a knife?'

'Because she thought I was able to save her.'

'She knew you were there?'

Some of them do, Elkyne. Some are very attuned to us.'

A short silence, then Elkyne spoke.

'So, you have been floating here ever since? Are there others like you who have not completely turned sides, ones that have remained "just" free floaters?'

'Yes, there are many of us, only that number is diminishing as quickly as they are being discovered. I was free until the sirens found me near the water's edge. Once they explained Duergar's intentions, it all made sense to me. So, I let the darkness enter. Many have not seen fit to follow us, but they will. Eventually, they will have no choice, and when they do, they will experience true expansion.'

She pointed to her core to show Elkyne where the darkness rested, then looked at the three Eathians.

'One of the ones that didn't join us is tethered to that woman over there.

She guards her.'

Elkyne found himself admiring the Soul Guardian for her tenacity.

'How is this going to make anything better? It feels like all this is being forced on Eathians and Soul Guardians alike.'

She turned to look directly at Elkyne.

'Look, you know the darkness was Eathian born. It's been growing among them regardless of our actions. Now, because of them, it resides within us. Like it or not, we are now more like them, only floating among them freely. Here on Eathia, we can help by tethering directly to them instead of through The Realm's portals. We can aid their survival. The Realm has done all it can for them. It is now defunct and of no further use to them. This is the reason behind Duergar's plan for them and us.'

'That is the opposite of what The Realm was to them. We were never meant to be directly involved in the Eathians' lives. Not like this.'

'Their own darkness and torment have permeated the space between us. While The Realm remains intertwined, the Eathians will willingly relinquish their responsibilities and darkness for us to address.'

Elkyne looked away to consider what she had said. He could understand her argument partially, but his underlying sense was that it was wrong and strangely misguided.

She continued with her story of her Eathian.

'If my tether had sensed the danger, taken her own action against those men, and not relied on being saved, she might still be alive. If I had the darkness within me then, as I do now, I could have reacted with the same anger they showed her.'

'But her husband sensed it, sensed the danger. Why didn't she?'

'Because she gave over her fate to another "me", and what is even more astounding, she was happy to do so.'

'Then surely, she deserves our respect, not our damnation?'

'Oh, I don't damn her, Elkyne. I wanted her to feel she had the right to survive and to fight for that right. Now, I feel like I let her down. At the time, I was powerless. Well. Not anymore. Duergar has allowed me a chance to put things right.'

She stopped their conversation abruptly.

The Eathians were moving on.

'We must follow, stay veiled and close by.'

As they followed, Elkyne found it easier to manoeuvre over the land. As they continued silently, he realised he didn't know her name. As before, she heard his inner thoughts.

'What difference does it make if you know my name or not? It's not like we will see each other again after this.'

In the distance, a vast opening awaited the Eathians, but it was too far to reach that evening. So, they watched as the Eathians settled within a sheltered woodland area a short distance away, near a cavern. The man led the way, and the young girl had managed to walk alone for a while. Elkyne wondered if she was getting stronger and contemplated possibly staying on Eathia a little longer. The thought brought him inner peace. He felt inclined to stay if it meant she could live.

The Terranean responded to his thoughts.

'Her energy is borrowed, Elkyne. I assisted somewhat while I was tethered to her, but that has all but faded now, and there is no need for me to re-tether now that you are here. She is already aware that she is dying. I have been listening in while she converses with her dead father's soul in her sleep.'

'Is that normal?'

'No. She is a special little one, and so was he by all accounts. Her father's tether was one of the first Superior Soul Guardians, Ashtar. You have heard of him I assume?'Elkyne had, of course. He wondered if this was why Nephelia had been so disdainful about the girl. Was it fuelled by the feud between Ashtar and Rammasus after all this time?

Her voice was soft, then, almost becoming aware of that, she changed her tone. She chose to ignore Elkyne's inner conversation.

Something fell into place about the Terranean he was with. Then she spoke.

'You must be prepared to leave at nightfall.'

'I know who you are now, Illiandra?'

'I am. You got there in the end.'

'I have heard rumours of you in The Realm. You weren't always on Duergar's side, were you?'

'That was then. A lot has changed since then. Leave it at that.'

They waited until the light diminished and an orange hue on the mountainside turned to the deepest shade of purple. A new fire lit. The woman was being comforted by the man. The child was wrapped tightly in a blanket, sleeping deeply, too deeply. Her petite, beautiful face, now with all colours fading, left her eyes shadowed by her impending fate.

'We have to get nearer, Elkyne. It's happening quickly. De-veil.'

Elkyne froze, unable to take any further action.

'Look. I'll stay. I want to stay. I can't do this.'

'Nephelia said you were going to be a pain in my side. You have no choice; either you do it, or I will. This is a gift, you idiot; take it. Now unveil.'

She prepared to continue, whether he liked it or not.

The woman turned, aware of Angelica's anxiety, sensing something was happening. She threw herself towards the child and covered her tiny frame with her own body as she had done time and time again, from the guards at home to the sirens in the ocean. Only this time, she knew she couldn't save her. Her heart and her beloved husband, in her conversations with him, had told her so. Her instinct still wanted her daughter to prevail. She was her mother.

She screamed out, and Elkyne watched as the man rushed to her side to lend extra strength to them all.

'She sees us.'

'You never said that she knows we are here.'

Elkyne could see that she was keeping a secret.

The woman's voice reached them, and Elkyne continued to stare at Illiandra.

'You can't have her; she should stay with her mother. Please don't take her after all we've been through; I beg of you.'

She looked directly at Elkyne and he saw the anguish in her eyes.

Now, her tether, Angelica, could see him and de-veiled instantly. She shot towards him and shrieked at him, sending him off balance. He retreated, shocked at her sudden appearance above the woman.

Then, in a brief moment, someone else entered the scene. A young woman stood on the shore watching them. Her red hair blew about her face while she watched on silently.

Elkyne's attention was drawn towards her, or rather, the strangeness of her appearance. Her face showed little expression, as if she were monitoring what was going on but had no connection to it.

Illiandra yelled at him to act, furious at his lethargy.

'There she is. Elkyne, fight back. You are more than strong enough to block her pathetic attempts.'

'No, I can't do it; stop this now.'

When he looked back for the woman, she was gone. Then the force hit him from behind, and the momentum pushed him towards the child. His aura was propelled forward until it joined the child's weakened energy. This caused an immediate tether with her. The girl suddenly burst back to life. The woman, crying uncontrollably, held her daughter's face in her hands, pleading with her to stay as the girl's eyes looked helplessly back at her.

Illiandra, shout out to Elkyne.

'GO NOW! Look up towards the vortex. GO ELKYNE.'

Angelica screamed at Elkyne not to go through with it, but he had no choice. The tether had been created the minute his aura had merged with the girls.

He pulled his attention away from the distraught mother and looked up. The pain was excruciating as he tried to free himself from Eathia's dense energy field. The darkness of the vortex beckoned him upward, but now there was no sign of light. It had been eclipsed and overpowered by the dark energy that emanated within him.

Finally, it reached out to him and began to pull him towards it. The familiar feeling of The Realm beckoned, and he resentfully let it take him.

He spoke to Angelica and the Eathian child.

'I'm sorry, I am so sorry.'

As he lifted away from Eathia, the lasting image was of the woman looking up at him and screaming.

Her daughter was lying lifelessly in her loving arms.

Illiandra slowly turned and left the Eathians to mourn their daughter.

She had a mixture of emotions to contend with and couldn't be seen to be in conflict by her group of mercenaries.

She damned Elkyne for stirring things up in her again. Those feelings were best left hidden deep within her core.

The child had been one of the Eathians on Duergar's hit list. A child. Did he have no mercy? She couldn't tell Elkyne what she knew, especially that, not if the reaction about the girl was to be believed, she couldn't risk him knowing any of Duergar's future plans. The truth was that the whole family had to be destroyed. The woman in particular.

Duergar had made that clear. She wondered what he was so afraid of. There was much she didn't know.

Over three eras, there were two family trees whose roots had found each other and intertwined. Unfortunately for them, both would now have to be cut down if Duergar's plan were to be successful.

~

Chapter 50
The Realm

Expendable Souls

Nephelia had informed Duergar that Elkyne would arrive at any time, so he went to the portal and waited anxiously for his arrival. He hoped that he had the common sense to veil before entering; otherwise, certain nosy Superiors would notice and it would be another predicament he would have to talk himself out of.

The Solescence Chamber was dimly lit and devoid of occupants, much to Elkyne's relief. His now veiled and unexpected return had gone unnoticed, except for the occasional flashes from the lake, which provided the only discernible evidence that it was inhabited.

Although Illiandra had not told Elkyne of the child's importance, he could see for himself as the lake continued to exhibit radiant light formations, which he knew to be a sign of a highly evolved Eathian lightworker. This child had been important.

His anger stirred as the pain he felt for being a part of her demise seemed to feed the swirling vortex within him.

A voice punctuated his feelings of melancholy.

'Be still, Elkyne.'

Makaria had been waiting patiently by the lake. Her sister, Angelica, had already informed her that he would travel back through an Illumacytes portal. Mattia, the child's tether, stood sullenly next to her.

Makaria moved towards Elkyne.

'Quickly, we must leave here. I would stay veiled, Elkyne, if I were you.'

Elkyne felt uneasy.

'Why are you here and who is she?'

Elkyne looked straight at Mattia, who ignored him and turned to leave without a word.

Makaria explained.

'She was the child's Soul Guardian. She waited for you before completely re-entering The Realm. To keep the portal active. You can imagine how she is feeling about you right now? Wait here.'

Elkyne winced at the thought.

Makaria briefly re-entered her own Psybiencian Chamber, checked it was clear, then returned and grabbed Elkyne, pulling him in with her.

'What were you thinking? You followed Duergar right to the Accumulator. Did you not expect him to do something like this?'

Elkyne pulled against Makaria, fed up with being dragged against his will.

'Just stop. I don't understand what is going on myself. It's carnage down there. You should have seen it.'

'I saw what happened to you up here, Elkyne; I saw Duergar draw you into the Accumulator; I thought you had been destroyed until I heard from Angelica that you had made it to Eathia. Was that his intention? He took such a risk sending you in there through that thing.'

'Apparently, it was, but he failed to tell me why he thought it necessary. I didn't think I would make it there, let alone back again.'

Makaria went cold.

'And here you are, nonetheless. You had better go and let Duergar know you are here.'

She went to move on, but stopped.

'Oh, and I would leave it a while before you approach Verra Mica if I were you.'

'Why? None of this was of my doing. I had no idea where I was going.'

'Not where you were going, but you knew how you would return, right? You still went ahead with it. I have to go. That part was of your doing.'

Elkyne sensed Makaria was holding something back from him.

'Wait, has something else happened in my absence?'

'Yes. While you have been away, Verra Mica has approached Duergar and asked that you be considered to tether "legitimately" with an Eathian soon to be born. Weirdly enough, he has agreed. It appears you are to join Corpus and Christi; you can only imagine how Verra Mica will feel once she finds out what you have done.'

With that, Makaria left, leaving Elkyne confused at her animosity. *None of this was of my doing*, reaffirmed in his mind. *Verra Mica would understand that surely, and now she had come through for him. He would make her aware of his appreciation after he had met with Duergar,* he decided.

Elkyne approached the outer entrance to Duergar's quarters with apprehension. He stopped and listened. He was in conference with another Guardian and could only hear Duergar's responses. Remaining veiled, he waited, wondering if now was the right time to approach him.

'What do you mean? How could you lose him through the portal? I put you in charge, and you let him out of sight. Where is he?'

Elkyne realised he was listening to an internal message from someone.

'So where is he now? What? What "girl" do you mean wasn't ready?'

'Fool! Why didn't you say this earlier? I was waiting at the Accumulator. Once he left my command, you were supposed to take over and guide him back through that portal and that portal only. The one he entered Eathia through in the first place! Now, it would appear he has gone and got himself obliterated instead. Fantastic, another one is gone! Am I to do everything myself?'

'How? On his own? Even Elkyne isn't clever enough to navigate through one of those.'

Elkyne winced at the sound of his name and how it was used. Was Duergar upset or angry at the thought of his demise? He couldn't tell.

'If he were here, I would know it. You have used a completely unorthodox method of bringing him back, which leads me to believe I overestimated both of your intelligence, so I must now consider that something has happened to him. Go back and use all of the abilities vested in you and try to locate him. I want to know where he is. NOW.'

Duergar's tones softened slightly, and he adjusted his aggressive stance.

'Nephelia, before you go, did you at least find it? I sense you did.'

'Finally, some good news. All of you, be ready to de-tether. I will give the order very soon. Our time is running out here, and I don't want to be caught out, do you understand?'

Elkyne decided to leave Duergar for the time being. The fact that Mattia had waited for him meant he had been directed. Undetected, to the Illumacytes chamber. There was no way Duergar would have known this. It bought him some time before making his presence known. Makaria had warned him not to approach Verra Mica, but that made little sense.

How bad could it be? he thought as he headed towards her order.

Chapter 51
The Realm

Core Values

It was finally nightfall on Eathia, and Corpus and Christi were in their Solescence chamber. Corpus appeared slightly confused by a request of Verra Mica's. She had contacted them, explaining to Corpus that she would need his blessing for something. She was due to meet with them there.

Elkyne had left Duergar's chambers and was on his way to see Olpheria first when he felt a new connection within his core. He was becoming aware of a section of The Realm opening up. The feeling fascinated him, so he headed towards its source instead. Then he felt Christi's presence there too.

As Corpus and Christi waited, they sensed a shift in the atmosphere of the chamber. Some of the other Soul Guardians were welcoming someone who had just entered. They both assumed it to be Verra Mica but turned to see Elkyne approaching them.

They looked at each other in shock.

'He's back from Eathia?' Christi whispered, astonished he had made it back somehow in safety.

'Elkyne!'

Christi rushed over to welcome him.

'You are actually here. Are you all right? We've been so concerned.'

Considering what he had just been through, Elkyne felt slightly uncomfortable with the attention. He joined them.

'I can assume I have finally been granted a tether by being here with you. This chamber just opened up to me. Is this how it works?'

Corpus nodded, still feeling mistrust towards him. He wanted an explanation, but this probably wasn't the time or the place.

'We heard. Verra Mica has been a fundamental part of you being able to be here and join us.'

Corpus moved towards him, and the brothers stared each other down. A silent acknowledgement that they had both seen each other on Eathia.

Christi hadn't noticed the exchange.

'Are you aware of who you are to be tethered to?'

Elkyne glanced across at Christi and beamed.

'No idea.'

She moved forward.

'Come and see.'

Guiding him over to the lake, she drew him into her aura so that he could see the image clearly. Below them, still sleeping peacefully, were Beatrice and Gabriel.

'You will be tethered to their new baby.'

She observed his reaction. An innocent, natural excitement flickered across his face, but for some reason, he regained his composure and offered a measured nod as though accepting an order issued by a Superior.

Corpus stood back, watching his brother cautiously. He couldn't continue as if nothing had happened.

'Where have you been, Elkyne? We have feared for your safety.'

'Duergar has been pushing me through the system at a ridiculous rate. It has been almost impossible to reach you both. It is so good to see you; you can't imagine how good it is to be back …'

Elkyne immediately realised his mistake in mentioning his absence from The Realm.

Corpus moved further back from them both. There was something not quite right about Elkyne. He looked somehow different. Not just because he now had a tether connection, but his form was denser.

Aware that Corpus had retreated slightly, Elkyne took the opportunity and turned discreetly to Christi, desperate to thank her, now understanding that they both knew where he had been.

'I heard you calling me, Christi, telling me to shield when I was in the Accumulator. I can't thank you enough. I feel you might have saved me.'

Christi looked confused.

'It wasn't me, Elkyne.'

Elkyne realised that it would be impossible for them to understand without them seeing for themselves what had happened to him. He disengaged his inner veil, allowing both Corpus and Christi the chance to scan him.

Corpus was horrified.

'I think Duergar was trying to show me another way into Eathia. Admittedly, it was dangerous. I have tried to recall what happened in the portal on the way down, but I can't remember anything apart from thinking I heard your voice, Christi. I met with someone on Eathia, a Dark Soul Guardian, a siren named Nephelia. Duergar sent me to her.'

'And you entered Eathia through the Accumulator. Willingly?'

'It felt more like being pushed at the time, but yes, I went into its portal.'

Corpus had been watching Elkyne's energy and noticed something alien about his core. He stepped forward and confronted his brother.

'Elkyne, that is a forbidden zone and for good reason. That energy destroys Soul Guardians; why would he take such a risk only to have you discover something he could have told you?'

Elkyne turned on Corpus. His anger flared, suddenly uncontrollable. Corpus had touched on the one question he himself couldn't answer. Instead, he chose to defend Duergar's actions rather than admit wrongdoing.

'That is precisely the attitude Duergar has been trying to warn me about. All this time, he has endeavoured to enlighten me that without some degree of awareness towards the dark matter, we lack an understanding of how to protect ourselves and the Eathians. We must be fully armed to achieve that, and yes, we may be compelled to experience the forbidden things in The Realm.

Christi moved back from him, completely appalled by her brother's stance.

Corpus stood strong and composed. Now, it was making more sense.

'Spoken like a true Psybiencian with the tight grip of Duergar at his reins.'

Unbeknownst to any of them, Verra Mica had entered the chamber and had unintentionally happened upon Elkyne's unfounded political attack on Corpus. While his veil was down, she jumped at the opportunity to scan him, although she knew most of what had happened to him by now.

'Elkyne!'

Her voice boomed.

'How can you still support a Superior that put you into that black death hole, knowing full well you may not survive? If my understanding is correct, you only made it through because of the intervention of another loyal Soul Guardian?'

Christi moved forward to try to soothe him before he said anything he couldn't take back. Corpus became aware of the energy intensifying at Verra Mica's core and realised the implications of Elkyne's darkened addition. He wondered if Verra Mica had noticed it too. A dark, swirling vortex was beginning to form within Elkyne. He reached out to prevent Christi from getting too close.

Elkyne felt hopelessly lost. His words and justifications were alien to him, but he thought that his words were somehow feeding something deep inside him, something that hungered for anger and hatred.

Unfortunately for Elkyne, he hadn't finished.

'To be blinded to the "whole truth" is just as dangerous, only you will never admit it. You might understand more of what he stands for if you'd only listen to him. I did make it through, and I am better off for it.'

Elkyne winced at his explanation, unable to believe, deep down, that it could be true; yet, what ought to be true if he was indeed a genuine Psybiencian?

Verra Mica's core was at the critical point, but Elkyne, full of his own compromising situation, didn't see what was coming.

'Superior Verra Mica, I am grateful for your concern. However, I must trust in Duergar's plans in my search for truth. I might not completely agree with his methods, but I will continue to support him, even though my future seems slightly unclear.'

That was too much for Verra Mica and she erupted.

'DOES THAT TRUTH INVOLVE MURDERING AN INNOCENT CHILD?'

Her high-pitched voice pierced Elkyne through his growing vortex. The extremity of the Source's awakening within him, in a core that was now predominantly darkened, unintentionally caused a scorching where they connected. Elkyne fell backwards; both Corpus and Christi were in shock. Neither of them understood what was happening. Why would Verra Mica attack Elkyne in this way, and why the mention of a child?

Verra Mica continued, unaffected by Elkyne's reaction.

'You were complicit in the murder of what used to be my Eathian child, so you could return to The Realm; you used her life. Where does that fit into your new awareness, your so-called truth? My Eathian child is dead because you killed her, and while you were doing that, I was asking your almighty Superior to give you a chance at tethering, a chance to be whole. The right way of being whole. Not this atrocity of an ideal of being whole.'

She gestured to Elkyne's core.

'You have no idea how valuable an Eathian life is, how much goes into each and every one of them, and you just used her as a stepping stone to get back to here.'

Elkyne bowed his head at the horror of what Verra Mica was saying. He now understood the gravity of Makaria's warning. The chamber fell into silence.

'That thing that's growing inside you, that darkness you have brought back with you, just might signify the end for all of us; you fool, how dare you preach to me.'

Verra Mica backed away in an attempt to diffuse and disconnect her anger; she was uncomfortable with these Eathian-born emotions, a by-product of tethering and witnessing so much sadness in her time on Eathia. Still, the sadness continued.

'Enough of this.'

Her anger was in remission, and with her composure forced to take the lead, she turned her attention to Christi.

'I wish to speak with you privately after we have finished here. Corpus, please keep us informed if the need arises for Christi to return to her tether.'

He nodded. She then turned to Elkyne and spoke with a sense of resolution in her voice.

'I am saddened that you feel it necessary to openly support that which is against the very essence of The Realm. I sincerely hope that your current journey brings you back to the only truth. I wish you well with your tether.'

She went to turn and walk away, but could not help herself.

'Try not to kill this one, won't you?'

She glanced across at Christi and Corpus. She could see their bewilderment at her loss. She stayed fixed on them.

'If you wouldn't mind, Elkyne, I would like to first speak with Corpus and Christi. I bid you leave.'

Elkyne exited from the chamber without looking back.

Corpus addressed Verra Mica.

'We had no idea what had happened until now. We are so sorry about your Eathian daughter, your Honour.'

Christi moved forward, knowing how much this meant to her and felt her pain and anguish.

'This is what Ashtar meant about the darkness approaching her, and it was Elkyne he was speaking of when he said don't let him come back, wasn't it?'

'Apparently so. Who could have imagined it was one of our own he was warning us about?'

Corpus looked doubtful.

'Surely he couldn't have meant Elkyne, your Honour. It's our brother we are talking about. What possible reason could Ashtar have to leave him on Eathia? I am sorry, but I can't accept his reasoning.'

'Nor I, but there it is,' she said bluntly.

Verra Mica tried again to compose herself. The chamber had grown quieter, allowing her to feel comfortable enough to continue.

'We must move on quickly. It's no wonder Duergar agreed to my request for Elkyne to tether to the newborn. I might have even given him the idea; I am a fool. He now has a spy within our Eathian family, that is, if he doesn't already.'

Corpus realised she was referring to Nemius, Avery's tether.

'This has become so cloak-and-dagger. This is where veiling and deceiving gets us. None of us know where we stand. I'm sure that's the point of all this chaos.'

'We know what we are doing and will stick to our plans,' Corpus exclaimed.

He looked across at Christi. Wondering if there was anything else she needed them for. Verra Mica noticed.

'Now, my reason for imposing is that it is not without consideration, please be assured. I require some time with Gabriel, Corpus. Would this be problematic?'

Corpus was taken back.

What possible reason could she have for wanting to speak with Gabriel? he wondered.

Elkyne wasn't the only one who had taken an Eathian's life into his own hands. If it wasn't for Verra Mica, he and his brother would have more in common than he wished for.

Chapter 52
Eathia - Third Era

Family Tree

Bertha stared at her ceiling, or rather, where she knew her ceiling to be within the darkness of the room. She noticed, instead, tiny, illuminated floating particles as they darted across her field of vision.

She had to focus on anything other than those images conjured up within the story of those poor men and the many more people that the Dark Soul Guardians had taken over.

'Where did they go? What became of them all? Had they just filtered into Eathia, never to be seen again? Were they still existing among those who lived now, after all those years?

The questions were becoming too much for her to cope with. She couldn't see past her dread that her father and Denis might have somehow fallen prey to their cruelty.

She threw her body to one side. She knew it was pointless to try and speak to the woman. It would have been to do with her life, and she wouldn't divulge any information on that subject.

The sadness caught up with her and gnawed away at her throat. She buried her head in the pillow and cried.

When she awoke, she felt angry and headed back to her uncle's. She needed answers.

The Emporium was open, but no lights were on, so she headed through the front of the shop towards the back.

Anamaya was in the kitchen with Maddox. Her arrival made her aunt jump. Bertha suddenly felt guilty for bursting into their home unannounced in the way she had.

'Bertha. I wasn't expecting to see you so early. Is everything alright?'

Anamaya wished immediately that she hadn't asked such a ridiculous question. Of course, it wasn't.

Feeling light-headed, Bertha sat herself down at the table. Anamaya could see she was distressed. She pulled her dressing gown tightly around herself and tied the sash. She sat and reached out for Bertha's hand.

Bertha spoke quietly.

'I'm sorry. I'm finding it hard to separate what I've learned from the story about the past and what is happening around us now. My head is trying to make sense of all of it, trying to find reasons behind losing my father and Denis.'

She burst into tears. Maddox ran to her and held onto her legs, in an attempt to try and make her happy again.

Her aunt knew exactly what she meant. At some point, she knew Bertha would question the significance of all she had been through thus far and what it had to do with the story.

Anamaya took a slow, deep breath in and let it out gradually.

'Talk to me, Bertha. What is on your mind? I promise to try and help if I can.'

Bertha wiped her face with the back of her sleeve. She thought about what it was she wanted to say.

'Uncle mentioned some time ago that one day, someone would be transcribing my story.'

Bertha continued.

'I didn't realise it then, but that bothered me. I feel I'm caught somewhere between history and the future, but my present seems completely out of my control. Like, Father and Denis were always going to die, and she knew that, but she didn't warn me about it, so I could have stopped them from going.'

Anamaya could hear Bertha's anger mingled with the anguish.

Bertha turned on Anamaya.

'Did you know they were going to die? Did Uncle?'

Anamaya was taken aback.

'No, Bertha. Why would you think such a thing?'

The kitchen fell silent.

Maddox reached up to Bertha's face and touched her cheek gently. He whispered to her.

'You'll see.'

Bertha's mouth dropped open. She looked across at her aunt and back at Maddox.

'I'll see what, Maddox. What will I see?'

'Why.'

With that, he wandered off and rummaged through his toy box.

Anamaya raised her eyebrows.

'Well, I'll be. That's a philosophical first.'

Bertha went to grin, then flushed, remembering she had just accused her aunt and uncle of having prior knowledge of what had happened to her father and brother.

'I'm sorry. I had no right to …'

Anamaya shook her head to brush it off.

'Have I introduced you to my son? Maddox, the all-knowing, all-seeing.'

Bertha laughed.

'Where did that come from?'

'He does spend an awful lot of time at the castle. Maybe the orb is rubbing off on him somehow.'

She shrugged her shoulders. Then, reached for a bag of flour.

Bertha watched as she continued to scatter the flour over the table. She smiled at the memory of her Nana Nora and their many days baking together.

'Right,' Anamaya said assertively.

Her voice brought her back into the room.

In the middle, she drew two parallel, thick lines that went upwards. At the top, there were many sections dividing off from what Bertha realised now was the main trunk of a tree. She continued to draw the roots. Many spurs branched off to create more and more until the whole of the table was filled with roots and branches.

'OK. This is my "non-Ashen" understanding of the story's cycle.'

She drew circles around some of the sections of roots; for each one, she drew a line up the trunk and circled the many branches directly above, connecting them.

'The trunk is the essence that takes the life and turns it into a story for the transcriber to understand. That act keeps the story and that section of the tree alive. Yes?'

Bertha nodded, trying to grasp the point her aunt was making.

'So …'

She pointed at a root cluster in the centre of most parts of her drawing.

'… this is your life. It feeds the essence, which gets drawn up through the trunk and out into the branches to be understood and transcribed. By being visible and transcribed, the essence is kept alive and active. Are you with me?'

Bertha shook her head.

Her aunt pointed at her cluster of roots again.

'All of the above can only happen if you live your life your way. You are connected to the whole, but the whole isn't controlling you. You are creating your own story, and so are all those connected to you.'

She pointed at the rest of the root system.

Bertha sat back in the chair and thought.

Anamaya continued.

'You are a part of something very special, but aren't we all? No one gets told what to expect. That's life, Bertha. The story isn't controlling you. The only person I have ever heard of who could see into the future lived a life of turmoil. I can't imagine the pain she must have gone through. She wouldn't want that for you.'

Bertha realised who she was referring to: her great-grandmother.

'Your ability to transcribe is not related to how you feel right now. They are completely separate. You are in mourning, Bertha. Out of everything you've had to grasp as a child until now, this emotion is a natural response. Please don't see it as anything more than it is, an awful accident.'

She stood up and went to get a cloth to remove the flour.

'Someone, in the future, will know your story, and they will learn so much from you, young lady.'

The back door flew open and Augustus walked in.

'Bertha, what a surprise. I'm not staying long. I just wanted to collect this little one. Did you need me at all?'

Bertha shook her head and smiled at Anamaya.

As Augustus picked Maddox up, his son saw his mother's drawing and pointed to the table.

'Tree.'

Augustus's face lit up.

'You did this? You clever boy. Ladies, I think we have an artist in our midst.'

With that, he shot back out the door.

Anamaya put her hands on her hips and looked at Bertha.

'Charming'

Chapter 53
The Realm

Last Flight

Corpus wasn't sure if he had heard Verra Mica correctly.

He stepped back, shocked by her request; he looked at Christi, who was already looking at him, having been forewarned of her request.

'Did you know about this, Christi?'

'I had already worked out that this was one of our options. We only have a few left, Corpus, and we must act quickly. Things are moving rapidly and this affects our tethers, especially Gabriel. He is so significant that The Realm cannot let his likes slip out of our reach. We need him to work with us knowingly.'

'But we, I mean he, hasn't had the best of experiences with The Realm thus far. Admittedly, that was my fault, but I assure you he is aware of why we need him. Am I missing something here?'

Corpus stopped, unsure why he felt he had failed Gabriel and Verra Mica, besides the obvious 'nearly ending his life' issue.

He didn't wait for a reply.

'I apologise for questioning your reasons. Of course, your Honour, you have my sanction. He might be a little wary, that's all.'

'There are things I need to show him, and certain explanations will be vital if he continues to work under our guidance. They are advancing in years, and there is still much to do, and it seems we are being forced to stay one move ahead of Duergar. He is more calculating and organised than I initially gave him credit for.'

Corpus looked at Christi again. He felt slightly bewildered by her comprehension and acceptance of everything that was happening. She caught his look and realised what was bothering him, and so did Verra Mica. The time to act ruthlessly was fast approaching, and some choices they had left, however desperate they appeared, were all they had, and Corpus would not be a part of them now. Not this time.

'Christi, I think that while I am with Gabriel, you should take some time away. I will arrange for a watch on Gabriel and Beatrice in case of disruption. Please, both of you, make sure your shields are lowered so you are always contactable.'

'Of course, as you ask, your Honour.'

Corpus and Christi bowed once again, and as Verra Mica went to leave, she glanced back at Christi.

'Would you accompany me for a while?

As they were about to exit the chamber, Elkyne reappeared, veiled and silent.

Verra Mica turned, and they both left, unaware of his presence.

He walked over to the lake's edge and looked down into the mist. He let his veil drop.

Corpus, shocked to see him reappear, watched as the multicoloured energies began to flow through the mist towards his brother.

He turned to look at Corpus and gestured towards his core.

'This wasn't meant to create a fight, Corpus. Do you know how hard this has been? I've never been part of your and Christi's world, watching you both go in a direction I thought I was meant to join. I didn't understand my separation until I entered that Accumulator. I feared I would be torn apart in there. That immense strength was unlike anything I've felt before – a force that destroys weakness, yet it left me with a sense of completeness, filling a void I didn't know I had. That strength will guide us through dark times ahead, Corpus. I will gladly use this gift to support us all.'

'That strength you refer to, unless it has certain reins attached, will ruthlessly barge into this world and others to cause havoc and mayhem. It bears little pity or remorse and holds no value to our natural state of balance. We have been taught to wait for awareness to grow and walk gracefully and respectfully into that space. Only then will order follow. There is a vast difference, Elkyne. That egotistical arrogance has been our eternal and relentless enemy on Eathia, and now, it appears to be our new emerging enemy here in The Realm.'

'What are you suggesting? That I have fallen prey to this arrogant, self-righteous behaviour and that now, I am your enemy?'

Corpus moved closer to Elkyne as a gesture of unity.

'No, brother, you are not my enemy. If true balance is what you seek, you must learn to control it, even if darkness simmers within you. I trust that you genuinely mean what you say, but you must manage it; no one else can do it for you. Do not let anyone manipulate you through that thing. Light and dark coexist, but don't compromise your soul or essence by engaging in endless inner conflict. Ultimately, that is all you will perceive. I don't want to lose you to that, brother.'

Now, Corpus pointed towards the darkness at the core of Elkyne.

'I hear you, don't worry. An excellent teacher prepared me, but I must guard against him. I've sacrificed much for this knowledge. We will work well together, Corpus, the three of us. I'm here for a reason. Let's harness my strength. I chose to return to you instead of following Duergar. I'll meet him now and let him know I'm back. Please trust in me.'

Corpus observed Elkyne depart. He pondered what had truly transpired during his time in the Accumulator and whether Duergar would ever face consequences for his actions. He was also confused about why the Source was allowing this to unfold in the way it was, which troubled him. Why had he not been made aware of any of this?

As Elkyne left the chamber to find Duergar, he passed Christi, who was returning after her conversation with Verra Mica. She completely missed his presence, still caught up in her thoughts, unaware of his proximity.

'Christi?

She glanced up at him, surprised to see him there. Elkyne tried to explain himself for his earlier outburst.

'I apologise if I spoke out of turn. I …'

'I have to go back now, Elkyne, to be with Corpus … but …'

'What is it? What happened with Verra Mica?'

Christi was blank. She looked through him with little or no recognition. He feared that he had upset her, possibly beyond repair.

'Christi?'

'It's alright, Elkyne, really, it's alright. I have so much ahead of me. It is there that my thoughts lie.'

She walked back towards him, looked deeply into his eyes and smiled.

'Just remember, it will be alright; it has to be. We are all becoming clearer about what is required of us. And that's a good thing. I feel that you are with us once again.'

He understood. He did feel a shift, and as a result, he felt more settled.

'You are the last soul I want to disappoint or hurt.'

Aware that she needed to go, Elkyne quickly reassured her.

'I will be back very soon to join you both, and we can all finally be together.'

Christi didn't answer. Instead, she smiled at her brother, turned and entered the chamber to join Corpus. She saw him at the edge of the lake. He turned as she approached.

'What has happened to him, Christi?'

'The Accumulator, that's what! We understand the deep impact it had on Duergar. It's hard to believe it wouldn't have influenced Elkyne in a similar way. However, he appears to be managing it, which is a relief. I really don't want to dwell on this any longer, Corpus. Can we please leave while we still have time?'

'Before we go, Christi, did Verra Mica say any more about why she wanted to tether to Gabriel?'

She remained silent, looking at Corpus imploringly.

Corpus didn't want to pressure Christi. He could see that something was troubling her. They could go anywhere together for the time being, and he knew precisely where he intended to take her.

They moved closer to the edge of the mist.

'Shall we fly with my winged friends?'

Christi looked back at him with apprehension.

'Since when did you become such an accomplished Airian?'

'Since the raven chose me as his flying companion. Now I am choosing you. I promise not to take us too close to the ocean's surface.'

A warm, green and golden glow swirled within Christi that Corpus had never seen before. He tried to read it, but as she looked down, the colours disappeared. She stood silently, looking at both of their Eathian tethers as they slept.

'Actually, can we watch them for a while before we go?'

Christi silently gazed down at Beatrice while Corpus watched, trying to interpret her thoughts. He knew something was bothering her, but didn't want to push the point; she would tell him when the time was right.

'Christi? You are somewhere else.'

Christi diverted his attention away from her.

'She has a new child, Corpus. Isn't it truly wonderful?'

'Feel sorry for me, if only for a moment, please. First Nemius and now Elkyne, both tethers to our Eathian children.'

She smiled.

'Look at them; through everything they have endured and are yet to endure, their love for each other goes from strength to strength.'

Again, Corpus heard something in her tone that he couldn't fathom.

He knew things would change for them all. He could feel it. These two beings were to be the next pioneers of The Realm's force on Eathia; they just needed a little more time to accomplish their purposes.

He moved closer to her.

'You know he's done it, Christi; he has been able to make the machine using Eathian materials. I'm not sure he really realises just how significant his invention is yet, but he has achieved it. I'm sure Verra Mica will be pleased when she finds out.'

'She knows.'

She turned to look at him. Christi had already been aware that it had been completed.

'I never doubted either of you for a moment,' she whispered in Beatrice's affectionate tone.

Corpus smiled.

'Of course you did, you're my wife after all. There isn't much that gets past you two.'

Christi laughed.

He turned towards her, a little more serious.

'I witnessed something amazing and have been waiting for the right time to tell you.'

'Go on.'

Corpus quickly explained what had occurred during the final process of making the machine and how Gabriel could sense and understand Corpus as he tried to help him.

'He listened and heard, Christi.'

This was something she had not yet experienced with Beatrice. This made her happy for him, more than he could ever understand.

She patiently waited for Corpus to relay the final moments as he continued excitedly.

'Gabriel's invention was scattered about the floor of his workroom, and I urged him, with all the power vested in me, to complete it, once and for all.'

Christi nodded understandingly at him.

'As the Reflectorscope – his name for it – began to shape up, I recalled the information shared while in the source. It was remarkable how identical it was. The Source showed me how the machine would look and how it would go on to influence Eathia and The Realm's future. It'll be a beacon of the Source's energy, its very essence, guiding Eathians if they ever became de-tethered from the Source or their Soul Guardians. This is big, Christi.'

Smiling at his enthusiasm, Christi signalled to leave for Verra Mica's chambers to find the ravens before time ran out. She sensed the urgency more than Corpus did, and they moved on as he continued.

When they arrived at the chamber, they entered together. She loved hearing the excitement in his voice at their new creation, but at the same time, she couldn't let him see how much pain it was causing her.

'You did it. You made that stubborn, beautiful man listen to you.'

Corpus stopped and composed himself.

'Right. That's enough about me. Let's go to the mountains.'

Smiling, Christi followed him as he called on the ravens.

Chapter 54
The Realm - Eathia

Stranger Happenings

A little over eight months had passed since the loss of Tobias and Denis. Sophia had promised Guss that she would make the journey to Sirenguard with two gravestones so they could be placed under the oak tree by the cabin. That day had come. Sophia had packed up her cart with provisions, and the two slabs had been laid carefully between blankets.

'I can't believe I'm actually doing this, especially with the number of babies due any moment. Shall I leave it another week?'

Bertha laughed and linked her arm with her aunt. Both of them argued that they would cope just fine. Bertha shot forward and hugged her mother.

'Please be careful. I know it's a straightforward route, but take it steady.'

'Bertha, now who's worrying? This will be good for me. I need to do this. You know I do.'

Sophia leaned in to hug Anamaya.

'Look after her, won't you? I shouldn't be longer than a few weeks.'

With that, she jumped up onto the cart and took hold of the reins. The horse shifted and fidgeted, ready to get going. She clicked her tongue and it bolted forward, and she was on her way. Giggling, she turned back, waving at Bertha and Anamaya.

They watched as she disappeared down the cobbled street. Bertha sighed.

'This is going to be weird. She will be alright, won't she?'

Her aunt smiled back at her.

'Bertha, your mother is well-travelled. I think she is right. She does need this, and so do you. You have time to concentrate on yourself for a change.'

Bertha frowned.

'That's what I'm worried about. I hate my own company. I'm boring.'

Anamaya tutted at her niece and led her back into the cottage.

Little did Bertha realise that she had only a few hours of silence before her and Anamaya's world would ignite into action.

After a frantic knocking on Bertha's door later that afternoon, Martha now sat on the opposite side of the kitchen table from Bertha. Her cheeks flushed and her red hair stuck to the skin on her forehead as she perspired through the pain. Her breathing was purposefully controlled to try to calm her next imminent contraction and wave of panic. This would be her third since she arrived at the cottage. Martha's hands clasped tightly onto the edges of the table as she focused intently on Bertha.

Bertha had come to terms with the fact that Martha probably wasn't going to make it home again anytime soon. She had just popped across for a check-up, but things had started before she had even made it there. Her husband, Alais, was working in the fields and wouldn't even realise she had gone until later that evening.

'That's it. Slow your breathing down and it will pass. You aren't due quite yet; these might be phantom contractions.'

'They feel real to me. What if I'm having it now?'

'Let's just take it one step at a time. We might need to consider getting you upstairs while we can.'

There was a loud bang at the front door.

'That might be Alais. Just wait and keep breathing slowly, and we'll be straight back.'

Martha dared not move. She closed her eyes and focused on her breathing.

Bertha opened the front door to see another father-to-be.

'Ben? Is everything alright?'

'It's Clara. I think she's going into labour. Can you come quickly? She's screaming for you.'

They both jumped as Martha yelled from the kitchen.

'Bertha, it's coming. This can't be happening.'

Ben's face drained of colour.

'Oh, cripes, sounds like you've got your hands full already.'

'Can you go and get Anamaya for me? Tell her it's urgent and she needs to come here. I'll go to Clara as soon as she arrives.'

'That's grand. Listen, I'll go via the barn and turn the furnace down on the way back and shut things up. I've left it all open. See you back at mine.'

Bertha ran into the kitchen, helped Martha to her feet and led her towards the stairs. They carefully made their way up to her mother's bedroom. She checked Martha for signs that her baby was on its way, and it was.

She waited until she heard her aunt's voice downstairs.

‘Anamaya is here now. I need to pop out, but I’ll be back.’

Martha nodded and blew out at the same time, and continued to nod with the next breath in. Her nodding continued long after Bertha had left the room, seemingly to reassure herself that she would be fine.

Bertha ran down the stairs and through the open front door straight into the path of her friend, Albert.

She screamed in shock, her mind already racing to get to Clara’s quickly.

‘Oh, Albert, is everything alright? I’m just flying out on a call.’

Bertha ran past him and talked, running backwards as she did.

He shouted back.

‘It’s Lottie.’

Bertha stopped in her tracks.

‘Don’t tell me she’s going into labour too?’

He looked shocked.

‘Too? Who else? Martha?’

‘And Clara. I’m just off there now.’

Bertha’s arms fell to her side as she lost hold of her coat and her bag. They both plopped onto the ground. She thought for a moment.

‘Can you get her here? Anamaya is inside with Martha. It would help if we can keep everyone together.’

‘No. I can’t move her. She’d have my head if I tried. This past month she’s been a right …’

Bertha stopped him.

‘Albert? Have you still got your cart?’

‘I have.’

‘Right. Follow me.’

Martha’s high-pitched scream shot out from the window above them, and Albert instinctively ducked, bringing his arms up to protect his head. Bertha frowned at him, confused.

‘See? I’m a nervous wreck. You’ve no idea what I’ve been through. There’s not one piece of china left in our place that hasn’t got a crack in it.’

‘Albert, concentrate. We need to go and get Clara and bring her to yours. I can’t be running around the town.’

Albert ran down the path, looking back at the window, then followed Bertha towards his house.

Once Clara had eventually been taken to Albert and Lottie’s house, Bertha realised no one had let Ben know the change of plan. It took a while for him to find the right scream from the right woman. When he did, he was just in time to see Clara give birth to a beautiful boy. As Bertha passed him to Ben, he greeted him by his chosen name.

'Hello Burnie, what a gorgeous little tyke you are.'

Ben looked down at his son; his tiny eyes seemed to glow almost as though they were being lit from behind. Ben blinked, and they looked normal again. He glanced at Clara, wondering if she had noticed, but her eyes were closed as she took a moment to recover.

'What a beauty, hey, you clever girl,' he whispered.

Beaming at Bertha, he gestured for her to go and see Lottie. She was still in the throes of labour. Albert was sitting next to her on the bed, her hand in both of his as he held onto her.

'No change. It's like it's all starting to calm down.'

Bertha examined her, and it did appear that she wasn't as ready as they thought she was.

'Albert, I'm just going to run back to the cottage and check on Martha and Anamaya. I'll be back as soon as I can.'

'Go on, you go, just don't forget us, alright.'

Bertha pecked the top of both of her dear friends' heads and ran out the door.

As she approached her cottage, all was quiet. She looked up at it, feeling the same empty feeling and trying to push it to the back of her mind. The cottage was just a shell without her mother there to greet her, and it hadn't even been a day yet.

Anamaya welcomed her at the door.

'All good here, Bertha. How are the other two? What a strange turn of events, don't you think?'

Bertha walked in and hugged her aunt. She heard a baby cry upstairs and smiled.

'A boy, Dante. Isn't it a beautiful name?'

'Another boy.'

As they walked into the kitchen, Bertha updated Anamaya on the progress of Clara and the lack thereof with Lottie. Ana lifted her cardigan off the back of the kitchen chair.

'I'll pop in on them and leave you here with Martha. I'll let Alais know that she is here. I'm sure no one has bothered to let him know that Martha's condition has escalated. Poor man missed everything.'

Bertha thanked her aunt and gave her a second squeeze, and went to see Martha and her new baby.

As she walked into the room, she realised there was something wrong. Martha was still panting. Dante was swathed in a blanket and was contentedly lying next to her.

'Martha, what is it?'

'I'm still getting contractions.'

'They'll pass Martha; it's natural for you to have a few after.'

'No, no, no, these are coming back.'

Bertha felt Martha's stomach.

'Oh.'

A wave of pain swept through Martha, and she gripped Bertha's hand so tightly that the pain seemed to continue up into Bertha's arm, too.

'Ouch! Martha, let go. I need to help you with the other one.'

'WHAT OTHER ONE?'

Martha screamed and burst into tears, then her face contorted, seeming to smile oddly. Then she started to laugh, still with tears falling down her cheeks, and then the crying started again. Once her hysteria had settled down, she tried to come to terms with the fact that she was having twins. A misplaced rage swept through her body as a new, much higher-pitched yell escaped from her.

'ALAAAAAIIIISSS, YOU DID THIS TO ME.'

Ten minutes later, Rossetta was born. Her hair was as red as her mother's, her skin as pale as ivory silk.

Martha reached out for her and held her close to her cheek and sobbed.

'Is that it, Bertha? I don't have the energy for any more.'

Bertha laughed and joined her, sitting beside the bed with Dante.

'No more, I promise.'

Through her transcribing, Bertha now knew just how important every single birth was. She looked down at Rossetta in wonder. All the generations before her, their lives, hopes and dreams, were manifesting and igniting within this little child. She felt herself well up.

It didn't go unnoticed by Martha as she reached for her friends hand just as they heard the door open downstairs.

'That'll be Alais.'

Bertha went to hand over Dante, but Martha shook her head.

'Take him down to him, then when he comes up, we can surprise him with Rossetta. I have to have some fun out of all this. The look on his face will be worth it.'

Alais quietly entered the cottage, went into the kitchen, and waited patiently for Bertha to come down.

As she walked through the door, he saw his son for the first time, and he ran to him, excitedly holding them both, feeling a deep sense of relief that it was all over.

'Thank you, thank you, Bertha. Is Martha alright?'

'Come and see for yourself'

She passed him Dante and took his arm to lead him upstairs. Halfway up, Rossetta gave a small cry and Alais stopped, looking up at Bertha in confusion. Her smile gave it away, and he ran with Dante, passed her and went in to see Martha.

Outside, the light had faded to night. As Bertha came down to turn on the lights and shut the curtains, the hairs on the back of her neck suddenly began to rise as she approached the kitchen window. She rubbed her neck and leaned closer to the glass to peer out into the darkness.

Unseen by her, a strangely disfigured man stepped back into the shadows. He had watched Bertha embrace a man, both cooing over their newborn baby. He pulled his collar up around his neck and lowered his hat over his face, his body involuntarily shivering.

She looks so happy, he thought.

***They** look so happy,* he corrected himself.

The feeling of betrayal overwhelmed any sense of love and loss. As it rose through his body, anger joined the betrayal, embracing it as though it were a long-lost friend. Memories, long gone, were starting to come back to him.

'So, you have a new family now.'

He was alone after all.

As he made a move to leave, something stopped him: a movement and approaching footsteps.

The woman he didn't recognise was with a man who had his back to him. His voice was unlocking bits and pieces from what felt like another life and time.

'Please take all the time you need, Ana. It's been a ridiculous night for you and Bertha. The castle will be fine unattended for a while. Give her my love and tell her that I am proud of her, today of all days. If only Sophia were here to see it.'

'I do hope she has made it safely. Sirenguard is a long way to travel on your own. Can you believe it's nearly been a year since Tobias passed?'

Augustus pursed his lips together and gently shook his head.

'She will be fine. She knows the route well enough.'

Anamaya leant in and kissed Augustus on the cheek.

'I will go in and check on her now and let her know that Deverill arrived safe and sound this evening.'

Augustus turned to leave.

'Very strange. I'll go to collect their reflectors and deliver them in the morning. It's a job lot this time. See you later, my love.'

Anamaya chuckled. As she listened to Augustus's footsteps retreat, she took a moment to gaze up at the night sky, which glistened with tiny stars. The man watched as she inhaled the cool air.

As she did, she was aware of another smell in the air. Something claggy and musty.

'Smells like somethings died out here,' she muttered.

She crinkled her nose and walked into the cottage, making a little mental note to let Bertha know.

The anger bubbled inside the stranger's chest.

'Not one mention of me,' he seethed.

He had to get away. He felt suddenly suffocated with his spiralling thoughts. So, he left quickly and ran as fast as he could, hidden, through the back streets of the town to escape the pain.

No one missed him, not even a mention of who he had been.

He was forgotten.

The old man who had nursed him back to life again had been right.

What was the point of having memories if all they did was deepen his pain? Why, if none of the others, had these memories returned to him? These were the two people he had been sent to kill. So why was this suddenly feeling wrong? He had an overwhelming urge to run. He had to leave and get as far away from her as possible.

He found himself still running as he neared the outskirts of the town. It wasn't until now, as its illuminated spire rose into the moonlit sky, that he realised he was heading for Castle Raphael.

Chapter 55
The Realm

The Last Tether

Elkyne headed towards his order. He lowered his veil, knowing that Duergar would immediately become aware of his return. Sure enough, a message came through instantly.

Elkyne scanned his whereabouts. He was leaving the forbidden area, no doubt returning from the Accumulator and heading for his quarters. When they finally caught up with each other, Duergar launched a verbal attack on Elkyne.

'I am incensed, dumbfounded and completely overcome with concern, all at the same time. The prodigal Guardian returns and graces me with his presence. Where have you been, may I ask? You just disappeared. Poof!'

He created a sudden burst of mist in front of him as if he needed to make his point theatrically to enhance his outrage.

Elkyne was justifiably angry, too. He wasn't going to take anything from Duergar, not after what he did to him.

'It's frustrating not knowing what's happening around you, isn't it? Well, welcome to my world.'

'Not the response I was expecting, Elkyne. Would you like to try that again? Wait, not until we have some privacy, come this way. Who else knows you are here? Forget it. It doesn't matter anymore.'

Duergar led him into his chamber, his internal core visibly starting to ignite as his frustration increased. He spun around and confronted Elkyne, ready to reprimand him where he stood for messing up so astonishingly, but he stopped as soon as he saw his addition. The beautiful, darkened vortex pulsing deep inside Elkyne's core.

'It worked, you have it.'

His demeanour changed instantly.

'He was so right.' He bellowed out a laugh.

Elkyne was confused.

'Wait, who was right?'

'Rammasus, of course! A Superior Guardian totally ahead of his time. He understood more than the whole Realm put together. Anyway, that's not important right now.'

'No, it is important; you sent me into that thing knowing full well what was going to happen to me, regardless of the possible dangers, all because some ancient guardian had some fixation with that death trap?'

Duergar smiled. Elkyne's anger seemed to please him regardless of whether it was aimed at him or not.

'I told you that you wouldn't be the same again, and I said you would expand your knowledge by going to Eathia, OK, it wasn't in so many words, but that's basically what I meant. Expansion hurts, knowledge has to be earned and you earned it.'

Duergar pointed to Elkyne's core to support his argument.

'So, my visit to Eathia was pointless after all? It was just about the Accumulator the whole time?'

'Not pointless.'

Duergar became serious.

'How did you get back, may I ask? Not by any means, I am aware of that's for sure.'

'I got pulled back through Mattias's portal, who I have to say, isn't thinking kindly of me at the moment, and nor is Verra Mica. The girl was her and Ashtar's Eathian daughter when they were tethered.'

Duergar's aura ignited. He couldn't believe what he was hearing.

'It was Sara, Mary's daughter? Is that who you speak of?'

Elkyne glared at him.

'What's wrong with you?'

'You have no idea how happy that makes me. One less to worry about.'

Elkyne roared at his indifference.

Duergar was unfazed.

'Why do you care? Well, at least you're back now, it doesn't matter how.'

'A young Eathian child died, and I piggybacked her Soul Guardian. It does matter, actually.'

'That had nothing to do with me, you knew very well what the consequences were, and you decided to return that way all the same.'

'She sounds just like you.'

'Sorry, who?'

'Nephelia. You trained her well. She's as ruthless as they come.'

'High praise. Thank you.'

Ignoring his sarcasm, Elkyne changed the subject.

'So, what happens now? Would you care to enlighten me, or am I still to be kept in the dark?'

Smirking, Duergar slowly moved forward as if to tell Elkyne a secret. His tone deepened.

'Don't underestimate the power of being "kept in the dark", Elkyne.'

As was his wish, Duergar's voice seemed to seep into every corner of Elkyne's being. He moved back to break the energy.

'You are to be tethered, aren't you?'

'Apparently, as a spy, yes.'

'Oh, come now. Stop being so overdramatic. When is it happening, do you know?'

'It could be anytime. May I give my leave? I have things I need to do. I just wanted you to know that I was back.'

'Of course.'

Duergar moved forward and, for a moment, seemed sincere.

'Elkyne, do you realise what I see when I look at you?'

Elkyne silently braced himself for another insult.

'Perfection.'

That wasn't what he was expecting, but it felt like an insult all the same.

'I am proud of who you have become, regardless of what you may think of me at this time. We might need to brush up on your charm a little, from what I understand from Nephelia.'

He smiled at Elkyne and turned away from him.

As Elkyne went to leave, he thought about what Corpus and Christi had said and wondered why Verra Mica would want to tether to Corpus's Eathian.

Duergar was on to him instantly and demanded an explanation.

'What is it, what have you heard?'

Elkyne's veil was down, yes, but how did he know what he thought? He hadn't sent a message to him.

'It's a by product of the Accumulator; I maybe should have told you about that. I can hear your thoughts. What was it you overheard Elkyne? Something about Verra Mica and a Gabriel, was it?'

'You can't do that. I want your word that you stop reading me in that way.'

Duergar looked intently at Elkyne. Elkyne suddenly started to hear his deepest thoughts. As soon as Duergar realised what he was doing, he cut them off and stood back from him.

'It works both ways, you see. So, there'll be no more secrets between us from now on.'

Duergar gestured at the vortex lying peacefully within Elkyne.

'Don't worry, I have it now anyway. Do you know when she is to tether with him?'

'No.'

'Very well, that's all for now. I'll call for you when I require you.'

Duergar waved him away and grinned, veiling just before Elkyne had a chance to read him in the same way Duergar had done to him. He didn't want to give Elkyne a reason to back out of tethering; he needed him there.

Elkyne left to update his friend Olpheira about all that had happened, but felt the pull of his tether. He excitedly detoured to the Seraphytes' Solescence Chamber. As he entered, the pull intensified. He anticipated seeing Corpus and Christi but remembered they were elsewhere. He approached the lake's edge and glimpsed the family he would join. As he looked into the mist, it cleared to reveal Gabriel and Beatrice in their kitchen, chatting, with Gabriel appearing concerned as he rested his arm around her.

It looked like the baby was due soon. Excitement bubbled up again in Elkyne. He wished his brother and sister could have been there for him at least.

The two Guardians who had kept a watch on Gabriel and Beatrice moved back into the shadows. Veiled and out of sight of Elkyne.

Elkyne jumped, not wanting to wait anymore. The blissful journey took him to the baby. The tethering process jolted Beatrice, and she held onto her stomach tightly as a wave of nausea washed over her. Gabriel had seen enough and ran to his study.

The two Guardians had moved back to the lake and watched as Elkyne fell through his tether portal. They moved back in disbelief when they realised where Gabriel was heading.'

'Is he going to do what I think he's going to do?'

'Is this part of the plan?'

'I don't think so. She wasn't expecting any movement during the night. We need to message Verra Mica. She should have been here by now.'

Olpheira walked nervously in her quarters as she waited for Elkyne. She had received his message about his arrival, but she could sense his presence fading until he was gone entirely. Frustration washed over her as she realised he must have already tethered without a chance to say goodbye. Baquarrah's voice broke through her thoughts, signalling his arrival in her quarters.

'You look perplexed, Olpheira, are you well?'

'I am your Honour, I was merely concerned at the absence of Elkyne, but it appears he had something else to do that was more important.'

'I can't imagine there to be anything more important than his tethering, can you?'

Olpheira looked away. Of course, he was right.

'Olpheira? I need to talk with you. Is now a good time?'

'About Elkyne?'

He smiled.

'No, not about Elkyne. I want to know if you have any concerns. What I mean is, are you coping with supporting the work we have been doing on Eathia?'

'What strange questions. Of course. Why?'

Olpheira sensed it was not her that he was unsure of.

'Is there something I should be aware of, your Honour?'

'I fear Duergar may have coerced me into overreacting about our current situation with the Eathians. Council has been a bit tense of late, to say the least, and …'

Baquarrah trailed off as though listening to something.

'Something's happening, Olpheria.'

'What is it? What's happening?'

'It's Duergar. He has just sent out a message asking those who support him to meet in his Solescence Chambers immediately.'

'Why, what is he doing? Why have you been able to hear his call? You are not thinking of abandoning us, are you?'

He listened again to the final call.

'I will go and see what it is he wishes to tell us. That is all, I will return very soon.'

Olpheira was taken aback. Why was Baquarrah even contemplating this?

He paused before leaving. Aware that Olpheria needed some explanation.

'Please do not judge me. I have been listening to both sides of the Council for a very long time now, and Duergar has made valid concerns for both The Realm and Eathia. I have wanted to be seen as giving him the benefit of the doubt at least for the time being, so I have his confidence, that is all. I see no harm in hearing what he has to say, he still trusts me, even though unfortunately he cannot be trusted.'

'Please be careful, I implore you. Should I warn Elkyne? Is he aware of these meetings? I would rather have him back here than unreachable.'

'You must not worry about Elkyne, he will be back in good time. Leave this to me, Olpheira, I will find out all I can.'

'Where is Verra Mica? She should be aware of what is happening.'

'I have just updated her.'

With that, he was gone. Olpheira tried one last time to locate Elkyne. She hoped he was still here and had only veiled. She had to reach him, he couldn't go. Not yet, something didn't feel right.

Chapter 56
Eathia - Third Era

Soul to Soul

The strange, darkened figure approached the castle's door, then stopped. Leaning his head against it, he squeezed his eyes shut to force himself to enter. Deep down, he didn't want to.

His arm lifted and pushed at the door involuntarily. To his surprise, it was open. It was never open. Then, he remembered what the odd-looking man said outside Bertha's cottage.

He snorted at himself ironically. Who was he to make a judgement about someone looking odd when his face was enough to give anyone nightmares?

The castle had been left unattended because they were too busy with … whatever. He couldn't remember.

As he made his way into the main hall, he stood in the middle and gazed around at its enormity, taking in the grandeur and the secrecy that surrounded it. As he turned, his head dropped, and he studied the light coming from one of the rooms. Wandering over to it, he read a plaque fixed to the wall.

'The Orbitarium Room.'

He opened the door but recoiled. The light was intense, stinging his eyes. He retreated.

There, right next to him, resting on some armour, was a pair of goggles.

He knew he had to get into that room. It was the only place the book would have been hidden. Putting on the goggles, he entered and headed over to the sideboard.

The orb pulsed louder upon his arrival, and he registered the change in its vibration.

With the protection of the goggles, he wandered over to the orb and stared into it.

Just like the door, his arm lifted against his will and reached out towards the light.

Fear flooded his body, and he tried to back away from the orb. Something in it was willing him to move closer.

Back at the Emporium, Augustus felt his pocket mirror suddenly vibrate. He touched his top pocket to make sure he wasn't imagining it. He wasn't.

It was the only direct connection he had with the orb when he wasn't there himself. It was in distress. He grabbed his coat and Maddox and headed towards the castle.

'Why is this happening, tonight of all nights?'

Maddox shrugged, unsure whether the question was directed at him.

The man forced himself away from the glare of the orb and staggered over to the sideboard, where he started to open the doors and drawers. He became frantic as each section revealed nothing.

I have to return with it; otherwise, what use would I be without it? he thought.

It wasn't there.

'Upstairs.'

He ran back into the hall and up the stairs, his awkward movements making it difficult for him to tackle them easily.

He was following his gut, but with no recollection of the castle. No memories, just an inner voice that seemed to tell him where to go.

He entered the room that was directly above the Orbitarium. A small bed was over at the far end of the room. He ran to it and threw the mattress up in the air.

Nothing.

He lifted the bed and tossed it on its side.

There, tied to the underside of the slats, was Gabriel's book.

As he started to release it, he heard someone calling downstairs. He froze.

Augustus and Maddox had entered the castle. The door had been left open, and the inner door to the Orbitarium was ajar also.

'What on Eathia is going on, little man?'

He felt uneasy and cursed himself for bringing Maddox along, even though he had no choice.

'Hello,' he called.

The man slipped the book into his trench coat pocket and stood still on the wooden floorboards, trying not to make a sound.

He heard whoever it was shut a door downstairs.

'We can't leave this open.'

Augustus glanced over to Arthur and noticed his oculars were missing. He felt even more uneasy. He needed to get Maddox out of there. He grabbed his son's arm and darted across the hall and back out of the main door, shutting it with a slam behind him.

Once down the steps, he ducked under cover and waited. He was sure someone was still in there.

The man slowly made his way down the stairs. He had pushed the goggles onto his hat and completely forgotten about them when he exited the castle.

Augustus watched as a creature came out through the front door. It was slightly hunched and moved in a twitchy, jerky fashion. He whispered to himself, 'What is that? He's got my oculars, damn him.'

Maddox was intrigued and stood up to get a better look, but Augustus pulled him down again quickly and shushed him.

Maddox jolted. He had seen something. Deep inside, he felt a sense of sadness. There was something about the man, something about his aura, that made him burst into tears. He felt a strange connection to him. Augustus tried to muffle cries, not wanting to be discovered.

The man stopped, looked around, and then ran off. Remembering the conversation the two people had had outside Bertha's cottage, he now knew where he was heading next.

All Augustus could do was watch him leave and try to console Maddox.

Something had stirred the orb; that much was undeniable.

But the question lingered.

Why?

Chapter 57
The Realm

Fall Out

After keeping a close watch on Gabriel and Beatrice, the two Seraphytes were about to leave their chamber, searching for Verra Mica, when they saw large groups of Psybiencians heading for another Solescence Chamber and immediately realised something was wrong.

One of them stopped a Soul Guardian as he passed her.

'Hey, what's happening?'

'If you don't know already, you don't need to know.'

He pulled away from her and continued without looking back. She heard him laugh as the group eventually disappeared out of sight.

She turned to her companion.

'OK, I have an uneasy feeling about this. We need to find Verra Mica quickly. Why didn't she meet us at the chamber as planned?'

The other shook his head.

'Either way, we're potentially going to have done the wrong thing by leaving our post. Let's find her quickly.'

Unaware of Gabriel's current movements, Verra Mica prepared to leave her order for a second time after her briefing from Baquarrah. She now quickly headed for the chamber to visit Gabriel as planned. As she left, she was prevented yet again from continuing, this time by Duergar, who approached her. It seemed he had been waiting for her.

'I am surprised to see you still here, Verra, I thought you had a pressing meeting to attend?'

'What? I don't have time for your games now, Duergar.'

'And I don't have time to play them. You misunderstand Verra Mica. I am here to give you one last chance to support the recovery of The Realm and the natural evolution of Eathia. I would prefer it if you could be by my side. We have had our differences, but we want the same thing; we just have different approaches. Do you think you could trust me? Just for once?'

'Are you mad? We do not want the same thing, and we never have. How dare you waste my time with your egotistical endeavours? You really think that your ideas and values are such that you may appeal to any part of my being in the vain hope that I will cast aside all that I despise about you and your beliefs. Don't make me laugh. As I said, I am busy trying to save both The Realm and Eathia following the way of our Source. Who may I ask are you following, or have you grown too almighty to follow anyone but yourself now?'

Duergar smiled, unaffected by Verra Mica's verbal attack.

'A "no" would have sufficed.'

'Get out of my way, I am tired of you and your lies.'

Duergar moved aside and made way for her to leave. He was buying time to allow his order to make it to the chambers undetected. He hoped he'd given them enough. He wondered if her plan to meet with Gabriel remained unchanged, then immediately decided he didn't care. He was ready, and his followers were waiting. He couldn't resist one last dig.

'Sorry to hear about your Eathian daughter's demise. Strange how things turn out wouldn't you say?'

Verra Mica paused, fighting to keep some control. *Now was not the time, but there will be a right time and she'd be ready,* she consoled the ache deep inside.

Duergar turned and left, heading for his Solescence Chamber, and what would spell the end of their collaboration altogether.

Verra Mica finally made it to hers as planned. She saw that Nemius was outside waiting for her.

'Your Honour.'

'Thank you for agreeing to do this, Nemius. I recognise we have not seen eye to eye before now, but I hope you have witnessed enough to understand the actions I have been guided towards are justifiable.'

'I have your Honour, and I apologise for my conduct and for ever doubting you.'

'There is no need and little time left available to us. Return now, and please be ready. We will need you to help heal some of the unavoidable wounds.'

She paused and looked at Nemius.

'If I had known this was to happen ...'

Nemius reassured her.

'None of us could have foreseen this.'

Another voice interjected from a different direction, and they both spun around in surprise to see the two Guardians as they approached.

'Your Honour? We have been trying to find you.'

Verra Mica was surprised to see them outside the chamber.

'What are you doing here? I thought you were attending to Gabriel and Beatrice while Corpus and Christi were away?'

'Could we have a quick word with you, Verra Mica? Privately.'

Nemius made ready to go.

'I am due to leave now. I bid your leave, your Honour?'

'Thank you again Nemius. I will be in touch.'

She turned to her Seraphyte students.

'Why are you away from your posts? I will never be able to meet with Gabriel with all of these confounded interruptions.'

We thought you should be made aware that the male Eathian …'

'Yes, Gabriel, go on.'

'… appears to have fired up his machine slightly sooner than intended.'

Verra Mica wobbled and tried to compose herself.

'Oh, for goodness' sake.'

They continued.

'We fear he means to use the machine on the female subject.'

'BEATRICE? What now, right now, you say? But they are supposed to be asleep. Confounded people!'

Verra Mica stormed into the chamber to see what Gabriel and Beatrice were up to. Her core was fit to explode at any moment, and her voice was losing all recognisable pitch. Her students cautiously followed her.

'If I've said it once, I've said it a thousand times; Eathians are impossible subjects. They change their minds and direction like the Eathian wind.'

Within a moment, her form, which had all the signs of being about to self-combust, suddenly weakened in front of her students. She moved away from the edge of the lake.

'Does this mean your plans have changed, your Honour? Our plans?'

Verra Mica thought for a moment.

'No, not necessarily. If I could just get him away from that room. If I could get him to see me down there on Eathia safely. I might be able to draw him away. He's not ready. Damn it!'

She burst past the Seraphytes, yelling for them to stay and update her while she went to confer with her friend, Alma Tadema.

While Verra Mica was becoming unsettlingly delayed, Duergar had now entered his Psybiencian Chamber, where he had ordered his followers to congregate. The thunderous undertones of so many of his order, and a few others, finding themselves in one area, drove an almost deafening rhythmical pulse through the very core of the chamber's framework.

Duergar screamed at them, blasting a deafening tone directly from his core. For his subjects, it was like being hit by an invisible force. It had the desired effect. All became silent.

'That's better. I apologise for being late and for the necessity of using such extreme measures. We need to remain focused.'

Baquarrah pushed his way through the throng.

'Duergar, speaking as a fellow Superior of The Realm, can you explain your reasons for this emergency gathering?'

Baquarrah began to be jostled by those around him and fought to maintain his place and composure.

Duergar smirked as he worked his way through the crowd towards the vast, open lake.

'All in good time, my friend.'

He raised himself on the outer edges of the lake and addressed his followers.

'We have waited for this moment, my loyal followers. You all know why we are here, apart from you, Baquarrah, it seems.'

A few of the crowd laughed at Duergar's comment.

'You are indeed the only one who doesn't. I couldn't trust you, and I was right, wasn't I?'

Baquarrah remained silent and still, feeling slightly nervous about what was to come next.

Where was I? Yes, you know why we're here and what we need to do. Ready yourselves and take your positions. Baquarrah, you're free to leave.

He turned, not waiting for Baquarrah, and looked intently down through the mist of the lake.

Bolts of white light were already beginning to flash through the dense fog, rebounding from the edges and colliding with others, their velocity increasing with every impact.

'Nephelia, are you there?'

A voice echoed back.

'Yes, your Honour, I am here.'

'... and the others?'

'... all in place, as you requested.'

Baquarrah tried to move away slowly enough to catch some of Duergar's plan still.

Each Psybiencian Chamber was full to the brim with Duergar's disciples. Each with an appointed leader, who was now like Duergar himself, ordered their Soul Guardians to circle the lakes in the chambers and focus their energies down towards Eathia.

The mist within the voids in the chambers began to churn, swelling and convulsing with every lightning bolt that pushed through their subtle layers.

Baquarrah yelled at Duergar amid the din of the escalating noise.

'What is happening? What are you doing in here?'

All ignored him. The noise was becoming hypnotic.

The very essence of The Realm began to vibrate. Baquarrah fled as fast as he could before they finished, and their focus turned back to him.

He couldn't possibly have realised that this was just the beginning of something that would change their worlds forever.

Chapter 58
The Realm

Brother Nature

Oblivious to what was happening in The Realm, Christi admired the beauty surrounding her. Corpus glided next to her, observing her delight in the scenery before them.

'I knew you would love it. It's like nothing else.'

'I can see why you disappear up here, Corpus. It is truly magical. I can't believe you have waited so long to show me.'

He looked over at her and gave a sheepish smile. He could still sense an element of sadness about her.

'You have a heavy core, Christi. You are carrying something, and I feel it is a burden you feel necessary to cope with on your own. Now that we are away from The Realm, can I ask if I can help? Is there something bothering you?'

Christi looked away and focused on the blue-purple hue rising from the snow-capped mountain peaks ahead. Corpus glanced down, trying to divert her attention so she wouldn't feel uneasy. He noticed something winding its way through the forest-lined fields below as he did. He slowed down, attempting to spot what he had seen again, but it had disappeared.

'Did you see that, Christi?'

'What? What have you seen?'

She followed his gaze just in time to see them again as they reappeared.

'What are they?'

'They look like Terranean floaters. Let's get closer. But be careful. There appear to be thousands of them. Where are they heading, I wonder?'

Christi flinched as if hurt in some way.

Corpus noticed and slowed his raven down.

'What is it?'

'Beatrice is awake. Why have we not been called back?'

‘I haven’t been connecting with Gabriel, not while Verra Mica has been with him.’

‘We have to get back, Corpus.’

‘Christi, can’t we at least see what they are doing? They are gathering for a reason. I had no idea that there were so many of them here.’

‘I’m not sure this is a safe place for us to be untethered, Corpus. It feels as though we are running out of time.’

With that, Corpus guided them away from the group of darkened Soul Guardians on Eathia and back up towards the clouds, hoping to give them an element of cover so as not to be seen themselves.

On the other side of the mountain range, the jagged rock face descended into a deep valley. Tall sequoia trees towered hundreds of feet into the air, standing in perfect formation. They surrounded a natural spring formed from the icy air that condensed and trickled down the mountaintop. In the centre of the valley lay a beautiful, clear body of water, untouched by its gentle waterfall inlet. Its surface lay as still, perfectly reflecting the sky and the swirling clouds above. In tranquillity, it rested; no rain fell upon its surface and no breeze caressed its shores. A perfect location for the Dark Soul Guardians to gather, and many more like it could be found scattered across Eathia’s lands and continents. Soon, every lake, every still and clear reflective body of water was encircled by a thousand Dark Soul Guardians, who waited, ready and alert for Duergar’s command.

Within his chosen chamber in The Realm, Duergar began to rise above the group, hovering over the swelling mist in the lake’s centre. It began to move and undulate beneath him, shards of light intensifying as they bounced from edge to edge, lighting the torrent as they ignited and flashed.

Duergar began to increase his drone, which emanated from deep within him, from the darkest part of his core. The chamber seemed to reverberate it back in response, its fabric vibrating and shaking as the others began to match his tone. Those who were not Psybiencians joined with voices and illuminations.

A swirl of energy erupted from the group as it joined and rose to meet Duergar’s booming harmonics.

On Eathia, his Dark Soul Guardians had been given the order and started to do the same. Each group circled their lake, sending their vibrational tonal codes down into the waters, where the current now joined with those of the misty water held within the chamber in The Realm. The water in the lakes on Eathia started to tremble, causing waves to pass inwards over its surface, increasing with every tone. Over and over again, the thunderous sound impacted the water, and on and on into the night, the waters filled with the pulsating energy from The Realm. Suddenly, without warning, it stopped; the waters calmed, and all was eerily still.

All of the Dark Soul Guardians, some now re-tethered to previously fallen Eathians, were held in a mesmerising trance. The water's reflection, once showing an opposing image of the beautiful, dawn-filled sky, was now a white, hazy, undulating fog, twinned with that of the chamber's lake.

Duergar fell silent, and all in the chamber were lost, hypnotised by his music. From the depths of his being came another tone. Unheard and unsensed by the group. It was sent out solely to draw energy from two other sources. It passed through The Realm, knowing exactly where it was heading, then the stealth-like tone diverged, heading to two extremes of The Realm. Through the empty tunnels, passing quarters and chambers, they went. Lights filled the walls as they sped on and on. One into forbidden territory, the other to the life Source itself.

Those left outside of the Psybiencian Chamber felt the blasts as the light energy made its way through the many layers of The Realm towards their targets.

Chapter 59
The Realm

No Entry

When Baquarrah fled from the Psybiencian Chamber, he searched for Verra Mica. Duergar was out of control and he felt ashamed that he had let himself be manipulated to such a degree. As he reached the exit, Makaria shot out in front of him.

'Where are you going? You can't leave, not now.'

'This is not what I agreed to, Makaria. I can't be a part of this.'

'Nor I, but I must stay and try reaching Angelica. This could bring her back to us.'

The noise in the chamber had started to rise again.

'What is he doing? Do you know?'

The room flashed and started to vibrate. The pressure was too much for Baquarrah's sensitive aura. As a healer, an Illumacyte, they weren't built for such an intense onslaught.

As he left, he called back for Makaria to leave before it was too late, pleading with her to follow.

She couldn't understand him and struggled to keep her state together. She was unwillingly getting drawn away from him. He bolted for the chamber's exit, barely making it through in time.

In stark contrast, all outside was now calm; only the manner in which he explosively exited the room seemed unusual. Baquarrah wondered if anyone outside of the chamber would have a clue what was happening inside. At this point, he was unaware that Duergar had sent two bolts of light energy towards the Accumulator and the Source.

He sent out an emergency message to all remaining Superiors.

Verra Mica and Alma Tadema were returning to the Seraphyte order when they received the distress signal from Baquarrah. Diverting their route, they found him trying to compose himself, his energy dangerously depleted.

'Alma, get Olpheira. Quick.'

'What happened?'

'It's Duergar, Verra. We can't stop this. He's sealed off his chambers. He's in there now.'

'This is too much.'

She tried to enter the chamber herself but found what Baquarrah had said to be true.

'We need Corpus and Christi back here now. I need to get to my chamber. Will you be alright?'

'Yes, yes. Go on. Get them back, quickly, Verra.'

Once she had received a message that they were on their way back, she entered their Seraphyte Chamber and made her way to the lake as fast as she could.

Below her, Elkyne had descended towards his tether, having slowed his pace. He began to sense Duergar's thoughts. Until that moment, nothing had affected his journey, but then a sudden, violent light shard struck the side of his portal, nearly thrusting him out of its stream. Trapped, he could only observe in fear as the atmosphere around him began to shift. He fought desperately against panic, trying to avoid returning his thoughts to that place, the Accumulator.

Verra Mica watched helplessly as Elkyne fell into the tidal wave of the energy storm Duergar had created. She couldn't understand why he had left so soon.

Was this all part of Duergar's plan, too? Traitors at every corner of The Realm? she thought.

She had wanted to believe Elkyne so much.

She looked beyond Elkyne and saw Gabriel putting Beatrice in the machine.

'NO!'

She was too late. Her plan was failing. The implications began to shake her to her core.

And now, as if things weren't bad enough, she could feel the Source's energy beginning to wane.

~

Chapter 60
The Realm

Detachment

Corpus and Christi sensed the anguish in Verra Mica's call for them to return.

They swiftly began to make their way back with the ravens. Together with what they had seen on Eathia, things must be escalating.

'Verra Mica can't be tethered to Gabriel.'

He stopped his flight mid-air, and Christi brought her bird about once she realised he was not with her.

'What is it?'

'Do you think something has happened to Gabriel again?'

'Let's go and find out. I doubt it, Corpus. It has to be Duergar.'

As they were about to leave, what looked and felt like a bolt of lightning suddenly shot between them, sending them both in opposite directions. Christi screamed and immediately became separated from her raven. Corpus turned his bird around and stretched its wings out to try and reach her before she fell too far.

'Christi, I'm coming.'

The separation stunned her for a moment. Her consciousness was leaving her aura, and as it dissipated, she began to see visions of both Gabriel and Beatrice appearing before her.

'No, not yet. Not now.'

Corpus called for her.

'I'm nearly there, Christi; it's alright. I won't let you go.'

He stayed transfixed on her as she fell, as he increased speed, readying himself to collect her mid-air. Then, he suddenly saw something in her gaze that sent a frozen shard through his soul.

Chapter 61
The Realm

Eathia

As Christi looked up at Corpus, he could see the anguish and conflict in her eyes. They weren't the eyes of fear; they were the eyes of sadness and grief.

'It's too late, Corpus. I have to go. You have to let me go. I thought we'd have longer.'

'Christi no. What are you saying?'

She fell faster and faster away from him, her beautiful face full of resignation. Her Eathian-shaped arms reached up delicately towards him.

'What's happening to you, Christi? Please, what's happening?'

The ground was rising quickly beneath her. She was showing no signs of stopping. He would have to stop and pull back if he and the raven were to survive.

Conflicted, he pulled at the bird. As they both changed direction, he looked back and watched, realising now that she was getting dragged by something. She was tethering but through the Eathian atmosphere. Was that even possible? Her voice broke through his thoughts.

'I love you. I will always love you, Corpus; please forgive me. There was no other way.'

Panic flooded through Corpus, making him feel heavy and disoriented. The raven struggled to keep connected with him as the heavy numbness began to bleed through into him, too.

As they rounded the peak of the hill, a small village came into sight. He recognised it immediately as Gabriel's hometown.

Of all places, how had they ended up here?

Corpus pulled at the raven and turned towards Christi once more, this time approaching from underneath her. He sped up and began to gain ground on her. Why was he not feeling the pull from Gabriel? The baby must be coming. Is this what it was? Nothing else made sense.

The wind was absorbing her voice, and he was losing his connection with her. He wondered whether he should head back quickly and join her through the chamber's portal.

Then he finally understood what it was she was saying.

'Don't blame her, Corpus. This was my purpose all along. I love you.'

Then the lightning struck again, diverting him completely from his course. Christi swerved away from him, screaming his name as she disappeared out of sight. Corpus fought to regain control and follow her.

'Christi, wait!' he screamed at her, fear pulsing through him.

Through the stone-built houses and streets, he flew, now knowing for sure where she was heading.

As Corpus neared the cottage, the night was slowly giving way to a faint morning glow, but not enough to overpower the luminescence emanating from Gabriel's workroom. For a moment, he thought it could be the lamp in Gabriel's room. Quickly, he realised the light was much stronger; the source of the illumination was coming from behind the lamp, and something was shining out like a beacon.

It dawned on him.

The machine was on.

Chapter 62
The Realm

Shaken to the Core

As Duergar continued to hover above the Psybiencian Chamber's great lake, he started to manipulate the speed of the energy he had sent out to The Realm, slowing it just before it reached the Accumulator. Then a third, much higher-pitched tone exploded through him and travelled out at speed, out into The Realm; this one had another destination. The shriek could be heard by all who were left outside the chamber, sending a shockwave through those who were unveiled.

This time, it headed off in a different direction, finally resting outside of the Source's sector.

Verra Mica realised what was happening too late. She rushed to the Source in a vain attempt to protect it, but when the thunder hit, all felt the blast, and all knew at once what had happened. The Source and the essence had been disconnected from Eathia.

In one final attack, Duergar blasted energy out from his vortex and into The Realm. The thunderous bolts travelled into the Accumulator and into the centre of the Source, catching their energies collectively before travelling back to him in an almighty explosion, sending hundreds of lightning forks down from the lake towards the waiting Dark Soul Guardians that had surrounded their motionless lakes on Eathia.

Each lightning fork shot down towards the water. As Duergar had planned, each one travelled through the dense shadow matter held within a reflection and the lakes within The Realm. Feeding from the hidden particles, entangled in their magnetic charges the lightning bolts gathered speed and energy until they entered Eathia's atmosphere. They reflected off the water immediately, their velocity causing those within proximity to the lake to be blown backwards. The forks of light continued to spread, one bouncing off from another, reaching out, creating a network of latticed beams encompassing Eathia's surface.

Both dark and light energy spanned the great planet. An eternal beam of energy moving from one side of the world to the other, and with it, devastating consequences.

Once Verra Mica realised that alone, she was not strong enough to ward off the attack against the Source from Duergar. She fled back to the Seraphyte Chamber, passing Alma Tadema on the way.

'What's happening now? I thought you were with Gabriel.'

Verra Mica only slowed for a moment.

'Go and find Baquarrah. He'll update you. I have to go. I can't do anything from here. He's using the Source to charge an attack.'

As she entered the Solescence Chamber, she hurled herself at the lake, down she went riding on the stream of Gabriel's tether.

As Corpus, still tethered to the raven, flew to the workroom window, he watched in horror at the sight that greeted him. He frantically used the raven to bash at the window, trying to stop them, trying to stop Gabriel.

Then it all started to fall into place, and a new revulsion began to bubble inside him.

'No.'

Now, behind Gabriel stood Verra Mica.

Traumatised, he tried to take in the horror of what was happening within the machine.

Gabriel had not only ignited the machine Beatrice was sitting in the centre of, but what made the whole scene even more horrific was the sight of Christi, tethered to her and now visibly hovering over Beatrice's head, her evanescent frame shining in the glow of the machine. Gabriel appeared to be watching her as she lowered herself down to rest in front of Beatrice.

Then, Gabriel suddenly burst into action; something had spooked him.

Corpus retreated, trying to make sense of it and work it through in his thoughts.

'This was the plan all along.'

He tried to remember what Christi had said when she fell.

'Don't blame her, it was her destiny.' No, it couldn't have been. He started hitting hard against the glass, trying to break it or to get Gabriel's attention, anyone's attention.

He went unheard.

Something cold passed through his frame, a chilling sensation that made him turn and look away from the cottage.

Behind him stood the darkened shadow of a man, and behind him, a tethered hissing, Dark Soul Guardian with a face that Corpus recognised. The man reached out and tried to grab the raven. Corpus swerved away from him, but the second blow caught it across its back, bringing its body down hard onto the windowsill. The bird's face was pressed hard against the glass of the window. All he could do was watch the scene unfold before him.

Corpus stared in terror. He felt powerless, but only if he remained where he was. He needed to return and retrieve Verra Mica from Gabriel and regain his tether. *Was Verra Mica behind this? Was she manipulating Gabriel? Had she orchestrated my absence to provoke this?* he wondered.

Just as he turned to try and release the raven from the hidden man's grip, he saw what it was that Gabriel had seen. A faint outline of another Soul Guardian crouched in the corner of the room. He was hardly visible, and he hadn't seen Corpus at the window either.

Corpus realised it was Elkyne, and he was visible. He had already tethered.

Fury swept through him.

He had to get back to The Realm, and quickly.

He unleashed a surge of energy through the bird, prompting it to act. The man sensed this and instinctively relaxed his grip on the raven. Seizing the moment, the raven took flight. Meanwhile, Corpus swiftly manoeuvred back through the tether connecting him to the raven, racing to the private chamber of Verra Mica. Time was running out. He quickly traversed the mist, allowing the raven to recover on Eathia from the jolt's force and Corpus's abrupt departure from its body.

Corpus sped through to his own Solescence Chamber; he had to make it in time; he just had to. As he entered the chamber, he flew to the lake and fell immediately into the mist, ready to interject with Gabriel and put a stop to the machine. Abruptly, he hit a force field and was thrown back into the chamber. He tried again and again, but he couldn't find Gabriel's tether.

Then it dawned on him.

He was now trapped in The Realm until Verra Mica had finished with Gabriel.

He glared into the mist, his being vibrating and pulsing, unable to vent his anger.

A voice suddenly echoed towards him from the back of the chamber.

'You are too late, my friend. I am sorry. It is beyond any of us now.'

Nemius stood in the farthest part of the chamber and was, at that moment, de-tethered from Avery, Gabriel and Beatrice's son.

He spoke fiercely to Nemius.

'Did you know this was going to happen?'

'Corpus, stop! I only knew what Avery's role was to be. Only now am I realising the whole truth, and I want nothing to do with it. They are as bad as each other.'

'Avery? What has he had to do with all of this? Have I just slipped into some ethereal parallel Realm?'

'Quite possibly yes, my friend. You and I both.'

'I need to get down there and stop them, Nemius, please. Christi has been caught up in this, too.'

Nemius stood up and joined him at the edge of the lake.

'There is no time, Corpus. It's too late.'

'Why are you here and not with Avery?'

Nemius fell silent, not wanting to divulge any more information than he had to. Then, he had an idea. It could work, of course it could, but there was no time left – he would have to take the chance.

He grabbed Corpus and yelled for him to hold on, then dragged him over to the edge of the lake and jumped.

Down they fell together, Corpus fighting against his grip until he realised what it was he was trying to do.

Nemius was pulling him into his tether stream. It was working. Down they went until they both reached Avery. At the last possible second, Nemius pulled away and swerved from Avery's tether portal, leaving Corpus free to attach.

Nemius landed just away from Avery's sleeping body, now becoming a free-floating soul. Corpus, tethered to Avery immediately, turned to Nemius.

'You have taken such a risk, Nemius. How will you be able to return now?'

'Just go, will you? I will be behind you, my friend. You have my Eathian with you, remember?'

Corpus sent the image he was now seeing of Gabriel and Beatrice through to Avery. They reached him while he slept. He could use his tether to his advantage. The vivid scene shocked him awake, and Avery jumped to his feet, unsure if he had actually dreamed it or not.

The memory of a dream he had had before of a world called The Realm was still very much in his thoughts, and through his semi-wakeful haze, this image spooked him enough to believe it was real. This was exactly what she had shown him. *What was her name? Was it Alma? Was this it?* Avery rubbed hard at his face to try to wake himself up.

He ran from his Nan's home towards the cottage, not seeing the man he knew to be Marcus by the illuminated window to one side. He opened the door and hurried through the kitchen and into his father's workroom. It was precisely what he had been shown. There was his mam in some contraption, and his pa was standing next to her, frozen to the spot. Then Avery saw her, too.

A young spirit was hovering just above his mam. A voice inside him screamed for them to stop, and he found himself joining in with it. His pa came to life at the sound of his son's fearful voice and started to run towards the machine again, now alarmed himself at the intensity of the energy building up within it.

'That's it!' Corpus screamed, still attached to Avery. 'Stop it, stop the machine.'

Then Beatrice opened her eyes, and Corpus yelled at Christi to warn her.

'NO, CHRISTI. DON'T LOOK AT HER.'

Verra Mica, now aware that Corpus had entered the room, remained watchful but did not attempt to stop the experiment or to hinder Corpus's efforts to try and get Gabriel to act on Avery's behalf. She knew there was nothing he could do now.

Beatrice slowly turned her head towards Gabriel as he approached her again, and he paused, staying just out of reach of the machine's glow, its brightness becoming too difficult to bear.

She spoke, her voice almost inaudible under the thrum of the machine.

'I love you, my darling. I understand everything now.'

Christi was looking at him, too. Then, she moved her attention to Corpus and Elkyne.

'Please understand that I had no choice. Please forgive me, my brothers?'

Right at that moment, an immense, unexpected blast of lightning suddenly exploded into the room from the window, hitting the uppermost part of the machine where the globe was attached. The surge threw it to one side, almost sending it flying to the ground, although somehow, it managed to stay intact. It took most of the hit from the glare, repelling it into the centre of the machine until it struck the reflective pieces of glass, which sent secondary beams inadvertently back up to the globe and down towards Beatrice in a crescendo of multicoloured rays. Corpus watched helplessly as Beatrice gazed about her in wonder at the reflective, rainbow-coloured shimmers that were now highlighting her aura. She turned her head. Surely, she couldn't see Christi. Corpus willed Christi to stay looking at him.

'Don't, Christi, please don't do this. She will see you.'

But Christi's head was already turning. She was as clear to Beatrice and Gabriel as she was to Corpus and the other Soul Guardians in the room.

The moment their eyes met, the pulsating tone of the machine became deafening, heightened by the external force that had hit the machine.

'What's happening, Corpus? Is this normal?'

Elkyne moved across the room to where Corpus could see him clearly; he was trying to edge as far away from the machine as possible, his tether-cord with the unborn baby only permitting him to venture as far as Corpus was standing with Avery.

The intensity in the room increased, and to Corpus's surprise, Gabriel seemed to notice Elkyne too. Gabriel could see him, but why was that even possible? What was happening outside of the machine that was allowing an Eathian to see a Soul Guardian so clearly?

That moment in time would be etched in Corpus's memory for eternity. All of the Eathians could see all of their Soul Guardians. He watched Beatrice and Christi make contact, Soul Guardian to Spirit. The love on their faces emanated into the room. It was at that second that Corpus realised what was about to happen. He spun Avery around to try to get him to protect his father from the inevitable blast, but Avery was transfixed in the doorway, now staring at the sight of the Soul Guardians himself. He slowly turned and looked at Corpus, and his mouth dropped open when he saw they were attached.

Corpus resisted looking at him.

'Get back, Elkyne. Get away. It isn't safe for you to be near it.'

He looked back at the window just in time to see the distorted features of a siren still tethered to the man as she watched, captivated by the chaos, snarling at Corpus's attempts to hinder the process.

'Nephelia!'

There was another sudden crack that ripped through the small room, its walls unable to contain the force of the explosion. Gabriel was pushed hard up against the wall as he was thrown over his mother's tiny single bed. Elkyne screamed in pain, his core receiving a direct hit from the outward blast of the machine. Then he disappeared.

Shards of resin, paperwork and all that hadn't been weighed or fixed flew about the room, caught up in an invisible tornado of energy. Gabriel ducked, putting his hands instinctively over his face.

Corpus, still attached to Avery, was also thrown back out of the door, the impact severing his tether and causing him to fly involuntarily out of the cottage. Avery screamed in pain as he was torn from him.

Nemius grasped the opportunity and flew at Avery, re-tethering just in time before he, too, suddenly vanished from the room.

Corpus turned back and re-entered. Hovering over the desolation that lay before him, he could see Beatrice, now awkwardly lying on her back amongst the shattered broken machine, her swollen belly slightly grazed from the glass which had flown out of one of the reflectors. It was beginning to bleed.

Corpus scanned the room for a sign of Christi, but she too had disappeared. He looked straight across at Verra Mica for an explanation.

'What have you done here? Was this what you intended?'

She looked across at him, anguished and drained from the blast.

'It wasn't supposed to happen like that, Corpus; I'm not sure what happened; something intervened. I need to stay with Gabriel for the time being to help him get through this.'

'What? I don't understand.'

'Not now, Corpus. We never envisaged this. Go back if you can.'

'We? Did Christi want this, too? Did she know about this?'

He scanned the room again.

'Was all of this the Source's doing or yours?'

He hadn't been heard.

Too much devastation.

Too much pain filled the tiny, ruined room that was once Gabriel's workroom.

Corpus searched for Christi.

She was gone.

Chapter 63

The Realm

Christi's Secret

Corpus left the room once he knew Beatrice was out of danger and drifted out into the early morning light. How could he get back? He saw a movement in the garden, high up in the tree. His raven, Artius, had stayed through all of the commotion to help him home.

Next to Artius, was Christi's raven.

He wondered if Christi had made it back to The Realm safely. He had to find her and try to understand why this had happened. She was wrong. He didn't understand any of this at all.

Corpus entered the portal, hoping above all hopes that he would see his beloved Christi there, waiting for him with a sorrowful expression on her face. She would see him rise up through the mist and, in her own contagious way, laugh at the close shave they had all had.

But this was not to be the case.

As he entered the chamber, he saw Olpheira huddled over something on the floor. He moved closer and noticed that she was crouching over a Soul Guardian, its energy completely diminished. As he approached, he saw that its translucent form was grey and nearly devoid of life.

'Christi? Move away quick.'

Olpheira looked up at Corpus, her soul filled with sorrow. As she moved back, Corpus could see that it was not Christi but Elkyne's pathetically weak frame.

Olpheira was distraught.

'What happened, Corpus? Was this Duergar's doing?'

Corpus dropped down by Elkyne, relieved to see he was still conscious. The Source energy within him had been badly damaged, but his darkened core remained as strong as ever and appeared to be sapping the very life away from him.

'Elkyne, stay with us, my brother. You are safe now.'

He looked at Olpheira.

'Can you give him healing?'

He looked down at Elkyne and studied him.

'He looks like he has been scorched; look, he's losing the Source's energy. You must try and revive what little he has left.'

Corpus looked around, suddenly aware that Soul Guardians were beginning to pour into the chamber from the lake. He turned back to Olpheira in confusion, pain etched across his face.

'This is Duergar's doing, Corpus. He has found a way to de-tether the Soul Guardians from Eathia. All at the same time. They have been flooding back through all of the chambers.'

'All of them? How?'

'Most of them. By making them visible, I don't know exactly how he's done it, but as far as I can understand, he needed the help of others on Eathia, Dark Soul Guardians that were waiting for him to act.'

'So that's why Gabriel and Beatrice could see Christi? And us? I thought it was the machine doing that.'

Olpheira looked across at the entrance of the chamber. His answer came from another source.

'No, that is not why he could see Christi, Corpus.'

Verra Mica entered the chamber and made her way through the confused crowds of de-tethered Soul Guardians. They paused and stepped aside, hoping, too, for an explanation. She reached the spot where Elkyne lay and stood silently over all three of them.

Corpus sprang up to face her, but her attention remained on Elkyne.

'Continue to heal, Olpheira, quickly, he is very sick and will need your care for some time yet.'

Moving back, she beckoned for Corpus to follow.

'What do you mean, it wasn't because of Duergar?'

'It's a coincidence that Duergar did what he did at the same time. What happened in the machine was planned and told to Christi while she was still in the Source. She told me some time ago. This was the only option we had if things escalated. It was a last resort, Corpus. Christi knew this and formulated the plan herself, only …'

'It didn't go to plan, did it? You weren't expecting fallout.'

Corpus pointed at Elkyne.

‘Where is she, Verra Mica?’

‘You will still address me as your Honour, Corpus.’

‘Where is Christi … your Honour?’

Verra Mica, noticeably saddened, bowed her head.

‘That part of the plan was a success. I can’t tell at present what the impact of Duergar’s plan had on the outcome for others. Elkyne has suffered because of him. Only time will tell. As for Christi …’

Verra Mica looked directly at Corpus, his confusion evident in the way he stared back at her.

‘Christi has fallen, Corpus. She has become Eathian.’

Chapter 64
The Realm

Fallout

The words cut through Corpus as if he had splintered into a million fragments.

Olpheira heard, stunned; she accidentally broke free from Elkyne, who groaned as she did so. She wanted to be clear about what Verra Mica had said.

'She has fallen to Eathia. Did you say as an Eathian?'

Corpus stepped back from Verra Mica, unable to comprehend what was being suggested.

Olpheira stood up and moved in towards Corpus, showing support.

Verra Mica looked up at Corpus.

'She chose to fall. We have lost …'

Verra Mica was unable to finish. Her friend suddenly appeared behind her and continued.

'… a beautiful shining soul, and we all have to accept that her light will now be our own Source shining into the darkest corners of Eathia. And don't you dare for one moment cast judgement on your Superior or anyone else, for that matter. This is Duergar's doing, and if I had been strong enough to listen to Verra Mica's concerns at the beginning, all of this might have been avoided.'

Alma Tadema stood in solidarity with Verra Mica.

'No, Alma, no, it wouldn't. It was always going to be this way.'

Corpus erupted again.

'You both knew she was going to do this, and you let her sacrifice herself.'

Then the truth, the whole realisation of how he had been manipulated, hit Corpus.

'That was what the machine was for? And you asked me to help and guide Gabriel to this end. This arrangement didn't compromise you in any way. You lied to me the whole time.'

The atmosphere in the chamber suddenly changed. Someone else had joined them.

'That's what I have been saying all along, Corpus, if you had bothered to listen to me, that is.'

Duergar had now entered the chamber, moving past Verra Mica and then behind Corpus. He lowered himself to take hold of Elkyne as he feebly tried to raise himself. He looked in bad shape.

'See what your plan has achieved, Verra Mica? You never gave it a thought as to how this would affect those closest to you. You and your precious Ashtar and your pet Eathians. It is you who has had your own agenda, not I. I think we ALL understand now.'

Elkyne fought to raise himself. Now, more lucid, he asked Corpus where Christi was. Duergar turned on Verra Mica.

'You kept that little plan of yours quiet, didn't you, Councillor? Well done.'

Verra Mica fired back at him.

'How did you let one of your own get hurt, Duergar, may I ask?'

She gestured down at Elkyne and continued.

'You couldn't allow a traitor to hinder your plans, could you? You realised that once he found out what you were doing, his loyalty would shift. It was you who orchestrated this.'

A crowd began to form around them. Every Solescence Chamber throughout The Realm was reaching full capacity with returning Soul Guardians. Those who had suddenly become visible to their tethers on Eathia through Duergar's lightning shocks that spanned the entire surface of the world. His plan had succeeded. Each waking Eathian glanced at their own Soul Guardian, momentarily aware of their connection, before they disappeared. The others would follow in time. The few who remained tethered would eventually return or remain free-floating on Eathia, likely joining Duergar's growing force that remained solidly rooted to the planet.

'You have your way, and as far as you are concerned, you have succeeded, Duergar. You have brought our tethered Soul Guardians home. You have done what you set out to do, but don't think for one second that I was prepared to leave Eathia with nothing in its place. Your darkness will begin to rise from the depths of their despair, and you have left them defenceless against it. Christi will not let that happen, mark my words. It will be her that holds the essence now. You have failed on that count.'

The enormity of what was happening was beginning to dawn on all in the chamber as the Superiors started to confess their plans while trying to defend their actions. The natural pulse that had vibrated through the whole of The Realm had lessened and faded into a background murmur, a sign that Duergar's assault had also damaged the Source.

Duergar looked at the crowd in the room, then across at Elkyne.

'All those who wish to follow me, leave now, by my side. The rest of you have made your position clear. I bid you all farewell.'

He turned to Verra Mica.

'Then I will make it my mission to find her and destroy her, and anyone connected to her.'

He turned to leave. Verra Mica sensed that a few of those who had watched the events unfold were now questioning who was best to follow.

Duergar sent a message to all the remaining Soul Guardians in The Realm, asking them to join him if they wished for a better existence, one of freedom.

A few in the chamber joined him, and most remained, to Verra Mica's relief.

Once Duergar had left, Olpheira pulled at Elkyne to try to talk with him privately. He followed her warily, using her as support.

'Will you come back with me, Olpheira? We should all be together on Eathia, surely. Not stuck here helpless.'

'I cannot, Elkyne, and you should stay and be cared for. You will not make the journey through that portal a second time. It was so close to taking your life, your very soul was about to be blown into pieces when you journeyed to Eathia the first time.'

'It was you, you told me to shield when I was in the Accumulator.'

She nodded.

'Duergar does not have your best interests in mind. Verra Mica was partially right, your injuries were caused by him, but also by the machine. Baquarrah was a supporter, but when he became aware of Duergar's true plan, he pulled away and told me everything.'

'What am I to do? I was led to believe that I was to be tethered at Verra Mica's and Duergar's wish, both of them knowing it would be short-lived. Neither of them has my best interests in mind.'

'Verra Mica can't have realised the consequences that Christi's falling would have had on you, Elkyne. I am sure she didn't realise that you had already tethered. None of us could have foreseen that. Come with me now, I need to work on you further, I can't concentrate here.'

'What of the child, Olpheira? Do we know the fate of the boy I was supposed to tether to?'

Aware that Verra Mica had heard Elkyne's question, Olpheria turned to her for an answer.

It had completely escaped Verra Mica's attention. The child was just as important as Gabriel, if not more so now.

'He will be born safely, Elkyne, and he will no doubt grow to watch over Christi, or whoever she is to become as an Eathian. It will be his life's purpose, this I have seen. The same purpose that had been secretly programmed into you, Elkyne, by the Source. That is why you felt the pull to be tethered so soon and strongly.'

Corpus realised that some details of how Christi fell were missing. He knew the science behind Eathian's ability to be fully on Eathia, so surely Christi wouldn't survive there long term.

'What of her Eathian Star? How can she exist without that?'

A new voice entered the conversation. It was Nemius.

Corpus welcomed him, still feeling very appreciative of his help. Nemius remained solemn.

'She is to use Avery's Eathian Star.'

Corpus was shocked at the discovery.

'But what of Avery?'

'He has gone, Corpus. Christi has taken his place, and because of that, their memories of him will vanish too in time.'

Corpus turned to address Verra Mica.

'You really did have this all planned out, didn't you? What makes us any better than Duergar? You have distinguished an Eathian's life. How can you justify that?'

Verra Mica remained calm.

'By discussing it with Avery and giving him the choice.'

'You've spoken with Avery?'

'Alma Tadema has, and he wanted to help us. He felt it was the best thing he could do for all concerned.'

'By the sound of it, he didn't have much choice. So, as it stands now, Christi has no one down there?'

Verra Mica remained silent but thoughtful. Corpus continued.

'You have placed Eathia at the feet of one solitary Soul Guardian. With few tools to help her, and she is supposed to guide them? How?'

'She is Eathian now. She has to find her own tools. No different to the rest of Eathia that are now left without our guidance to help them.'

She sighed.

'I still need to speak with Gabriel, Corpus. Before you get back to him, his portal should still be active, as he hasn't seen you to sever it. He has even more to contend with now.'

Corpus had heard enough. He nodded. He was impatient to get back to him. At least he knew where Christi was now. He could still be close to her, for the time being, anyway.

Verra Mica addressed Elkyne.

'The baby boy will be fine, Elkyne. Let's get you better and see if we can see about getting you tethered again somehow.'

Corpus moved towards Verra Mica.

'I will leave now. Please let me know when I can return to Gabriel.'

He quickly left for Ashtar's private chamber and his raven. Unable to tether to Gabriel, they would return to Eathia to be with Christi. He no longer needed to be in The Realm. He felt lost without Christi. He wondered if this was how Elkyne felt when born into The Realm. He sympathised with him for the first time. No allegiance, no purpose. Suddenly, he realised he shared the same devotion to Christi as Elkyne. He would find her and never let her out of his sight again.

Reaching the chamber, he collected Artius, and together they waited at the edge of the misty lake. He looked down at the carnage below in the cottage. Beatrice was now in labour, and Gabriel was by her side. Eathia and its inhabitants were heading towards uncharted territory, and things would never be the same again.

It was time to go and be with them.

It wasn't until he was just about to jump that he saw her.

An Eathian girl who embodied all that Christi had been.

Chapter 65
The Realm

Gabriel

Within The Realm, Verra Mica waited for Gabriel to fall asleep, planning to tether to him then. However, she realised that she would need help this time, or rather, Gabriel would need help. She approached Nemius and asked if he would speak to him first. Nemius understood her concerns and was happy to be with her. Considering all the conflict in her world, it would be difficult for her to maintain a calm demeanour; however, she must remain calm. Gabriel should not be overly aware of their turmoil, as this would only complicate his situation. This is going to be challenging; she was barely managing herself.

Once tethered, Verra Mica was able to explain their situation to him loosely and what had happened that evening. It wouldn't make things any easier for him, but she hoped it might contribute a little towards his healing if he was aware of the bigger picture and where he fitted into it.

Seeing Nemius had been the right move, undoubtedly. It allowed Gabriel to grieve and brought him an element of peace, albeit for a short time.

The difficulty came when Verra Mica had to try to explain what Christi needed from Eathia to enable her to fall. The loss for Gabriel was almost unthinkable. Past, present and the future of Eathia had been recalculated by the Source. Even Verra Mica wasn't sure of the impact that would have on those who were there now.

The essence that had travelled to Eathia with Christi contained the Source's imprint. Once embedded into Eathia through the Eathian Star, their present time would be changed.

This was the complication that Verra Mica dreaded warning Gabriel about concerning his son, Avery.

She was aware of Christi's fate on Eathia. She explained all she could to Gabriel, so he knew some of what to expect. Her life wasn't going to be easy.

Long after Gabriel had left Eathia for good, Christi's purpose would come to fruition, but until then, her life would be challenging to say the least.

Before she let Gabriel leave, she briefly spoke of his Reflectorscope invention and how it would eventually become so much more. It was to be a prototype. She showed him the final construction and where it was to be placed, and that she would help again nearer the time.

It would be the final piece of the plan. She urged Gabriel to understand its importance.

He would soon realise that his work had only just begun.

Chapter 66
The Realm

Makaria's Decision

Once Verra Mica had spoken to Gabriel and was happier that he was now more in the picture, she retreated to her quarters after her meeting with Baquarrah. She sent Corpus a message to say Gabriel was now on his own without a tether. Corpus received the message but chose not to respond. Verra Mica didn't expect him to, not yet, anyway. She would wait for him to come around. He was shocked, and she was prepared to bear his anger for now.

Having just arrived, she was deep in thought when Makaria announced her approach.

'Please enter.'

'What an absolute mess.'

Makaria had been aware of Verra Mica's challenges and the impact the fallout would create, but she wasn't prepared for Elkyne's injuries.

'How is he?'

'Not good. His portal was scorched, and Olpheira is trying to re-establish his connection with the Source, but it is only through her that it reaches him at present, thanks to Duergar's party trick with the Accumulator. The Source received severe trauma from Duergar's ridiculous actions. None of us are sure of how it will recover yet. I hope that is why Elkyne's inability to connect and nothing more permanent.'

'You look completely drained, your Honour. Has Baquarrah spoken with you?'

'We have all lost so much. At this moment, I am unclear as to how we will recover ourselves, and yes, he has updated me.'

Verra Mica looked up at Makaria, shocked that she had overlooked her own loss.

'Please forgive me, Makaria. What of Angelica? Has she been forced to hide? I hope she has the good sense to keep a low profile for a while.'

'She is safe and still with Mary. She will be careful.'

Verra Mica's relief showed immediately.

'Well, that's one piece of good news at least. Do we know how she managed to stay unseen?'

'She and I risked a quick communication. Mary was meeting with Ashtar in dream state and did not wake through Duergar's attempts at revealing the Soul Guardians, so when Angelica became momentarily visible, Mary did not see her manifestation.'

'I am happy to hear Angelica and Ashtar are close to her. Still keep your guard up, Makaria. I wouldn't put it past Duergar to eavesdrop. He has a way of listening in to others' thoughts. Be careful of yourself.'

'Angelica said that Ashtar also told Mary about Christi. He feels their paths will cross at some point. Were you aware of this?'

'No, but he is a clever Soul; he knows Christi will need guidance, and Mary is the perfect person to help her. It grieves me to the end, but I cannot help in any way. She is on her own now.'

Verra Mica moved closer to her.

'What will you do, Makaria? I worry for you also.'

'If you agree, your Honour, I will try and get back to Eathia somehow, to be with Angelica. Unless, that is, you need me here?'

'How will you get to her?'

'This is one of the reasons I have come to you now. Baquarrah has had to speak with a group of his own Illumacytes to reason with them not to go. Duergar is collecting all remaining Psybiencians and other orders and asking them to meet him in his Solescence Chamber.'

'To what end? What is he up to now?'

'I think he intends to fall.'

Verra Mica stood, shocked at the thought of mass abandonment from The Realm.

'All of them? To Eathia?'

Suddenly feeling weakened, she moved herself away.

'He had no intention of leaving the Eathians alone to find their own way. What does he think they can possibly do down there, as so-called free-floating Soul Guardians?'

She looked at Makaria in horror.

'Christi, he's going after Christi! Do you think he knows what has become of her?'

It hadn't dawned on Makaria what Duergar's motives were behind his decision to leave, but of course, knowing now what Verra Mica and Christi had planned, he wouldn't, no, couldn't, leave her down there to ruin his plan.

'I must warn Corpus. Oh, when will this end?'

Verra Mica tried to reach him again, but he had gone from her sight now completely.

'Damn fool. He's veiled.'

'Then it is important that I leave with Duergar, still as if I am with him, your Honour. I will do my best to inform those still tethered on Eathia of Duergar's actions. This isn't over by a long shot.'

Makaria moved closer to the Superior.

'Give me your blessing to go, and I will do all I can to protect her.'

Verra Mica bowed and agreed.

'Very well, Makaria. Go safely, and I WILL see you again. Thank you for your trust in me.'

'I can see all that you have done. I appear to be one of a few in the Psybiencian order that can, but that won't be the way forever. My loyalties have always been with Angelica, first and foremost, so I have always been able to have a balanced, detached viewpoint. You will probably find, in time, that the Triplexes will have a similar outlook now that they are more detached. They are free thinkers and will always, I am sure, remain loyal to each other if allowed that freedom. They may be out of sight now, but you have given them a head start, and they will be grateful for that.'

'You are kind, Makaria. Go with my blessing, and when you eventually see Corpus and Christi …'

Makaria understood what she wanted to say, bowed in acknowledgement and left.

Verra Mica raised herself. Makaria was right. This wasn't over yet. She left in search of Duergar.

'If he thinks he will get away quietly, he has another thing coming.'

She requested Alma Tadema and Baquarrah to meet her at Duergar's Solescence Chamber immediately.

Chapter 67
The Realm

Cut Off

Corpus and his raven flew to where he had seen the girl through the lake in Ashtar's private chamber.

She stood beneath them, having just stepped out of the cottage.

Corpus felt his core shatter. The girl was crying, tears streaming down her face as she looked up towards the sky.

He didn't know if she could see him.

As she looked away, he realised she couldn't. Maybe she could feel him there.

He took the raven higher and began to draw in the moisture from the clouds. It was something he had played with in the past. He had made shapes in the mist for fun, but this time was for an altogether different reason.

He flew around, jettisoning the vapour as he went. He willed her to look up again.

Slowly, the girl turned, pulled her blanket tight around her, and went to walk back into the cottage.

Corpus waited patiently. Internally calling her name.

She stopped and, miraculously, glanced up.

There in the sky, she saw a vast kiss. Two lines crossed each other in the centre. It filled the sky.

Corpus saw her smile.

Then her head tilted as she noticed a solitary raven flying high up above her.

There was something familiar about it. It made her feel at home, like she wasn't alone after all.

The tears continued to flow as she walked back in through the kitchen door and closed it behind her.

Corpus felt elated. He had done it. He had been able to contact her.

At that moment, he received a message from Verra Mica letting him know he could return and tether to Gabriel.

He was ready.

Then, a more urgent message came through from her.

A call for help.

He turned and tried to connect with the portal through the raven to get back to The Realm, but it had vanished.

He raised his veil and tried again. Nothing.

He sent a message to Verra Mica but felt no contact with her or, for that matter, anyone in The Realm.

It didn't take him long to realise something more sinister had happened.

He was stuck.

He continued in vain to make contact and to re-establish his portal, but all had gone.

Is Eathia to become my home too now? he wondered.

He looked back down at the cottage.

Turning the raven, he flew downwards towards Christi, or whoever she was now.

~

Chapter 68
The Realm

The End is Just the Beginning

Alma Tadema was the first to meet Verra Mica once she had sent out an urgent call. She had only just arrived when the roaring sounds started.

Verra Mica was able to follow Duergar to a collection of Psybiencian Chambers when her connection to him disappeared. She waited anxiously for her friend to join her.

It was coming from the other side of the chambers. Explosion after explosion erupted, shaking the very structure of The Realm as each one ripped through the chambers.

Baquarrah arrived and was thrown back by the next one that hit.

'What in The Realm's name is happening? Have you tried to enter?'

Just at that moment, Makaria came flying towards them.

'Verra Mica! Verra Mica!'

She yelled back at her, desperate for an explanation.

'What is it? What's happening?'

Another hit, this time throwing them all against the outer walls.

'He isn't just leaving; he is destroying all of the Solescence Chambers. Every last one of them. We'll never get back, any of us.'

'How is he leaving? Through the Accumulator? Surely not all of them are risking that?'

'He's using a secret chamber. Someone said it used to be Ashtar's.'

Verra Mica's very being went ice cold.

'No, not the animals. How could he have known about them?'

Baquarrah looked at Alma Tadema, confused.

'What is she talking about? Verra Mica, what animals?'

'I don't have time. Quick, follow me.'

Verra Mica took them to the next level. As she approached the entrance to Ashtar's private chamber, she turned, quickly linked with all three of them, and entered.

The noise hit them first, then the chaos. One Soul Guardian after another launched themselves towards an unsuspecting animal with the sole intention of using their tethers to return to Eathia. Duergar was nowhere to be seen. Verra Mica turned to Makaria.

'Where is he now?'

Alma Tadema and Baquarrah were speechless, watching in shock at the horrific sight unfolding before them.

The Soul Guardians frantically sang their haunting tones, desperately trying to subdue the fearful animals, racing against time to grab and tether them, just as Corpus had done with the willing raven, which at least was free to choose its actions. They were then violently dragged to the lake's edge, where they were forced to leap into the abyss towards Eathia. The lake was a nightmarish whirl of chaos; terrifying screeches and agonised roars echoed their protests, while violent lightning shockwaves crashed off its sides, sending shockwaves through each Soul Guardian as they plunged into the unforgiving depths.

Verra Mica suddenly saw a Soul Guardian leap at Marla and screamed at them, flying across the chamber to stop them. A piercing, helpless shrill escaped Marla as Verra Mica reached for her. The Soul Guardian pulled away with Marla beneath her and dashed towards the lake. Then they, too, disappeared.

The shrill stopped, and Verra Mica stood motionless, taking in what was happening. It was out of her control.

'Where is he now, Makaria?'

From the depths of chaos, a haunting voice floated above the commotion, sending a shock through to her core.

'RIGHT BEHIND YOU.'

They all spun around to see Duergar. His vortex had grown and now encompassed most of his core; dark shadows spread wildly throughout his remaining frame. He was on fire; energetic rays were still discharging from his core towards where the Superiors stood, causing them to take cover or risk being scorched and suffering the same fate as Elkyne had. Beside him, a bull paced, as if in a trance, its strong chest swung side to side as it moved, its horns stretched out well beyond its girth, making it look all the more intimidating.

'You thought I didn't know about this place. I have always known. You have no secrets from me now, Verra Mica. You have been rendered surplus to requirements and so has The Realm.'

He looked across at the remaining Psybiencians, smirking as he watched them take their animals and leave.

He called to them.

'Hurry, we will be leaving Eathia's orbit soon, and this age will be over,' he said, looking across at the Superiors and grinning.

'You really did think this one through, didn't you?'

'There was no alternative plan, Verra. Only this one. The one that was going to see you all put in your place once and for all.'

He turned to the other two Superiors.

'Are you with me Baquarrah, Alma? Now is your last chance.'

They both moved away from him, sickened by what he was doing. He now looked at Verra Mica only.

'You didn't listen to me, and now you have created your own downfall. With all portals closed and The Realm out of its orbit, Eathia will slip away from your grip, finally and forever and in time, a very short time, it will have a new leader.'

Alma Tadema moved forward.

'You have gone mad, Duergar. This was not how you said it would be. I will have nothing to do with you.'

'So be it. I am disappointed in you, but it makes no difference to me.'

He flew above them, and the bull seemed to come back for a moment and ran, but Duergar immediately sent a deafening drone towards it as it was running frantically to escape the traumatic scene. It fell again, submitting to his harmonics.

'You are pure evil. This has only ever been about you. This is not the end by far.'

'Your move, Verra Mica. Meanwhile, I will be taking Eathia in my ward now and mark my words. I will find Christi and destroy her and anyone that has the misfortune of being associated with her.'

Duergar started to pull the large bull towards him. Mounting it, he roared back at Verra Mica as he moved over and hovered above the centre of the misty lake.

'Oh, and your precious Gabriel, I've had someone watching him for some time, a fellow Eathian, a tethered one at that. Nephelia will be keeping a close watch on all of them. I will not let Gabriel take one more step towards his destiny. I am Eathia's only destiny now.'

The bull was now positioned beneath him. They all watched helplessly as he fired up his vortex.

Then, he set his attention on Makaria.

Sending out a tendril, he snatched her up, raising her from the chamber floor. She screamed as the dark shadows running through the feeler began to sting as they penetrated her own soul.

'No, don't hurt her. She means nothing to you.'

'You're right, she doesn't. But she does to you. Hey, little spy.'

Duergar pulled her towards him, now tethered to the bull. he ignited the swelling vortex within him again. Red and orange energetic bolts ran through him as he turned and snarled at Verra Mica and dropped down into the centre of the mist. Makaria screamed as she fell, still attached to him. The sound of Duergar's own drone now faded slowly as he fell away from them. They heard his final words before he fell away from The Realm.

'Together we'll fall.'

Verra Mica ran to the lake's edge only to see the sparks lessen as Duergar left The Realm once and for all.

The remaining animals were still running around the chamber, trying to find cover. Baquarrah was running around trying to calm them.

He turned to Verra Mica, who was now slowly backing away from the lake.

'Get away from here quickly, we must get out of here. Something is building beneath the mist.'

Her voice was drowned out by a booming eruption from the lake. She saw it before she heard it. A rolling mass of dark matter was returning up towards them. The vibrations hit the whole of the chamber as it neared the surface.

Then it tore up through the mist. Spirals of twisted black tendril launched up and spread out above where Verra Mica stood.

Alma screamed for her to get back out of the way as she tried to fire up what little energetic bolts she could muster. But it was too little, too late.

Each tendril came crashing down, obliterating the lake's edges, one just missing Verra Mica. She flew backwards from the blast. The claw-like feelers started to turn, dragging the edge with them as they went. Faster and faster, it went until the mist turned black, taking on the nature of the vortex that had embedded itself deep inside Duergar. Slowly, it began to shrink, pulling all in the chamber towards it. Baquarrah ran to Verra Mica, and Alma followed. They held fast until the vortex was just a small opening. The pressure fell, and the chamber finally became quiet.

Then, Alma Tadema broke the silence as she saw something get thrown up and out of the vortex just before it completely disappeared, evaporating before their eyes.

Makaria's lifeless form was propelled hard against the top of the chamber and fell mercilessly against the scorched surface of where the lake had been.

Alma ran towards her.

She sobbed at the sight of her contorted, singed aura. All life force fading. She looked back at Verra Mica, who was frantically making her way over to them.

Makaria turned awkwardly to try and find Verra Mica as Alma Tadema comforted her.

'She is coming, Makaria.'

Baquarrah helped Verra Mica to Makaria's side.

Unable to speak, Makaria sent a final message to Verra Mica before the Source dissipated and her soul disappeared.

'I've seen him. I've seen Rammasus through Duergar. Rammasus is here.

He is the Accumulator.'

Chapter 69
Eathia- Third Era

Gabriels Journal

Something had woken Bertha with a start.

She thought back to what she had witnessed.

She was in a cold sweat and was still shaking.

It had been a long while since she had been able or required to transcribe; her nights had been uneventful, although she still found comfort in keeping her reflector close by as she slept.

That night, she had witnessed the birth of a baby boy, one she had only become aware of through her transcription of The Realm. A boy who had been eradicated from the story but still lived within its essence.

In the early morning light, she pushed open her bedroom window to let the warm summer breeze enter. It soothed her face as she inhaled the aromas of nature.

Slowly, she opened the drawer and looked down at the journal.

It was one of two that had been given to her by her Uncle Francis. She assumed that by now, there would be no need for it.

She hesitated before picking it up.

Was she ready to begin to transcribe again? Her mother was away, so she had the time and the boredom to allow it fully back into her life.

She wondered whether to consult her Uncle Augustus on the matter.

Her sense of adventure prevailed as it always did.

She dived her hand into the drawer and grabbed the journal.

Her hand began to tingle. A sure sign that she was transcribing.

She watched, grinning at the book as its title appeared before her.

Gabriel's Journal
Life and Times of an Inventor

It had been their baby she had seen born.

She knew only a small part of their life.

This would be the beginning of something very special: lives that were close to hers on Eathia. The essence was bringing her stories forward to another era. One that wasn't too far away from the one she was in now.

She felt elated.

As she held on to the leather cover of the journal, the words and images transferred themselves onto its pages.

Once the tingling sensation passed, she knew the story was there.

Bertha gently placed it back in the drawer and left her room.

In the years ahead, she would uncover the thrilling truths of that groundbreaking era, filled with twists and revelations that would forever change her understanding of her history.

Running down the stairs, she saw a brief shadow as it passed the kitchen window, moving towards the cottage's front door.

Not wanting to wait for the knock, she opened it quickly.

Her vibrant smile froze when she saw that it was Guss standing there.

Chapter 70
Eathia - Third Era

Torn

Sophia had arrived at Sirenguard two weeks previously. The two stones for Tobias and Denis had been placed next to Tobias's grandparents and aunt, Sara.

She now looked down upon them. The sun gently warmed the back of her neck through the dappled light under the oak tree.

She glanced across at the cottage, where smoke rose from its chimney. She smiled to herself. Guss always had a fire going regardless of the weather.

They had spent time together, discussing Tobias, laughing about the past when he was younger, and Guss's paternal care for him when they first went out on the ships. Tobias had been so alive to her during those discussions, but now, as she looked down at the gravestone, the words engraved made it impossible for her to feel anything other than the void losing him had left behind.

She stepped sideways and crouched down next to Denis's grave. Even though neither of them was there beneath the earth, she found some peace knowing that they would be remembered where they had both been together. Denis had been by his father's side. Somewhere, he had always craved to be.

'Oh, Denis.'

She lowered her head and cried.

'I never could make it right for you. I hope you have found peace now, my love.'

A guttural voice from behind her broke the mood. Sophia shot up, wondering who would be so crass as to have interrupted such a moment. She wiped the tears away with the back of her hand.

There was no one there.

She tried to remember what it was he had said. She wondered if it was just the wind and felt silly to have overreacted. Then she thought back and realised it wasn't words at all, it had been a low, gravelly laugh.

She didn't feel as though she was alone anymore.

'Guss, is that you?'

A whiny voice came back. Sarcastically mimicking her own words.

'I could never make it right for you.'

Sophia's heart began to pound against her chest.

'Who is it?'

There was movement behind the undergrowth in front of where she stood. She tried to peer in to see anything of the man that was mocking her.

'You didn't do anything to save him. You let him suffer for years as long as your precious Bertha was alright.'

Sophia flinched at the mention of Bertha. How could he know about her? She turned and glanced at her name etched on the tree and felt slightly easier.

There was movement.

A tall, dark figure began to emerge.

Sophia found her breath caught in her throat in shock at the man's appearance. She raised her hand to her mouth.

He was too lean. His black coat hung on him. His suede black trousers creased above high black leather boots, pointed at the toes.

He wore a ruffled, dirty white shirt with a purple, scrawny boa tucked under the collar of his jacket. His tall black hat was pulled down over his face so all she could see was a dark, closely trimmed beard. She was caught momentarily from the reflective glare as the sun hit the oculars that had been placed around the rim of the hat. Sophia raised a hand to her eyes and continued to stare at him.

The stranger knew she was scanning him up and down. He kept his head down for effect. His face would be the last thing he would let her see.

Slowly, he lifted his head.

Sophia stood back in shock and nearly fell backwards onto Denis's gravestone. She stumbled but regained her footing.

The man laughed.

As he reached for his hat, she could see his thin, grey-tinted hand, his emaciated fingers and black nails. But that wasn't what had scared her.

His face was birdlike. His nose stretched out and down his face, almost like a beak. The beard, or what she thought was a beard, was a series of minute feathers curving over his cheeks and neck. His eyes were yellow with dark centres.

He watched her as she took his features in. Knowing she was staring at his eyes, he blinked.

Sophia gasped again.

A second pair of eyelids closed from the sides before his main ones shut and reopened.

He advanced slowly, and Sophia could see his discomfort as he moved.

Sophia looked at the cabin, realising Guss was completely unaware of the stranger. She looked for somewhere to go away from him.

'I can't help you, I don't think. I have some money and food if you need some. You look like you do.'

She darted towards the bank that would take her to the cove, but she didn't want to get cut off down there. So, she ran up to higher ground, towards the rocks. Maybe Guss would catch sight of her. She didn't want to provoke the man by shouting out for him.

He continued to follow her slowly, almost menacingly. She yelled at him.

'What do you want?'

He snarled back.

'Nothing from you. Absolutely nothing. It's far too late for that. You'll pay for the secrets you kept, the lies you told, and the damage you have caused.'

He jumped forward towards her and reached out an arm.

Sophia screamed and fell backwards.

Inside the cabin, Guss heard Sophia's cry and ran to the cabin door. He looked everywhere but couldn't see her. His failing eyesight made it impossible for him to see at any distance.

Sophia scurried backwards on her hands and feet as she tried to navigate her route away from him.

She screamed again as the man launched at her, trying to grab her throat.

Guss grabbed his gun and started to load it, dropping the bullets as panic began to set in and make his hands shake.

Sophia kicked the man in the chest and he fell back, which only made him angrier.

With the small amount of space between them, she got to her feet and stumbled back further. She looked down and saw that she had reached the edge of the stony incline. There was a sheer drop beneath her.

'No!' she yelled at him, pleading for him to stop.

As the man screamed at her, he started to run towards her. His arms reached out, ready to push her over the edge.

Then, something stopped him. He raised his hand to his throat and coughed. He crouched down and started to sound like he was crying.

Then, a piercing roar, and he stood up. He started to talk to himself. Sophia tried to make sense of what he was saying.

'No, you can't. Leave her alone. No, she deserves to die.'

Sophia was horrified.

The man stumbled back and fell, his action almost self-inflicted.

She heard Guss yell from a distance that he was on his way.

There was something about the man that made her feel compassion. As he fell, his hat dropped backwards, and she caught sight of his matted black hair. It had been pushed back to reveal …

She gasped.

He spoke to her through the sobs. He tried frantically to get away from her.

'Ma, it's me. Get away from me; I can't control the anger; it's burning me from the inside.'

Guss appeared around the corner and raised his gun despite the shock of what he was witnessing.

Sophia screamed for him to stop.

'No, Guss. It's Denis. Don't shoot him.'

In that moment, Denis raised himself to full height and ran at Sophia again. He growled at her and held onto her shoulders, pushing her backwards.

Guss yelled at Sophia to try and duck while he aimed again.

One last push from the creature caused her to fall over the edge.

Guss fired, but in his pure panic, he hit high above the man, who had now collapsed in a heap, sobbing.

He turned to face Guss, his face contorted, and he ran at him. He yanked the gun from him and threw it over the edge of the hill where Sophia had fallen.

The man gripped his stomach as if in pain, pushed past Guss and ran.

'I have to get myself away from here. What have I done?'

Guss scrambled to his feet and ran to the edge of the hill. He looked over and saw Sophia lying face down on a rocky ledge. She was within reach.

Her body was contorted and she wasn't moving.

He sat back and cried at the horror of it all.

Only that morning, they had been sitting down over breakfast and laughing.

'What's happening?' he cried to himself.

The creature continued to run, unsure of where he was heading. He was losing himself more and more every day now. He needed to get back.

Back to Duergar.

He was lost. At least there were more of his kind there where he wouldn't feel such a freak.

His life here was over.

Bertha would only be safe if he was as far from her as possible.

He wasn't going to be the one who eliminated the final lineage and the Sources essence that lived within it.

Bertha's story would live on and so would its history. He would make sure of it.

The End of Tethered in Time – Volume One

Epilogue

Tether through Time

Although time did not exist within The Realm, many eras had elapsed on Eathia. , where almost three eras had passed.

The Realm itself had healed but had remained de-tethered. Its orbit taking aeons to return to be in line with Eathia again.

The Accumulator had remained intact. No Soul Guardian went near it. All tunnels leading to it were blocked.

That was until …

Elkyne felt the pull of a tether as he made his way through one of the tunnels of The Realm. He stopped, familiar with the sensation, but not entirely understanding why he was experiencing it again.

After Duergar's evacuation from The Realm, any chance he had to re-tether to Gabriel and Beatrice's child was a lost cause.

Olpheira had just messaged him and was patiently waiting for a response.

He messaged back.

'Something's happening, Olpheira, to my core. If I am not mistaken, I would say that a tether is pulling me.'

Alarmed, she messaged back and then contacted the Superiors.

'I'm coming to you; stay where you are.'

Verra Mica responded immediately.

'Are you sure he said tether?' Baquarrah interjected.

'It's not possible, surely?'

Verra Mica sped to Elkyne and arrived shortly after Olpheira. She could see immediately that Elkyne had not misjudged the situation. Olpheira turned to her, desperate for an explanation.

'It's getting stronger. I have to go or … or what? What is my alternative?

It is pulling me towards the Accumulator.'

'This isn't right. What if it's Duergar, or worse, what if this is Rammasus's doing? What if it's one of their tricks, Elkyne?'

Baquarrah, upon hearing Elkyne, rushed towards the group.

'Olpheira, try to block it to slow it down until we can decide our next move.'

Elkyne looked helpless amongst the chaos.

Verra Mica moved forward to stop Olpheira.

'What if it's Christi or even Corpus … this could be our only chance to connect with them. What if they have found a way to bring him to Eathia?'

'But he won't be able to return, Verra.'

'Listen, I've been in there before. I know what to expect. With both of your help …'

He looked at Olpheira and Baquarrah.

'… I can make it. As Verra Mica says, this might be my sister and brother.'

Alma Tadema finally joined the group and stopped when she saw Elkyne's core, from which a stream of twisting currents shone.

'It is a tether … look.'

'Yes, we know … it's what to do about it, Alma.'

'He has to go, can't you see? We are finally in alignment, not for long, mind you. It has to be Christi's doing. Baquarrah, can you feel anything attached to the other side of the tether?'

He couldn't.

'I have to go, I can't keep away for much longer.'

Verra Mica shuffled them all together and began to push them toward the Accumulator.

'We will come as far as we can, Elkyne. Olpheira and Baquarrah, can you help to put a force field around you for as long as you can while you're in the portal?'

'Of course, I've done it before.'

Verra Mica shot a look at Olpheira.

'Start as soon as you can.'

Her attention went back to Elkyne.

'Elkyne, we'll have no way of knowing if you have made it, or if Duergar is behind this, but …'

The group had reached the forbidden zone and was now fast approaching the Accumulator.

'Be safe and come back home as soon as possible.'

She trailed off, not knowing what else to say.

Elkyne started to move away from them. Olpheira and Baquarrah moved with him, both deep in concentration and forging a bright blue and white swirl of energy around his aura. He was disappearing now, becoming just a spiralling mass that quickly headed for the opening of the Accumulator. Baquarrah stopped, nervous of moving too far into the danger zone, but Olpheira continued with him. They could all hear her voice over the thunderous vibrations as it drew Elkyne into its grasp.

'Elkyne, Elkyne … please come back to us … please …'

Her voice faded as she poured all her energy into Elkyne, as he finally disappeared into the Accumulator.

Only she heard him respond. Only she sensed his panic as he fell into the void.

'I feel him. He's here. Stay with me …'

Then he was gone.

As soon as Elkyne entered the Accumulator, he felt something sharp pierce his aura. It threw him off balance, and he began to spiral out of control.

Olpheira's energy expanded as if she could feel the threat.

Elkyne recognised the process from before and veiled it; only this time, there was a definite portal. One that encased him.

As his connection to Olpheira weakened he sensed a stronger, lighter energy pulling him towards it.

There was no shattering this time. He remained whole as the portal increased his speed.

He watched his descent with intrigue. Colours, movement and noises were rising from beneath him.

Then there was Christi. He could feel her all around him.

Then, there was a baby.

En route to tether to him, he thought he briefly caught a glimpse of Corpus, tethered to a raven, and then he was fighting for breath. No, his tether was fighting for breath.

He heard him scream as he came to life.

He was indeed finally tethered to a beautiful baby boy.

An Ashen that went by the name of Maddox.

Browne Family Tree

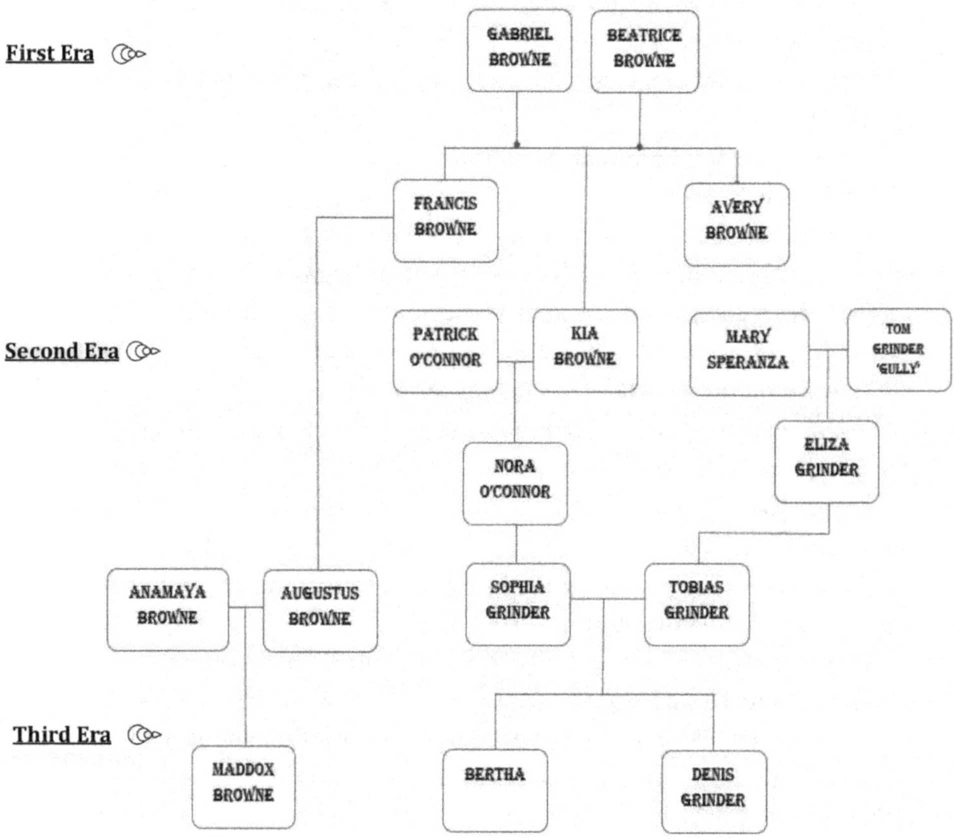

To my dad,
... a promise made so very long ago.

Over the years, there have been many friends and family who have constantly shown such an interest in this story as it has evolved. Admittedly, it has taken a while to get off the ground — life tends to run its own plans alongside our dreams.

Most of the story has grown with me. Inspiration has come from personal experience, music, lyrics, and certain interesting characters who have found their way into the voices of those now playing a significant role in my alternative dreamscape.

Bertha herself was created in 1992, and she encompasses so many of the amazing women I've had the privilege to know and hold dear.

I want to first thank her namesake, GD whose very essence gave Bertha the strength of character that underpins her true nature.

To my Mum, who has never lost her caring, supportive, and incredibly strong sense of drive and motivation.

To Molly, who showed me that simplicity, love, and creativity are the grounding of life itself — baking, painting, nature and family.

And finally, to Elly — my aunt, who always knew what to do, was always frank and sincere, cherished her family, and who created the most beautiful cakes in the shed at the end of the garden. Her Cake Hole.

To those who gently pushed me to put this other life down in words — a life that has become as real to me as any experience I could ever hope to have.

To Anna — for asking me why I wasn't getting on with it.

To my girls, Bex and Georgia — for always believing in me, in Bertha, and in her story.

To all those gorgeous people who asked, time and time again, "How's the book coming along?" (You know who you are!)

To my proofreaders — Caro, Julie, Caelia, and Georgia — who patiently endured my grammar.

To the many quiet corners where I've hunkered down to write — from Carcassonne, Vézelay, Grayshott, Tilford, Blackmoor, and many cafés along the way.

And to Julian — thank you for creating the space in which I could finally let the words breathe.

Not quite finally, to my sister, Amanda, for her contagious and inspiring bursts of creativity, and my brother, Stewart, whose wedding speech gave me the final stubborn push!

Ever since I was young, certain songs have sparked stories in my mind, and those imagined moments have shaped some of the scenes in this book, as I've purposefully tried to weave them into the characters' lives. Music has always been part of my creative inspiration. More recently, Bex's love of music has opened up my world even further, and many of the songs she's shared have naturally become part of the Tethered in Time soundtrack.

Pink, Genesis, Disturbed, Evanescence, Nickelback, Leonard Cohen… the list is endless — and they will all play throughout The Chronicles of Bertha at some point.

I see a playlist emerging.

My final two appreciations:
To those we cannot see — who linger beyond the veil of consciousness, guiding with love and compassion.

And to Dan — for making this dream come alive.
The story of Bertha has been a passion. A journey.
From a single idea to something greater than I ever imagined.
Within its lines are moments of pain that hurt beyond belief, nestled alongside the quiet grace of love — which, time and time again, has proven that it always wins.

"A quiet child with so much to say, finally finds her voice…"